Only you

Kate Eberlen was born in a small town thirty miles from London and spent her childhood reading books and longing to escape to the big city. She studied Classics at Oxford University before discovering she was much less interested in the world of academia than the world of work. Kate has had many jobs, from lift girl in Harrods, au pair in Rome and New York, to working in theatre box-office and a career in publishing, before becoming a mother, teaching English as a Foreign Language and writing novels. Kate now lives in London.

BOLTON LIBRARIES

BT 1993853 5

ALSO BY KATE EBERLEN

Miss You

Kate Eberlen

PAN BOOKS

First published 2020 by Pan Books
an imprint of Pan Macmillan
The Smithson, 6 Briset Street, London EC1M 5NR
Associated companies throughout the world
www.panmacmillan.com

ISBN 978-1-5098-1991-1

Copyright © Kate Eberlen 2020

The right of Kate Eberlen to be identified as the
author of this work has been asserted by her in accordance
with the Copyright, Designs and Patents Act 1988.

All rights reserved. No part of this publication may be reproduced,
stored in a retrieval system, or transmitted, in any form, or by any means
(electronic, mechanical, photocopying, recording or otherwise)
without the prior written permission of the publisher.

Pan Macmillan does not have any control over, or any responsibility for,
any author or third-party websites referred to in or on this book.

1 3 5 7 9 8 6 4 2

A CIP catalogue record for this book is available from the British Library.

Typeset in Meridien by Jouve (UK), Milton Keynes
Printed and bound by CPI Group (UK) Ltd, Croydon, CR0 4YY

MIX
Paper from
responsible sources
FSC® C116313

This book is sold subject to the condition that it shall not, by way of
trade or otherwise, be lent, hired out, or otherwise circulated without
the publisher's prior consent in any form of binding or cover other than
that in which it is published and without a similar condition including
this condition being imposed on the subsequent purchaser.

Visit **www.panmacmillan.com** to read more about all our books
and to buy them. You will also find features, author interviews and
news of any author events, and you can sign up for e-newsletters
so that you're always first to hear about our new releases.

For Connor and Becky
with all my love always

You live as long as you dance

RUDOLF NUREYEV

PART ONE

April 2018

1

Monday

ALF

The air is bright with sunshine, crisp with a lingering breath of dawn. As Alf steps out of the apartment building, his face tilting towards the clear blue sky, a sigh of contentment spreads through his body, releasing tension he didn't even know was there. This has become his favourite moment of the day. He has lived in Rome for six months, but the way the morning light gives a kind of beauty to the shabbiest of buildings still lifts him. It's a walk to the school, strolling past sites that in an hour's time will be thronging with tourists. It feels like a privilege, like being alone with a free pass in a theme park or something. First, there's the long slow climb through the posh residential area until the avenue meets a scrubby expanse of field that is the Circus Maximus, then a tree-lined road slopes up between the Palatine and the Caelian, two of the seven hills. Suddenly you're in front of the Colosseum. It never stops amazing him how it's just standing there, the colours as crude as the postcards they sell on the souvenir vans that are just opening for the day. He takes a photo and posts it on Instagram with the greeting: *Buon giorno! #Roma #Rome #colosseo #bella #beautiful.*

Alf scrolls through his feed, pausing as he sees a photo of his grandparents with big smiles on their faces. Cheryl, his gran, is wearing one of her old competition dresses that always reminds Alf of a cupcake, because the skirt has so much netting it stands up by itself without Cheryl being inside it. This one is a deep pink colour, with silver diamanté swirls on the bodice. His grandad Chris is in full white tie and tails. The caption underneath is: *Keep dancing! #slowfoxtrot #nevertoooldtodance*. Alf's never been on a cruise ship, but he knows that you stay in cabins. There are thousands of them, all stacked up like a block of flats. He can't imagine how there's the cupboard space for their dancewear. He pities the other old people who've gone on a cruise holiday fancying a gentle turn around the dance floor, and have the bad luck of finding themselves on the same ship as Cheryl and the dress that'll swish you out of the way if your floor-craft isn't up to much. And Cheryl unable to resist teaching as she swirls past.

'Let the man lead!' 'Sharper with your head!' 'Flower in a vase! You're wilting!'

Alf 'likes' the photo, not knowing whether his gran will be pleased or annoyed when she sees. He wonders if she ever looks at his posts. She never 'likes' them. She probably thinks that doing so would show approval.

Alf wonders what the weather's like in Blackpool. The default image that comes to mind when he thinks about home is a rain-lashed promenade, the water pewter, the clouds so grey it's difficult to tell where sky meets sea. But that's only because it was that kind of day when he left. When the sun shines, Blackpool can be as attractive as almost anywhere.

But not Rome. What he loves about Rome is the surprises. You'll be walking along a street – pretty enough, but nothing special – then suddenly there'll be a church with a tower and a tiled roof, so old it looks like a film set, or an even older bit of wall, with thousands of narrow red bricks made before there was technology, that's stood there for two thousand years.

As he winds his way up through the cobbled streets of Monti to get away from the traffic on the main road, he's tempted by the aroma of espresso wafting from every bar he passes, but he has to be on time. They give you a test before the classes start to see which one you're in. You don't have to write anything, just tick the correct box, the nice receptionist told him when she saw his face at the mention of exams.

Behind him, the hoot of a car's horn warns him to get off the road, and one of the old Fiat Cinquecentos passes, its engine as spluttery as a moped as it pulls up the hill. The driver has the radio tuned to a bright morning station playing Pharrell Williams's 'Happy' to get the day off to a good start. Jive, Alf thinks, his feet automatically kicking and flicking to the beat, until the car makes a right and the music fades and he's not even sure whether he can hear it any more.

Alf has no idea about the multiple-choice grammar test, so he just ticks what sounds best to him. Then he's told to see the director of the school to assess how good his speaking is. The door to the office is closed. Inside, he can hear a man asking questions in slow Italian and a woman giving quiet, hesitant responses. Then there's the sound of a chair being scraped back and, sooner than Alf expects, the door opens, and the girl who comes out gives him a look that makes him feel as if he's been caught eavesdropping.

It doesn't help his heart rate that she is stunningly beautiful and walks towards the staircase with her feet turned out, like a dancer.

'*Buon giorno!*' The director waves him into his office.

Alf thinks it's all about the gestures with Italian. He's watched how Italians talk to each other. Even when they're alone and on a mobile phone, the free hand is moving to emphasize a point, express surprise or despair. Sally and Mike, who share the apartment, have been here much longer than him, and speak much better Italian, but Alf is always the one who gets the compliments, because he puts his body into it. The director of the school isn't as impressed. He likes Alf's fluency, he tells him, but his grammar is non-existent. He hands him a piece of paper with the number of a classroom at the very top of the building.

There are seven others in the class. Six of them are trying to chat using the fragments of Italian they already know, but the girl he saw downstairs is sitting alone, concentrating on an Italian–English dictionary. She is wearing a long-sleeved grey T-shirt that could have cost two pounds or two hundred, because she's got the sort of body that makes cheap classy, and jeans with horizontal distressing – not tight like the girls back home, their pale flesh bulging through the gaps in the denim, but loose, held up only by her pelvic bones, the slashes giving glimpses of slim bare leg beneath.

The only chair that is empty is next to hers. When he sits down, she shifts slightly away.

The teacher, whose name is Susanna, is holding four lengths of narrow gold ribbon, the type that *pasticcerie* use to wrap the trays of tiny cakes Italians take along to Sunday lunch with their families. She bunches them in her hand, indicating for all the students to come up and grab an end, and then she lets go, leaving them each connected to another person.

'*Introduzioni!*' she says, pointing to useful Italian greetings she has written on the whiteboard.

The pairs stand smiling nervously, still obediently holding their ends of ribbon, until Alf decides to break the silence.

'*Ciao!*' he says to the beautiful young woman he has lucked out with. '*Come ti chiami?*'

As if given permission, the others peel away from the huddle, echoing his greeting and, amid little coughs of half-embarrassed laughter, the classroom stutters to life.

'*Mi chiamo Letty*,' the girl responds.

'Letty?'

'Short for Violet,' she says.

'*Piacere*,' he says.

'*Come ti chiami?*' she asks him.

'Alf,' he says. 'Just Alf.'

She asks where he is from.

'*Inghilterra*,' he replies.

'Two English people! Not a good idea!' says the teacher.

She tells them to change partners.

LETTY

There are eight in the class, and they continue swapping partners until they have all met each other. Masakasu is Japanese, Paola and Carla are Colombian, Jo is Norwegian, Angela is Austrian, Heidi is Swiss, and Alf is English. From the North, judging by his accent, Letty thinks.

She wonders if her Italian will ever be fluent enough to discover how these disparate people washed up like flotsam and jetsam in Rome, in April, in a dim classroom, in a virtually empty language school.

What stories brought them here? And will they want to know hers? If so, what will she tell them?

It occurs to her that she could construct a completely different version of herself if she wished.

Letty looks towards the window. The brilliance of the sunshine, which has not yet found its way into the classroom, makes the view seem as remote as a postcard: a splash of purple bougainvillea; a soft geometry of slanting terracotta roofs and bulbous black-green treetops; a flat blue sky.

I am here in Rome, she thinks. I know no one here and nobody knows me.

She sees that she has twisted the gold ribbon into a ring around her finger, almost without realizing.

The teacher switches on a recording of random Italians asking for each other's telephone number. The students have to compare what they hear with the person next to them.

Letty is paired with Heidi, a friendly Swiss woman in her thirties. Letty thinks ahead. Will they have to practise asking each other for their details? She has a new phone, a new contract. The only contacts in it are her family. She's not even sure she knows what her number is or whether she wants to give it out to strangers. She could just make one up, she thinks.

But making stuff up can get complicated.

Wafts of warm pastry rise up from the cafe in the basement, as the class traipse down the circular staircase for morning break.

Letty orders a cappuccino, checking her watch first as she remembers her grandmother Marina telling her, in that categorical way of hers, that no Italian drinks coffee with milk after midday. Ragu – never 'bolognese' in their house – must be simmered for three hours and served with tagliatelle, not spaghetti. Cheese and fish do not go together.

She sees that her class has divided itself by gender. The men are sitting at one table eating croissants. The women have not bought food, only coffee or fresh orange juice. After a few faltering attempts to speak Italian to each other, they revert to English, which they can all speak fairly well.

Back in the classroom, the teacher splits them into two different groups for a discussion about their home countries.

Letty isn't sure she's been placed in the right class. Perhaps it's the wrong teaching method for her? She finds it difficult to form sentences in Italian unless she knows them to be correct. In the level test she will have made very few mistakes in the grammar paper, but she struggled to say anything in the oral

8

exam. She suspects that most of the others in the class would have been the other way round. Masakasu, for example, has a way of holding the floor because he has learned various Italian linking phrases like *in fact* and *however* that make it difficult to interrupt.

'Tokyo is beautiful but it has a lot of motorways.' 'Japanese food is good.'

Everyone seems very positive about their home country, Letty thinks. Perhaps it's just because they don't know each other yet. It wouldn't feel polite to say that she doesn't like her country very much at the moment. And it would be beyond her linguistic capability to justify the statement, should anyone attempt to ask follow-up questions. So, when it is finally her turn, she contributes that London is beautiful. There are lots of museums. There is a big river.

'Are people in London friendly?' Paola asks her.

Letty doesn't know how to say, 'Not as friendly as Italians.' So she just says, 'Yes.' She wonders why Paola giggles at this response, then realizes it's because she doesn't sound very friendly. She's aware that people often think she is stand-offish even though she doesn't mean to be.

At the end of the morning lessons, the English guy, Alf, takes his time collecting his pencil and notebook, pulling on a jumper over his white T-shirt, and picking up his backpack from the floor. Letty senses that if they are left alone together he will want to speak to her, perhaps even suggest lunch. He is about her age and oozes confidence with his tousled-surfer looks and open smile, but his attention is the last thing she wants. She gathers her stuff together quickly, looking at her watch as if she has an appointment to get to, then hurries out of the classroom and down the stairs.

It's gloriously sunny outside, although there is a bite in the air. She has been in Rome just a day, but she has already been told three times – by her landlord, the reception staff at the school and her teacher – to beware of bad people in Termini station. As she crosses the concourse, she is offered tours by two unlikely looking guides, and is approached by several gypsy women clutching babies and holding out their hands woefully. She doesn't feel good ignoring them but, alone in the city, she knows she must take care of herself. They back off when she walks determinedly by, possibly mistaking her for an Italian.

Outside in the square, buses and trams seem to chase her from all directions, but the side street she chooses is suddenly, almost scarily, quiet. She passes several restaurants offering a menu of the day for a reasonable price, but she doesn't want to sit alone and be fussed over by too-eager waiters, so instead she buys a banana and a bottle of water from a fruit stall, feeling a little flip of triumph at making the transaction in Italian, including handing over the correct coins.

Vittorio Emanuele square is flanked by once-elegant colonnades, now spray-painted with graffiti. Where rich people used to promenade in the shade, the homeless now sleep on flattened boxes and filthy sleeping bags. Letty crosses the busy road to the park in the middle, where there are tall trees with lime-green leaves fluttering against the pure blue sky. A dilapidated bit of Roman ruin fenced off in one corner has become a campsite with bright blankets draped over rocks to catch the sun; groups of teenage boys perform clattering skateboard tricks on the steps and paths. Letty sits on a bench and peels her banana, then eats it slowly, sipping her water, alert to everything going on around her.

In her pocket, her mobile phone buzzes. She knows that it will be a WhatsApp message from her mother wanting to know how she is, but she doesn't want to send back the two blue ticks that show she's seen it yet. Not until she feels more settled. She glances at her watch. Not yet three o'clock. Two o'clock in the UK. She's surprised Frances has managed to restrain herself for so long.

Time passes slowly when you are alone, and it feels much longer than thirty hours since she arrived in the city. Letty can't decide whether that is a good thing or not. A whole month stretching ahead seems like a sunny eternity in which to sort her life out, and yet she dreads happy solitude turning into the cold ache of loneliness.

At the end of the square she chooses a route back to her apartment down a tree-lined residential street. Having lived most of her life in London, she's alert to a city's sudden changes in atmosphere. The street is quiet but it doesn't feel threatening, though she glances occasionally behind to check that no one is following her.

In a small supermarket, Letty buys an individual chicken breast clingfilmed to a yellow polystyrene tray, a bag of salad and a lemon. She thinks she remembers seeing a bottle of olive oil when she arrived at the apartment the previous evening, and her landlord gave her a cursory tour of the kitchen, opening cupboard doors and saying, 'Here, everything for cook, yes?'

The end of the avenue intersects with a busy dual carriageway. Opposite stands the imposing Baroque frontage of a church, set back from the boulevard. There is a tour bus parked outside. Letty hovers on the edge of a group of Americans listening to their guide telling them that this is Santa Croce in Gerusalemme, one of the seven pilgrimage churches of Rome.

Letty follows the group in, then sits down alone in front of the altar and gazes up at the almond-shaped mosaic of Christ in the dome of the apse. She wonders what adjective would best suit the brightness and clarity of the blue background. Is this cerulean blue, a description she has only ever seen written down? Celestial sounds better, but is that even a colour?

An image of her grandmother's face, on hearing that the first thing Letty has done in Rome is go to a pilgrimage church, crosses her mind. She pictures Marina sitting up in bed in her silk dressing gown, with her four beloved Victorian prints of Roman ladies on the wall behind her.

She wonders if her grandmother ever came to this church when she was a child, whether there is some minuscule fragment of her DNA left here in the wooden pew, a relic of her visit. Did Marina's eyes gaze up at golden Christ in his blue Heaven? Or does she seem somehow present only because Letty is thinking of her?

The phone vibrates in her pocket again. She does not look until she is outside.

There are now two messages from Frances. The first says simply, *Well?*

The second, *Are you OK?*

She texts back.

Fine. I'll call later.

The apartment Letty has rented looks better in real life than the photos on Airbnb. One entire wall is glass with a far-reaching vista to the west. In the foreground stands a stretch of the ancient Aurelian wall, and beyond the cathedral of San Giovanni in Laterano.

If Letty opens a window and cranes her neck to the right, she can see the dome of St Peter's in the far distance, and to the left, the soft purply shadows of distant hills. But she's tentative, standing a foot back from the glass, not quite trusting it as a barrier to the ten-storey drop to the street.

Letty lies on the sofa and gazes at the sunset. Stripes of duck-egg blue and grey intersperse with shades of pink, from the fiery coral of the horizon to the palest candyfloss of the highest cloud.

Finding herself in near darkness, she realizes she has been transfixed by the changing expanse of sky, lulled by the incessant hum of the city's traffic, for almost an hour. She is suddenly aware of a low thump of bass, and the clatter and sizzle of cooking emanating from a neighbouring apartment. She likes the sensation of being alone, but with the knowledge there are people around her. Wafts of garlic remind her of the need to eat. She fries the chicken breast in olive oil, empties the bag of salad onto a plate, then squeezes lemon juice over it. She eats her meal slowly, chewing and swallowing methodically as she watches the last embers of light disappear from the sky. Then she washes up. Finally she calls her mother.

'I've always hated the term empty nest,' Frances declares, as if it's a phrase Letty has greeted her with, when all she's said is, 'How are you?'

'I never was that cooing, clucking sort of mother, was I? Although, of course, it was me who paid for all the feathering.'

A lifetime in advertising has made Frances arch with words, as if she's testing copy. Or maybe she was always like that, and that is why she chose it as a career. Letty's never known.

'I've spent all day trying to make the place look presentable,' Frances goes on. 'I've got a viewing tomorrow. Ivo's done f-all, of course. So much bloody stuff. I'm honestly thinking of buying a new-build, all glass and nowhere to store anything. What do you think?'

'Can't see that working for Ivo,' Letty says.

'No,' says Frances.

Is her mother's tone bitter or wistful? Would she actually like to live in a glass tower? Letty can't tell.

Her parents are selling the house that they have lived in all their marriage. It had been informally agreed that when Marina died, the house would be left to them. But it turns out that her grandmother never changed her will, and Letty's father Ivo, Marina's younger son, shied away from raising the subject with her. So the house, which has always been their family home, now half belongs to her father's older brother, Rollo. Or what's left of it after inheritance tax, as Frances often remarks. There must be quite a lot left, Letty thinks, because one-bedroom flats in the area are selling for over a million and their property is big enough to make five of those, but it does nevertheless seem terribly unfair that Frances has to leave the house on which she has paid all the expenses for years, including a new roof and underpinning.

The constant tension between her parents is one of the reasons that Letty needed to escape.

'Anyway,' says Frances, with a prolonged sigh. 'What's it like where you are?'

Her mother sounds so uncharacteristically defeated, Letty doesn't dare tell her that she has a great glass window, with a view that makes her feel happy and free.

'OK,' she says.

There's a long pause.

'I've just had supper,' Letty finally says. 'Chicken with lemon and a bag of salad. There's a supermarket quite near.'

'A bag of salad. In Italy! Who knew?' Frances says. Then, slowing down: 'Good you've found somewhere easy to shop.'

The effort to keep the conversation going is suddenly too much for Letty.

'I've got some homework to do,' she says.

'OK, I'll let you go, then.'

'OK, bye!'

Letty tastes a familiar bittersweet cocktail of guilt and relief as she presses the end call button.

2

Tuesday

ALF

Alf wakes up before his flatmates. Usually he clears up the debris left over from their after-work drinking before brewing a pot of coffee. Now, as he closes the door carefully so as not to disturb anyone's sleep, he feels guilty for leaving the stale smell of Peroni on the air.

As he leaves Testaccio, he takes a photo of the Pyramid – so white and modern in shape you could believe it was built two years before, not two thousand – and posts it with the caption: *Buon giorno! #Roma #Rome #ancient #modern.*

Within a couple of seconds, he has his first 'like' from Stuart. It's eight thirty. Which is seven thirty UK time. So he's probably having his breakfast before heading off to work, catching up on all the stuff that's arrived overnight. Alf pictures him sitting at the table in the huge kitchen-diner that looks onto the golf course before snatching up his keys, asking Alexa to open the garage door, and giving the Porsche a rev before driving off in a swirl of exhaust.

Alf decides to take the tram up the long hill to the Colosseum, because he doesn't want to be late. He thinks she's the sort of person who will get to class early. His mind runs through the things he knows about her. She is called Letty. Short for Violet. Violetta, the teacher calls her, which he likes the best. She is English but she doesn't sound like the usual English person trying to speak Italian, and she doesn't look like any English girl he knows. Her hair is dark and long and she uses it as a curtain to hide behind. The way she hurried out of the classroom has stayed with him, as if she had somewhere to go, but he knew she didn't somehow. Or maybe she did. Maybe she is just shy, or maybe there is a reason she doesn't want to be friendly. Maybe she has a jealous lover, or a partner.

'*Buon giorno! Ci vediamo dopo!*' Alf tests his Italian on one of the stallholders as he walks past the Forum.

He's on nodding terms with most of them now. They've watched him taking clients on tours. They give him a discount on bottles of water and throw in a free one for him. The other day when a restless American kid was clamouring for a plastic Roman helmet, Alf negotiated a free sword to go with it, and the tip the appreciative parents gave him was far more than the price they would have paid.

'*Parli bene Italiano!*' the stallholder replies.

Alf knows he doesn't speak Italian well. If he learned anything from yesterday's lesson, it was that. But it's the fact that Italians generally encourage any attempts to speak their language that made Alf decide he wanted to learn it properly. If he's going to live here, he wants to be able to hold a conversation.

If he's going to live here . . . The original plan was to go travelling, but they kind of got stuck. There are worse places to be stuck, though, Alf thinks now, crossing the piazza in front of the basilica of Santa Maria Maggiore.

Today Violetta is wearing a black vest with her slashed jeans. No bra. Her hair is braided in two plaits across her head then falls loose down her back.

16

The teacher tells them to walk around the classroom greeting each other, seeing if they can remember everyone's name, and then asking how they are.

They all say they are well because they don't know any other words. Until you can speak, you can't express anything different or complex. It's like babies, Alf thinks. They cry because they can't tell you why they're unhappy.

The teacher tells them that today's lesson will be about personal information.

'How old are you?' is a question that he's not used since primary school, when it seemed to really matter who was five and who was only four and three quarters. With a September birthday, Alf was always oldest in his year. People said it gave an advantage with sport and stuff.

He's paired with Angela, the Austrian woman, and he feels a bit awkward talking about age. He estimates she is in her late fifties – could be early sixties because she's had Botox and fillers. You can always tell. He doesn't understand why women do it. He thinks it ages them more than wrinkles.

'Give me wrinkles any day,' he once said to Gina, and she said, 'Well, that's a relief!'

'*Ho sessanta anni,*' Angela says.

Alf doesn't have the Italian to say, 'You don't look it!'

And even if he did, he doesn't think it would be appropriate, because it would make it sound like sixty is really old.

Sixty is a difficult one for women to admit to, he's noticed. Forty, too. Whatever they say about life beginning at forty, all his mum's friends dread that age. Fifty doesn't seem so much of a problem – a lot of women who come to his mother's dance school have big fiftieth birthday parties. But sixty isn't good. His gran, Cheryl, has been fifty-nine for several years.

He's observed that when women get to seventy, if they're still in fairly good shape they quite like saying it, because they want to hear, 'I can't believe that!'

And weirdly, the older they get, the prouder they seem to be of their age, especially since it's often the ancient ones who can get around the dance floor really well because everyone learned to foxtrot in the 1950s.

'Eighty-seven? You are kidding me!'

He likes the feeling of making their day.

He can't stop glancing over to where Violetta is sitting with Masakasu. He thinks she is probably in her early twenties. He can't work out why he wants her to acknowledge him so much. The only thing they have in common is that they're English. It's not like it's his duty to befriend her. She's probably from London: nobody in the North would call their child Violet. It would be like your great granny's name or something.

Angela is saying she thought Alf was older than nineteen. He knows this not because of her faltering Italian, but because everyone always says it.

Even when he was a little boy, people were constantly praising him for being the man of the family, ruffling his hair, telling him he was doing a great job of looking after his mum. He remembers being terrified that he would be found out. Someone would see that he didn't have a clue how to look after her, especially when she was crying in the kitchen after doing the washing and everything when he had gone to bed. Sometimes he came down and allowed her to give him a cuddle and kiss his hair as her tears made it wet. Mostly, though, he pretended not to see, creeping back up the stairs to his bedroom and lying awake agonizing about how to make her happy.

It got better after she met Gary when he was ten, although he still remembers her saying, because he's heard the story and the accompanying shrieks of laughter so many times, 'You don't mind me having another man in my life, Alfie?'

And him confiding to her in a whisper, 'I'm not really a man, you know.'

*

18

At break, Alf orders a cappuccino and a cornetto filled with apricot jam that erupts over his fingers and drips onto his T-shirt as he takes a bite, causing Masakasu to roar with laughter. He glances in Violetta's direction, but she isn't looking at him, and when he comes out of the cloakroom with a wet patch down the front of his T-shirt, having removed the jam, it's Heidi he bumps into. She's in her late thirties, pretty in a Claudia Schiffer kind of way, and wearing a black leather jacket with tassels and shorts with patterned tights. He imagines she is used to being the sexiest woman in the room. She's flirty in the entitled way that older women often are with him.

'Now with a wet T-shirt,' she says in English. 'What, I ask, are you trying to do to us girls?'

He smiles because she says *vet* instead of wet and *vot* instead of what. There's something about her keenness to be friendly that makes him think she is a lonely person, although he cannot see why she would be.

The teacher hands them worksheets about jobs.

They have to match words with cartoon pictures of people working. Doctor, lawyer, teacher, labourer, waiter, cook. It's all pretty obvious.

The teacher asks them what they do.

Jo from Norway says he's a doctor.

'*Vero?*' asks the teacher. 'Really?' As if Jo has misunderstood the instruction and simply said the first word on the sheet.

'*Vero*,' he says.

Then she asks Alf.

'*Sono avvocato*,' he says with a grin, choosing the next item on the list.

The two Colombian girls giggle.

'*Dai!*' says the teacher.

It's a word that Italians use all the time. It's like 'C'mon!'

Alf doesn't know which job to go with. In Blackpool, he's always helped his mum out at her dance classes, but he knows what sort of looks he'll get if he says he's a dance teacher. It's ironic, he always thinks, that although he spent his adolescence being called gay because of his dancing, he was the first of his year to have a girlfriend, the first to have sex. Women like a man who can dance.

He spent a year as a waiter in a pizzeria after school and at weekends. The summer before that he did the deckchairs on the beach. Since living in Rome, he has worked as someone who stands near a restaurant handing out flyers offering a 15 per cent discount, but he doesn't know how to say that. He's also promoted Segway tours. For a while he led the tours too, after Yuri, who owns the Segways, took a corner too quickly and broke his arm, which wasn't a great advertisement. That was what gave Alf the idea of becoming a tour guide, but he's unofficial, so he isn't sure the teacher will approve of that. She's quite strict. In the end, because it's one of the words on the worksheet, he says he's a waiter.

Heidi works in a hotel as an events manager, which makes sense. The teacher moves on to Violetta.

She says she is a student.

She doesn't look like a student. Alf wonders what the Italian word is for model.

The Colombian girls are also students, as is Masakasu – a student of lyric opera, the Japanese boy elaborates, which is why he needs to learn good Italian pronunciation. To demonstrate, he stands up and gives them 'Nessun Dorma'. He has that operatic way of singing where your face contorts with the effort of making such a loud noise, but it sounds brilliant. He'd be great on *Britain's Got Talent*, Alf thinks. He gets out his mobile phone, holds it up to ask Masakasu's permission. The Japanese boy nods, delighted, as he continues softly, then gets louder and louder until the final '*Vincerò!*'

Everyone claps when he finishes the song, and they can hear applause coming from the classroom next door.

Finally, the teacher puts a Post-it note with the name of a celebrity on each person's forehead. They have to ask each other questions, using the language they have learned, to find out who they are.

When the class finishes, Alf stays seated while the others are leaving as he posts the video of Masakasu singing, with the caption: *Cool guy in my Italian class #opera #Rome #Roma #singer #BGT #Italy'sGotTalent?*

He shows it to Masakasu as they walk down the circular staircase together, and he says, 'Cool guy!' happily.

Out in the street, Alf looks hopefully in both directions, but Violetta has vanished. The feeling of disappointment is like someone clutching his heart then letting go, although if he saw her in the distance walking up the street, he doesn't know what he'd do.

Alf's phone buzzes in his pocket and keeps buzzing. The video is the most popular thing he's ever posted. It must be the BGT hashtag. He resets the phone not to vibrate each time there's a notification.

3

Wednesday

LETTY

There's a border as bright as white neon around the edges of the blind when Letty wakes, telling her that it is already sunny outside. She is going to be late for class. Rolling from the middle to the side of the bed, she remembers just in time to duck rather than hit her head on the concrete beam.

The landlord was keen – a little too keen, she initially feared – to scamper up the ladder and show her the sleeping gallery. But it was the beams he was concerned about.

'You stay alone?' he asked.

'Yes.'

'Maybe not so much a problem.' He winked.

She'd looked at the bed, and the ceiling, maybe a metre above. Was he saying that previous guests' rearing throes of passion had been cut short by concussion?

'It's perfect,' she told him, wanting him to go.

'Everything necessary,' he'd said, ducking expertly as he moved around the bed.

After he left, she'd found a collection of condoms in a wooden box with the word LOVE stamped on it. She wondered if the apartment was his shag pad between Airbnb bookings.

Now she pulls up the blinds on the vast window. The sky is a very pale blue, the saints atop San Giovanni in Laterano lit by the clarity of the morning sunshine. Letty finds herself thinking that she has found what she wanted, even though she didn't really know what it was she was looking for.

'What do you like doing in your free time?' the teacher is saying when she arrives at class.

'*Violetta, che cosa fai nel tempo libero?*'

Hearing her name spoken in Italian, as Marina always did, makes Letty panic a little, feeling slightly fraudulent for not being better at the language.

'*Mi piace leggere,*' she says.

And then she wishes she had come up with anything other than reading, because it makes her sound like a swot. It's the first impression she gave when she arrived at her secondary school aged fourteen, when all the social hierarchies had already been established, and she never seemed to be able to move away from it, however hard she tried to make herself look like one of the cool ones.

The teacher tells the class to ask each other questions about their hobbies.

Jo, the Norwegian, likes cross-country skiing and skating.

Does Letty like skating? he asks.

When Letty says she doesn't, he looks surprised, even a little offended. She doesn't have the language to try to explain why not.

The teacher divides them into two groups for a more general chat. Letty's pleased to be with Heidi, who likes yoga. Alf likes football. Playing or watching? Letty asks, using the vocabulary they have just learned. Both, he says. She doesn't know how to ask which team he supports, so she starts listing Premiership clubs.

'Manchester United? Liverpool?'

'*Italiano!*' the teacher warns, seeing that she's inadvertently put the two English people together again.

'*Lago Nero*,' Alf replies. 'Blackpool.' Then, in a whisper: 'Sounds better in Italian.'

Letty knows she's meant to laugh, but she doesn't. In her head, Letty can hear her mother saying, 'The furthest I ever went as a child was bloody Blackpool!'

She knows exactly what her mother would be saying about Alf now.

'Men can be too good-looking. Makes them think that life is easy.'

It's one of Frances's categorical statements that's also a sideswipe at Letty's father.

Alf's face is objectively handsome and he smiles a lot. His hair has lots of blond in it, but is more dark than fair.

Letty feels colour spreading over her cheeks, as if Alf might be able to read her thoughts. She says, '*Si chiamano i Tangerini, no?*' (They're called the Tangerines, aren't they?)

He wasn't expecting that.

One of her attempts to be cool at school was to become very knowledgeable about football and, as she has an almost photographic memory for facts, she can remember all the nicknames of the clubs as well as the grounds they play in. She's only done a pub quiz once, but the team she was in won because of it.

Letty leaves the class just in front of Alf. She knows he's behind her as she walks down the stairs and across the marble-floored lobby of the building, and she can feel that he wants to say something. Outside in the street, he catches her up, and asks, 'Do you dance?'

She stops.

'You walk like a dancer,' he says.

'*Italiano!*' she says, using the strict tone of the teacher, then

24

smiling to show she's joking. She sees him struggling to think of Italian words.

'*Sei ballerina?*' he asks.

'No, I'm not a ballet dancer,' she tells him.

There's a moment when they could fall into step and start a conversation, but she can see he's lost his nerve and she doesn't want to elaborate.

Instead, she smiles and says, '*A domani!*'

She walks smartly on. Looking back when she gets to the top of the street, on the pretext of checking before she crosses the road, she sees he has disappeared and wonders if he wasn't going in her direction after all, or whether he has nipped down a side street to avoid the awkwardness of walking just behind or just in front of her.

Letty's surprised how familiar the layout of Rome feels, even though she hasn't been here since she was eight years old. On that occasion, she and Frances and Ivo arrived on the airport train at Termini. Perhaps because it was her first trip to an Italian city – they'd always been to villas in Tuscany or Puglia before – or perhaps because she was at an age where she took everything in, she remembers being in the taxi to the hotel, feeling very low to the road as they bumped over cobblestones, swerved around buses, and accelerated away from traffic lights amid swarms of mopeds. It was night-time and she remembers craning to see the full height of the towering white Vittorio Emanuele monument, thinking that it looked like a model, not a real thing, and speeding past random floodlit columns and bits of temple that just stood beside the road as naturally as parked cars or newspaper stands.

The lunchtime traffic is very heavy and the air is thick with exhaust. It's not pleasant walking so she decides to get on a bus. In the crush of passengers, Letty is squashed up next to a young man in a shiny grey suit. His hair is slicked back and he smells strongly of cologne. He is talking to someone she can't see who's sitting down. As the bus stops suddenly, the standing passengers are catapulted forward, and she sees that the young man's companion is a bride in a big white wedding dress. At the stop near the foot of the Campidoglio, the young man shouts at the other passengers to let them through, and Letty decides to get off too. The groom jumps the bride from bus to kerb. She is wearing trainers under the many layers of net skirting that have acquired a grey border from swishing along Rome's grimy streets.

The groom takes the bride's hand. In his other hand he holds his mobile phone, filming their ascent of the wide, flat steps up to the square. He's chatting all the time in Italian, too fast for Letty to understand. She tries to keep to the side of them, not wanting to appear in their video like a poorly dressed brides-maid following on behind. There's something gloriously un-selfconscious about the couple in their finery, the way the bride keeps scolding him for the poor angle, the way he pro-tests that his arm isn't long enough! *Mamma mia!*

At the top of the steps, the bride adjusts the flowers in her hair, using the phone as a mirror, and then she turns, smiles at Letty and asks, in Italian, if she will take a photo of them.

'*Certo!*'

They pose, first with Rome behind them and then the other way, with the equestrian statue of Marcus Aurelius as the background.

The groom checks the photos, says thank you, shakes her hand.

'Congratulations!' says Letty, wishing she knew what you say in Italian. Is it *Saluti*? Or *Auguri*? Or is that just for toasts and birthdays?

'You are English?' the groom asks.

'Yes. I hope you will be very happy!'

The bride asks what she has said. The groom translates. The

26

bride rushes to Letty and plants a kiss on both her cheeks. The groom shakes her hand again. They look so utterly delighted by the good wishes of a stranger that Letty wonders if it is a tradition, like first footing on New Year's Eve in Scotland is. She smiles, then with a shrug says, '*Ciao!*' and walks away, not looking back in case they decide to invite her for a drink or something. She wonders whether, if she stays in Rome long enough and becomes more fluent in the language, the Italian side of her will start to prevail over the English reserve that makes her feel embarrassed at this brush of intimacy with two strangers.

How odd that she will be in their lives forever as the taker of the photo that will sit on the sideboard in their parents' houses. She wonders if they will ever say, 'Do you remember that an English girl took that?' Or whether they will just see their smiles and remember how it felt to be newly married under a perfect blue sky with statues sculpted by Michelangelo looking down on them.

A bride on a bus is somehow much more romantic than a bride in a white vintage Rolls-Royce.

Letty decides that if she ever gets married she will use public transport too.

Not that it's likely. She has been in love twice. The first time, it was really more of a crush because she was only eleven. She had just gone to board at ballet school. Vadim, the Russian boy, was in his final year and he danced like no one she had ever seen. After the end-of-year performance, she'd hung around, trying to get up the courage to take this last chance of speaking to him. When he appeared, she knew she only had seconds alone with him, but found she had no idea what to say, even though she'd imagined the moment many times.

'You are amazing!' she blurted.

He'd smiled right at her – modest, uncomprehending, amused, she couldn't tell – but the image stayed with her for two years as she practised relentlessly, knowing that ultimately words did not matter, dancing would be their language, and she would make herself good enough to wear Aurora's rose-pink tutu, or Odette's white feathers, and be a worthy partner for his Prince.

But then she'd got injured. After that she couldn't bear to have anything to do with ballet.

Letty's first proper boyfriend was Josh. Maybe spending her entire adolescence in a world of fairy-tale princesses made her believe Josh would rescue her from the ordeal of life after ballet school. She was fifteen when he asked her to go out with him, and she was quickly enveloped in a blissful haze of wonder that this could be happening to her. When he betrayed her, it was as if her body and her mind shattered into nothingness. The still searingly painful memory blots out the warm sweetness of her encounter with the newlyweds, like a cloud passing over the sun.

Letty blinks back tears of self-loathing that well automatically in her eyes if she ever allows herself to think about Josh and all the other mistakes she has made. If only she hadn't been so naive, so trusting, so stupid. If only she could rewind those bits of her life where she has allowed herself to think 'Why not?' instead of sticking with her natural caution.

4

Thursday

ALF

Alf can't sleep. At first light he gets up, washes and dresses as quietly as he can, and leaves. He'd like to go for a run to kick off the fidgety anxiety that's made him toss and turn all night, but he'd have to come back and shower and risk waking the others up, and they're usually pretty grumpy in the mornings, especially if they've drunk a lot the night before.

The streets are empty except for the refuse men. The sudden loud shattering of a thousand bottles, as a recycling bin is lifted and emptied, startles awake the homeless man who always sleeps at the tram stop in the middle of Via Marmorata.

Alf walks into the only bar that's open this early, and stands at the counter stirring sugar into an espresso while he scrolls through his Instagram feed.

His mum has posted a photo of his bedroom, except it's painted pink, with two identical cots with frilly canopies and matching frilly curtains. The caption says: *Almost ready! #twins #babies #excited*.

He's happy for her and Gary after all this time, he really is, and he's glad she's feeling confident. He thinks it must be a good sign that she's posted a photo, because normally she's superstitious. His instinct would be to put a comment saying 'Good Luck!' but he doesn't dare, in case having babies is like performing in competition and it's bad luck to wish good luck. So he just 'likes' her post. And then he wonders if she'll read something into that. Maybe the photo was meant as a kind of message to him that he's not welcome back? Usually her posts are about the school rather than about her personally. Endless shots of her dancers holding up silver cups. He wonders if she boxed up his football trophies. His dancing trophies are displayed in the dance hall cabinet, alongside the photo of him and his mum dancing on the beach when he was a little boy. He can't imagine her binning them. His football ones, yes, but his dance trophies are as much hers as they are his.

Alf realizes suddenly that he's not cross with her any more. Whenever he's thought about her over the past months, his body has tensed with resentment. Now he just feels weary and a bit sad. He knows she didn't mean to do what she did. At least, she did mean it, but she didn't realize what the consequences would be. And he wishes that he hadn't had to take sides, but at the time he hadn't been given a choice.

Mum's due date must be quite soon now. On the spur of the moment, he decides he'll ring her, wish her well. Why not? Somebody has to make the first move. He pulls her number out of his contacts, then realizes it's only six thirty in the morning at home. If he rings now, he'll wake her and she'll think there's something wrong.

He puts his phone back in his pocket. He's too old to be missing his mum.

Alf orders *un cornetto vuoto*, which is what they call a croissant with no jam or custard in it. Icing sugar falls like a tiny smattering of snow over the shiny black counter as he eats it. He downs his espresso in one, pays, then orders another cornetto, which the bartender hands to him in a paper napkin. Alf crosses the road and gives the pastry to the homeless guy.

Gina says that you shouldn't give them money because they'll only use it on drugs, but she doesn't like it when he gives them food either.

The guy accepts the offer with wary surprise. Alf has no idea how old he is. Could be Alf's age, could be forty. His skin is burnished and etched with grime and the hardship of keeping alive. It's an interesting face. Alf would like to take a photo. Sometimes he thinks the photos he posts of daily life in Rome are too pretty. There are so many homeless people in the city it seems wrong to ignore them, but he wouldn't want to intrude on the little privacy that they have living on the streets.

Today's theme is food.

The teacher asks them what they ate the previous evening. In Italian you say 'I have eaten', not 'I ate'. Violetta gets it straight away. She's very good at grammar. She says she had *tagliatelle al ragu*. There's something about the way she hesitates and thinks before she says the name of the dish that makes Alf think that she probably didn't. She doesn't look like a pasta eater.

Alf ate *zucchini fritti*. It was Mike's turn to cook and he's pretty good. Alf had never eaten a courgette before he came to Italy, and now he likes them a lot.

The teacher announces that they are going to do a listening, which means gathering around the CD player and listening five times to the same conversation between two Italians. After the first time, they have to pair up and say what they've understood.

'*Niente!*' says Masakasu, laughing.

Alf tells him that it's a conversation about two people setting up a vegetarian restaurant. He seems to understand more than the rest of the class, probably because he's been in the country longer. He's used to hearing Italian spoken at speed.

31

He's done more shopping, read more menus, watched more adverts on television.

By the fifth listening, he's bored. He lolls in his chair, unable to concentrate. The teacher tells him to get a coffee in the break. *Un espresso!* she advises.

Alf thinks it's weird how the class members always sit in the same places in the cafe. It reminds him of the time he went on a coach tour of Devon with his mum and her sequence class, when he couldn't understand why everyone always returned to the same seats they had randomly selected the day they left Blackpool.

The boys always get something to eat; the girls don't. Today, after a flurry of chat, Heidi stands up and walks over to the boys' table. She says they are thinking of going out to lunch together and would the boys like to come? There is a restaurant around the corner from the school where they do a buffet for eight euros. You can eat as much as you want.

When they return to the classroom, Heidi tells the teacher their plan excitedly, almost as if she's expecting to get a gold star for practising today's theme. She's quite a needy person, Alf thinks. She wants to be everyone's friend and she wants to be the teacher's pet, but it's useful to have someone like her in a class. If she were one of his beginners, he would pick her out to demonstrate a step with. She'd giggle and pretend not to be able to do it, but she'd give it a go and probably be quite good, though you can't always tell from how pretty someone is whether they'll be able to dance.

The teacher is handing them yet another sheet of paper with sentences about the meaning of colours. The idea is to guess which colour goes with the description. It's pretty obvious, because a lot of the words are almost the same as they are in English. Red is the colour of love and passion. White is the colour of purity, of angels, of brides. *Passare la notte in bianco* means not to have been able to sleep, which is very relevant to Alf today. Yellow is the colour of sunshine, but also, in Italy, of detective novels, he reads, fidgeting in his chair. He hates spending so long sitting down. Mr Marriot used to say there are seven different sorts of intelligence and everyone has a different way of learning. He thought Alf was a kinaesthetic learner, which means he learns better through physical activity than reading or listening. Sometimes he wonders whether that was his teacher's way of reassuring him that he wasn't thick.

He doesn't think Susanna has heard about the seven intelligences. Perhaps they're not a thing in Italy? Even when she says they're going to play a game, it's still sitting down, taking it in turns to describe someone in the class and see if the others can guess who they are thinking of.

'She has black hair and violet eyes,' Alf volunteers.

'*Violetta!*' the others chorus.

'*Violetta è bella!*' adds Masakasu.

Which makes Alf regret choosing her, because she's clearly not someone who likes attention – unlike Heidi, who's looking slightly put out.

He wonders if her parents called her Violet because her eyes are such a deep blue? Aren't all babies born with blue eyes? Or is that kittens? Perhaps she wears contact lenses to emphasize the depth of the colour? He doesn't think so. She is not vain. She wears no make-up. She doesn't even paint her toenails. The only adornment she has is a tiny tattoo of a heart with a knife through it, inked over the third and fourth metatarsals of her right foot. He wonders about the story of that tattoo. It must have been painful because the skin is very tender there.

As if she knows what he's thinking, Violetta slides her feet under her chair.

Finally, the students are allowed to stand up and circulate freely, asking each other questions about the cultural significance of colours in their own countries. He wasn't aware that they had cultural significance until he starts thinking about it. Blue is sad. Green is envy.

When Alf approaches Violetta, she turns, looking in another direction, but by sidestepping across her back, like the sliding doors movement in the cha cha, he ends up facing her. But the only question he can think to ask is, 'What's your favourite colour?'

He feels like he's back at primary school. He wants to be able to ask why she's here, what's important to her, who she is.

She thinks for a moment, before saying it's black. She asks what his is.

'*Blu.*'

Normally he's good at this, he thinks. He never has a problem chatting to people. But with her, he's just inept. He hasn't a clue how to make her interested in him, or even to make her smile. She's as absent as a model in a monochrome photograph advertising some cool perfume.

Then she says, 'Like the Azzurri?'

'The Blues' is what Italians call their national football team.

Distantly beautiful, she knows about football and she's remembered something about him from the day before. Alf's mood see-saws.

On their way to the restaurant, he falls into step with her, hoping she's not going to insist on Italian.

'How long are you here for?' he asks.

'In Rome?'

He doesn't know what else his question could mean. For the first time, he wonders if the remote quality she has is simple nervousness.

'A month, maybe.'

'You're a student, right? What subject?' he tries again.

'Latin,' she says.

He thinks she must mean the language rather than the dance style.

'You've come to the right place then,' he says, and then feels like a dick because it's such a dumb thing to say. He's finally managed to start a chat with the person he's been obsessed with all week, and he comes up with the sort of line he'd use on a barmaid.

'That'll be why you're good at grammar,' he says.

'Yes,' she says.

Most girls he knows would say 'I'm not really . . .' He likes the fact she doesn't.

Then she says, 'You're much better at speaking.' Which surprises him, because he didn't think that she had noticed him particularly.

'I just don't care so much if I get it wrong,' he says, adding, 'And I usually do.'

'I wish I could be more like that,' she says.

Not: 'Don't be silly, you're really good!' as Gina would say.

The restaurant has a big table laden with a variety of dishes. Chargrilled vegetables, arancini, various types of pasta. Heidi beckons Violetta over to the space she's saved next to her, and Alf finds himself with Jo and Masakasu again.

When he sees Violetta going up to the buffet, he scrapes back his chair mid-conversation, and stands beside her as she helps herself to a small portion of tomato and mozzarella salad garnished with basil leaves.

'*Rosso, bianco, verde,*' he says. 'Like the Italian flag.'

'Oh,' she says. 'I knew it was called *insalata tricolore* but I never thought of the flag. Is that why?'

Suddenly he doesn't know whether it's something he's heard, or just made up.

'I think so,' he says carefully.

'What are you having?' she asks, watching as he ladles *gnocchi alla Sorrentina* from the steaming bowl that a man wearing a white chef's jacket has just deposited on the table.

'It's Thursday and Romans eat gnocchi on Thursdays.'

'Really? Is there some reason for that?' she asks. 'I mean, like fish on Friday?'

He has no idea. It's just something he's picked up.

He asks the cook why Romans eat gnocchi on Thursdays, seeing from the wince on Violetta's face that he's got the grammar wrong.

The cook thinks about it for a moment. It's true, he says, on Thursday, a lot of people eat gnocchi, but he has no idea why.

They all laugh.

When she allows herself to relax, Alf thinks, she seems younger, less intimidating, and her smile is warm and genuine. He wants more, but he senses that if he pushes her she will retreat again, and he knows that Heidi is watching them talk. He doesn't want his interaction with Violetta to be public property.

'I'm just going to get a picture,' Alf says, putting down his plate and taking out his phone to snap a shot of the colourful table. 'I post about stuff in Rome, you know, not the usual tourist things.'

Violetta steps back as if he's told her to get out of the way, and returns to her seat.

Alf posts the photo with the caption: *Buon appetito! #Rome #Roma #lunch*.

Heidi suggests that they get some wine for the table.

It's a strange feeling being with the class away from the school. In the classroom, there's a certain camaraderie. It's a bit like you're all stuck in a lift together, Alf thinks. You know you're going to be with these people for some time, so you try not to like or dislike them too much, or say anything controversial, because if you get on with each other, the experience will be more pleasant. Outside there's not so much reason to do that.

Even though he's spoken very little to anyone, he's formed quite definite opinions about them. Paola and Carla are good-time girls. They've no interest in learning Italian, which is why they turn up late if at all. Studying is just the way they got their rich daddies to fork out the money for an extended holiday. Angela is nice enough, but she's old enough to be his gran. Jo is boring; Masakasu is a pain in the arse. It was cool the first couple of times he gave them a song, but it's now getting irritating. Heidi is physically attractive and he kind of knows he could, but also that she would be a nightmare afterwards.

Then there's Violetta.

He hasn't felt so disorientated and tongue-tied by a woman since he was twelve years old, when he saw Flavia Cacace doing an Argentine tango show dance. He and his mum waited for her at the stage door, and when she came out Donna took a picture of them together and told her that Alf was North-West Ballroom and Latin Champion in his age group, and that when he was older he wanted to dance with her. Flavia was sweet and said she'd look forward to that, which she probably said to everyone, but for weeks he thought about the way her eyes shone when she spoke to him. Then he overheard his mum talking to Leanne, his dance partner Sadie's mum, about how he kept the photo by his bed. Hormones, Leanne had whispered knowingly. And Sadie had overheard and mocked him mercilessly, even though she fell for a different one of the male professionals every single season of *Strictly Come Dancing*, and wrote them fan letters and everything.

It's a crush, Alf tells himself. He knows less about Violetta than he did about Flavia. She is beautiful, her favourite colour is black, she is a student of Latin. For heaven's sake. I'm too old for a crush, he thinks.

Alf pushes back his chair, says he has to go, and leaves a ten-euro note to cover his share.

Outside, he checks his phone. Gina's dad has liked his photo. Alf sometimes wonders how Stuart ever gets any work done, since he always seems to be looking at his feed when Alf posts. It might be a bit spooky, like he's checking up on Alf, if he weren't such a great guy.

It's quarter to one in the UK. Perhaps he's having a sandwich at his desk. Alf pictures him sitting in the luxurious office where he and Gina once met him for lunch. He remembers the soft depth of the carpet underfoot, and how underdressed he felt in jeans, even though he'd put on a shirt.

Stuart was wearing a blue suit, the shade that's just lighter than navy. He took them to a sushi restaurant. When Alf saw the prices, he ordered very little, but Stuart told him to have whatever he wanted because today, for the purposes of his expense account, Alf was a billionaire oligarch.

The dessert had a bit of gold leaf on it, which Alf had left on his plate, and Gina had laughed and said he was meant to eat it, but her dad said, 'Listen, young lady, you don't tell an oligarch what to do.'

And Alf had said, 'Yeah, I had gold for breakfast,' then, gaining confidence: 'I find it a bit rich with every meal.'

And Gina's dad had high-fived him.

Alf remembers the feeling of pride at gaining his approval. It was like confirmation that he could cut it in the world outside Blackpool.

It was only six months ago, Alf calculates. But it seems longer.

5

Friday

LETTY

Letty is in the Forum. She is standing on an empty pedestal, one arm shielding her eyes from the sun.

'Put your arm down!' Frances is shouting.

'I can't see!'

'You don't have to be able to see! It's a bloody photograph!'

Letty hears the camera click.

'Can't you do an arabesque?' Her mother's voice. 'Or fifth position or something?'

Letty obliges by putting both arms in the air, fingers held precisely as her ballet teacher demands.

'Lovely!' shouts Frances.

'All done!' Her father's voice, his hands on her waist, jumping her down.

Letty wakes up. As returning consciousness fuses sensations with memory, she thinks, I'm in Rome, then closes her eyes again.

The photograph of her on the pedestal in a sundress, feet turned out, arms aloft in fifth position, eyes blinking in the sun, always stood on Marina's mantelpiece.

'My fifth little Roman lady,' Marina called it.

Letty doesn't know if she really remembers it being taken, or whether a memory has formed because she has seen it so many times.

There's an end-of-the-week feeling to the class and a slightly flat mood in the break, with everyone concentrating on their phones instead of talking to each other. It's almost as if their lunch together was a date between work colleagues that didn't quite pan out, and none of them is sure how to recalibrate the relationship.

Letty and Heidi ended up being the last in the restaurant and finished off the wine together, which was a mistake because Heidi got confessional and revealed that she and her husband were having a trial separation, which was slightly too intimate a conversation given how little they knew each other. It made Letty feel that she should reciprocate with a secret of her own, but she wasn't going to do that, so she ended up agreeing to meet Heidi for brunch on Sunday, which she didn't really want to do.

The theme of today's class is family. They learn the words for brother, sister, aunt, uncle, grandparents, children. Then they sit in groups to talk about their own families.

Letty is with Angela and Alf.

Angela asks Alf if he has a brother.

No.

A sister?

No, but his mum is having twin baby girls soon.

'*Che meraviglia!*' Angela says.

Letty thinks she probably meant to say 'How lovely!' instead of 'What a miracle!', but Alf takes it to mean that his mum is old to be having babies.

'She's only thirty-seven,' he protests.

Angela has three grown-up children. She's been married to her husband for thirty years. She has two grandchildren.

'You're a grandmother?' says Alf disbelievingly.

Oh, please! thinks Letty.

'*Mia nonna era italiana*,' she volunteers. '*È morta.*'

Now that she's told them her grandmother is dead, they don't know what to say. There's a moment of awkwardness, then Alf asks if she has two parents.

Yes. She's a little surprised at the question.

'*Mia papà è morta*,' he says in explanation.

'*Mio papà è morto*,' Letty corrects him automatically. 'The ending has to be masculine for a man. I'm sorry,' she adds, meaning for correcting him, but it must sound like she's sorry about his dad because he says, 'It's OK, I didn't know him. It happened a long time ago.'

He gestures with his thumb over his shoulder, like a half-hearted hitchhiker.

When the bell goes for the end of the morning lessons, everyone is keen to get away quickly, as if to avoid the possibility of someone suggesting another lunch.

The Forum is swarming with tour groups led by guides brandishing scarves on sticks, to make it easy to follow them. Letty hears snatches of English, French and Spanish as she weaves past, trying to find a peaceful space to look at the map and work out the location of the pedestal that she stood on for the photo. She has it in mind to send her mother a selfie from the same spot. She's surprised not to have heard from Frances again, and feels a little guilty for being monosyllabic when she spoke to her.

Letty is sitting on some steps, looking at the map, trying to match the dots and lines to the bits of wall and column, when she hears a familiar voice.

To her left, a small group of middle-aged women are learning about the Arch of Septimius Severus. The guide is speaking in English. He has his back to them because he's pointing out the features on the arch, but it's unmistakably Alf from her class.

'The arch was originally dedicated to the Emperor Severus and his two sons, Geta and Caracalla,' he's telling them. 'But you know how brothers are? Always fighting? These guys took it to another level. Caracalla murdered Geta.'

One of the women says, in an American accent, 'Oh my, those Romans were so bloodthirsty!'

'So when Caracalla became emperor,' Alf continues, 'he got his people to put another inscription over the top that doesn't mention Geta, so it's like he never even existed. It was the Roman way of wiping all his data. It's called *damnatio memoria*.'

Letty winces at the incorrect Latin.

How awkward. She remembers talking to him yesterday, him asking about Latin. She would never have imagined that he knew anything about Ancient Rome, let alone worked as a guide.

Letty stands and walks smartly off in the opposite direction. The House of the Vestal Virgins, she has worked out, is nearer the entrance to the Forum. Once she enters the space, she remembers exactly which pedestal it was that she stood on. She waits for a group of Chinese tourists to hear the history in Mandarin and move on. Then, finding herself alone for a moment, she stands next to the pedestal to take a selfie. Unable to get an angle that shows her and the pedestal, she moves further away.

'Do you need a hand?'

Alf, with the American ladies a few steps behind him. His white T-shirt has his Instagram handle @rometourguidealf printed on it.

'No, I'm fine,' she says automatically, and then, 'Well, actually . . .'

'Give me one minute,' he says.

Letty wants to say, really, don't bother, but he's already caught the women up and is saying goodbye, his arms outstretched, as if awarding them a symbolic farewell embrace. She sees the delight on their faces as he tells them what a pleasure it has been showing them around, and that he hopes they will enjoy the rest of their stay. They fumble in their purses, drawing out a note each to give him, without even looking at how much. She notices how he makes taking the money part of a handshake, then stands back, shrugs and, as if he can't resist, gives each of them in turn a warm hug and kiss on the cheek. It's done with a kind of chivalrous respect, but she sees the sparkle in their eyes. After a couple of steps away, they huddle together excitedly, like the schoolfriends they probably once were, discussing their latest heartthrob.

'It's *damnatio memoriae*, by the way,' Letty says, when he returns with a smile on his face.

'I'm sorry?'

'What Caracalla did to Geta. *Damnatio memori-ae*,' she says, emphasizing the last phoneme. 'Not *damnatio memoria*, which is what you said.'

Alf's uncomprehending look shows her that he didn't see her sitting on the steps, and now she's going to have to explain and she doesn't know why she felt the need to correct him anyway.

'I overheard your talk,' she says, waving towards the end of the Forum where the arch is.

'Tell me again,' says Alf.

'*Damnatio memoriae*,' she says.

He repeats it after her.

'Thanks,' he says. 'I'll remember that. Maybe I'll check with you before attempting any more Latin.' Again, the smile. There's an attractive openness about it.

Letty wishes she hadn't said anything. What was she thinking? Who in the world, apart from her, would care? The equable way he has dealt with her means he is not the arrogant person she took him for, and she feels slightly ashamed of herself for making assumptions based solely on his good looks, and the fact he is male. It's the sort of thing Frances does. Now she's irrationally annoyed with her mother for being like that, and wonders why she's even bothering to try to amuse her by sending a photo.

'So, where do you want this photo?' Alf asks, holding out his hand for her phone.

'Over here.' Letty points. 'I came here with my parents when I was eight, and there's this photo of me on a pedestal, and I just thought it might be fun to recreate it . . .'

'Not a problem,' he agrees. 'Do you want a hand getting up?'

Before she can say no, he has lifted her effortlessly, his hands confident on her waist, as if he lifts women onto pedestals all the time. Perhaps he does? Perhaps this is where everyone has a photo taken and it's not unique to her family?

She finds her footing and takes a moment to decide on her pose, before standing with one leg slightly bent at the knee, arms by her sides, like a statue. The sun is behind her, so there is no need to shield her eyes.

She attempts a self-mocking pout to overcome the embarrassment of the situation.

'That's good,' he encourages. 'Turn a little bit more so that I get your profile. That's great!'

She goes from feeling silly and self-conscious to quite enjoying it, even raising her arms into fifth like in the photo on Marina's mantelpiece, laughing at herself as she does it.

'I knew you were a dancer!' he says.

She drops her arms and jumps down from the pedestal.

'Thanks,' she says as he hands her back her phone.

She's about to walk away, when he asks, 'So was that the last time you were here? When you were eight?'

'Yes. We came because of a series of books.'

Why did she say that? Nobody needs a reason to come to

Rome. It's Rome, for heaven's sake. But Alf is nodding, waiting for her to continue.

'They were about a group of children having adventures in Ancient Rome,' she explains. 'By an author called Caroline Lawrence. The main character was a girl, so I suppose I identified with her. I loved them so much my mother decided we should come to Rome, check out the location . . .'

It was one of Frances's typically extravagant gestures. The first book in the series had been a birthday present from her uncle Rollo, who had read Classics at Oxford. It irked Frances that Rollo provided the book that switched Letty on to reading, because Frances, while working long hours, had always made time to read to her daughter at night.

Letty understands the family dynamic now better than she did then. She remembers her grandmother Marina at Sunday lunch remarking how wonderful it was that Rollo had introduced Letty to these books she loved, and Frances, clearly slighted, upping the ante with, 'We thought we'd go to Rome at half term, to see where it all happened.'

Then her father saying, 'First I've heard of it!'

Letty can still remember the invisible flames of Frances's wrath flaring across the table, and not understanding why her mother was cross with him.

And so the three of them had come to Rome. They'd visited Ostia Antica, where the first of Caroline Lawrence's books was set, and taken a fast train to Naples to spend a rushed day in Pompeii, where the characters lived in another of the stories. She remembers turning pirouettes on the stage in the theatre there, imagining she was Flavia Gemina, the books' heroine.

'Is that how you got into Latin?' Alf asks.

'Yes, my uncle taught me.'

Alf lets out a little laugh.

'What?' she asks.

'No, it's just that I was thinking in class today, you know

when we were learning the words for relatives? *Lo zio*, wasn't it, for uncle? I was thinking, why are we learning this? Who-ever talks about their uncle? And' – he looks at his phone – 'now less than three hours later, here we are talking about your uncle!'

At the Sunday lunch following their return, when they were describing what a brilliant time they'd had, Letty had mentioned the sign in Pompeii that said *Cave Canem* – Beware of the Dog!

And Rollo had said, 'Why don't I teach you Latin?'

And even though Frances had bought her every subsequent Caroline Lawrence book as soon as it came out in hardcover, those stories were quickly replaced in Letty's affection by the tale of Aeneas and his adventures, written by Virgil, whose words Rollo taught her to decipher using the rules of grammar and a vast dictionary, which was far more enthralling than reading something everyone else could read in English.

Alf smiles at her. She notices that his eyes are deep brown, not blue. With his blondish hair, it's a striking combination. As they amble in no particular direction, the silence between them is comfortable. Part of her nags that she ought to find an excuse to get away from him, but mostly she's quite enjoying the company. She's spent a lot of time on her own during the week, trying to think things through, yet nothing has become any clearer.

'Should we be trying to speak Italian?' Letty asks.

'No offence,' says Alf. 'But we're not really good enough to say anything interesting, are we? I mean, I've known you a week and all I know is that your favourite colour is black.'

'I only said that because most of my clothes are black. I haven't had a favourite colour since I was little.'

'When it was . . . ?'

'Pink, obviously,' says Letty.

He smiles at her.

'Have you seen Santa Maria Antiqua?' he asks.

'I don't think so,' says Letty.

'I think you'll like it,' he says, turning towards a church that backs on to the Palatine Hill.

'How long have you been a tour guide?' Letty asks. 'I thought you were a waiter.' It sounds as if she's accusing him of lying.

'I'm a man of many talents,' he says with a broad smile. 'I followed a few of the tours round, you know? I thought, how hard can it be?'

Letty can't imagine how anyone could have the self-confidence to show people round the Forum, unless they were a classical scholar.

'What people like are stories, you know, that bring it alive for them,' says Alf, as if he's read the expression on her face. 'People like you who know about stuff don't take tours, do they?'

It's true, Letty thinks. Her family wouldn't have dreamed of taking a tour. Frances always had a guidebook. Ivo preferred to wander alone, 'soaking up the atmosphere', he called it. Letty was somewhere in between. She was fascinated by the history that Frances was reading out, but she also liked to stay a while in places, let her imagination roam, trying to imagine what life would have been like in the past. Ivo got bored easily. He said it was a nightmare sightseeing with Frances, because it was as if she wanted to own everything. She retaliated that if you'd grown up working class, you didn't take foreign holidays for granted, as he did. Ivo said she always had to have the last word, and Frances said actually he wanted to have the last word himself, so why was it so objectionable for her to? At which point, Ivo usually gave in, catching Letty's eye and shrugging in a gesture of exasperation. It was all good-humoured sparring, but holidays were never that relaxing.

The church is unusual because, unlike most churches that

47

were built on ancient sites, this one was buried by an earth-quake and was untouched by Renaissance or Baroque architects and artists, so that the frescoes that remain in the apse come directly from the Byzantine era. The air inside is cold and smells slightly of the brick that has been hacked away in the recent excavation.

There are a couple of steps leading up to a small chapel to the right of the altar. Faded fragments of ancient wall paintings are visible, but Letty cannot see quite why Alf was so eager for her to see it until, suddenly, the chapel becomes dark and from some hidden 3D technology, the walls light up with the Roman mosaic that would have adorned the original temple. And just as she is taking in this virtual spectacle, the patches of fresco start to expand into complete early Christian paintings, with inscriptions showing that a thousand years ago this was a place where people came to be cured of their ills by prayer.

In the coolness of the chapel, with the soft rhythm of the commentary and colourful saints emerging from the walls around her, the frown that always seems to be stretched across Letty's forehead relaxes, as if she herself has come as a pilgrim and found balm for her troubled mind.

Alf smiles at her as they emerge from the dimness of the church into the golden sunshine of late afternoon, but does not say anything, as if he knows that she needs time and peace to process the experience.

'Thank you,' says Letty. 'That was absolutely fascinating.'

'*Prego!*' he says.

They both stop walking, as if unsure what happens next.

'Don't you have to work?' she asks.

'No, but if you'd rather I left you . . .'

'I'm quite enjoying my own private tour!' she hears herself saying.

'I'm glad!' he says. 'The Palatine?'

He indicates the route with a bow and an exaggerated flourish of his arm, like a bestockinged courtier in the presence of royalty.

'I like it up here,' Alf says, as they wander through the Farnese Gardens. 'When the tours have gone, I sometimes come up here for a think.'

About what, she wonders, but doesn't ask, as it would be an intrusive question.

The afternoon sun is mellow, and the air that separates them feels softer somehow. There is no need to fill it with talk.

Alf leads her over to a viewpoint where they can see the whole of the Forum and Rome beyond.

A large seagull swoops, hovers, then perches on the wall in front of them.

Alf takes a picture of it.

'The seagulls here look different from home,' he says.

'In what sense?' Letty asks.

'Like they own the city,' says Alf.

'You're right. They are kind of imperious. Julius Seagull,' she suddenly says, laughing.

'Hey, can I borrow that for my post?' he asks.

'*Prego!*' she says.

He taps the words into his screen, then posts the image.

'Can you speak Latin?' he asks, as they mooch on.

'It's not really a spoken language.'

'What if you bumped into an Ancient Roman?'

'I'd probably be as useless as I am with contemporary Romans.'

'So what is it?'

'What's what?'

'Why do you study it?'

'I like working the language out. It's almost mathematical.'

'That's a reason to like it?'

She laughs.

'For me, yes. And obviously I like being able to read the literature as it was written,' she says. 'Because you understand that they were just like us in so many ways.'

'Who's your favourite Roman writer?' Alf asks.

She wonders if he is really interested or whether he is humouring her.

'Catullus,' she answers. 'He was a poet.'

She remembers the thrill of reading him for the first time, and how there was one poem that seemed to sum up how she felt, speaking to her across time.

'What sort of poems?'

'Love poems,' Letty says. Then, feeling slightly embarrassed, she hears herself babbling, 'There's this poem called "Odi et amo". It's only two lines long, but it says everything I feel about love, somehow.'

'*Amo* is "I love", right?' Alf says. 'Same as Italian.'

'And *odi* is "I hate",' she says. '*Odi et amo,*' she recites, translating as she goes. 'I hate and I love. *Quare id faciam, fortasse requiris.* Perhaps you're asking why? *Nescio.* I don't know. *Sed fieri sentio et excrucior.* But it's the way I feel and I am torn in two.'

In the silence that follows, Alf stares at her, and she feels that in her enthusiasm for her subject she has revealed too much about herself.

'*Excrucior,*' she says briskly, like a schoolteacher. 'It literally means "I'm on the cross". Crucifixion being a common method of elimination in those days, as we know.'

And then she walks on, slightly ahead of him now, feeling the colour in her face.

What possessed her to quote that poem to him? Letty asks herself. Now the space between them feels all jangly again.

In the Palatine Museum there is a set of wings, in marble, that must have been attached to some figure that no longer exists. Victory, she thinks. Or Cupid?

Alf asks her to take a picture of him in front of it, so that, when she lines up the shot carefully, he appears to be wearing a winged helmet, like the gods' messenger Mercury.

'Would you like me to take one of you?' he asks, as she hands him back his phone.

'No thanks,' she says. 'I'm not usually keen on having my photo taken.'

'Shame,' he says. Then, almost under his breath: 'Because you are very beautiful.'

She spins.

'What am I supposed to say to that?'

Why can't she just say thank you like anyone else would?

'Sorry. I was out of order,' he says, holding up his hands as if to defend himself.

'It's just that people say it to me all the time, especially in Italy.' She tries to dial down her frustration. 'People don't usually comment on your appearance, do they? Not people in bars and things, anyway.'

'It's just what Italians do,' Alf says. 'I don't think it really means anything apart from trying to brighten your day.'

He looks at the screen as his phone buzzes with a notification.

Now that his eyes are lowered, she thinks it is he who is beautiful. With his wavy hair framing a face with strong cheekbones, a long straight nose and a square chin, he could actually be the model for a classical statue. Because his face is usually animated, talking or laughing, she hasn't quite seen how sculptural it is when still.

Should she tell him? she wonders. To even things out? Or would that make her seem even more odd?

The bell is ringing to say that the Forum is closing.

'So, where are you heading?' he asks, as they walk towards a different exit he knows that leads onto the road between the Palatine and Caelian hills.

'I'm staying near Porta Maggiore,' she tells him.

'So, you can get the number three tram from here,' he says, pausing for a moment at the stop.

And then he's gone, strolling off down the hill, and she watches him, now talking on his phone.

6

Weekend

ALF

Alf always meets his flatmates after they finish work on Friday. There's a bar in Testaccio where the students drink. Alf doesn't know why that's the one they choose, since they're always complaining about their job – teaching English as a Foreign Language – but it has a deal on cocktails early in the evening, which is probably reason enough. The first people he spots are Mike and Sally. Mike's brooding over a tall glass of beer while Sally's chatting brightly, holding a glass of Coke, or probably a Cuba Libre, trying to cheer him up. Mike is always morose. Alf doesn't know what a nice person like Sally is doing with him. It seems more like a habit than a relationship to him. Alf sometimes wonders if Mike resents him being there, but Sally has reassured him that no, Mike's always like that. He resents everyone, she said laughing, as if it's an endearing side to his character.

Alf says hello to them.

Sally says, 'She's over there!'

Gina is sitting on a semicircular banquette with a group of Italian lads drinking Aperol Spritz. She's telling them the story about when they went to see Roma play, and how a loose ball coming from the foot of Daniele De Rossi flew into the stands and hit her on the head, so, technically, she headed a ball from De Rossi!

The Italians love that. He recognizes the look that passes between them as Gina drains her glass. He's seen it often enough amongst his mates. They think she's an easy touch, possibly worse. He feels a pang of protectiveness.

Gina looks up and waves him over.

'This is Alf,' she says.

He notices that they say *ciao* to him, recognizing him as somebody of their own age and status, rather than *buona sera*, which he thinks they would probably say to Gina.

'Don't you ever learn?' he says to Gina as he sits down next to her.

'Jealous?' she asks.

'No,' he says, giving her a quick kiss.

He doesn't like the bitter taste of Aperol.

'I thought it would be good practice for you to talk to these guys,' she says, as if she's arranged this for him. She's started doing that a lot recently, making out that the stuff she does is all for him. Maybe she always did and he never noticed before.

Gina tells her students that they should speak to Alf in Italian now, not English.

'I don't get paid for overtime,' she declares.

They ask him where he is studying. Does he like it? And then he has run out of things to say because he's not going to ask how old they are, what they do in their free time, or how many brothers and sisters they have.

He feels depressed at his lack of progress. The cost of his lessons is eating into his savings, but after a week, he doesn't feel he's learned anything.

'Can we go eat?' he asks Gina, wanting to get out of the bar. 'I'm starving.'

'My boyfriend is very hungry!' Gina tells the boys.

Alf's not sure whether there's a double entendre in Italian, but there's a lot of nudging and smiling knowingly at him.

Perhaps it's just that they fancy her, Alf thinks, as they say their goodbyes. Why wouldn't they? Gina is very pretty and bubbly. All his mates thought he'd struck gold. And so did he, he reminds himself.

'Let's walk, shall we?' Alf says, when they leave the bar. 'Shoes OK?'

Gina, who is self-conscious about being small, often wears shoes with heels that are impractical on Rome's cobblestones.

'Yes, Mum,' Gina says, looping her arm through his.

It's a joke between them that Alf behaves like the one who is older. He has never lost his credit card or his phone or his keys. If they go on a train, he holds the tickets. He doesn't get drunk. Petite and blonde, Gina doesn't even look that much older than him.

They cross the river and wind their way towards a pizzeria they have eaten in before, which isn't too expensive, unlike some of the tourist traps in Trastevere.

'Outside or inside?' he asks Gina, hoping that she'll say inside. You never see Italians eating outside, especially in April when they still consider it cold. But Gina likes to.

'I want to feel I'm in Italy,' she says, scraping a chair across the cobbles.

It makes you look like a tourist, Alf wants to say. But isn't that what they are? He doesn't know why it bothers him so much.

He orders a *napoletana*; she takes an age to choose between a *quattro stagioni* and a *capricciosa*.

'What do you think?' she asks Alf.

'Up to you,' he says.

He's learned not to decide for her, because nine out of ten times when the food arrives she'll say, 'Oh, I wish I'd had the other one now,' even though, with a pizza, there's barely any difference.

He orders a beer. Gina orders a half carafe of white wine.

Italians always drink beer with pizza. It's one of their things. If you ask an Italian why, they don't know the answer. It doesn't matter that Gina prefers wine, he tells himself. It's a free country.

They've been together almost a year now, the longest relationship he's ever had, and maybe this is what happens when you're with someone a long time. Little things that used to be cute start to grate. When you know what someone is going to say before they say it, that's a sign of closeness, isn't it? Not boredom.

'This is nice,' Gina says, leaning forward. 'Just the two of us for once.'

'Yes,' he says.

Because Mike and Sally were in the flat first, it's like their territory, even though he and Gina are paying half the rent. It was good of Sally to offer them the spare room because it's cheap and Testaccio is a cool place to live, but it's a small room, so Alf often has to leap over piles of Gina's clothes to get to the bed. The flat's on the interior of the building, so there's virtually no light. And he never feels quite comfortable in the communal kitchen-diner.

Sally and Gina were best friends at uni. It was Sally who got her the job. They get on really well, but Mike, not so much.

Alf's gran Cheryl says that there are two types of people in life, radiators and drains. Mike is a definite drain.

Sally's a radiator. He used to think that Gina was too. Recently, he's not so sure. He's not even sure what he is now, although he once was Blackpool's brightest radiator – according to his gran, anyway.

Everything in Blackpool has to be the best. This rollercoaster is the highest; this shop on the seafront sells the finest

Blackpool rock; the pubs compete to sell the cheapest beer. If you believe the signs, there isn't a single fish and chip shop that hasn't won prizes.

Gina drinks her wine as if it's water. Before their food has arrived, she's ordering another *mezzo*. She can get touchy when she's had a lot to drink, reading things into everything he says, so he tries to choose a neutral subject to talk about.

'What are we thinking of doing this summer?' he asks.

'Why? Aren't you happy?'

'I just thought . . . we said we'd go travelling.'

'But we don't have the money,' says Gina.

The fact is that they do, just not for the way Gina likes to travel. Gina likes nice hotels. For her, travelling is about getting somewhere as quickly as possible then having a luxurious time, whereas what he had in mind was going on a journey, not really having a destination in mind, seeing where they ended up. They probably should have discussed it more before they left.

'I thought you liked Rome,' Gina says.

'I love Rome.'

'And me?'

'Of course and you,' Alf says, because it would be impossible to say anything else, even if he's not sure any more whether he still does. Or ever did.

LETTY

The place Heidi has invited Letty for brunch is on the roof of a high-end hotel in the expensive area at the foot of the Spanish Steps.

After the oppressively opulent reception area, the view from the terrace over the rooftops is unexpectedly luminous and uplifting, a bit like Rome's dark church interiors with their shining domes of painted sky above, a short ascent from Earth to Heaven.

Heidi is already there, sitting at a table looking at her mobile phone, but when she sees Letty she jumps up and kisses her on both cheeks as she arrives at the table.

There is a lavish breakfast buffet with an array of cold cuts, smoked salmon, fresh fruit salad, and baskets of tiny patisserie that make the air so sweet and buttery Letty feels she's taking in calories just by breathing.

'Or you can order something,' says Heidi, handing her a menu where the charge for egg dishes made to order is twenty-seven euros.

Letty helps herself to a small bowl of fruit salad and a miniature croissant, and is relieved to see that Heidi is equally abstemious, taking just a sliver of smoked salmon and a slice of pumpernickel bread.

There is a moment when they sit down that they both look at each other's plates and then they look up, catching each other's eye for just a second. Neither of them says anything, but Letty suspects they are thinking the same thing.

'So how do you like my hotel?'

'You're staying here?' Letty is amazed.

'It's in the same group as the hotel I work for,' Heidi says, explaining how she can afford it. 'All it lacks is a spa. But next weekend I will go to Capri for the spa.'

'Capri. How lovely!' says Letty.

She saw the island from Naples when they went on the day trip to Pompeii, a distant jagged rock floating on the bluest sea she had ever seen.

'I've always wanted to go there,' she says.

Marina used to sing a song called 'Isle of Capri' when she was babysitting her as a child. Letty suggested it when Rollo was asking for music for Marina's funeral, but neither Ivo nor Rollo remembered it, and decided that an aria from *Così fan tutte* would be more appropriate. When Letty googled 'Isle of Capri', she found that it wasn't an Italian song at all, but an American one that was popular in the dance halls of the 1950s, and she'd wondered if it had held romantic memories for her grandmother. Perhaps she and her grandfather had danced to it? Or maybe there had been another admirer? The song is all about a flirtation with a married woman, and Marina was a great beauty in her day.

'So, why don't you come?' Heidi is saying. 'I can get us a deal.'

Letty doesn't know how to cope with Heidi's over-familiarity. Her natural instinct is to shrink away, and yet why? Why be so suspicious of everyone? Why not use some of Marina's money to go to Capri? She knows her grandmother would approve.

'Actually, that would be lovely,' she says.

Heidi's face lights up. She comes across as pushy, Letty realizes, but it is because she is lonely and insecure. People often think that life is easy for people who are pretty, but she knows it isn't. Maybe that is why Heidi has latched on to her.

'Shall we leave Friday? Make a long weekend? We miss a day, but that's OK, yes?' says Heidi.

It's not in Letty's character to skip class, but when she thinks about Friday's lesson and how bored she was, she doesn't object.

'The class is quite slow, yes?' says Heidi.

'Maybe that's how it has to be when you begin to learn a language,' Letty says, unwilling to criticize.

'And what about our classmates?' Heidi asks.

'Mostly, they seem nice,' Letty says.

If she's learned anything from this week, it is not to make assumptions about what people are like from appearance. A shy Japanese boy who suddenly bursts into song; a gorgeous Swiss woman who is lonely and troubled.

'Do you like Alf?'

For a moment, Letty wonders if Heidi saw them together in the Forum.

'He's good-looking, no?' says Heidi.

'I suppose so.'

'Lots of – what is it?' She searches for the word. 'BDE, yes?'

'BDE?' Letty assumes it's a social media acronym that everyone else knows; even Frances said 'YOLO' when she told her she was going away to Italy.

'Big Dick Energy!' says Heidi.

Letty wasn't expecting that.

'Don't worry,' says Heidi, laughing. 'It just means like cool, you know, with charisma, but not making a big deal.'

It's amazing, Letty thinks, that someone who isn't a native speaker of English knows these things and she doesn't.

'I don't really do social media,' she says.

'He likes you,' says Heidi.

'No more than anyone else, I'm sure,' says Letty. She's never been good at girls' talk.

'I would,' says Heidi. 'But it's not me he's looking at all the day.'

Letty's about to ask 'Would what?' when she realizes exactly what Heidi would.

'I'm having a break from relationships!' she says quickly.

'Also I,' says Heidi, suddenly sad.

'How long have you and your husband been apart?' Letty asks, relieved to have withstood the pressure, and now able to relax as she knows that Heidi doesn't share any of her inhibitions talking about personal matters.

'Four weeks now. I was staying with my sister and her family, but it made me too sad with the children.'

'Why Rome?'

'Honestly? I worked here as a nanny a long time ago, and I know Italians love a blonde woman. I need this boost to the confidence,' Heidi says. 'And you?'

'My grandmother left me some money,' Letty says. 'I also needed to get away.'

'So it's a holiday?'

'Yes, in a way,' Letty says.

It's not the whole truth. But it is true. And that will do for now.

ALF

Alf decides to make Gina breakfast in bed because he's feeling guilty.

It wasn't really a row, but it was enough for her to get up from the table and walk away, leaving him to get the bill, pay, then run after her. Worse than that was her remorse when she realized that she'd got herself into a state for no reason, and kept asking his forgiveness all the way home.

'There's nothing to forgive,' he'd told her.

And she'd said it didn't sound like he meant it.

And he'd said, 'Well, what do you want me to say?' Because it was like he couldn't win with her.

She was all over him when they got in, wanting to make love, but she was so drunk she'd passed out in the middle of it. And then he'd felt bad that they'd even started because he hadn't wanted to, and so he'd withdrawn limply and lain awake listening to her snoring and wondering how the hell it had come to this.

He goes downstairs to get a couple of croissants from the bar. In the square of garden in the courtyard of their apartment building there's a shrub that, in the past week, has produced a crop of exotic-looking red flowers. On his way back, Alf picks one of them, hoping that none of the other residents is watching. He puts it in a small glass of water, and carries it in on a tray with the coffee he's just brewed.

Gina's face lights up for a moment when she opens her eyes as she hears him coming in. It's the look he wanted to see. Gina loves a gift, and the pleasure on her face is as innocent as a child's when their birthday cake comes in all lit with candles.

'That's so cute!' she says, but as she sits up, her face contorts with pain.

'Actually, do you mind if I have a bit more sleep? Splitting headache.'

'Take as long as you like,' he says, picking up the tray.

'Do you forgive me?' she says, stretching out to grab his hand.

'Nothing to forgive,' he says, then drops a soft kiss on her lips.

The smell of stale wine is weirdly at odds with her angelic appearance.

'I'm going for a walk.'

'Later, babe!' she says, turning over.

In the kitchen, Alf eats both croissants and drains both espresso cups of coffee. He can hear the unmistakable sounds of sex happening in Mike and Sally's bedroom. Mike has this habit of shouting 'Go on! Go on! Go on!' as if he's whipping a horse to the finish in the Grand National. Alf's only ever seen him clothed – in cheap jeans, usually, and a Smiths T-shirt at weekends. He doesn't like to imagine him naked.

Rome doesn't make much of its river. With main roads running along both banks, the Tiber sometimes appears like a bigger-than-average central reservation in the middle of a busy motorway.

There are walkways at river level, but very few people use them, Alf has discovered, so it's a good place to go if you want a think. He has walked the entire length of the river northwards – towards the Olympic stadium, where Roma play – but he has never gone southwards towards San Paolo fuori le Mura. As the ancient city gives way to a more contemporary suburban landscape, he is on his own, apart from an occasional runner jogging past with earphones.

Walking at a steady pace, he suddenly realizes that the only noise he can hear is the trudge of his footsteps. It's so quiet it's like going for a country walk. A family of ducks swim alongside him. He takes a picture of them, realizing it's one of the few photos he has posted that could have been taken anywhere in the world. Anywhere there are ducks.

Gina will love the photo. She loves animals, especially baby animals. Almost every picture he's seen of Gina as a child is with a kitten or a puppy. Gina can be as vulnerable as a puppy herself. The first time he saw that, it made him want to protect her, and he liked that feeling. That, and the sex, and the thrill of being with her.

Has she changed? he wonders. Or does he just want to think that because he has?

Alf replays last night's row in his mind.

She was asking him about his class, having recognized, maybe, that she's always talking about her own students.

He ran through his classmates. Showed her the video of Masakasu singing. And then she pointed and said, 'Who's that?'

He didn't realize that Violetta was visible in the background, staring amazed at Masakasu's unexpected performance.

'Just an English girl,' he said.

'You didn't mention her.'

'Didn't I? I don't really know her,' he said. 'The teacher never pairs us up because of speaking English, you know?'

He thought he'd got away with it, but the 'didn't I?' and 'you know?' were too much. Gina's extremely sensitive to nuance when the subject is other good-looking women.

'I'm just surprised you didn't say,' she'd persisted, looking at her pizza, not at him.

'Maybe because you didn't ask,' Alf retaliated. 'You haven't shown any interest in what I've been doing!'

It was unfair to throw it back at her. He has avoided talking about school, and now he feels like a shit for trying to make out she was the one in the wrong.

The stakes didn't need to get that high – he doesn't really know what's going on with Violetta and needs a bit of time to figure it out. Or does he? Maybe he's kidding himself as well as Gina.

As he approaches a bridge, he notices that the walkway has graffiti on it in white chalk, a message to be viewed from above. The words are: *Non cercavo niente, ma con te ho trovato tutto!*

He thinks the first bit means 'I'm not looking for anything, but with you I've found everything!'

Ti amo!

Amo, I love, the same as in Latin.

LETTY

The thing Letty likes most about Rome is the way that ancient and modern coexist. Most European cities, like London, date back to Roman times or before, but the traces of the past are buried. Here, there are houses built into bits of aqueduct. The ancient is integral and present even in Pigneto, the neighbourhood she's living in, which is a couple of miles from the historic centre.

When she arrived a week ago, in a taxi from the airport, she was alarmed by all the graffiti around, and by the cardboard city just opposite her building, but in daylight it isn't really scary at all. The main street has cafes and bars, a dry cleaner's, a library, a couple of small supermarkets.

Her landlord mentioned a famous cafe called Necci that

appeared in a film. In such a normal neighbourhood it seems unlikely, but eventually she is directed to it, feeling a ridiculous sense of achievement for being understood on the third time of daring to ask.

She orders a sparkling mineral water and sits at an outside table. There are several people of about her age working at laptops. She doesn't yet feel confident enough to ask them about exchanging English conversation for Italian, but she promises herself that the next time she comes, she will.

Finally, she feels relaxed and resilient enough to ring Frances. She appreciates the fact that her mother has left her be for a whole week.

'*Come va?*' Frances asks.

'*Bene, grazie,*' Letty replies.

'That's such good news.' Frances has reached the limit of her Italian.

'And you?' Letty asks.

'Oh . . . fine, I suppose,' says Frances distractedly, which makes Letty wonder if her mother is doing something else as well as talking on the phone. Frances is always multi-tasking, but sometimes she's not as good as she thinks she is at focusing on two things at once.

'No offers on the house yet,' Frances informs her. 'The market is dropping like a stone.'

Letty thinks that's probably an exaggeration.

'Loving the photo,' Frances adds. 'Who took it?'

Letty bristles. Why does Frances have no sense of the boundaries around her privacy?

'Just someone in my class,' she says.

'So there are some fun people for you to go around with?'

Perhaps it was just an innocently curious question because, after all, it was Frances who took the original photo.

'Yes,' she says. 'I had brunch with a friend from class. Heidi. She's Swiss.'

'She would be with a name like that!'

'I'm trying to seek out some Italians to talk to, though.'

'That all sounds excellent,' says Frances.

Letty thinks her mother is probably looking at something on her computer.

'Are you OK?' she asks.

'I'm fine.'

Is there a tiny crack in Frances's voice?

'Your father . . .' Frances says.

'How is he?' Letty asks. She's a little hurt not to have heard from him, but she thinks he's probably trying to give her space. That's what she said she wanted, after all, and Ivo has always treated her like a grown-up.

'Oh, you know. Out and about,' says Frances briskly.

It sounds to Letty as if they've had a row.

'It would be nice to speak to him if he has a moment.'

Letty's surprised by the silence at the other end. Usually Frances has lots to say.

'Oh well, I'll let you go,' she says, using her mother's phrase back to her.

'Keep having a lovely time . . . Missing you!' Frances says, as Letty taps the end call button.

Her mother has never missed her. Certainly never said so, anyway.

Perhaps, Letty thinks, being made redundant and having to sell the house has had more of an effect on Frances than she admits. For a woman whose identity depended so much on having a successful career, it must be tough.

Back in the apartment, Letty opens her books. There are pages and pages of verbs to be learned and another beautiful sunset to gaze at.

7

ALF

The language point they are learning is called the imperfect, the tense you use to talk about things that happened in the past. Alf wonders who decides these things.

Susanna wants them to practise by talking about when they were young. What did they like doing? What pets did they have? Where did they go on holiday?

Alf partners up with Masakasu, who says he wasn't good at school so his parents made him do extra work during the holidays.

Alf didn't really go on holidays, either, because he was always dancing.

Sometimes, the competitions were in holiday places like Bournemouth, sometimes in cities like Stoke, but it didn't really make any difference because you spent the whole day inside a ballroom, trying to hold on to the bit of space where you'd put your bags, listening out for if you'd got through to the next round and being ready to go again, changing your costumes in cramped cloakrooms alongside dozens of other sweaty boys in clouds of Lynx body spray.

Masakasu says that when he was young, he had a pet peach,

although he probably means fish. The words are similar. He used to talk to the fish because he didn't have any brothers or sisters.

Alf says he had two dogs.

In fact, they were his grandma Cheryl's dogs. She's always owned pairs of little white Westies, so cute they could feature on the cover of a calendar of dogs, and gives them slightly royal names. The most recent two are Wills and Harry. They sit in a basket in the corner of the dance hall during Cheryl's advanced classes, wearing bow ties that match Cheryl's dresses.

Alf has one ear trying to listen in to Violetta on the other side of the room. He thinks she says that she used to dance, and she glances at him at the exact moment he looks at her, giving him a rueful smile, as if to say, yes, you were right.

She has dimples. He hasn't noticed that before. Her smile has a modest sweetness, a kind of old-fashioned vibe, like a girl in a costume drama catching a man's eye across a dance floor, hoping he'll invite her for a gavotte.

In his dreams.

To his dismay, Alf is getting a semi. Concentrate on something, he thinks, employing the tactics he used when he was pubescent and doing a rumba with his dance partner Sadie. Think of a list, a very boring list. There's a map of Italy on the wall. How many cities can he name in a minute? Genova, Torino, Milano, Verona, Venezia, Padova, Firenze, Parma, Modena, Arezzo, Siena. Some of the cities have masculine endings and some feminine. He's never noticed that before.

When he asks Susanna why that is, she looks a bit annoyed because it's nothing to do with the lesson, and she doesn't know the answer either.

'Why? Why?' she says in English. 'All the time, with you is why? Here in Italy, there is no *why*!'

*

As he walks up the road towards the station, Alf hears footsteps behind, catching him up.

'I liked your question,' Letty says.

'It's just there are so many rules you have to learn, but then nobody can tell you why a road is feminine and a tree is masculine. It does my head in,' he tells her. 'It must seem dumb to you.'

'No,' she says. 'In fact, I've always just accepted that some things are masculine, and others feminine. Latin has neuter too. I've never asked why. So I thought it was a very intelligent question, actually.'

If anyone else said that to him, he would find it patronizing, but with her it comes out like it's a simple statement of fact, not a judgement.

She smiles at him. Did he really not see the dimples before, or was it that she never smiled?

'So where are you off to this afternoon?' he asks.

'The Villa Giulia. It's a museum the other side of the Villa Borghese,' she says. 'I thought I'd walk there.'

'Are you sure it's open? Most museums here close on Mondays,' he says, then looks it up on his mobile phone. 'Yes. Closed. Sorry!'

'Oh,' she says.

'The Villa Borghese is nice,' he says. 'I can get you a free Segway tour if you like.'

'I've never been on one.'

'It's a blast,' he says.

'But aren't you working?'

'Mondays are usually pretty slow.'

It's not true and it's the sort of thing she'll figure out, because she's got this logical way of thinking. He half expects her to say, 'That seems odd if the Forum is one of the only places that are open on Mondays,' but she doesn't. And he tells himself not to mislead her again. It's too nerve-wracking.

'Well, if you're sure?' she says, which is what she said to him in the Forum, and it feels like they've taken all this time to get back to the same point. He's never had to work so hard with a woman, but he likes that he has to be at his sharpest with her.

They walk across the huge square in front of Termini station and past the Baths of Diocletian. He points out the international bookshop Feltrinelli, where you can buy books in English. They cross the road that leads towards the Quirinale, and down past the American embassy towards the Via Veneto. This is the place where they shot scenes for *La Dolce Vita*, he tells her, as they walk past expensive cafes with waiters dancing attendance on their rich international guests.

'It used to be where Italians came to watch the world go by, but now it's mostly the world watching Italians going by,' he says.

'Did you just make that up?' she asks.

'Yes,' he says, taken aback.

'I thought perhaps you'd read it in a guidebook.'

'I don't think so,' he says, wondering now if he did. 'When I first came here, I bought a Blue Guide and went all over the city with it. I wanted to know what everything was – you know how it is?'

She nods.

'You're from London, right?' he says.

'Yes.'

'People who live in cities never see any of it. They just take it for granted.'

'You sound like my mother,' she says, adding, 'Not in a bad way. I just mean she's the same with a guidebook – and she comes from Preston.'

'That's near Blackpool,' he says.

He doesn't think he's ever been actively pleased to hear someone comes from Preston before.

It allows him to suppose that Letty is not so very different from him after all.

'So when did she leave Preston?'

'When she went up to Oxford.'

Still pretty different, he thinks.

'Is that where you go?' he asks.

'Yes,' she says.

Very different. Very, very different.

Too intelligent, too posh, too beautiful. All he has to offer her is a free Segway ride, and he's not even sure that he hasn't over-promised there. Yuri is pretty tight with favours.

The sounds of the city drift away in the park. Their pace slows as if to harmonize with the tranquillity.

'Do you have Italian friends?' Letty is the one to break the silence. 'You've been here a while, right?'

'Five months,' he says.

There are people – the guys on the ticket kiosk at the Forum, a couple of lads he's seen a few times in the same seats when he's gone to Roma matches. They travel back on the Metro together talking as best they can in bits of English and Italian, and they always fist-bump him as he gets off the train at a stop before theirs. But they've never suggested having a drink in a bar, or going back to theirs for a beer. Italians are very friendly, but there is no one he would call a friend.

'I'm trying to find someone who would like to exchange Italian conversation for English,' she explains.

'There is a bar where people go on Tuesdays,' he suggests.

The bar they were in on Friday. Why is he telling her that?

'But it's mainly a pick-up place, you know,' he adds quickly. 'Italian guys go there to pick up Scandinavian au pairs.'

'Oh, I don't think I'd like that,' she says.

His heartbeat slows down again.

There's one of Rome's ubiquitous painted vans selling soft drinks and snacks. The word 'Emporio' is written on the side.

'What a big name for a little van,' says Letty, as Alf photographs it.

He posts the photo, stealing her words as a caption.

Alf sees the look that Yuri gives her as they approach the clearing where the Segways are. And then his surprise as he clocks Alf with her.

'*Ti presento Violetta,*' he says.

'Letty,' she says, shaking Yuri's hand.

Alf doesn't even have to ask for free hire, Yuri's so keen to impress her.

She listens very carefully to Alf's instructions, shadowing as he demonstrates, as if she is learning a dance step. First they practise along the flat avenue that leads up to the viewpoint at the Pincio. Apart from a yelp as she first sets off, she gets it straight away. She has good balance.

They go as far as the zoo, past little temples and the theatre, then back up to the field where the military exercise their horses. Letty isn't as tentative as he expected her to be, but keeps pace with him, even races him, as they go faster and faster, and on the final descent back to Yuri, overtakes him, long hair blowing behind her, right arm punching the air as she beats him to an imaginary finish line.

'That was brilliant!' she says.

It's as if her body has suddenly come alive.

'You're pretty brave,' Alf says, as they walk away from Yuri.

'Reckless, maybe?' she says. 'It was like . . . it was like the first time it snowed in London. Well, not the first time, obviously, but the first time I had seen it. My father found this wooden sledge that he had as a child. When we got to Primrose Hill, it was like the whole of London had come out to play.

People were shrieking and laughing as they careered down the hill, and at first I was reluctant, but my dad just gave the sledge a little push with his foot so I didn't have time to think about it, and I went hurtling down the hill. I loved it so much, I ran back up and went down and up again until it got too dark to see!'

It's the most he's ever heard her say and, as she talks excitedly, he can see what she must have been like as a little girl, and he wonders what happened to make her so reserved.

'Do you want to grab something to eat?' he asks as they pass the park cafe.

She thinks about it, then says, 'Why not?'

She chooses a *tramezzino*, a single sandwich; he a panino. He offers to pay for both, but she insists on paying her share.

He feels pleased about prolonging their time together, but now he can't think of anything to say, and she, as if regretting her breathless enthusiasm, has gone back to silence as she eats her sandwich slowly. A pigeon pecks around their feet, picking up crumbs.

'You only get to know people when you can talk in the past tense,' Alf says.

'What do you mean by that?' she asks, either genuinely curious or hostile; he's not sure.

'Well, today, with the *imperfetto*,' he says, 'I learned that Masakasu wasn't taken on holidays as a child because he wasn't good enough at school, so his parents made him do extra study. So, Masakasu's a pain in the arse, right? With all his singing. I mean, great at first, but now it's like any excuse and he'll break into song . . .'

She lets out a little blurt of laughter.

'But when I saw him as this only child with strict parents, talking to his pet peach – or fish, I think he meant . . .'

She laughs again.

'. . . I could understand exactly why he's always having to

73

show off something that he's good at now. It made sense. And I liked him more because of it, somehow.'

Letty rarely responds immediately. She considers what he's said as she chews each small mouthful methodically.

'You're right,' she said. 'Oddly, I'd never associated that with the imperfect tense.'

He doesn't know whether that's a good thing or a bad thing. He wants to say, 'What made you like you are? When did you get so measured and precise and thoughtful?' But he knows it is too soon to ask.

At the edge of the park, he says, 'We can catch the number three tram here. All the way back to Porta Maggiore for you.'

She looks surprised, possibly irritated, that he has remembered where she lives.

'And Testaccio for me,' he adds.

'Where is that?'

'Beyond the Aventine. It borders the river. It was Ancient Rome's dump. There's this hill called Monte Testaccio that is made entirely out of discarded crockery. You can see bits of terracotta poking out of the grass, I'm not kidding.'

'You really are a walking guidebook!' she says, as a tram pulls up in front of them and its doors open with a loud hiss.

'I sometimes tell my Americans, if you want to see *la vera Roma*, just get the number three tram,' says Alf. 'It takes you everywhere.'

There's a fairly steep hill up the side of the park, and then the tram trundles through Parioli, which is the posh bit of town where the embassies are. After that it goes through the university area and San Lorenzo, which comes alive at night with music pounding from clubs that you wouldn't even know were there during the day.

As he points everything out to her, Letty swivels on her seat looking this way and that, and he knows that all the other men in the tram are staring at her. Their envy feels like sunshine on his skin. Every time her thigh accidentally bumps against his, or her hair touches his arm, he can feel the point of contact for seconds after.

'You're the next stop,' Alf says as the tram rattles through a tunnel under the main railway lines from Termini.

'Oh!'

Is there disappointment in her voice, or is he just reading that in? He hates the idea that tomorrow will be Groundhog Day again: they will meet in class and she will ignore him, and then she'll say a few words and finally feel comfortable enough to say more, and then it will be almost time to leave her.

'Would you like to do something tomorrow?' he says, as the tram screeches to a halt in the middle of the busy roundabout next to the enormous triumphal arch.

'Yes!' she says.

No thinking. Just yes!

'What did you have in mind?' she says.

He wasn't expecting that. He hadn't got beyond the likelihood of rejection.

'Surprise?' he says.

She looks doubtful, but there isn't time now to think of suggestions.

He watches as she walks away from the tram towards the pedestrian crossing, trying to get clues about what she's thinking from her body language. As the tram pulls away, she turns and looks for him, and when her eyes find his, she waves with fingers splayed, her hand at shoulder height, like a child who has just learned how to.

8

Tuesday

LETTY

According to today's worksheet, people born with the star sign Leo are very sociable and easy-going. But – *attenzione!* – you shouldn't put too much trust in them. Letty wonders if Alf is a Leo, and then tells herself not to be so silly. Her star sign apparently means she is a happy, optimistic person who needs a lot of affection and falls in love easily. But – *beware!* – she adores change and novelty. She can't think of a description that suits her less.

Susanna wants them to guess their partner's star sign.

Without thinking, Letty says Heidi is Libra because the description says: *Very attractive, but vain and wants to be the centre of attention.*

And Heidi, twisting a lock of her perfectly straightened and highlighted hair, retaliates with Gemini, described as: *Intelligent but also irritable and anxious. They have many intellectual interests, but living with them isn't easy.*

Luckily, they both think it's funny and they're both wrong.

Today, Alf doesn't try to partner up with Letty or get into her group for discussion. He doesn't even hang back at the end of class. But when she leaves the building, he's already waiting in the place they've started talking twice before.

As she joins him, he says, 'Do you have a ticket for the Metro?'

'Where are we going?'

It's a long journey, and the trains are hot and noisy, so it's difficult to sustain any sort of conversation. They're almost at the end of the line when they reach a nondescript station called Ponte Mammolo, and Alf says, 'This is us.'

The heat outside is intense and the place they have arrived in looks unpromising. It's a bus station. At last, Letty discovers their destination. Tivoli. The emperor Hadrian had a villa there. It is one of the places she was intending to visit. Alf buys four tickets in the bar, one each for the journey there and the journey back, and two big squares of pizza cut from a giant tray that has just come out of the oven.

'Lunch,' he says, handing her one.

The oil from the pizza slab has already turned the paper napkin translucent. It's hot and heavy in her hands. She's about to say that she doesn't want it, but remembers she hasn't eaten since yesterday's sandwich in the park.

It's food she would never normally dream of eating, but it is delicious, although it's far too much for her, and the melted mozzarella and long watery strips of courgette make it impossible to eat decorously.

Standing at the bus stop in the searing heat, with the air full of diesel fumes and her fingers and face oily from the pizza, it's the most unlikely place to feel a sudden bolt of happiness. I'm in Rome, I am free, Letty thinks, and nobody in the world knows where I am.

Just before the bus arrives, they are suddenly crowded out by people with shopping and babies in pushchairs. Alf helps others on, but he's also assertive, holding a couple of queue jumpers back with a firm arm across the steps to allow Letty in. He knows which side will have the sun, and chooses the other. There's a breeze from the open window when the bus is moving, but it's swelteringly hot when stuck in traffic through the miles and miles of car showrooms, out-of-town discos, bowling alleys, McDonald's. It's an Italy Letty didn't know existed, more like she imagines the urban sprawl of a big American city.

'It will be worth it. Promise,' Alf tells her.

'How often do people in Italy change their sofas?' Letty asks, as they pass yet another sofa showroom.

He asks the woman in the next seat, in broken Italian.

'Italians like new sofas, yes?'

She smiles and says only if they can afford it! She rubs her thumb and fingertips together to indicate money. Letty notices that Alf does the same. He talks with his body, she thinks, like Italians do, and the woman responds, asking him where they are from. He introduces Letty as his friend from London.

'*Bella*,' the woman says, smiling at Letty, and somehow she doesn't mind so much this time.

As the road begins to climb, fruit stalls appear beside the kerb, and they trundle through villages with shops and schools and five-a-side football pitches. Then the road becomes steeper, and the bus grinds around hairpin bends to the hilltop town of Tivoli.

They get off in a square with a vast panorama of the plain below and hills all around. She wonders if they are the ones she can see from her apartment window.

'Come on,' Alf says, eager to get to show her what they have come to see.

The Villa d'Este is a sixteenth-century villa built into the hillside.

The plain stone walls of the outside give no indication of the splendours within. Each of the rooms has long windows at the level of treetops; the walls are covered with extraordinary paintings of Arcadian scenes, making it feel like there is nothing separating the interior from the gardens. One even has trompe-l'oeil windows opposite the real windows, with painted billowing curtains.

'This would be a great place for a ball, wouldn't it?' Alf says.

He dances an imaginary partner around the room, arms in ballroom hold. Even though he's wearing shorts and a plain white T-shirt, his movement is as formal as if it were white tie and tails.

'May I have the pleasure?' he asks, bowing in front of Letty.

'I don't know how to!'

'That's OK. I can teach you.'

'Truly, a man of many talents!' She echoes the phrase he used in the Forum, but turns away from his invitation.

There are steps leading down into the gardens.

The elegant way Alf allows her through the door first speaks of the formality of dance training. She wonders why she didn't immediately realize that he was a dancer when he recognized her as one. It now seems so obvious from his posture and the ease with which he carries himself.

She's conscious of her own feet, turned out as she walks down the stairs, abs pulled in, bottom tucked under.

'So you're a ballroom dancer?' she says, as they wander through the formal terraced gardens. The air is loud with the many fountains. Alf and Letty appear to be the only visitors.

'My grandparents own a dance hall,' Alf tells her. 'They were ballroom champions. My mum was a Ballroom and Latin champion. I didn't have a lot of choice!'

'Were you a champion?' she asks.

'I was, yes,' he says.

It's the first time she's seen him a little flummoxed, as if he realizes that he invited the question but wasn't intending to show off.

'Everyone wanted me to turn professional, but I had other ideas.'

'What other ideas?' Letty asks.

He laughs, like she's put him on the spot and he didn't expect that.

'Yeah, still trying to work that one out. Don't get me wrong – I love dancing, but I didn't want ballroom dancing to be my whole world.'

He smiles at her, unaware of the emotion the phrase has triggered. The number of times she has said, 'Dancing was my whole world' or heard people saying, 'Dancing was her whole world' to explain her.

Amid the constant splash of water, she hears herself saying, 'I wanted to be a ballet dancer . . . but I snapped my cruciate ligament.'

She looks up at him, sees the pain on his face.

'I'm so sorry,' he says, and she knows that he means both for the injury and for reminding her of it.

Ivo had taken her skating in the quad of Somerset House. It was always just the two of them during the school holidays because Frances was working. Usually, they didn't stray very far from their area of North London. Tennis in Regent's Park, kite-flying on Parliament Hill, matinees at the Everyman cinema. It was the first time that ice rinks at Christmas had been a thing in London. Letty had pleaded with him to go, assuming that since she was good at ballet, she'd be good at skating. Mistake. She'd actually heard the ligament snap as she thumped down onto the ice, and the pain was so acute she'd passed out.

The next thing she remembers is Frances screaming at Ivo on the other side of the curtain around the bed in A&E where the doctor was examining her knee, swollen to double its size.

'How could you?'

And Ivo, protesting.

'It's not my fault. It's nobody's fault! This isn't helping!'

And Letty thinking, It is my fault. I have ruined my own life.

'It recovered, but never well enough to go back on pointe. So that was it,' Letty says with as much lightness as she is able to muster, because if she ever thinks about it, her knee aches and tears gather just behind her eyelids, as if the ghost of the thirteen-year-old lying in A&E still remains inside her, even though she has tried so hard to leave her in the past.

'Don't you dance now then?' Alf asks.

She thought he understood, but it turns out he didn't.

'Ballet is all about perfection,' she says.

'But what about dancing? Don't you miss it? Dance is in me all the time.'

She looks at the shape of his face, polished by the sunshine, and for some reason she thinks of something she read about sculpture: that the figure was always inside the marble; the sculptor simply set it free. Is dance like that? Is it an integral part of a body that is liberated by training? It's never crossed her mind before. She always thought of dancing as the product of endless practice, and she's suddenly confused, as if she's never properly understood the thing that gave her identity.

'You should try ballroom,' he says. 'Or salsa. Have you ever tried salsa?'

'I don't think I'd like it.'

Frances tried it once, as one of her many 'perfect solutions' to the problem that she didn't get enough exercise but hated going to a gym. Rowing on the Thames was another, as was swimming in the Ladies' Pond. Frances would get tremendously enthusiastic, sign up for an entire course, buy all the kit and then find that she didn't like the river in the rain, or the mud in the pond, or washing out her wetsuit, or, in the case of salsa classes, the company.

'My mother says it's speed dating men with sweaty palms.' Alf jokingly wipes his hands on his shorts.

'Come on,' he says. 'I'll teach you.'

'I couldn't.'

'Why not?'

'Because we're in this . . . place!'

They're standing on a flat terrace beside two long rectangular pools that guide the eye towards the ornate fountain built into the hillside. They are the only people there, like figures in the foreground of one of the wall paintings in the villa.

'It's not a church, is it?' Alf says. 'It's a palace Cardinal D'Este built for weekend parties! People have probably been dancing here for hundreds of years!'

She glances around again. No one is there to watch. It is such a magical setting it almost invites abandon. What's to lose? Nervously, she allows him to take her in a loose hold, one hand clasping hers, the other on her waist. Though he gives a confident appearance, she can feel the slight tremble of his fingertips through her T-shirt.

Alf counts the rhythm, stepping on the first three counts, holding on the fourth, talking her through the basic step. She gets it straight away.

'Hold on!' He drops the hold, leaving her feeling self-conscious again as he gets out his phone. 'We need music.'

He chooses a gentle Cuban track with the volume low, and offers his hand. She takes a step towards him, feels her body responding to his touch, swaying to the lazy beat, following his moves naturally, as if the ability to dance has lain dormant inside her for many years and has just awoken.

'This is the most incongruous thing I've ever done!' Letty whispers as he guides her into a spin, with the fountains dancing around them. No longer caring whether anyone is watching, she gives herself to the steps and the music, enjoying the sense of achievement as he smiles at her, and the freedom from any thought except dancing, as if nothing else in the world matters. When the song begins to fade, she wants to say, 'Again! Again!' like a child.

Instead, she gives Alf a little curtsy as he drops his hold and they walk side by side, his arm trailing around her shoulder for one brief moment, drawing her towards him in a friendly squeeze before letting go.

Letty's aware of her accelerated heartbeat, the sheen of sweat sticking strands of hair to her forehead, the ground beneath her feet, the blood still dancing in her veins as they climb the steps at the side of the main fountain.

At the top, there are three grottos with pools to feed the flow. Inside the caves the air is dank. A single trailing fern hangs down like a stalactite. Outside, the bright sunshine makes diamonds of droplets thrown high by the jet below. The ferocious roar of the gushing water seems to fill the space. It feels almost elemental, as if the two of them have always been there, inside the earth, gazing out at the glittering ether.

Letty glances up at Alf and he is already looking at her, his eyes as dark as deep brown glass. A slight shiver ripples through her body, because she thinks he is going to kiss her and she doesn't know what she will do.

'What's your star sign?' he says suddenly.

It's so not what she expected – Letty takes a step back, bewildered.

'Do you believe in astrology?'

'No,' he says.

Whatever it was just now has vanished.

As they walk back up towards the villa, Letty hears music like an old-fashioned fairground carousel.

'It's an organ powered by the water,' Alf tells her. 'Waltz.'

They both stop to listen, but he doesn't hold out his arms and offer to teach her, and she's relieved. She's feeling let down, although she doesn't really know why.

The main square is thronging with the people of the town taking their early evening *passeggiata*: young families pushing buggies, children playing games of tag while mothers on benches chat, couples at pavement tables toying with glasses of Aperol Spritz as bright and luminescent as Christmas tree baubles in the late-afternoon sunshine. It seems strange that all this quotidian life is going on just metres away from the peaceful paradise on the other side of the villa's walls.

It would be natural to suggest an aperitivo, but as the Rome bus passes them, they both start running towards the bus stop to catch it.

As the bus rattles down the mountain again, they have nothing to say to each other. Alf seems deep in thought and fidgety.

It's only when they're nearing sofa warehouse territory that he finally speaks.

'What I said, back there,' he begins. 'I don't believe in star signs . . .'

'It wouldn't matter if you did,' Letty tells him, still staring out of the window.

'No?' he says, with a slight note of challenge in his voice. 'It would matter to me. I'd think I was a dickhead!'

Suddenly they're both laughing.

'It's just my mum's really big on them,' he explains. 'She says that some signs are air and some are water, and if you're both water or air or something, you attract or you don't. I'm not sure, one or the other . . . In that cave, it was like we were water, and looking out at the sky, it was like we were air, and I . . . I don't know what I was thinking.'

She thinks he is trying to describe the strange sensation that something bigger was happening, something not quite earthly, as if time had been suspended.

'I felt it too,' she says.

And suddenly the tension is gone, and they both allow their heads to relax against the back of their seats, hands by their sides, little fingers almost touching.

9

Wednesday

ALF

'Listen,' says Letty. 'What can you hear?'

Alf concentrates.

'Nothing,' he says.

'Exactly!'

They are only a couple of miles from the Forum but they are in the countryside. The bikes they have hired lie beside them on the grass.

Alf's never felt more like he could actually be in Ancient Rome. When Letty announced that the Via Appia Antica was today's destination – as if meeting each afternoon was what they did now, as much part of the routine as school – he wasn't expecting so many miles of perfectly preserved original road lined with cypress trees and dotted with Roman tombs. Some of the monuments are as big as temples, some much smaller, which are more affecting because they look so homely.

'They're little houses,' he says, looking at the figures carved on the one that is nearest to them. 'Where you can stay with your family forever.'

'Romans used to come and visit their families, bringing offerings of wine and food,' Letty tells him.

'I like that idea,' he says. 'More fun than bunches of flowers that wilt and go brown. It makes death part of life, instead of hiding it away like we do. Why did we ever start burying people underground?'

'It's a Jewish thing originally, I think, then it became Christian. Jesus was buried, wasn't he, before he rose from the dead?' says Letty.

Alf wasn't even expecting an answer to his question, but he's getting used to her being serious about stuff. If she doesn't know the answer, she tries to work it out logically. When he's with her, he feels his brain working harder.

Gina doesn't really talk about facts, only feelings. If they were having this conversation – which they wouldn't be, because Gina's not really interested in history – by now she definitely would have said something like, 'You really know how to cheer a girl up!' or, 'Can we stop talking about death? It's depressing me.'

'Even now, Italians don't bury people underground, do they?' he says. 'You see those cemeteries outside cities. I always think they look like little towns.'

'You're right,' says Letty. 'I hadn't made that connection.'

He loves the hit of excitement he gets when he inadvertently observes something that interests her.

'My grandmother didn't wanted to be buried,' she says. 'I wonder if that was why.'

'She was Italian, wasn't she?' He remembers from the lesson about *la famiglia*.

'Yes, but she only lived here when she was a very little girl. Her parents came to England in the thirties. Her father worked as a hotel manager. But when the war came, he was interned. All Italian men were.'

'I didn't know that.'

'Marina learned to speak with the most cut-glass English accent you've ever heard, because it was dangerous to be known as Italian in those days.'

87

'Marina?'

'That was her name. We call each other by our first names in our family. Marina didn't like being called Granny. She was too elegant somehow.'

With Cheryl, his gran, it was that she felt too young to have a kid running round the dance hall shouting for Granny.

'Were you close to her?' he asks.

'Very,' Letty says with a fond smile. 'But not cuddly close like a typical Italian *nonna*. Marina held herself very upright. She was quite distant, in a way.'

Like her granddaughter, Alf thinks.

'We spent a lot of time together when I was growing up, because we all lived in the same house and my mother worked.'

'That's in London?'

'Yes, Belsize Park. It's an expensive area now, but it wasn't when my grandparents bought the house,' she adds, as if she's trying to assure him that she's not rich. 'At the time it was all divided into little bedsits which had sitting tenants, apart from the basement. That's how they could afford it.'

He tries to imagine what such a house might look like, but he's only been to London a couple of times. Gina's dad lives in a gated estate of detached houses and he works in Hampstead, but Alf doesn't think ordinary people live there. He's seen Buckingham Palace and Big Ben, but otherwise his only points of reference are *EastEnders* and *Mary Poppins*.

'My gran looked after me a lot too,' he says, searching for something they have in common. 'She wasn't very cuddly either, come to think of it. She's quite strict. "Longer strides! No skipping! Flower in a vase!"' He imitates Cheryl's barked instructions.

'Flower in a vase?' says Letty.

'It means leaning back from your partner when you're in hold. Here, I'll show you.'

He pulls her to her feet, positions her head looking left, away from him, then takes her in hold, forcing her torso away from his with his arms. He'd love to teach her to quickstep. But not here, among the tombs. It would be too – what was her word? 'Incongruous.' He loves that she uses words he's only ever read as naturally as girls he knows would say 'random'. For a moment, they stand in hold, very formal. And then she glances at him, and starts giggling at the ridiculousness of the pose in this setting. He drops her arms and they sit down again.

'We were close too,' he says. 'I only had one set of grand-parents because my dad died before I was born. Motorbike accident.'

'Oh, your poor mother!'

'She was only sixteen. He didn't even know she was preg-nant. I don't know if they would have stayed together. Mum says so, but she has to really, doesn't she?'

Letty is frowning, trying to process the information. He hopes she doesn't think he's looking for sympathy.

'It must have been very strange for you.'

'I didn't really know any different, did I? I was so used to being called the man of the house that I didn't even realize until I went to school that other kids had dads.'

She smiles.

'We lived in this flat above the dance hall, and I really liked it there, because I had my own bedroom in the eaves, and when it rained, I'd lie there listening to the rain on the roof and the music drifting up from classes. It was like my little space, you know? When Mum met Gary we moved into a proper house with him. My grandparents converted the flat into studios.'

'Dancing really was your whole world,' Letty says.

'What about you? What did you do after you left ballet school?' he asks.

She twists a spike of grass around and around until eventu-ally it breaks.

'I went to the local comprehensive,' she says. 'It's not a bad school, but it was so different from what I was used to. I'd been one in a year of twelve. Now there were more than two hundred in my year, and by the time I arrived, I was fourteen and I didn't fit. And my dad teaches there, which made it worse. Teenage girls can be very unkind.'

She looks at him with sad eyes.

'I know about that,' he tells her. 'I was dumped by my first dance partner. She grew up quicker than I did. She was thirteen going on thirty.'

He remembers how vicious Sadie could be, and how her gang used to taunt other girls for wearing glasses, or being fat, or, worst of all, being prettier than them, which would have been Letty's crime. At that age, some girls still look like children, while some are fully grown women. The teachers used to refer to Sadie's crew as the Pink Ladies, even before they did *Grease* for the Christmas show. He'd never really understood that, because they were always having anti-bullying days and Sadie and her mates were classic bullies, but the name gave them the status they were looking for. Sometimes he thought the teachers were a bit afraid of them too.

'But you found another partner?' Letty asks.

'It's easier for boys. There aren't that many of us,' he says.

'That used to be true in ballet too, but there are a lot of boys now.'

'Since *Billy Elliot*?'

'Maybe. But there have also been several really fit and definitely heterosexual stars, so being a ballet dancer doesn't automatically mean you're gay any more. Not that it ever did, or that there's anything wrong with being gay, obviously. My brother's gay,' she adds, so hurriedly that he wonders whether she thinks he is.

'I didn't know you have a brother,' he says.

'He's much older than me,' she says. 'My mother says that

Oscar's the reckless-passion child and I'm the biological-clock child.'

Alf doesn't know how to react. Her mother sounds very different from his. He doesn't want to say that she sounds like a piece of work, because people always stick up for their relatives. Even now, he'd never let anyone say anything negative about his mum.

'I auditioned for *Billy Elliot*,' he says.

'Really?'

'Not that I knew ballet or anything. But I looked the part. I could dance. But when they offered it to me, it meant living away from home to do the training. I couldn't leave Mum by herself.'

Although, as it turned out, they moved in with Gary soon after that, so she probably would have been all right without him.

'Do you ever regret not doing it?' Letty asks.

'The way I see it, I liked my life in Blackpool and I don't know if I would have liked the Billy Elliot School. So no point regretting it,' he says.

It was his mum who had all the regrets, he thinks – probably because she felt guilty.

Every time he succeeded at anything after, like captaining the school football team or winning ballroom or Latin titles, his mum always had to say that he wouldn't have been able to do that if he'd gone to the Billy Elliot School. And if the film was ever on television, she'd always wonder what happened to the other Billies who'd been in the musical. You never heard of them, did you? she'd say.

He wonders if she ever feels guilty now. She's probably too busy to think about him at all.

Letty's still plucking at the grass, deep in her own thoughts.

'Did they teach Latin at your school?' he asks, trying to move away from reflection.

Letty looks up, startled.

'God, no!' she says, then, after a long pause, 'Actually, I got ill. I had to go into hospital for a while. My uncle came after work twice a week and taught me. So I'm kind of home-schooled. Or, more accurately, hospital-schooled.'

'Is your uncle a teacher?'

'No, he's a lawyer.'

He imagines a rather formal man in a dark suit sitting by a hospital bed, both of them bent over books.

'That's why you are like you are!' he exclaims.

'What do you mean?' she asks.

'I mean, you're so precise, a bit like a lawyer . . .' He stops. The only lawyers he knows are in television dramas, so what's he talking about?

Letty frowns for a moment, and then her face relaxes.

'I suppose you're right,' she says. 'Rollo does analyse every-thing in rather a lawyerly way. I must have picked some of that up. You're very thoughtful,' she tells Alf.

'You're well now?' Alf asks.

'I'm well now,' she says, still looking at the grass, and then she looks up and smiles at him. 'Thanks for asking.'

But there's something in the way she says it that makes him think she's really saying, 'Thanks for *not* asking.'

'Shall we push on?' he suggests, picking up her bike and holding it for her before getting on his own.

She leads the way, her hair blowing behind her. Her long legs and arms are bare today – she's wearing shorts and a white T-shirt. She tilts her head back to get the sun on her face. It's an expansive gesture of happiness, as if the pedalling has set her free. When she is in motion, she is truly gorgeous, he thinks. When she is still, it's like she's shackled by invisible chains, a prisoner in her own beautiful body.

'This was such a cool idea,' he shouts.

'I know!' she shouts back.

*

92

The bus back into town is crowded, so they strap-hang facing each other, and each time the bus stops and his body is flung against hers then back, he looks into her eyes, her mouth so close to his that he can breathe her breath. He badly wants to kiss her but he knows he cannot, must not must not must not.

They alight near the route of the number three tram, and he waits with her at the stop.

'How about tomorrow?' he says.

'Your turn to choose,' she says, and his lungs feel like they're filled with pure joy. Then she says, not quite looking directly at him, 'Do you have any plans for this evening, by the way?'

It's so unexpected he panics, and speaks too quickly.

'It's my turn to cook.'

He could text Gina and say some clients have invited him for dinner, which sometimes happens, and would they mind if he did his turn another day? It's not like his cooking is something they're all looking forward to. But the moment has gone.

'Can you cook?' Letty asks, perfectly pleasantly, but looking into the distance as if she'll conjure up a tram if she stares hard enough.

'I'm learning. I do a pretty good carbonara. How about you?'

'Not really,' she says.

Is something happening here? Or is he imagining it because he wants it so much? She's on her own and likes having company, and it's probably nothing more than that. She just doesn't give out the normal clues. He's never been in this position before. He's tempted to say, like a contestant on *Love Island*, 'I feel this connection with you. I'd like to know what you feel about me?' But nobody talks like that in real life. Or maybe they do. But not him, and definitely not Letty. He doubts she's even heard of *Love Island*.

10

Thursday

LETTY

'Have you seen *Roman Holiday*?' Alf says, when she catches him up at what has become their meeting place on the corner two streets up from the school.

'Ages ago,' says Letty.

'So, we're going to do my *Roman Holiday* tour.'

'Didn't they see Rome on a Vespa?' she asks, not sure whether she'll feel safe in the crazy traffic.

'I was hoping you wouldn't ask that,' says Alf. 'Because I don't have a moped.'

'That's a relief!'

As they set off walking, he says, 'It's the one thing I promised Mum. Couldn't do that to her twice.'

His father, Letty remembers. It's rather sweet that a grown-up would admit to honouring a promise to his mum. She thinks about all the things she promised Frances she wouldn't do when she was a teenager, how she got a kick out of doing the opposite, and how self-destructive most of the betrayals turned out to be.

Alf hands her a postcard with *Saluti da Roma* written on it, surrounded by about a dozen miniature views of Rome, including all the famous sites.

'How many of these have you seen?' he wants to know.

'Only the Forum, the Colosseum, St Peter's . . . oh, and the Spanish Steps.'

'Good,' he says. 'The rest are walkable, once we get down into the centre.'

'Do you always give out postcards with your tours?' she asks.

'It's that little bit extra. Like a free gift,' he says, quite serious about his work. 'People really like them, but nobody sends them now because of Instagram.'

'You do Instagram,' she says.

'Doesn't mean I don't remember how great it was to get a postcard from my gran when they were doing competitions abroad,' he says. 'I think it's what made me want to travel.'

Normally he seems so mature, as if he has everything under control, but just sometimes you get glimpses of how he must have been. She sees a little boy with curly fair hair looking up at postcards stuck to the wooden joists of his bedroom under the roof.

'Did your grandparents compete in Italy?' she asks.

'I don't think so,' he says. 'There's a fair number of Italian dancers though. Do you remember Flavia and Vincent on *Strictly*? And now there's Giovanni.'

'I don't really follow *Strictly*,' she says, adding quickly, in case he thinks she's a snob about reality television, 'Frances does.'

'Frances?'

'My mother. She's always saying she wants to learn ballroom dancing. *Strictly* must have been good for your business?'

'You'd think. In January, sure, when everyone's followed the programme and it's their New Year's resolution to learn. By February the weather's bad, and weekday nights there's usually some big new crime series on television. Then it starts to tail off.'

Letty thinks of Frances and her enthusiasms. She'd buy the shoes and the dress, and then they would disappear into a drawer with the wetsuit and the swimming goggles.

They get off the bus at Piazza Venezia, then walk through the backstreets to the Pantheon.

With Alf, Letty sees aspects of Rome she knows she'd never notice alone. On the Via del Corso, she would go to the Palazzo Doria Pamphilj and study all the paintings, but she would walk past the official AS Roma football club shop, where you can buy merchandise and tickets for the matches, which is an equally important part of the culture of the city. She would marvel at the structure of the Pantheon, but not know about the statue of an elephant by Bernini in the square behind it, which, according to Alf, is beloved of Romans. On her own, Letty wouldn't go into Rome's most famous gelateria Giolitti, where they stop for an ice cream. Sitting in a tea room with gilded mirrors on the walls, she can imagine people eating dishes of gelato in the fifties, wearing proper tea dresses and slingback shoes, attended by the same waiters in waist-coats, who bring little glasses of iced water with their coffees, which, she knows from Marina, is the proper way to serve an espresso.

On her own, Letty would never venture into a little shop whose walls are covered with dozens of wall clocks painted with different designs and mottos, all ticking frenetically. Alf takes a short video on his phone.

The writing on one of the clocks says *Carpe Diem*.

'It means seize the day,' she tells Alf when he asks for a translation. 'It comes from a poem by the poet Horace.'

'And what's "seize the day" supposed to mean?' he asks.

She remembers the phrase from her first Latin textbook, the one Rollo had also learned from at school, where the outdated translation was 'Gather ye rosebuds while ye may'.

Today, she thinks the closest phrase might be 'Have fun while you can'.

'Live in the moment?' Alf offers.

'Yes, that's much better,' she says, pleased with his more contemporary translation.

It occurs to her that living in the moment is what she is doing right now, and maybe it is the reason she finds herself increasingly craving Alf's company. Alone, she tends to worry about the future, or ruminate on the mistakes she has made in the past. She came to Rome to try to sort her head out, imagining that with enough time to think, a solution would emerge. But when she is on her own, she tends to panic that nothing is becoming clearer, that she's somehow running out of time. When she is with Alf, she simply experiences the beauty of the places they see, the feeling of sunshine on her skin, or wind rushing past her face, the taste of food.

She hears the accordion player before they reach the Piazza Navona. He's standing outside one of the restaurants in the far corner where tourists are eating lunch, but the tune drifts down the long piazza: the drinking song from *La Traviata*.

'Viennese waltz,' says Alf suddenly. 'Shall we dance?'

And before she has a chance to reply, he takes her into hold, pushing off with his right thigh against hers, so that she has no choice but to follow him. They waltz around and around, with her feet somehow following his, her hair flying out behind her, the golden stone *palazzi* racing around like images in a magic lantern against the constant luminous blue of the sky. Her feet skip across the cobblestones, knowing he is strong enough to hold her if she trips. As they twirl and twirl, surprise becomes pleasure, fear becomes trust, and her body fills with such elation that when the music finally ends and she collapses against Alf's chest, breathless, giddy and laughing, she wants to tell him that this was the best moment of her life.

She's suddenly aware that an audience has gathered. People are filming them on their phones. For a second she's alarmed that something so intensely personal has become public property, but it's cancelled out by the undiluted joy that she feels. Together they take a bow.

Then, just as suddenly as he took her in his arms, Alf lets her go and they walk on, side by side, as if nothing has happened. But she is very aware of her hand dangling next to his, like two strands of a broken live cable sparking towards each other with crackling flashes of electricity, just too far away to make a connection.

'When I'm dancing I know who I am,' Alf says. 'Other times, I'm not sure if I'm anything at all.'

The confession feels like something precious he has given her. She does not want to devalue it with platitudes. So she says nothing. And then worries that she should have said something, but has left it too late.

In the Campo de' Fiori, the market stalls of flowers and fruit are packing up for the day. They sit at a cafe table drinking *acqua frizzante*.

At the foot of the statue in the centre of the square, a lone guitarist is strumming 'Every Breath You Take' with a backing track.

'Tango,' says Alf.

'I've never known why people think this song is romantic,' Letty says. 'It's about a stalker.'

'I've danced to it many times, but never really listened to the words,' Alf says.

'What's your favourite dance?' she asks.

'The one I'm best at is probably quickstep,' he replies. 'But there's nothing quite like a Viennese.' He stares so emphatically into her eyes that she feels her cheeks flushing. A week ago, she thought him arrogant, and felt uncomfortable when he looked at her. Now, she has to look away because she's scared of betraying what she's beginning to feel.

'I loved it,' she says simply, taking a sip of her water.

'Next time,' he says, 'try to allow yourself to lean back. I won't let you fall. It looks better when our torsos make a kind of V shape.'

'Flower in a vase.'

'Correct!' he says, glancing at his watch.

She wonders if they are done for the day. They usually part around this time.

She makes herself not ask. She is living in the moment and the moment is now, not what happens later. It's as easy to spoil the present by thinking about the future as it is about the past. She will not ask him about the dinner he cooked for his flatmates yesterday evening. She does not want to know if he has a girlfriend. But it's hard to imagine that someone as attractive as him isn't in some sort of relationship.

'Two more sites,' Alf says, scraping his chair back across the cobbles, just as a man with a bucket of roses approaches their table. 'We shouldn't have to queue too long at this time of day.'

The only scene Letty remembers well from *Roman Holiday* is when Audrey Hepburn and Gregory Peck visit the Bocca della Verità. Situated in the portico of a church, it's a huge round carving of a face with an open mouth. Gregory Peck tells Audrey Hepburn about the legend that if you have lied, your hand will be bitten off when you put it in the mouth. Audrey, who plays a princess pretending to be an ordinary person, hesitates, her hand wavering, before she dares him back. Gregory puts his hand in and screams as if it has been taken, but he is only joking.

She was a princess. He was a journalist. They were both

lying to each other. What started as an undercover sting had become an impossible love. Their worlds were too different.

Letty wonders if the film would still work today when a princess can marry anyone she likes, although a journalist would probably be the last person she'd choose.

'You first,' says Alf.

It's strange how powerful superstition can be, and how Letty's hand trembles as Audrey's did as it approaches the mouth, even though she isn't much of a liar. Her rational self knows very well that it is only the decorative end of a Roman drain, but she still finds herself asking it silently, as if it's an oracle, Am I kidding myself that something is happening here?

When all she can feel is the coolness of the air inside, her heart skips a beat with the most ludicrous rush of optimism. She withdraws her hand.

What is she thinking?

At the Vittorio Emanuele monument, they take the lift up to the terrace between the two giant four-horsed chariots. The 360-degree view is breathtaking.

'It's good to wait until the sun is going down,' Alf tells her, 'when the city turns from gold to rose.'

Letty scours the skyline, trying to see the building where she is living, finding first the statues on top of San Giovanni in Laterano, and then locating it in the far distance.

'Wow,' Alf says. 'That's a tall building for Rome.'

'How about you?' she asks.

He points towards Testaccio.

'We have an interior apartment,' he says. 'No view.'

She tries not to let the 'we' affect her, pondering whether it would be weirder to ask, or not to ask, who the 'we' is, since the word seems to hang in the air between them.

Alf takes photographs, then puts away his phone, then gets

it out again, unable to resist taking more as the sky becomes ever more spectacular.

Eventually, and quite suddenly, darkness falls, and flood-lights turn Rome's golden stone as white as the monument.

'Your turn to choose, tomorrow,' he says, glancing again at his watch as they descend in the lift.

'I'm going to Capri tomorrow.'

'Oh,' he says. 'Well, in that case, there's one more thing we have to do today.'

They dodge the hectic traffic of Piazza Venezia and cross the bottom of Via Nazionale, running past the Palazzo Colonna and beyond, through the maze of pedestrian streets full of souvenir shops with colourful boards of fridge magnets and replica football shirts hanging outside. Then, quite unexpect-edly, they're in the square that contains the Trevi Fountain, its statues bathed in yellow light, its pools as turquoise as the tiny photo on her postcard. The sound of foaming water fills the air.

Alf searches in his pockets for a coin.

'So I know you're coming back to Rome,' he says.

He watches her as she stands with her back to the fountain and throws the coin over her shoulder.

'You too?' she says.

'I'm not going anywhere!'

The streets are emptier now; workers have returned home, tourists are eating dinner. The Piazza San Silvestro is deserted, apart from a busker strumming a guitar.

'Waltz?' Letty says hopefully, but Alf seems preoccupied now.

'Yes,' he says. 'That's a Viennese.'

As the bus pulls up beside them and the doors open with a hydraulic hiss, he says, 'Take care,' very gently, and plants the quickest kiss on her cheek.

She watches him getting out his phone as he walks away,

the deep breath he takes before putting it to his ear, and how he's already talking as the bus passes him and doesn't look up at her. Elbow against the window, she cups her cheek against her palm, as if to hold his kiss there.

11

Friday

ALF

By now, she will be on the train, Alf thinks. He imagines her sitting on the Frecciarossa to Naples with the countryside rushing by.

'Alf!' the teacher interrupts him. *'Come va?'*

'Bene grazie,' he says automatically.

The students laugh. He's meant to say that he's suffering from a medical complaint.

Today the class is all about ailments. My stomach aches. My head aches. The doctor says it's probably due to stress. Stress is the same word in Italian as it is in English, as if Italians didn't have the concept before they heard the word.

At break, the teacher keeps him back. What is his problem?

Alf tells her that he slept badly, quoting the phrase they've just learned. She laughs, but when he tries to tell her that he feels the class is too slow, she says that the next class up would be too difficult for him. To learn a language you need to work hard, she says, making him regret slouching in his chair, which she has pulled him up on twice this session.

Instead of going to the cafe in the basement with the other students, he goes for a run round the block – just enough to get the blood flowing in his veins and his mind thinking again.

The school is expensive, and since he has been seeing Letty in the afternoons, he hasn't earned any money. It occurs to him that he doesn't really talk to her in class, so maybe that's the thing he should drop. He could get in at least one tour in the mornings and meet her at lunchtime. On his way back to class, he informs the receptionist that he won't be renewing. Unfortunately, it's Olivia, the strict one, who deals with the paperwork and wants to know the reason to put on her form.

'*Non ho soldi!*' he says, hoping that's the correct way of saying, 'I don't have the funds.'

The nicer receptionist, Chiara, giggles.

By now she'll be on a ferry, motoring across the Bay of Naples. He wonders how long the journey takes and whether it's calm or there's a breeze blowing her hair around her face.

Nobody seems interested in a tour of the Forum. Alf hangs out with a dumpy Romanian guy he's talked to before, who's on a cigarette break. He used to work in a fish-processing factory in Grimsby, but in Rome he makes his living dressing as Cupid in a short white dress with a golden bow and arrow, wings – the lot. With his hairy legs, five o'clock shadow and Marlboro Light hanging out of his mouth, he's the most unlikely looking god of love. Incongruous, Alf thinks. He's about to get a photo to Instagram, but changes his mind when the guy starts grumbling about the tourists who take pictures of him without paying the five euros that he demands.

Alf scrolls through his Instagram feed. Cheryl has posted a picture of the Tower Ballroom with the caption: *Home Sweet Home! #Blackpool #goodtobeback*. They've returned from their cruise in time to be there for the birth of their grandchildren.

His mother has posted a picture of Gary performing at an

event that looks like it might be a wedding, with garlands of balloons around the stage, along with the hashtags #shelovesyou #yeahyeahyeah. Gary is Paul McCartney in a tribute band called the Stag Beetles. They sing pretty well, but they look like a bunch of electricians wearing floppy wigs. His mum always says it was Gary's voice that attracted her, but Alf thinks it had a lot to do with him fixing the lights and glitter ball when she shorted the dance hall just before the annual Christmas party.

Alf still hasn't sent her a message, and if he waits any longer, she's going to have had the babies. He crosses the Via dei Fori Imperiali and takes a photo of a bucket of pink flowers on a stall at the bottom of Via Cavour. Then he posts it, tagging both his mother and Cheryl and adding #thinkingofyou.

Eventually, Alf's approached by a British family with an overbearing father who bargains him down on the price. Alf much prefers Americans, who always tip. He knows that his patter will be interrupted constantly by the father telling his hyperactive son to get down from there, to be quiet and listen because he might learn something. Standing in front of the Arch of Septimius Severus, he tells them about the *damnatio memoriae* of Caracalla's brother Geta, wishing that Letty were sitting on a nearby step smiling at the corrected Latin.

Just about now, they should be disembarking, he thinks, imagining her and Heidi from the point of view of the tour guides and taxi drivers waiting on the quay.

'Hey up! Who are these two beauties?'

Capri is a playground of the rich. The sort of place that film stars and Formula 1 drivers go on holiday. Letty and Heidi will look like two models arriving for a photo shoot.

Alf walks up onto the Palatine Hill, retracing their steps of a week ago, when she told him about the poem she liked.

'I hate and I love.'

She said that it said everything about love, and he wondered why she thought hate came first, but he still hasn't found the words to ask her.

Alf's phone buzzes with a notification. His mum has replied to his photo with the simple message: *Thanks, Alf #meansalot.*

Gina wants to see the new horror movie that everyone is talking about. Alf knows she won't like it, but he's quite glad to be doing something where they don't have to talk for a few hours, instead of sitting across from each other at a dinner table.

'Hi hon!' She greets him outside the cinema, wearing the dress that he once told her was her sexiest outfit. She's done her hair and make-up, so he feels underdressed in shorts and his work T-shirt.

She's standing in front of a poster advertising a live screening of a Royal Ballet performance in London. The ballerina has her back to the male ballet dancer, her arms stretched behind her. He is on his knees, gripping her hands, as if he is pleading with her to turn and recognize his love.

About now, Letty and Heidi are probably being whisked off to dinner by guys in Ferraris. Heidi will like that; Letty not so much. With Letty there's a protective barrier, but once it's stripped away, there's a quality of innocence underneath. She doesn't have the usual layers of flirtation in between. She gives nothing, or she gives everything, but only for such fleeting moments it's like finding tiny diamonds in the sand that disappear when you reach to grab them.

He realizes that Gina has asked him twice where he wants to sit and he hasn't replied.

This has to stop. Gina has done nothing wrong except love him.

Maybe he should just stay away from Letty? Now that he has left the school, it will be possible. But when the trailer comes on for the live relay of the ballet, he straight away finds himself trying to think of a good excuse to be out the following Thursday evening.

Usually, after they've seen a horror film, he does stupid things to make Gina jump. She's pretty easy to tease. But this one was so disturbing they're both silent on the way out.

'Would you like a gelato?' Alf asks, as they amble in the direction of the Spanish Steps.

'After that, I need a drink,' Gina says.

She has a glass of Prosecco; he has a beer. Sitting at a table outside, it costs as much as a full bottle and a week's supply of Nastro Azzurro.

'It's worth it though,' says Gina. 'Because when I'm somewhere like this, I really think I'm here, in Rome – you know?'

By the fountain, the same busker who was in San Silvestro twenty-four hours ago is playing the same song: 'Where Do You Go To My Lovely?'

It was a hit in Alf's grandparents' youth. His grandad, Chris, once showed him the clip from *Top of the Pops* on YouTube. The singer looked like a comedy 1970s tribute with his long hair and moustache, but the song has the pure simplicity of a classic. Cheryl and Chris often do a demonstration Viennese to it towards the end of their fortnightly social. Last night, he was desperate to dance again with Letty, but he knew that if he did, they would end up kissing in that empty square. He didn't want to kiss her then leave her; and he knew he couldn't stay with her. But it took all the self-control he had in his body, because the connection was so strong between them you could almost see the sparks flying in the darkness.

Now, she'll be sitting on the terrace of an expensive restaurant, chinking champagne glasses with some smooth guy with a permanent tan, who'll be telling her about his speedboat and how, in the morning, he'd like to take her to a secluded beach he knows . . .

Gina is chatting about what she'd like to do this weekend,

as a flower seller approaches their table with a bucket of roses. You can't sit down for a minute in one of the tourist spots without it happening. Alf doesn't know how they make their money, because the buckets always seem full and he's never seen anyone buy one.

Gina is determinedly ignoring the vendor, but Alf knows it would make her happy for a week if he bought her a rose. As he hands the guy the ten euros he demands, he realizes how they make a profit. It's guilty men who buy roses for their partners, not men who are all loved up, which is what Gina calls it as she comes around to his side of the table so she can take a selfie with him and the rose to send to her father.

'By the way, Dad's coming to Rome!' she suddenly remembers. 'Arriving Sunday and staying someplace on the Via Veneto . . .'

'Is this a holiday? Business?' Alf enquires. 'I thought he had Rome down as a pile of rubble?'

'Think he just wants to see me,' Gina says. 'It's been quite a long time . . . and you. He likes you.'

'Mutual,' says Alf.

Unlike his own family, Stuart has always smiled on Alf's relationship with Gina. Stuart idolizes his daughter and subsidizes her, although he's always saying that he doesn't believe in 'the bank of Mum and Dad' because he never got any help, and that made him get off his arse and make something of his life.

Stuart left Gina's mum when Gina was five, but he always saw Gina regularly, and paid for her to go to a posh private school in the South so he could spend weekends with her.

When they stayed with Stuart on their way to Rome, he took Alf to see Arsenal play. Stuart had not just one but two season tickets for the Emirates Stadium – so that he could always take a mate, he'd said, smiling at Alf as if that was how he thought of him.

That evening, the match they'd seen was first up on *Match of the Day*, so they watched the highlights in a room Stuart called his den, which was really a small cinema. And Gina had said, 'Not more football!'

But Alf could tell that she liked it that they were bonding so well.

'I said we'd see him Monday,' Gina is saying. 'I'll go over and spend the morning with him while you're at school, and then we can all hook up for lunch at his hotel, maybe?'

Alf knows that this is the moment to tell her that he's given up school. If he leaves it any longer it will be too late, because she'll start asking why he didn't tell her before.

But instead he says, 'Sure,' adding a quick 'great' too, in case he didn't sound enthusiastic enough. Any other time, he'd be really happy that Stuart was coming. Just not now.

Gina picks up her rose, twirling it between thumb and finger and smiling at him. The rose has bought him time to decide how he's going to handle this, Alf thinks.

And it's not like he's done anything wrong.

12

Saturday

LETTY

There's a mist hanging over the Bay of Naples. The road is as precipitous as the guidebook says, but without the promised spectacular view. Letty thinks that Heidi probably made the right decision staying in the hotel for pampering, rather than accompanying her on her expedition. Anacapri is on the other side of a mountain. It's a more modest town than Capri itself. The bus drops her at the bottom of a rickety lift of one-person chairs. It's still early and the operator tells her she is the first person ascending. The journey to the top of Monte Solaro is an eleven-minute hoist, dangling precariously over the rocky mountainside.

When she reaches the summit, the strength of the sun burns away the cloud, and the emerging panorama brings tears to her eyes. It feels like a privilege to witness such astonishing beauty. The sky is the purest aquamarine, the outline of Vesuvius a purply grey backdrop to the vast expanse of the inky blue Bay of Naples that is now glinting in the sunlight. Looking south, the rocky Italian coastline stretches away, past Positano and Amalfi and on towards Calabria.

Though Letty rarely takes photos, the vista is so incredible she fears it might fade in her memory, unless she captures it. Turning slowly on the spot, she takes a 360-degree video on her phone, and finds herself wishing that Alf were here to experience it with her.

She feels at ease with him, a sensation she's never had before with someone outside her own family, and often not with them either. He has a completely different take to hers when they see new things, but if she tells him about something she knows, he doesn't look at her as if she's slightly peculiar; he seems genuinely interested, and that gives her the same buzz of excitement as discovering it for the first time.

Up here in the dazzling sunlight, the mountain breeze blowing her hair back from her face, her body can still feel him dancing with her, the touch of his hand on her back, the delicious abandon of twirling again and again, trusting totally that he would not let her fall.

Glancing around to make sure she's the only person on the terrace, Letty takes a few tentative steps, arms by her sides, then bigger, bolder strides, pirouetting with her arms stretched out, hair flying as the view spins around her. Closing her eyes, she imagines him here with her, laughing with the immense good fortune of being in this heavenly place as they waltz around and around, then falling against each other, the warmth of his body on hers, staring into each other's eyes, and—

'Gee!'

Letty stops abruptly, unsure whether the American tourists who have just arrived are exclaiming at the view or at her.

'*Che bella ballerina!*' The operator smiles at her as she sits on the chairlift and he closes the single bar across her lap.

The hotel room smells of orange blossom and sandalwood. Heidi is lying on one of the twin beds in a white dressing gown, her hair wrapped in a towel.

111

'How was your mountain?' she asks.

'So beautiful!'

Letty takes off her shoes and flops onto the other bed. Her initial apprehension about sharing a room has disappeared. Heidi is good at chatting about nothing in particular – the facial she had that morning, and the colour of nail polish after her pedicure. She wiggles her toes backwards and forwards. She has chosen silver, but she's not sure it's a good colour without a deep tan. Letty assures her it is.

'What is the story of your tattoo?' Heidi asks, looking across at Letty's bare feet.

'My first proper boyfriend . . .' she tells Heidi, hoping that will be enough explanation.

Frances had stormed down to the tattoo parlour because you weren't meant to tattoo minors without their parents' consent, but they'd shown her the signed permission form that Letty had faked. Frances had threatened to make a complaint about Josh to the head teacher, but Ivo said what was done was done.

Letty can still hear her mother's comment in defeat: 'Well, if you have to self-harm, at least it's quite pretty.'

It annoyed Letty beyond measure at the time, but later seemed strangely prescient.

'Did he get one too?' Heidi asks.

'Yes,' Letty says, adding, so that Heidi doesn't get an impression of sweet, teenage romance, 'Apparently, he got one for every girlfriend.'

At fifteen, she thought the tattoo was a sign of everlasting love. Now she thinks of it as a brand Josh wanted to leave on her so that her shame would remain forever.

Afterwards, there was a part of Letty that wanted to gouge the tattoo out of her foot, but she left it there so that she would never forget. The knife through the heart, with the tiny red dot of blood falling from its tip – which she had thought of as a symbol of the pain she was prepared to endure for him – became a metaphor for the cruelty of love.

The lunch menu is simple and designed for people who are enjoying the well-being facilities. When Letty's pasta arrives, it is one large raviolo in a shallow pool of tomato concasse that is pale red in colour but tastes like the distillation of a thousand fresh tomatoes. Heidi's saffron risotto with a single langoustine is equally delicious, but both of them eat only half their dish.

'Eating problems, they never go away. True, no?' Heidi says.

Letty doesn't know what to say. Is it so obvious? Does Heidi know from the way she looks, or the way she eats? Then she realizes that Heidi doesn't mean to accuse her, simply to share something that they have in common.

'I didn't realize that you . . .'

She stops mid-sentence, in case Heidi will think that she's implying she doesn't look thin enough to have suffered herself.

'You look so healthy,' she says.

In hospital, she learned to speak about it as an illness.

'Yes,' says Heidi. 'But it's hard work, no?'

Letty laughs, knowing that she means the eating, not the starving. Starving is much easier.

'How long for you?' she asks Heidi.

'I was picked out by a model agency when I was fourteen. Funny to say that I was taking coffee and cake with my friends, and this woman came up to me and gave me her card. So they sent me to do promotional work, like lying on a car looking sexy, you know? My parents didn't like this, but now I was thinking I was a model, so I told the woman I would like to do catwalks instead. She laughed, said I was too fat. So, you know, I lost the weight and then—'

'You couldn't stop.' It's Letty who finishes the sentence.

It's easy to start, and then it becomes impossible to stop; like an addiction, except you're addicted not to substance but to a behaviour. She learned from the cognitive behavioural therapist she went to, during and after hospital, that addiction is never about your drug of choice, but the beliefs that led you to that behaviour.

Letty was always thin as a reed, like her father's side of the family. She didn't get puppy fat in adolescence as some of her friends did. At ballet school, she used to eat more than any of her peers, constant physical activity making her hungry.

'I used to do ballet—' she begins to tell Heidi.

'Oh yes,' Heidi interrupts, as if she understands.

'No. It wasn't *because* of ballet . . .' Letty corrects her.

That's what everyone thinks, even the doctors. They'd seen the film *Black Swan*, so they thought they knew all about it, but they didn't.

Ballet had given her control over her body. It was the injury, the sudden shock and lack of discipline that allowed the illness to creep in and take over. She'd gone from ballet school's strict regime to her father's school, where she was 'free' but had no idea how to cope. Compared to the other girls there, she was tiny and undeveloped, and so frightened that she made an easy target for the cliques of 'cool' girls. They called her Ballerina and said she had been kicked out for being too fat. It was true that she had put on a little weight, having been unable to exercise for months, and so the seeds of the belief were sown.

By the time Josh rescued her from the bullies it was already a problem, but it was still her secret. When he betrayed her, it all spiralled out of her control.

'I was taken into hospital,' she tells Heidi.

'*Mein Gott!*' says Heidi. 'This was catastrophe, no?'

For some reason, this makes Letty smile.

A stranger had been concerned as she walked past Letty on the bridge. She had called the emergency services, then doubled back and started talking to her.

Would she have jumped if the stranger had done nothing? Letty doesn't know any more.

It was so hot that summer. They said she was severely dehydrated. She couldn't remember how or why she went to the river, or how long she had been standing staring down into the water.

In the hospital they asked her how she felt on a scale of one to ten. The truth was she felt nothing, a total void, so she said zero. Had she thought of harming herself? The honest answer was that she just wanted to disappear.

The night she was admitted, one of the agency nurses, running out of patience at the end of a long shift, told her that if she didn't eat and drink, she would die. At the time, Letty had thought, yes, that would be so much easier for everyone.

She remembers Frances sobbing beside her hospital bed, thinking Letty was asleep. She'd never seen her mother cry before. It had made her hate herself even more for making everyone unhappy.

A lot of it is a blur now, like a nightmare whose details she can't quite grasp. She doesn't really know what it was that made her finally respond to the routine of the hospital, the regular mealtimes and her uncle Rollo's visits.

When she was stable enough to leave, she'd continued with therapy and Marina had provided the routine at home. While Letty studied for her A levels each morning, Marina prepared a light lunch which they would eat together. If Marina was worried about her, she never let it show as her parents did. Frances and Ivo couldn't understand how it had happened right under their noses. It was as if they thought that anything

115

they inadvertently said or did might make it happen again. Certain words became taboo. Eat, fat, thin, sick, river, death.

'Come!' Heidi says, pushing back her chair from the table, leading the way out onto the pool terrace, where there are vast umbrellas and loungers with deep cushions. She takes off her wrap and dives into the temptingly blue pool, and Letty follows her. The water is unheated; the late spring sunshine has only taken the edge off its coolness. The shock feels gloriously cathartic, as if she is washing the bad memories away, and when they both come up for air, they are laughing like old friends together.

The streets of Capri town are really alleyways, where shops built for grocers and bakers now offer the designer brands found on Rome's Via dei Condotti, London's Bond Street or New York's Fifth Avenue. Heidi likes to window-shop, but these are places even she cannot get a deal. As she walks on to Tod's, Letty stays behind in Louis Vuitton. When they meet up again in the main square for an aperitivo, she pushes an orange cardboard carrier bag across the table towards Heidi.

'Just a little something to say thank you for arranging all this!' Letty says. 'And it really is tiny,' she adds.

Heidi leans across the table and hugs her, then lovingly extracts the gift box inside the carrier bag, unties the blue ribbon bow, and slides out the tray to reveal a Louis Vuitton dust bag inside. It's such a ridiculous over-packing of a cheap item, Letty's suddenly slightly nervous that Heidi will think she is mocking her.

From inside the dust bag, Heidi draws out a packet of Post-it notes with the Louis Vuitton logo. She bursts out laughing.

'It's perfect,' she says. She pulls one off and puts it on her forehead.

'Who am I?' she asks, remembering the game they played in class.

116

Heidi has an Aperol Spritz, Letty a glass of white wine.

After the swim, Letty's body feels so clean and purified the wine goes straight to her head. The pleasant feeling of well-being has remained with her, and it's nice just watching the world go by. Heidi is talking about her husband and how, after four years of marriage, he suddenly told her that he wasn't sure he loved her.

Letty listens, nodding, not saying a lot but offering as much reassurance as she can.

'What I need is an affair,' Heidi tells her. 'Because now, I have no self-confidence. Did you know that Jo asked me for a drink?'

Letty didn't.

'But I'm not so desperate,' Heidi laughs. 'And you and Alf?'

Letty knew this conversation was inevitable. Heidi has seen them leaving the school together. She's surprised that it hasn't come up sooner.

'We've spent a few afternoons together,' she hears herself saying.

'You like him?'

'Yes, I do.'

'So . . . ?'

'So . . . I don't know.' Though she's trying to appear nonchalant, Letty can feel the colour in her face.

'Do you fuck?'

Letty's just taking a sip of her wine. She splutters it back into the glass.

'No!' she says.

'Such a waste!' says Heidi. 'You know you want to.'

'I don't!' Letty insists, but it sounds a little half-hearted.

'What happens in Rome stays in Rome, yes? It's an expression?'

'I'm sure nothing is going to happen in Rome,' Letty says,

thinking how prim she sounds, like a spinster schoolteacher. 'We hardly know each other!'

'He's tall, he's ripped, he has a sexy smile – what more do you need to know?' Heidi asks.

Letty's about to say, 'Well, I'm not like that.' But she finds herself thinking, Like what? What am I like?

So I know you're coming back to Rome, he'd said at the Trevi Fountain.

What's to lose?

But she's had that thought before, and the answer was so much more complicated than she intended.

13

ALF

'Non cercavo niente, ma con te ho trovato tutto! Sei il mio tutto. Ti amo!'

The chalked graffiti on the walkway is still there.

Now that Alf knows the imperfect tense, he can translate it correctly.

'I wasn't looking for anything, but with you I've found everything! You are my everything. I love you!'

Alf always thinks better when he's walking beside water. In Blackpool, in winter especially, there are miles and miles of empty beach where your worries and doubts are blown away by the gale coming off the Irish Sea. Here, with the softer sounds of the river around him, he stands with a handful of gravel, throwing it, stone by stone, into the water with gentle plops.

Letty will be in class by now.

He tries to remember if he felt like this when he and Gina first got together. He was made up, yes, turned on, without a doubt, and shocked because he wasn't expecting it. It was definitely a good surprise, but then the secrecy became all bound up with it and made it a bigger deal than it really was.

Gina hasn't changed. He has. But she's had to give up so much, he doesn't know if he can bring himself to let her down.

He owes it to Gina to discuss what's happening, but he can't do that when Stuart's here because, if he's honest, it's not going to be a discussion; it's going to be an ending. Or perhaps now's the best time? Perhaps Stuart will come to her rescue, provide TLC and a few grand to set her back on her feet?

His hand is empty of stones, but there are still random splashes in the water. Alf realizes it is raining. In central Rome, within seconds of it starting to rain, vendors appear on the streets, their forearms hung with umbrellas, their hands proffering packets of plastic ponchos in candy colours. He never knows how they get there so quickly. It's almost as if they're waiting in the drains below the streets listening for the patter of raindrops. Here, by the river, it's too remote for street vendors, and the shirt he has worn for their lunch on the Via Veneto gets soaked.

When he arrives back at the apartment, dripping from head to toe, there's no one home. The flat feels different when it's empty, not so oppressive. On his own, taking a shower with the bathroom door open, he wonders if it's simply the lack of space that is making him feel cramped. If it were just the two of them, would he be happier? The thought of undiluted Gina is even more restrictive, though, than the thought of them all together. Alf negotiates a path through her stuff to his suitcase, and puts on his only other good shirt – a white one that he brought in case he got a job as a waiter – hoping the creases will fall out as he wears it because there isn't time to iron it.

Gina and her dad are sitting at a pavement table, which today is encased in thick plastic sheeting because of the threat of rain. He shakes Stuart's hand and gives Gina a quick kiss. Stuart pushes a designer cologne he's bought him in duty free across the table. The chair that they've left for Alf is situated just beneath the corner seam in the plastic. Drips of water fall directly into the gap between his collar and the nape of his neck, and trickle down his spine. Alf shifts his seat a couple of inches.

'No Roman would ever eat out in this weather,' he tells Stuart.

'Probably couldn't afford it, with the state of their economy,' says Stuart. 'Total disaster, the Euro—'

'No politics, please!' Gina intervenes.

'How was your flight?' Alf asks.

'Not bad, not bad at all,' says Stuart. 'How was your lesson?'

'I told Dad you're trying to learn Italian properly,' Gina chips in.

'Back to school, eh?' says Stuart, winking at him.

Does he know Alf has packed the classes in? How could he? This is why he should have told Gina, Alf thinks, before not saying anything became telling a lie. But he can't tell her now.

'The pace is a bit slow for me,' he says, picking up the menu.

'What about you, princess? How's your Italian?'

'I don't really need a lot,' Gina says. 'It's best I can't explain anything in Italian at school, because then they really do have to learn the English. And when we're out, Alf is really good.'

'Why don't you order then?' Stuart says.

Alf would normally have no problem communicating in Italian with the waiter, but because he's being scrutinized he's hesitant about doing the expansive Italian gestures. Also, Stuart wants a hamburger. The waiter is used to dealing with international guests, and all Alf's attempts in Italian are met with responses in English.

'Must try harder!' Stuart chuckles.

Is there something slightly aggressive about his mockery, or is it only that Alf's banter has become a bit rusty through lack of use?

'Shame about Arsenal not qualifying for Europe,' he says, hoping to land one where it hurts.

'Shame about Blackpool not qualifying for anything ... Well, just shame about Blackpool, really!' Stuart replies.

Alf laughs.

The mood seems to relax, equilibrium restored.

'What brings you to Rome?' Alf asks, as the waiter opens a bottle of red wine for Stuart, and a bottle of sparkling water for Alf and Gina.

'Do I need a reason?'

'No. I just—'

'Haven't seen my princess for, what is it?'

'Nearly six months,' says Gina.

Alf thinks it's cool that Stuart treats them as equals, but sometimes the father–daughter bond feels awkwardly close to flirtation. If someone were looking at the three of them together, would they see a father, a daughter and her boyfriend? he wonders.

If Letty were walking past, what would she think? This exact time last week they were strolling up this street, he remembers, suddenly grateful for the plastic sheeting obscuring them from the casual glances of passers-by.

Gina eats her spaghetti with a spoon and a fork. It's a stupid thing to get irritated by because it's how most English people are taught. But it's so much easier the Italian way, which is to use the side of the bowl as the anchor for the fork. Just because they're in Rome doesn't mean they have to do as the Romans do, but if you see a better method used by people who eat pasta every day, why not change? Afterwards, she orders tiramisu and complains that the alcohol in the sponge is so strong she'll be drunk for her afternoon class, which is what she always says when she eats tiramisu. Alf knows that he used to find all her little girly habits as adorable as Stuart clearly still does, but now they grate like fingernails on a blackboard. He's glad when she picks up her bag and goes off to work, leaving the two of them together.

They order coffee. An espresso for Alf, a cappuccino for Stuart.

'In Italy, nobody drinks cappuccino after midday,' Alf tells Stuart.

'What kind of a rule is that? I usually have about five per afternoon! Costs me a bloody fortune.'

It's not a rule, Alf thinks; it's just a cultural thing. But he doesn't say that.

'So what's this school of yours like?' Stuart asks him. His face is pink from the red wine, his lips black round the edges.

'What can I tell you?' says Alf. 'It's a school. We learn some grammar and then we try to practise it . . .'

'Is everyone there English?'

'No, not at all. There's only one other English person in my class. There's a Japanese guy, a Norwegian, a Swiss woman, two Colombian girls . . .'

'Colombian girls? Maybe I should learn Italian,' says Stuart.

Alf remembers similar laddish conversations in the cafe before the Arsenal match, and how much he liked being accepted as one of the guys. It's not Stuart that's changed, he thinks, it's me. It's just banter, he tells himself. It doesn't mean anything.

'Anything you fancy doing this afternoon?' Alf asks.

There's no particular reason for them to move from their table, but he feels trapped and restless. It's still raining, so there's no point in suggesting a walk in the Villa Borghese, and it's a Monday so most of the museums and art galleries will be closed. He doesn't think that Stuart would be interested anyway.

'Are we anywhere near the shops?' Stuart asks.

'The expensive shops, yes,' says Alf, realizing as soon as he says it that those are the only ones Stuart would go to.

'I like an Italian fabric,' says Stuart. 'And you look like you could use a new shirt . . .'

Stuart buys an umbrella from one of the street vendors, beating him down from ten euros to eight, although Alf knows that he could have got it for five if he had been charming instead of aggressive. They walk towards the Spanish Steps.

'Why are they the Spanish Steps when we're in Italy?' Stuart wants to know.

'I think it's because the square is called the Spanish square,' says Alf.

'Duh . . .' says Stuart.

Alf consults Wikipedia on his phone.

'It's because the Spanish embassy is here. Thanks for that,' he says. 'I like collecting facts for my tours.'

'How much do you get paid?' Stuart asks.

'I'm self-employed,' says Alf. 'Normally, I use an algorithm to fix my price.'

'Impressive,' says Stuart. 'How does that work?'

'The information I put in is how skint am I, along with, do I like these people enough to want to spend a couple of hours with them? The computation is almost instant,' he says, watching Stuart's facial expression shift from listening carefully to knowing he's been had.

'Very enterprising,' he says. 'Have you thought about what you're going to do when you come back to England?'

'Don't have any plans right now.'

'Gina's not going to want to stay here forever though, is she?'

He says it as though it was Alf's decision to come to Rome, although it was only Sally telling Gina about the job that brought them here in the first place. Teaching English as a Foreign Language was falling-off-a-log time, she'd said, when Gina had been nervous about working abroad. Alf wonders if Gina has been talking to Stuart, expressing a wish to return home.

'What do we think about this suit?' Stuart says, stopping outside Armani, pointing at a summer suit in a very pale grey.

Alf isn't really a suit person, except for dancing and those have to be specially made.

'What size do you think I am in Italian?' Stuart asks.

'I'm sure they'll be able to tell you.'

'Will you translate?'

'Sure, but I think they'll speak English on this street,' Alf says, relieved that he wore a shirt with his jeans because he's noticed that Italians expect you to dress properly if you're browsing in their smart shops. He went into Gucci once with Gina, because she'd seen a bag in the window, and the staff glared at him like he had no right to be there.

Stuart looks good in the suit. A little flashy, but Stuart's quite a flashy kind of guy. The shop assistant sells him a shirt to go with it. It's just a white shirt but it costs ten times as much as any shirt Alf's ever bought.

'Time is money. I don't spend time shopping in London, but when I'm on my holidays . . . can I get you one?' Stuart asks.

'No thanks,' Alf says. 'I've got a couple of new ones at home.'

Gina should be here. She would be loving it. The bag she wanted cost more than all the money he'd ever earned. She'd replaced it on the stand, saying, 'Oh well, when you're rich . . .'

Alf didn't tell her that even if he had all the money in the world he wouldn't spend it on a handbag, but now he wishes he'd taken a closer look at which one it was, because he's sure Stuart would get it for her, and that in turn would win Alf brownie points for remembering the item she coveted. But if he chooses the wrong one, it might backfire. Instead he suggests, 'You should bring Gina shopping. She loves this street.'

'I bet she does,' says Stuart.

Outside Prada, Alf makes the mistake of admiring a short-sleeved shirt created from two contrasting fifties prints. Even though he protests that he really doesn't want it, once Stuart's decided on something there's no persuading him otherwise.

As with the duty-free cologne, his only option is to say, 'That's incredibly generous of you, Stuart. Thank you very much.'

'Not a problem. Grateful to you for taking care of my girl,' says Stuart, adding with a pleasant smile as he hands over the cardboard carrier bag, 'I really don't know what I'd do if anyone hurt her.'

It's the kind of thing that Stuart says, Alf reassures himself, because he works in London where everyone seems to put on more of a performance than people in the North do. It's not a threat. If Stuart really knew what was going on in Alf's mind, he wouldn't be buying him a shirt, would he?

Stuart insists on taking a taxi to the hotel with his shopping, although it would be much quicker to walk, and then they're in the same position as they were two hours before, with Alf wondering what to do with him.

It's too early for aperitivi, too wet for Alf to take him up to Stadio Olimpico to see where Roma play. They end up in Stuart's suite, playing *FIFA* on the PlayStation, until it's time to head to Trastevere to meet Gina for a pizza.

'Grateful for your time this afternoon, son,' Stuart tells him in the cab. He gets out his wallet and for one awkward moment, Alf thinks he's going to try to pay him, but instead he extracts a flyer from the hotel advertising a two-day trip to a track near Modena where you can drive Lamborghinis.

'I thought I might give this a go,' he tells him.

'Wow!' Alf says. 'That looks like a lot of fun.'

'Be happy to treat you ... if you can drag yourself away from school?'

'Stuart, I haven't even got a driving licence. I don't think anyone's going to let me in a Lamborghini!'

It's a relief to know that he will have a couple of days without Stuart breathing down his neck to figure out what to do.

14

Tuesday

LETTY

Anima gemella, principe azzurro, colpo di fulmine.

Susanna is writing words on the whiteboard.

'What do you think these expressions mean?' she asks. 'Do you have similar expressions in your language?'

She hands out a reading with the beginning of a love affair described first by the woman and then the man.

'It wasn't love at first sight,' Letty translates the woman's side. 'We fell in love little by little, day by day . . .'

'I fell in love with her immediately,' Heidi translates the man's side. She glances up and smiles at Letty, still trying to look encouraging even though Alf hasn't appeared in class for the past two days.

In Capri, where the air seemed to shimmer with anticipation, Letty made up her mind that she would do something. *Carpe diem*. Live in the moment.

Yesterday, she was nervous on her walk to school, but looking forward to seeing him again. When he wasn't there, and the weather was wet in the afternoon, she returned home and studied, feeling pleasure trickling through her body whenever she thought about him.

But today he's absent again and she wonders whether it's something she's done. Or not done. If she hadn't been so distant, would he be here? It's probably nothing to do with her. Perhaps he's ill?

At break, she goes down to reception and asks if they have heard anything from him.

'He's left the school!' one of the women says.

For a moment, Letty stands stupefied, not knowing how she could have got it as wrong as this.

Even Heidi seems embarrassed for encouraging her.

'Men are bastards,' she says, when Letty tells her in the cafe.

But he isn't, Letty thinks.

After the break, they practise the language they have learned.

'Do you believe in love at first sight?' Masakasu reads the sentence slowly from his notebook.

'No.'

'Are you in love with someone?'

'No.'

'How was your date?'

'*È stato un disastro,*' Letty says solemnly, which makes him laugh.

Today the sunshine is bright, as if the rain has rinsed the dust and diesel fumes from the air. As Letty walks away from the school, she keeps reminding herself she is in Rome to sort out her life. She is absolutely not here to get involved with a guy. Each thought coincides with a determined stride, as if she is inventing a mantra of positive thoughts. There is still so much to see. She hasn't even started on the Vatican Museum yet. She is just taking out her phone and looking at Citymapper to find the best way of getting there when she hears footsteps approaching.

'Come on, Lets!' says Alf. 'We've got a train to catch.'

She stands still, unwilling to be pulled up the street towards the station, annoyed that he just assumes she'll go with him. But when she sees him looking at her bewildered, she realizes that she's the one who has been making assumptions. For her, the last four days have been a journey of admitting that she likes him, deciding that she wants something to happen between them, then feeling let down and humiliated. But he doesn't know any of this.

'Why did you leave the school?' she asks brusquely.

'I couldn't afford it,' he tells her. 'Not without working. And I didn't want to spend my afternoons working . . . so I thought I'd work mornings instead.'

His smile is slightly mischievous as he watches her processing this information.

Now, she feels silly for asking him.

'So where are we going?' she asks, letting him take her hand as they run towards the station.

'Anzio,' he says.

The train journey takes an hour and when they arrive, there's a short walk through the town to the seafront.

'At the weekend, the whole of Rome comes here for lunch,' Alf tells her, but today they are one of only three couples in the restaurant.

He orders the pasta with lobster and encourages her to try it, but she decides on spaghetti with clams. He asks if she'd like some white wine. She's got into the habit of drinking a glass with Heidi. Why not? *Carpe diem!* When it comes, she drinks the first glass quickly, enjoying the sensation of cold liquid slipping down her throat and the warm relaxation that suffuses her body just after.

The lobster arrives on top of the pasta, still in its shell and coated with sauce. She's glad she chose the clams, because she doesn't know how she would begin to tackle it. Alf tucks his napkin into the neck of his T-shirt before diving in.

'I never had lobster before coming to Italy,' he tells her. 'It would be way out of my price range at home.'

'Mine too,' she says.

She has eaten lobster once, in Venice, accompanied by so much champagne that the sour taste of excess seemed to stay in her mouth for days.

'So what did you do in class?' Alf asks.

'Is the idea that you get the lessons free from me every day?' she says.

'Hadn't thought of that, but now you mention it . . .' he says, smiling back at her.

'So, today it was all about meeting someone, going on dates,' she says, getting halfway through the theme before becoming self-conscious, then trying to recover. 'In Italian they say Blue Prince instead of Prince Charming . . . and *colpo di fulmine* for love at first sight.'

'Struck by lightning,' he says, looking straight at her.

She looks out of the window at the sea.

'Wasn't Anzio where the Allies landed in the Second World War?' she asks.

'The Americans, yes. The Brits at Nettuno, which is just down the coast. We can walk there along the beach, if you'd like to.'

'I'd like it very much,' she says.

The beach is wide and empty, apart from a mother with a pushchair and a small toddler in the distance. The sand is wet and flat.

'Beaches are good places to think,' Alf says. 'It's kind of like you've got life on one side' – he points inland – 'and nothing-ness on the other.' He waves his hand at the open expanse of sea.

'Liminal places,' says Letty.

'Is that the word for it?'

'It comes from *limen* in Latin, which means threshold.'

'Liminal,' Alf repeats, stopping for a moment as if savouring it.

The woman with the buggy and the toddler has a radio on. As they draw closer, the tune that's playing becomes recognizable.

' "Don't Get Me Wrong". The Pretenders,' says Alf. 'It's what I did my first junior quickstep to.'

'Your best dance,' Letty remembers.

'Yes. That particular one not so much, because we only came third, but the quickstep's great.'

He demonstrates the steps. She's amazed how far he travels in just a couple of bars. It's funny that he always dances with his arms in ballroom hold position, even without a partner.

'The hold's the most important thing,' he says, realizing why she's laughing. 'Takes a lot of muscle strength. Important for you too,' he says. 'Look!'

He takes her in hold.

'You have to keep pushing those elbows up. You can't just rely on my strength. So,' he explains, looking at her feet, 'it's slow, slow, quick, quick, slow. That's good,' he says, as she mirrors his steps. 'What you have to remember is that the quick steps are quick but not too short. That's how you cover the distance. So . . .' He waits for a moment in the song, then leads her through the steps she's just learned.

'You could just do basic step all the way round the room,' he says.

'The beach,' she says.

'Yes, it's probably the best step for the beach,' he says. 'But if you want to get round a corner or just look a bit more impressive, then you can do a spin turn. First we need to learn a lock step . . .'

He shows her how to cross her feet travelling backwards.

'That will get you out of any situation,' he says. 'And now, the spin turn.'

Which involves putting her foot between his while he spins her to change direction.

'Now, a lock step out of it – good . . . You're a natural!'

They're fifty yards past the surprised mother now, and can no longer hear the music.

'Shall we put it all together?' he asks, scrolling down his phone screen to find the song again.

They're on a beach and there's no one about, but there's a road above with cars; villas with windows where people could look out and see them.

'Here!' Alf puts his mobile quickly in his back pocket and holds out his arms.

The music comes on before she has a chance to protest, and then they're quickstepping across the flat sand, and it feels wonderful, as if she's the star in a Busby Berkeley movie.

When the track ends, he does a final spin turn and she collapses against his chest laughing breathlessly, with rivulets of sweat trickling down her temples. Through his T-shirt, she can feel his heart beating fast against her cheek, his chest firm and warm and smelling of some expensive scent that she suddenly recoils from.

'What?' he asks.

'Nothing,' she says, looking away.

'It's just . . . your aftershave . . .'

Alf laughs.

'You're saying I smell?'

'Not a bad smell. Well, not to most people, I'm sure. But to me . . . it's just I hadn't got that close before and . . .' Everything she says makes it somehow sound worse.

'It's the first time I've worn it!' he tells her. 'And I wasn't sure myself . . .'

'Sorry,' she says.

'It's fine. I appreciate the honesty ... and I'll promise to keep my distance until I can wash it off.'

He steps deliberately away from her as they continue walking.

'Why didn't you want to be a professional dancer?' Letty asks. 'You so love it!'

'That's a long story,' he says.

'We have a lot of beach ...'

'Well, the short answer is that I did think about going to study dance, but it didn't work out.'

She would be more interested in the long answer, but she's already conscious of having asked something he's uncomfortable about. With Alf, you can tell from his gait – when it goes from long easy strides to hesitant, more staccato steps.

There is no way round the headland at the end of the beach, so they have to climb up to the promenade. She glances back at the beach. The mother and toddler have gone. The sun is dropping in the sky, turning everything golden.

Alf checks his watch.

'We need to be getting back,' he says, checking the quickest route to the station.

Letty tries not to feel disappointed. They've had lunch, they've chatted, they've danced on the beach – what more could she ask in an afternoon? If the train leaves soon, they will get back to Termini around six thirty. That's generally the time they split. Except for the *Roman Holiday* tour when it was dark by the time they parted, and he walked away talking on the phone without looking back.

The train is a double decker and they sit upstairs.

Alf asks her about Capri, and she is trying to describe how beautiful it was, when she remembers a video she took and shows it to him. He moves to sit next to her to look at it. As she watches the video again, pointing out the places to him –

Ischia, Procida, Naples, Pompeii, Sorrento – she remembers dancing alone round the terrace, wishing he were there with her. She can feel his arm along the back of the seat, fingertips just touching the edge of her T-shirt sleeve. She allows her thigh to relax against his, then feels the gentle, tentative stroke of his forefinger on her arm. She glances up from the screen at his profile, his eyes focused on the video. Then, sensing her looking at him, he turns his face and their mouths are so close she can feel his breath on her lips, his eyes staring into hers.

She wants to say, 'I thought about you when I was there.'

Suddenly, there's a clatter of feet behind them as an excited teenage couple dash through the carriage, barging against them, then collapsing into the seat nearest the stairs, laughing.

'They're fare dodging,' Alf whispers. 'When they see the conductor coming upstairs they dash down, and then come up when he goes through the downstairs bit.'

The couple are now snogging.

'Fare dodging, eh?' says Letty.

Alf laughs.

'Looks amazing, Capri,' he says, shifting back over to the opposite seat so neither of them has to look at the teenagers.

'It really was,' she says. 'Have you ever been to the Bay of Naples?'

It's as if they've gone back to the stilted language of the classroom.

'I haven't,' he says. 'But I'd really like to one day.'

They spend the rest of the journey comparing notes on the places they've been in Italy, although Alf hasn't been anywhere except Rome and the surrounding towns. Tuscany is beautiful, she tells him, and Puglia too, although the landscape is very different. Venice? Yes, she's been there. It is as amazing as everyone says, but she wouldn't want to go there again. She's relieved that they're pulling into Termini so there's no time for him to ask her why.

The tram is crowded with workers who have finished for the day and there's hardly room to breathe, so when they get out at Porta Maggiore, the air feels cool and sweet on her skin. They walk slower than they usually do.

She knows that she wants him. She thinks he wants her too. But something is holding him back. Or maybe it has to be her. Maybe that is what he's waiting for. Does she dare?

A number three tram is rattling towards them. It has to be now. It has to be.

'I was wondering . . .' she says, as the doors open.

'Yes?'

'I was wondering . . . if you were doing anything tomorrow afternoon?' she says.

Alf smiles, then suddenly takes her face in both his hands and kisses her lips with melting tenderness.

'Seeing you, I hope,' he says, then leaps onto his tram just as the doors are closing.

15

Wednesday

ALF

He stands in the shade of the building opposite the school waiting for her, and when she comes out, his heart misses a beat
at how beautiful she is and how she wears her looks so casually, like a dress she picked up in a charity shop with no idea
that it's couture. She glances up the street towards the place
they usually meet, frowns when he isn't there.

'Over here!' he calls.

She doesn't even look before she crosses the road, causing
a moped to swerve to avoid her.

'Why are you standing here?' she demands, as if it's his fault
that she nearly got killed. She stops in front of him, just too far
away for them to exchange kisses.

It's taken two weeks to understand that her reticence is
because she is unsure of herself in all sorts of ways, almost as
if she's a much younger person, a virgin, unconscious of the
signals she is giving, or even wants to give.

He wants to be able to reassure her, 'It's OK, I won't hurt
you.' But he's determined not to lie to her. Whatever has happened in her life has damaged her, and he wants to be part of
the solution, not the problem. But the restraint is killing him.

Today she's wearing a short pinafore over a black vest. The skirt is loose and wouldn't have a chance of staying up if it weren't for the dungaree bib and straps that criss-cross over her back. He wonders if she knows that every man who sees her will yearn to put his hands on her waist beneath the loose circle of denim.

'So, what's the plan?' he asks, taking her backpack from her hand.

'I was wondering . . .' She looks at the pavement. 'Well, I wondered if you'd like to see my apartment. I mean, there's a little Sardinian restaurant right near which looks really good, and they do a lunch menu for less than ten euros and—'

'I'd love to see your apartment,' he says, before she talks herself out of it.

'I found a quicker route to walk,' she says, setting off in the opposite direction from Termini.

Inside, he's dancing.

Her new route follows the Aurelian walls along the side of the clubbing district of San Lorenzo, which is shabby and empty during the day.

They have to go single file through a dark tunnel to get back under the railway. He doesn't like to think of her here alone.

'Do you come this way by yourself?' Alf asks, as they walk past a dodgy-looking guy with a fierce dog at his heels.

'I figure the dealers are unlikely to bother me,' she says. 'And I don't really carry anything that's worth mugging me for. It looks dangerous, but that's only because it's poor. It's just a city neighbourhood.'

She's grown up in London, he remembers. She's street smart. She's such an odd mixture of frailty and confidence; she's always surprising him. He likes that. He likes not knowing what to expect.

Her apartment building is part of an industrial complex that used to be a pasta factory, she tells him.

Letty hesitates outside the gate.

'View first, or lunch first?' she asks.

View view view, he's crying inside.

'You decide,' he says.

'Shall we just dump my stuff then?' Letty says. 'Thank you for carrying it, by the way.'

In the hall, she says hello to the caretaker. He's a big bear of a man who gives Alf the once over, as if assessing whether he's a suitable companion for this precious charge, before shaking his hand.

Just as the lift doors are closing, an old Italian man puts his stick out to stop them and gets in. The lift doesn't appreciate the interruption to its cycle. The doors open and close a couple of times, and then there's an agonizingly long wait with the three of them inside before it finally decides to start moving up. And then it stops between floors. They all exchange cautious smiles, but inside Alf's wondering how long they need to wait before pressing the emergency button. Will it work if they do? What if they are trapped there for the time it takes the fire service to arrive? Why did the old man choose that exact moment? Why didn't he wait for one of the other lifts? Finally, the lift starts moving again, the old man gets out on the fourth floor, and it's just the two of them until the tenth.

As Letty turns the key in the lock and pushes open the heavy door into the apartment, Alf is as nervous as he's ever been in his life. This will be their first time properly alone, out of the public gaze, he suddenly realizes, and it would be so easy to make a mistake, do something that frightens her off.

'Come in,' she says.

The apartment is flooded with sunlight through the wall of window and feels as hot as a glasshouse. Letty turns on the ceiling fan and comes to stand beside him at the window.

'That's San Giovanni in Laterano.' She points to the line of statues along the top of the facade, spiking the pale blue sky.

'There's the Vittorio Emanuele,' he says, spotting the black quadriga chariots, tiny in the distance, with just a sliver of the top of the white marble monument visible.

'I have never noticed that before!' Letty exclaims, delighted.

'We could see your building when we were there, couldn't we?' he says. 'So . . .'

They're standing next to each other and though there's no contact, Alf can feel the tremble of her body close to his.

'Would you like a glass of water?' she asks him. 'I have a bottle in the fridge.'

She walks across the room into the kitchen area, puts two glasses on the counter and pours some cold water.

Alf looks around.

'The sound system is pretty high end for an Airbnb,' he says.

'I think it's the landlord's shag pad between rentals,' Letty says matter of factly.

In her own territory, she seems more at ease. He's the one who's tongue-tied.

'He likes the Beatles,' Alf says, flipping through the array of CDs, finding the red album of early hits, including the songs Gary likes singing best.

'Mind?' he asks Letty.

'Go ahead!'

But when he looks down the tracks, he can't find anything that won't sound like he's being suggestive. 'Please Please Me'. 'She Loves You'. 'Love Me Do'.

Alf quickly chooses another album. Beatles tunes aren't usually that easy to dance to anyway.

It's only when they dance that he and Letty seem to communicate perfectly. They speak English, they're learning Italian, but dance is their language.

Alf puts on the track 'Dos Gardenias' from Buena Vista Social Club, thinking that even if the words are inappropriate, they're in Spanish.

'Dance?' he says.

Her face lights up and she comes out of the kitchen area, leaving the two glasses on the counter.

It's a slow salsa. He takes her in a loose hold, his left hand clasping her right, the other gently cupping her elbow, amazed how well she remembers the steps. She hears the music as he does, he thinks, not rushing at it nervously as some girls do, but responding to every bit of it, so that her movement is languorous, as if the rhythm is taking her body with it, her hips naturally tracing the figure of eight that most beginners never master. He longs to put his hands on her waist and draw her towards him.

He lets go with one hand, leads her into a spin, then goes to spin her a second time, but she isn't expecting it and stumbles slightly towards the vast window. Instinctively he grabs her to stop her fall, and then they're kissing and he doesn't even know if it was he or she who made the first move, just that they both want it so much, and when they stop to look at each other, she pulls him back in.

He slips the straps of her pinafore over her shoulders and it falls to the floor. She is wearing plain black cotton briefs that turn him on more than any satin or lace has ever done. Where the panties end and the vest begins there is a gap, a perfect curve of waist that he has longed to touch. He kneels and kisses her perfect smooth skin, her perfect belly button, his tongue trailing up her body as he inches the vest up and over her perfect breasts, her perfect clavicle bones, her perfect chin, her lips. As he kisses her mouth, she arches her body into his, letting her head loll backwards, drawing his tongue deeper in.

Suddenly aware that they are right in front of the window,

he pauses, looks out, hears her whisper, 'It's the tallest building for miles. Nobody can see.'

And then she's lying on the floor, her fingers unbuttoning his shirt, spreading it slowly back across his chest as he kneels astride her. Then, vertebra by vertebra she curls her spine up to sitting, her mouth tracing a line from the top of his shorts to his neck, her hands on his head, pulling his mouth down onto hers again.

His erection is jutting against his shorts. He suddenly realizes that he doesn't have any protection. He wanted this. He wanted it so much, but he never expected it to happen so soon, so quickly.

'What?' she asks, her lips red, her long hair muzzy.

'I don't have any condoms,' he says.

'Oh,' she says.

He doesn't know if she means oh, she's disappointed, or oh, she had forgotten about that, or even oh, that's not what this was about.

He feels acutely exposed. Suddenly she jumps up, as if she's remembered something, climbs the ladder to the sleeping gallery and, crouching down to avoid hitting her head on the beams, disappears from view. He's wondering if he's supposed to follow her when she appears again, leaning over the rail, bare-chested in her panties, brandishing a selection of condom packets.

'*Fragola, ciliegi o naturale?*' she says.

'*Ciliegi?* Tomato?' he says.

She laughs.

'That's *ciliegini*!' she corrects. 'Cherry tomatoes. *Ciliegi* is just cherries.'

'You choose,' he says, thinking of all the times he has imagined how this might happen and how it was never this bizarre.

'*Naturale*, then,' she says, carefully stepping down the ladder. 'I like the taste of you.'

'I showered four times to get the cologne off,' he says.

'I know,' she says, sitting down beside him, putting the condom on the coffee table. 'Or at least, I don't know how many times you showered, obviously, but you smell nice again today.'

Always, always precise.

'You feel nice,' he says, drawing her body towards his again.

'You taste nice,' she says.

'May I?' he says, fingering the top of her panties.

'That sounds nice,' she says.

Now the pace is less frantic as they gently encourage each other to explore the things that turn them on, finding the sweetest places and moving in lilting rhythm to a climax that obliterates his senses, and for a moment he doesn't know who or where he is.

They lie next to each other on the wooden floor, shining with sweat, in a pool of sunlight.

He doesn't want to move, or to say anything to shatter the exhilarating feeling that somehow he has lived all his life for this moment.

Eventually she sits up and puts her hand on his cheek, as if checking to see that he is real.

'Would you like some water?'

'Yes.'

He holds her hand there for just a moment, staring into her eyes and finding there what he feels in himself.

'Violetta,' he says.

'I prefer your nickname for me,' she says. 'What you called me yesterday.'

'Lets?'

'Sounds so positive,' she says. 'You make me feel positive. Thank you.'

'I'm glad,' he says.

She gets to her feet and, suddenly modest, pulls her vest and panties back on.

She brings the glasses of water. Puts them on the coffee table beside him.

'Can't think of a poetic way of saying this. That was the best sex I've ever had,' he tells her.

'For me too,' she says simply.

He sits up to kiss her again but midway she breaks off, as if she's just remembered something important.

'How much sex have you had, though?'

Typical of her not to simply accept a sweeping generalization. For Letty, all words have to mean something.

'Enough,' he says. There are some things he's not going to be pinned down on. 'How about you?'

'Not enough, it seems,' she says, kissing him again.

The second time it's more experimental. Her body is strong and flexible and easily reaches positions he has never tried before. But what he loves the most is looking up into her face, with her hair falling around them, like they're in their own private little tent, their bodies moving in sync and so, so slowly that they both cry out with pleasure so intense it is almost pain.

The Sardinian proprietor of the restaurant is dragging the tables indoors when they turn up for lunch. It's an unprepossessing, windowless building with graffiti around the door. Like a lot of shops and restaurants in Rome when they're shut, you'd walk straight past without even knowing it was there.

'*Ho sentito che il vostro cibo è buonissimo!*' Alf says, which he hopes means, 'I've heard your food is very good.'

He's learned that if you're paying a compliment, it doesn't really matter whether the grammar's correct.

The proprietor hesitates, looks at them, smiles as if he can see from the glow around them what they've just been doing, and allows his romantic side to get the better of him. He beckons them into the restaurant, saying that they can only have what's left. He's already told the chef to go home and he's not cooking them anything new.

Inside it's as cool as a cave and painted bright pink. Chandeliers hang from the ceiling, giving it the most unexpected ambience: part Disney, part boudoir.

'Incongruous!' Alf whispers to Letty.

Despite the fact he's told them that they can only have what is available, the proprietor keeps dashing to the kitchen, returning with slivers of raw fish to taste, a batch of mussels he cooks up especially, a delicious bowl of stew with squid and fresh peas. He encourages them to take a quarto of Sardinian wine, giving them the history of the vineyard, and by the end of the meal, they feel they have enjoyed a tasting menu in a very good restaurant for only the – nine-euro – price for lunch.

He's pleased when Alf asks to Instagram a photo of his business card with the restaurant details. Alf writes the caption: *Cibo buonissimo! #restaurantsinRome.* Then, on impulse, he gives the man a hug, feeling suddenly sentimental because their lives will be forever linked. He will always remember this place.

Ambling back to her building, he walks as slowly as he can, trying to stretch out the time before he has to tell her that he's not going back up to the apartment. The only thing he wants is to hold her again, feel her skin on his, make love and fall asleep together and, waking, make love again, but the closer they become, the less likely it is that she will forgive his duplicity. No point in trying to explain that it is over with Gina. It has to actually be over. He has to act.

Even now, he wonders if he has left it too late.

'Can I see you tomorrow?' he asks, as she puts her key in the lock of the gate.

'Oh!'

'Believe me, the last thing I want to do is leave you, but . . . there's something I have to sort out.' Please don't ask. Please don't ask.

She doesn't ask in words, but her eyes search his until he looks away.

'I'm sorry,' he says, stepping closer to her, taking her in his arms.

The body that was so pliant now stands stiff and straight.

'*Ti adoro*,' he says, dropping kisses into her hair.

'No, don't adore me.' She takes a step back. 'I don't like people adoring me.'

'What do you like?'

She hesitates.

'Kindness,' she says.

'I am kind,' he says, feeling like a total shit. 'I'll meet you tomorrow. Promise.'

'Tomorrow then,' she says, not looking at him.

'Tomorrow,' he says, and walks quickly away. When he turns, expecting to see her wave, she has gone in and he wonders if he has already lost her.

It's not Gina's fault, it's his. But there's nothing he can do about it. It's like being struck by lightning. No. Keep it simple. He's sorry. He never meant to hurt her. Alf silently rehearses his speech a final time before opening the door to their apartment.

'You took your time,' Stuart says.

'I thought you were driving Lamborghinis,' Alf says, unable to disguise his shock.

'By the time I woke up, the coach had already left.'

Stuart looks as if he's been drinking. Alf wonders where he has been for the past two days.

'So, what have you been up to?' Stuart wants to know.

'Some clients asked me to a late lunch,' Alf says, as casually as he can.

'*Buonissimo seebo*, I believe?' says Stuart, pronouncing it wrongly.

He's seen the Instagram post.

'Yes.'

'Maybe you should take us there?'

'I'm not sure it's your kind of place,' Alf says casually. 'It's pink and very camp.'

'There's nothing Alf wouldn't do for a tip!' Gina jokes.

'I waited for you outside the Forum today,' Stuart says.

Is that a normal thing to do? Alf wonders. If he wanted to meet up, why didn't he just text? Is he being paranoid, imagining that Stuart can sense the cheating?

'Which exit?' Alf asks.

'There's more than one exit?' Gina asks.

'Yeah, I often use the one on Via di San Gregorio,' Alf tells them. 'It's better for the tram.'

'Alf loves trams,' Gina tells her father.

'It's coming from Blackpool,' he says, grinning at Stuart, but inside he's panicking.

He can't deliver his speech with Stuart there staring at him.

He's going to be flying back Saturday morning, to be there for Arsenal's last home match on Sunday.

That's three more nights, Alf thinks, not sure if Letty will wait that long.

16

Thursday

LETTY

When she wakes up, she wonders whether she dreamt it. She closes her eyes, trying to think herself back to the blissfully terrifying sensation of taking him inside her, her muscles slowly opening to him until she felt full of him, and his sigh, as if he had finally found the place he was supposed to be, and how he moved, so gently and slowly and with such control that she found herself begging for more, more, more, wanting him to go further into her body, into her mind, into her soul.

There's something I have to sort out.

It has to be a girlfriend.

Letty's desperate to know, but she doesn't want to know. What is the point of knowing?

Live in the moment.

She and Alf exist in the present tense.

If she doesn't ask him about his past, he will have no right to ask about hers.

In class, she wonders if anyone can tell from the way she looks, the involuntary smile that keeps creeping to her lips. She

147

knows Heidi would, but her friend is on another long weekend, this time to Florence.

The theme of the lesson is where you live.

I live in an apartment.

He is there to meet her out of school. They run all the way back.

It's on the tenth floor. Fortunately, there is a lift.

He stabs the 10 button again and again to make sure no one gets in with them, then pushes her against the mirror at the back, kissing her as the lift climbs, his hands under her vest, his crotch pressed against hers.

It has only one room.

The door slams behind them and they're kissing each other, tearing at each other's clothes.

And a wooden floor.

She pulls him down onto her.

E una vista meravigliosa.

The word can also mean miraculous. A miraculous view.

'It's like making love in the sky,' Alf says afterwards.

At the restaurant – *their* restaurant – they order pasta with spicy Sardinian sausage, another quarto of the light white wine. Two tiny cups of espresso, barely a mouthful, but the perfect end to the meal.

The proprietor calls her *'cara'*, as if they have known each other for years. He shakes Alf's hand like an old friend.

Back in the flat, they make love on the sofa, lying together after, with Alf stroking that place near the top of her arm with his finger that feels almost more intimate than all the things they have done together, but she can tell that he isn't fully present.

'Let's go away together for the weekend!' he suddenly says.

'Where?' she asks.

'How about Florence?'

'Heidi's in Florence.'

'Not there then. How would you feel about Naples again?'

'We could go to Ischia!' Letty says.

He looks up the Trenitalia site on his phone.

'There's a train at one o'clock tomorrow. If you come straight out of school, we can get that?'

'I'm there,' says Letty.

He taps the phone a few more times.

'So that's done,' he says.

He looks at his watch and stands up. It's his usual time to leave.

Letty braces herself. 'Come on. Get dressed,' he says. 'We're going out.'

'Going out? Where?'

'It's a surprise!'

Half past six is too early to eat again, except maybe a gelato. It's too far to come for an ice cream, she thinks, as they get off the tram at Termini. He guides her across the roads to Piazza della Repubblica, and stops outside a cinema. She tries not to be disappointed. Going to the cinema is what people do at the beginning of a relationship, isn't it?

'Surprise!' he says, pointing.

On the poster she recognizes Vadim, the boy she had a crush on, now grown up and apparently dancing the principal role in the Royal Ballet's live transmission of *Manon*. Letty hasn't been to see a ballet since her accident. The prospect triggers a rush of conflicting emotions: excitement, nostalgia, regret.

'It's a good surprise, isn't it?' Alf says, as if picking up on her ambivalence.

Is it? Is she really going to deny herself a lifetime of watching ballet just because she can't be on the stage with the dancers? She looks at Alf's troubled face, sees how much it matters to him that he hasn't made a mistake.

'It's a lovely surprise,' she says.

'I've never seen a ballet before,' he says. 'Except on television at Christmas.'

'You picked a brilliant one to see live,' she tells him. 'It's all about class and sexual exploitation, and not a tutu in sight!' She realizes that's exactly how she's heard her mother describing *Manon*.

Frances often goes to the ballet by herself, although she never mentions it to Letty, for fear of being tactless. Frances loves any kind of theatre. She wanted to be on the stage herself, and met Ivo in a garden production of *A Midsummer Night's Dream* during the Trinity term of the first year they were both at Oxford.

'You could call it love at first sight,' Frances always says, when she recounts their meeting. 'Or you could say that, unlike the stuck-up cow who played Titania, I was prepared to put out, much good that it did me.'

Ivo was playing Oberon; Frances Puck.

Frances never fulfilled her acting ambition because of getting pregnant with Oscar in her final year.

'Being an actress was far too precarious an existence,' her mother said when Letty once asked her why she didn't return to it. 'One of us had to earn some money.'

For many years, her mother supported Ivo's ambition to be an actor himself, but it never really happened for him. Eventually he became a drama teacher, which was great for Letty because he was always there for her in the school holidays.

Letty just manages to WhatsApp Frances before the lights go down. *I'm watching RB Manon live in Rome. Are you there at ROH?*

The ballet is set in the demi-monde of eighteenth-century Paris. The first act is about Manon, a beautiful innocent country girl, arriving in the city where she meets a young romantic poet called Des Grieux. In the sensual bedroom pas de deux,

Manon and Des Grieux declare their love for one another. But Manon's brother Lescaut is a crook and a social climber, who tries to buy his way into society by pimping Manon to a rich admirer, Monsieur GM. Manon, seduced by the luxury of wealth, agrees to become his mistress.

'Wow!' says Alf as the curtain comes down. 'I didn't see her doing that!'

'It wouldn't be a three-act ballet if they lived happily ever after,' Letty says.

The screen is showing the auditorium of the Royal Opera House during the interval, where people in London are filing out to the bars. Letty looks at her phone.

'Hey, my mother's actually there!' she tells him, seeing Frances's text.

'Tell her to go down to the front and wave to us,' Alf suggests.

Letty doesn't know if she can bear the humiliation of seeing her mother waving to all the cinemagoers who are watching the transmission in hundreds of cinemas worldwide.

'OK,' she says, texting Frances with Alf's idea, wondering whether she'll be game.

Sure enough, after a couple of minutes, the small but distinctive figure of Frances walks determinedly down the left aisle and stands in front of the orchestra pit, waving not just one hand, but both. If she had a piece of cardboard, she'd probably write 'Hello Letty!' on it. Seeing her there, so small and faraway, and so very Frances, she feels a lump of homesickness in her throat.

'That's her!' she says, pointing.

'That is *so* cool. Your mother is one cool lady,' Alf says.

Letty's never thought of her like that. Embarrassing, over the top, yes. Cool, not so much. She knows Frances would enjoy the description.

She texts her: *OK, we've seen you! You can stop now! Enjoy Act 2.*

It's surreal to see Frances checking her phone. Blowing a big kiss at the camera before returning to her seat.

In the second act, Des Grieux tries to win enough money to get Manon back by cheating at cards in a brothel, but as they return to their bedroom to pack and run away, the police arrive, and they are arrested and banished to the colonies.

'I never knew ballet could be so sexy,' Alf says when the lights come up again. 'The dancers are on fire!'

'I was at ballet school with Des Grieux,' Letty tells him.

'You know that guy?'

'Well, not exactly.'

She tells him about her fleeting encounter with Vadim when she was just a pubescent girl. 'I don't think he even noticed me,' she says.

'He would now,' Alf whispers as the lights go down again.

It's a lovely compliment, because it's so guileless and unplanned.

In the final act, the two lovers land in the penal colony of Louisiana where, as her past sins revisit her, and in the most challenging and emotional pas de deux, Manon dies in Des Grieux's arms.

The performances by the two leads are so full of artistry and so moving, tears are rolling down Letty's face by the final curtain. Even though there is no chance of the dancers in the Royal Opera House hearing their cheers, the entire audience in the Roman cinema rise as one to their feet and applaud.

Alf is silent on the walk to the tram.

'What did you think?' Letty asks him.

'Didn't the word passion originally mean suffering?' he says.

And when she nods, he says, 'It was the most beautiful and passionate thing I have ever seen.'

The tram is full of restaurant workers who have just finished their shift. It reeks of garlic and bodies that have been toiling in hot kitchens, and it's so noisy that neither of them speak, but Letty can hear the haunting music of Manon's theme going over and over in her head.

Back at her apartment, the lights of the city like a sparkling carpet below, they embrace, carefully and with agonizing tenderness, and she somehow knows that Alf is hearing the poignant music in his head too as skin on skin, stroking, kissing, their bodies synchronize in a slow sensual dance.

Afterwards, she lies naked in the moonlight, gazing at him gazing at her.

'*Quanto sei bella!*' he says.

She sits up, puts her finger on his lips.

'Don't . . .'

'Why?'

She sighs. Will he feel the same once she has told him?

'Someone else used to tell me how beautiful I was . . .'

If he runs away, better now than when she has further to fall, because she knows she is falling for him, and it is scaring her.

'I told you that when I left ballet school, I went to the local school and there were these girls . . .'

'. . . who bullied you.'

'Yes. But there was this guy they all fancied, called Josh.'

Even now his name has a romantic ring for her. She used to say it into her mirror, watching how she looked when she spoke – casually (*Oh, hi Josh!*) or brightly (*Hi Josh, how you doing?*) or seriously romantically (*I love you, Josh*) – moving in close to see how she appeared when being kissed. Eyes open? Eyes closed? Impossible to tell, because she had to squint to see it.

'He was two years above us, and he was really fit, and he started taking an interest in me. It felt like being picked out of the crowd by the one everyone fancies in a boyband. At first I thought it was some kind of trick. I mean, I was flat chested, immature, didn't wear make-up or anything. But then he asked me out. I'd never been out with someone, and I had no idea what to say. Turns out all I had to do was listen because he spent the whole time talking about football – he was a Spurs fan. So, when I came home, I learned everything there was to know about Spurs, and the rest of the Premiership . . .'

Alf chuckles.

'. . . and the next time he came out of school with me, I had a lot to talk about. He thought it was pretty cool. He got me fake ID and took me to the pub with his mates. He was like, this girl is really pretty, but she knows stats and stuff, so I suddenly had a kind of identity, I suppose.'

Alf smiles.

'So, then there was this kind of courtship ritual. First he told me he adored me . . .'

Alf winces.

'Then there was the tattoo. Frances went ape, but there was nothing she could do, which made it all the more exciting, obviously. And then we had sex. Frances and Ivo were out at work. My room is at the top of the house, so Marina couldn't hear. Afterwards, it was so strange because I felt completely different, but nobody noticed . . .'

She glances down at Alf.

'He said I was so beautiful he wanted to film me. And so, one weekend, in the flat where he lived with his mum, I let him.'

An anxious frown appears on Alf's face, as if he knows what's coming.

'It felt amazing actually. I trusted him so much, like this was really love,' Letty says, thinking that she might as well be totally honest. 'So . . . he posted the film on the internet.'

The film wasn't there on the Monday morning, when she checked his status and profile picture as soon as she woke up, as she did every day to confirm that he still loved her. But by lunchtime something had happened, because when she walked past the lockers, the cool girls started panting and calling, 'Yes, yes, yes!' after her. And in the queue, she kept hearing the word 'slut' without realizing, for several minutes, that it was being directed at her. And then she turned on her phone . . .

'Idiot!' Alf says.

'I know, but I was naive. I trusted him,' Letty says sadly.

'God, not you! Him! He's the idiot!' Alf sits up and holds her close, as if to hug away the damage.

Nobody's called Josh an idiot before.

To Frances, Josh was a rapist.

Letty could hear her parents discussing it late into the night as she sat on the stairs down to the basement kitchen.

'Nobody could say she wasn't consenting,' Ivo had argued, and Letty felt as if her heart would break with the shame of her father having to exist in a staffroom of teachers who'd seen it too.

'In law, you're not able to *give* consent at fifteen!' Frances had screamed at him. She wanted to press charges.

'But what good would it do?' Ivo asked.

'Never mind what good – what harm has it done to her?'

'More if you make it into a big deal . . .'

'How much bigger a deal can it be?'

Letty remembers thinking it was as if her whole life had become public property.

Idiot. The truth is, if you take away the permanence of posting it, it wasn't that big a deal. It probably happened in Alf's school too. It probably happened in every school in the country. Josh wasn't an evil tormentor, but a seventeen-year-old boy showing off.

Maybe if someone had said 'idiot' then, it wouldn't have got so out of hand.

'So that's when you got ill?' Alf says.

'Yes,' she says. 'Eating disorder. I think I was literally trying to disappear.'

'But you got better. You're here,' he says, kissing her forehead, then holding her close again.

'I learned to eat. I learned that I control my food intake. It doesn't control me.'

In therapy, she learned that recovery is a process, not something that's ever finished.

'And you got to Oxford, after all of that?' Alf says.

She smiles. Comparatively, Oxford was the easy bit.

She'd felt safe there because of the structure and the meals at set times. For one happy year, she lived in Oxford's cocoon, until she decided, bizarrely, to behave recklessly again.

But she doesn't tell him that. She doesn't know if there will ever be a time to tell him why she came to Rome.

In the middle of the night, she wakes with a start, aware of Alf getting out of bed, crouching to avoid hitting his head. When she hears the toilet in the downstairs bathroom flush, she drifts back off and wakes again, unsure whether five minutes or five hours have passed. The slivers of light around the blinds are grey, not bright silver as they are with the morning sun. Dawn, she thinks, stretching out her hand to find his, but the space is empty. A click. The front door.

Rushing down the ladder to pull up the blinds, she leans as far out of the window as she dares, and sees him walking away from the building.

In the still of the dawn, there is barely any traffic. If she called out, he would probably hear her. But what would she shout? Don't go? Come back?

Was it too much information for him? He's young. Younger than her, although he doesn't seem it. Why would he want to take her on?

Alf is all about living in the moment. So why did she have to bring up the past?

She watches him disappearing from sight, turns sadly away from the window, and only then sees the postcard on the table.

The picture is a collage of sepia stills from *Roman Holiday*.

On the back, he has written: *I didn't want to wake you. I have to pack. Ci vediamo all'una! Don't be late!*

17

Friday

ALF

It's too late and too early for the number three tram. In the grey dawn, Alf walks past Santa Croce in Gerusalemme and down the avenue towards San Giovanni in Laterano. Beyond the cathedral, a narrow street leads all the way to the Colosseum. He enjoys hearing the echo of his footsteps, the feeling of being the only person awake in the city.

The first pale beams of sunlight are beginning to illuminate the arches of the amphitheatre, grey against an almost white sky. Cleaners are hosing down the streets, freshening the air. He can smell the pine trees of the Palatine as he walks towards the Circus Maximus, arriving in Testaccio to the clatter of the shutters going up at his local bar. He stands at the counter to drink an espresso, eats a cornetto, then buys another and puts it on the bench beside the homeless man, who is still sleeping.

As he climbs the four flights of stairs to their apartment, he is dreading the impending confrontation. He told Gina that he was playing five-a-side with a group of the lads from school. She was spending the evening with her dad, so she wasn't that bothered about the details. At least he won't have to tell her that he ended up getting drunk and crashing at the imaginary apartment of an imaginary classmate, because he can't wait any longer. He has to finish with Gina this morning.

As he opens the apartment door, he breathes slowly, looking at his watch. In a couple of hours it will be over. He just has to get through this. And then he will be free.

He pushes the door of their bedroom open carefully, so as not to wake her abruptly, but the bed is empty. Her work clothes are scattered around. Two pairs of high-heeled shoes tried and discarded, matching handbags abandoned on the bed. She obviously came back from work in a hurry to get dressed up. She has probably stayed over in Stuart's suite.

Alf recalibrates his plans. He will get packed up and wait for her to return. He stands on tiptoe to slide his backpack down from the top of the wardrobe, clears Gina's possessions from the bed, then starts packing up his clothes, leaving the shirt Stuart bought him still in its Prada bag, complete with the receipt.

Then he sits on the bed, not wanting to lie down in case he falls asleep, and waits.

In the kitchen, he hears Mike pouring cereal then eating it noisily. Sally is in the shower. Then she's in the kitchen, brewing coffee. They exchange a few brief words. Mike's not a morning person. Then Sally calls out, 'Gina? Alf? Bathroom's free! Catch you later!'

The front door clicks shut. By nine o'clock Gina still isn't back.

Alf has a shower and puts on clean clothes, shoving the dirty washing into the top of the backpack. He sits in the kitchen, wondering if it would be better to encounter Gina there, on neutral territory.

Alf wakes up suddenly as his head lolls and bangs down on the table. The waiting and tiredness must have overcome him for a moment. He looks at his watch and panics. It's half eleven. In an hour and a half, he and Letty have a train to catch. And Gina is still not here.

He decides to ring her. He hears the mobile ringing so loudly it could be in the flat. It *is* in the flat. He follows the sound to the bedroom and peers over Gina's side of the bed. Her phone is on the floor, still plugged into the adaptor socket, charging, where she must have left it. She was in a rush. It's happened many times before.

'The person you are calling is not available. Please leave a message after the bleep.'

Alf taps the off button.

They've been together for nearly a year. He cannot dump her by voicemail.

Time is running out.

Would leaving Gina a note actually be kinder? It's the coward's way, but is it any worse than all the lies he's told her so far? He's tried to do the right thing. He can't put it off any longer.

He fetches a piece of paper and a pen.

He waits opposite the school, the anticipation of seeing Letty again making him so happy he forgets everything else. Then she is there and her beautiful face lights up as she spots him, and she is about to run but, seeing his alarm, looks both ways before crossing the road. Then she comes to him, and he puts his hands on her waist and lifts her so that their faces are level. He kisses her for a long time, until she slips down his body to standing and says, looking at his backpack, 'Are you bringing your whole life with you?'

'Something like that. I'll explain on the train.'

He reaches for her hand and, as he does so, glances in the direction of Termini station.

He sees the couple walking towards them as Letty might see them: the woman dolled up for a night out – red dress, high heels tapping on the pavement, the chain of her black quilted evening bag slung across her cleavage; the older guy in smart jeans and an expensive white shirt, sleeves rolled up. In this area, close to the station, they look like a prostitute and a pimp.

Terror spasms through his body, and he drops Letty's hand.

'We've come to take you for lunch, Alf!' says Gina.

She has clearly not been home, not seen the note.

She walks straight up to him, putting her hands on his waist, and plants a kiss on lips that have just kissed Letty.

He feels Letty freeze beside him, hears her sudden intake of breath.

'No!' she says.

Then she's running down the street, picking up speed until she reaches the corner and disappears.

PART TWO

Twenty months earlier

18

September 2016

LETTY

It was a late September day, just like the one a year before when Letty had first arrived in Oxford. The leaves on the trees lining St Giles' were beginning to turn from green to gold. There was a crispness on the air whispering that summer was almost gone. As she walked into town from the road in North Oxford where she had a room for her second year, she felt as nervous as she had done then.

The Randolph hotel wasn't a place students normally frequented. It wasn't a place that really felt like Oxford at all. Letty walked past the tall windows of the restaurant a couple of times in the hope of catching a glimpse of her date before their meeting, but she couldn't see any likely candidate waiting. When she asked at the reception desk, she was shown in the opposite direction to a lounge with swathes of soft peach and eau de nil.

The word that came to mind when she first saw Spencer was 'masculine'. His blue suit seemed a very definite colour against the pastel tea room. She suspected he was a little older than thirty-eight, the age stated on his profile. In good shape though, longish hair swept back from his face.

This was a silly idea, she thought. She hadn't even remembered to turn on her phone's voice recorder, and it was too late now because he was smiling at her, hand outstretched.

'Elle?' he said.

'Yes,' she said.

The collar and top three buttons of his shirt were undone, as if he'd removed a tie in an attempt to appear relaxed. His openly appreciative look made her feel exposed. She realized that 'yes' wasn't a proper greeting.

'Spencer?' she said, suddenly unsure if she'd remembered the name correctly. To her relief, his smile remained.

His handshake was dry and firm. She was never sure she got handshakes right because she always forgot to think about how her hand should be until the moment was over. Handshakes were important. Frances had once met the Chancellor of the Exchequer at a function, and had never been able to hear his name since without remarking on the weakness of his grasp and how it had undermined her faith in his fiscal policy.

Letty wondered what Spencer did for a living. Not politics, she thought, although from the look of him he could be an ambitious Tory MP, but if he were, they probably wouldn't be meeting in such a public place.

He gestured at the sofa he had been sitting on. It was low and squashy, big enough for two people to sit at each end without touching, but she'd have preferred to sit on a separate piece of furniture.

'What would you like?' he asked.

'Tea,' she said. 'Would be nice.'

'Scones? Cake?'

'No, thanks.'

'You must have to be careful,' he said.

'Why?'

'A figure like yours.'

'Oh . . .'

166

'You could be a model. Perhaps you are?'

His way of dealing with the awkwardness was to flatter her, slightly too loudly. Or perhaps he didn't find it awkward? Perhaps he had encounters like this all the time.

This was such a mistake, Letty thought, shifting deep into the corner of the sofa.

A waitress appeared.

'Are you ready to order?'

'Pot of tea for two.' He took charge. 'English Breakfast – unless you'd prefer . . . ?'

Letty shook her head, grateful at least that he hadn't forced the issue of food. The scenario would be intolerable with tiers of dainty plates between them; the question of whether to use a cake fork and risk shooting a macaron across the damask.

'Do you come here often?' he asked.

Her blurt of laughter came from nowhere, like a sudden sneeze.

'Never,' she said. 'How about you?'

'First time,' he said. 'First time in Oxford, in fact.'

'Well, this is not representative,' she said.

'Representative?'

The repetition made it sound almost as if he didn't understand the word.

'I just mean that most of the buildings are medieval rather than ostentatiously Victorian.' Letty could hear herself talking quickly, nonsensically, making things worse not better.

'You're interested in property?' he asked.

'Not especially.' Architecture was the word she would have used.

'I'm a property developer.'

'Oh!' Letty didn't think she'd ever heard the phrase spoken before without the falling cadence of disapproval. 'How interesting!' she said.

'You're a student at this university?'

'Yes.'

'Clever as well as beautiful. Well, not exactly beautiful. Striking,' he said.

'Would you like my honest opinion about your looks?' she asked him, suddenly finding a kind of courage.

'I'm thinking probably not, from the way you said that,' he laughed.

'You're too old for hair gel,' she said. Then, seeing his surprise, 'I think almost everyone is too old for hair gel, by the way.'

'Point taken,' he said with a raised eyebrow.

She was grateful for the arrival of the waitress because she felt she was floundering at some strange card game where she didn't know the rules, a bit like when Marina had tried to teach her to play bridge.

'You're clever, you'll soon pick it up,' Marina had said. But Letty never really had. And Marina had eventually given up, claiming one Sunday lunch that Letty's intelligence was more deductive than strategic, which had made Ivo laugh and Frances protest: 'Don't you dare try to put limits on the sort of person she is!' Which was rich coming from Frances.

Letty watched Spencer pouring the tea. Steady, at ease with himself, clean, shiny nails. Could they even be manicured?

'Milk?' he asked.

Frances had some rule about milk in tea that Letty could never remember. Was it that you showed your modest origins if you added milk to the poured tea, or the other way round? Frances always put her milk in first, but Letty wasn't sure whether that was her in her 'I'm as sophisticated as anyone else' or 'I'm proud of my working-class roots' mode.

'Just a little.'

The two cups and saucers remained on the table.

'What do you study?' he asked.

'Classics,' she said.

'*Pride and Prejudice*, that kind of thing?'

'It's what they call Latin and Greek here,' she explained. There was no reason why he should know. Most people didn't. She waited for him to ask what was the point of studying dead languages, which was often the next question.

'Now I'm really out of my depth!'

She quite liked that he laughed, as if it wasn't going to affect his view of himself. She thought he could be quite attractive, if you didn't know why he was there.

'What's the endgame?' he asked.

She wasn't sure whether he was asking about her degree or this meeting.

'What do you mean?'

'Latin? Greek? What do you do with that after?'

'I'm not sure yet . . .'

Spencer picked up his tea. The china cup looked very delicate in his big, masculine hands.

'What sort of property do you develop?' she heard herself asking.

He took a sip of his tea, looking over the top of the rim at nothing in particular.

'Residential, mostly,' he said.

'The market's very hot, isn't it?' she said, using a term she thought a property developer might use.

He gave her a stare she couldn't quite read.

It crossed her mind for a second that maybe he thought she was flirting. Or maybe he was bored.

'Cut to the chase,' he said, holding her gaze. 'What are you looking for?'

It felt a bit like a who-blinks-first contest as she struggled to remember the backstory she'd created. She hadn't really thought through the questions he might ask her, only the questions she might ask him. The persona of Elle was fairly sketchy.

'Fun, mostly,' she heard herself saying, in the least fun voice she'd ever heard. 'As a student, you know, you're always on a budget and, well, it can get a bit dull . . .'

'And what sort of things do you like doing – apart from Latin and Greek?'

That probably seemed like the dullest thing in the world to him.

'Opera,' she said. 'Reading.' She was only making it worse. 'I also like travelling, exploring other cultures,' she added, feeling like a contestant in a beauty contest.

'Don't we all?'

'Do we?' she asked. 'Lots of people want to go back to the same place, to lie in the sun or whatever. I prefer finding out about a place and its history.' She was conscious of sounding sanctimonious and unsophisticated whilst trying to sound the opposite. 'What about you?'

'What do I like? Good food, good wine, lying in the sun . . .' He winked at her.

'I didn't mean—'

'Don't worry. I'm pretty easy-going.'

He gave her a long appraising stare.

'Cards on the table. We're different, but I like the look of you. I don't do tea. Why don't you come up to London one evening. See how we get on? No obligation on either side. Sound reasonable?'

It did sound very reasonable in the circumstances, Letty thought, but it wasn't something she had any intention of doing.

'Will you excuse me for a minute?' she said.

She could feel his eyes on her back as she walked across the room, and asked the waitress for directions to the Ladies' room. Locking herself in a cubicle, she sat down and considered her options. This was moving faster than she had anticipated. Why had she ever thought it was a plausible idea? He didn't seem like a bad person, but she had to keep reminding herself that his intention was to buy the services of a much younger woman. What services exactly they had yet to discuss, but she couldn't imagine from the look of him that sex wouldn't be involved. He was fit and attractive. She didn't really understand what he was doing here.

What she did know was that she wasn't capable of going through with the deception.

Should she therefore go back, explain and apologize for wasting his time? If he were insulted or angry, she didn't know how she'd cope in the pastel gentility of the tea room.

Should she suggest they go for a walk? Somehow she didn't think he would 'do' walking any more than he 'did' tea. And she would run the risk of bumping into someone she knew.

It wasn't as if she owed him anything, Letty thought. A cup of tea. It would be ridiculous to go back and offer to pay her share.

He had no way of contacting her again apart from via the site, and she'd given false information on that. She ran through what she had told him. Only the subject she was reading. Not the name of her college, or where she lived.

She decided to leave. But how, without the possibility of running into him? She weighed up the likelihood of him coming to find her or sending someone to look, but she didn't think a man of his type was going to suffer the indignity of asking someone to search the Ladies'.

All she needed to do was wait.

Luckily she had a book in her bag.

'You sat there for five hours?' Oscar said, when she told him the following day at Browns.

The words struck some distant memory of him reading to her as a little girl. Beatrix Potter, she thought. Didn't a cat sit on a basket with Peter Rabbit inside for five hours?

'I got involved in my novel,' she told him.

'Let me check I've got this right . . . for your first attempt at student journalism, you decide to go undercover to honeytrap a complete stranger?'

Letty nodded.

'What were you thinking?'

'Frances kept banging on about me doing something extra-curricular like journalism to put on my CV. So I went along to an editorial meeting and they were talking about the cost of student loans and this sugar babies thing a lot of female students are doing, where they get rich men to pay their fees in exchange for, well, company . . .'

'I heard something about that on the radio.'

'Yes. It's been in the news.'

'You know Frances wanted me to do that . . .' Oscar said.

'Sell yourself to an older man?'

'Ha ha! No, student journalism. Frances has some notion that if she'd done journalism when she was at Oxford, her life would have turned out differently.'

'Frances would have been a good journalist,' Letty said.

'Frances would have been a good columnist,' Oscar corrected. 'Frances is all opinions.'

Letty always felt at a disadvantage when talking to her brother about her mother. Oscar was so much more like Frances and the two of them blossomed in each other's company, vying to top each other's puns or waspishness. Whereas she, in Frances's company, seemed to shrink and wilt.

It was one of the reasons she'd been keen to confound her mother's expectations.

'I found girls who did it, but none of them were willing to speak to me about it. I mean, why would they? So, I thought I'd do the research myself . . . I created a profile and was inundated with men who wanted to meet me.'

'You don't say?' said Oscar.

'I chose the least creepy-looking one. He seemed pretty normal, to be honest. But I had no idea how to handle it. Somehow, I thought I'd be the one in control.'

'Obviously . . . with your vast experience of relationships,' Oscar teased.

'I know, I know. It was a crazy idea.'

'Well, no harm done, anyway,' said Oscar, leaning back in his chair and holding the menu as far away as his arm would allow. Too vain to admit to needing glasses, Letty thought; it would indicate the onset of middle age, and for a man coming up to forty, he looked much younger.

'What are you going to have?' he asked.

Sometimes Letty wondered if her family had a secret rota, where each of them visited to take her out for lunch at the weekend and make sure that she was eating.

'The chicken Caesar salad?' she said.

'Are you sure? I'm having a burger.'

'Oh, good. I'll share your chips,' she said, knowing it would please him.

Oscar was full of the new off-Broadway musical he'd brought over from America for a six-week run in a theatre that had suddenly become vacant. The musical had received such good reviews that he was now transferring to another West End theatre.

She watched as he talked while eating his food, barely stopping to chew, waving each chip to emphasize a point he was making.

Letty took a chip, dipped it in the tomato sauce, and took a small bite from the end.

'Oh, and . . .' said Oscar, mouth still full. 'We're getting married!'

'Congratulations!'

Oscar and his partner Raj had been together a long time. Everyone liked Raj. Raj was a good thing.

'Raj asked,' Oscar said, 'totally out of the blue. We were having a TV and Doritos night in. Sad, but true. They were talking about unusual proposals, you know – bungee jumping, getting the chef to put a ring in the dessert, that kind of thing . . .'

'Bungee jumping?' Letty interrupted.

'. . . so Raj said, "I've been trying to think of an imaginative way of asking you." So I'm like, "What?" through this enormous mouthful of tortilla chip. So he says. "I'd like us to get married." I said, "For real?" and he was like, "Yes." So I was like, "Bugger the Doritos." We went to the Ivy.'

'How brilliant.'

'I mean, not the most romantic proposal . . .'

But that made it a better story, Letty thought, and one that Oscar clearly enjoyed telling. She wondered if they'd really been eating Doritos, or whether that was a little flourish he'd added.

'We can't decide whether to do a big thing, or just get married then have a party.'

'You've been engaged for less than twenty-four hours . . .'

'I hate the word engaged,' Oscar said. 'Sounds like a public convenience. I prefer betrothed. Much more fairy tale.'

'But that means promised, normally by someone else,' Letty said.

'OK, Miss Pedantic. Suggestions?'

'Pledged?'

'Furniture polish.'

'How many times are you going to have to say the actual word anyway? You can just say you're getting married.'

'True,' Oscar said. 'And what about you? Apart from Sugar Daddy, obvs?'

'Promise you won't tell anyone about that?'

'Of course not.'

'Not Frances, not Raj, not anyone?'

'No one,' Oscar said solemnly. 'Not that there is anything *to* tell. I wish there was. Some sex at least. Honestly, Letty . . .'

'What?'

'You had a bad experience with Josh. Very bad. Doesn't mean you have to run away to a convent.'

Oscar knew her well. It was exactly the idea of a monastic existence that had attracted her to Oxford, with its libraries with windows like churches and medieval colleges secluded from the outside world.

'I haven't met anyone who I feel anything for,' Letty defended herself. 'I'm not closed to the possibility.'

But she wondered if that was true. Trust was something that built over time, but since Josh, she never let anyone near enough to try to put down foundations. Sometimes she wondered if the bit of her brain that dealt with human interaction had simply been destroyed by what had happened.

Oscar was looking at her bowl. There were a few croutons concealed under the last couple of iceberg leaves, but she had eaten all the chicken.

'Pudding?' he asked.

'Why don't we share one?'

She could almost hear Oscar reporting back to Frances, 'We shared chips and dessert!'

The profiteroles arrived with two forks. As soon as Oscar launched back into wedding plans he forgot to keep track, and when the plate was empty, he stared at it enquiringly.

'You *are* eating, Letty?' he said.

'Yes.'

'I mean during the week?'

'Yes.'

'Not just lettuce?'

'The effect of eating too much lettuce,' Letty quoted Beatrix Potter, 'can be soporific!'

They finished the sentence together.

'Such a long word for a children's book,' Letty said. 'I don't think I've used it once in my entire life, but I've never forgotten what it means. People think that children acquire language easily, but when you imagine the incredible complexity of the neuron links for me to go from being three and asking you what soporific meant, until today . . .'

Oscar was staring at her.

'Is this the sort of thing you think about?' he asked.

'Don't you?'

'No. I'm essentially a shallow and trivial person and you, Letty, are essentially a clever and serious person. All the same, you really should get out more.'

19

October

ALF

Auditions were being held in the school hall. Alf could hear Mr Noakes on the piano playing 'There Are Worse Things I Could Do' to accompany the girls auditioning for Rizzo. It was a difficult song, he realized; requiring power for the defiant bits, but also a softer, poignant quality.

The song he'd chosen didn't involve layers of meaning, but his mouth was still dry and his legs like jelly. Alf looked at himself in the cracked mirror of the boys' toilets. You needed the nerves to give the performance, but you never got used to them.

Alf ran the cold tap, splashed water on his face, then pulled a comb through his wet hair, slicking back the curls from his forehead. He took a deep breath and did a Danny Zuko thumbs-up at himself.

Mr Marriot, his English teacher, was sitting at a table in the hall alongside the newly qualified teacher, Miss Jones, who'd joined the department after doing her teaching practice at the school. The two other judges were Nathan and Bryony, the head boy and girl. John, another prefect who was good with tech stuff, was filming the auditions.

Mr Noakes, the music teacher, was sitting at the piano.

'Hello!' said Bryony. 'Who are you?'

She'd been Alf's girlfriend before the summer holidays, but she was clearly channelling *Britain's Got Talent* for the video.

'Alf,' he said, grinning at her.

'And you're auditioning for?'

'Danny.'

'And you're going to show us?'

'"Greased Lightning".'

'OK. Should be interesting.'

Alf heard Mr Marriott saying to the new teacher, behind his hand, 'This boy's very special.'

Alf loved the feeling when people who didn't know him first saw him dance.

When he finished with a full knee slide towards the judging table, everyone in the room, apart from the Pink Ladies, applauded.

'Judges, what do you think?' Bryony said.

'It's a yes from me,' said Mr Marriot.

'And from me,' said Miss Jones.

'It's a yes from me,' said Nathan.

Bryony paused to give it a bit of drama for the video.

'Alf, you've got four yeses!' she said.

'We'd like to see you with a potential Sandy,' Mr Marriot added. 'So could you and Sadie take ten minutes, then come back and show us "Summer Nights"?'

Alf kept smiling, but inside the nerves had started churning again.

He had been sure Sadie would be going for Rizzo, not Sandy. Alf couldn't see it. The final scene with the skin-tight black leathers, yes, but fresh-faced, virginal Sandy would be a stretch. Alf couldn't remember ever seeing Sadie without make-up, even the first time she'd come to his mother's Ballroom and Latin Little Stars class. Donna had spotted her and partnered them up. He could still remember Sadie's first words as she'd twizzled over to stand by his side.

'I will dance with you, but I won't marry you.'

She must have been all of five years old.

They had danced together through the junior competitions, but Sadie had grown up more quickly than him. At twelve, her mum, Leanne, announced that they were thinking of finding Sadie a new partner, because Sadie preferred the Latin. They all knew the real reason was that she could have passed for fifteen, while Alf was still a weedy kid.

'He will grow. His dad was tall,' Donna had protested, but it turned out Sadie had already committed to a sixteen-year-old from a rival dance school in Manchester.

For a couple of years, Sadie and Kyle had smashed the competitions, but when Alf had grown a foot taller and found Aimee they'd taken over. That hadn't gone down well.

At school, Sadie mostly acted like he didn't exist. He sometimes wondered if she had registered that he was now six foot two, because she still kind of looked down on him.

'I've got an idea,' she said, when they left the hall and found an empty classroom to practise in. 'We start on opposite sides of the stage, and then, in the bits where we're describing what happened, we kind of dance it?'

They'd only choreographed about half by the time they were called back, so they had to improvise the rest. It was a bit of a shaky start, with Mr Noakes at the piano speaking the 'tell-me-mores' in a bored teacher's voice between verses. Alf and Sadie could both hold a tune, but it wasn't like they were proper singers. However, the last verse, where the voices harmonized, worked perfectly. There had always been chemistry between them when they performed.

By the time Alf got home, Leanne had already been on the phone to his mum, saying wasn't it exciting how they were going to be together again?

Donna met him at the door. He could tell she had already

been crying. He hadn't told her about the audition because he didn't want to worry her before he knew he'd got the part. Which was stupid. If he'd learned anything from the *Billy Elliot* audition, it was not to do something expecting to fail. And in this case, the competition wasn't all the talented eleven-year-old boys in the country who could dance, but Luke who used to come to Donna's tap classes but was too fat to do the routines without getting breathless, and Cal who couldn't sing or dance, and only went along because he was Alf's best mate and fancied one of the Pink Ladies.

His mum had immediately realized that rehearsing for the main role in *Grease* meant that he would have to give up competing in Ballroom and Latin, and that was another thing he hadn't discussed with her.

It had actually been Aimee's suggestion. She was at university in Leeds now, and all the rehearsing meant she was missing out on student life. They'd discussed it the previous weekend. Since neither of them wanted to turn professional, there didn't seem that much point in continuing.

But it wasn't as simple as that.

'How do we tell Donna?' Aimee had asked.

It was Alf's mum who coached them, who made Aimee's dresses, who enlisted Gary to drive them up and down the country to competitions at weekends, who invested all the money her classes brought in for them to compete abroad. The two of them went out onto the dance floor, but as Aimee often said – and it was one of the reasons Donna liked her so much – there were three of them in the partnership. 'Aimee and Alf' was a huge part of Donna's life, and Donna was fragile at the best of times.

'Maybe leave it till after Christmas?' Aimee had suggested.

Now delaying it was impossible.

'Sorry, Mum, I should have told you . . .' Alf said.

'Yes, you should.'

He hated it more when she went all clipped and huffy than when she was crying.

'I'm sorry.'

'It's your life.' Donna turned away from him. 'Just don't ever come moaning to me when you realize what you've given up.'

'When have I ever come moaning to you?'

'There's all these opportunities now that I never had . . .'

What she meant was the possibility of becoming a professional on *Strictly Come Dancing*, or *Dancing with the Stars* as it was called in other countries. Alf knew that Donna would have absolutely loved that. But he wasn't interested. The way he saw it, you might get a hot pop star one year, but a not-so-hot soap matriarch the next. He was good at making middle-aged, even elderly women feel like princesses at his grandparents' socials, but he didn't want it to be his life, even if it was offered him, and it was only his mum assuming that.

What he wanted to do was go to one of the dance schools where they taught musical theatre. Alf loved the feeling of freedom dancing gave him, and the unique exhilaration when an audience cheered. He did it for that more than the winning. He thought he'd enjoy being in a live show. With a new audience every day, it was always going to be different, and it would be fun to be part of a team. He thought it would combine what he'd liked about playing football with what he liked about dancing.

'Mr Marriot says I need to get different types of dance on my CV,' Alf told her. 'I think he chose *Grease* to give me the opportunity . . .'

'And Mr Marriot always knows best, obviously.'

His mother still resented Mr Marriot for suggesting Alf try out for *Billy Elliot*.

Donna breathed a huge sigh.

'Sorry, Alf,' she said eventually. 'It's difficult when some-one's your whole life.'

'I'm not your whole life. You've got Gary, and the school and your friends . . .'

'Yeah, but it's not the same.'

She meant children. She and Gary had been trying for a baby for ages. Donna was only thirty-five, and she was still in great shape, but it hadn't happened. From the whispered conversations he sometimes walked in on, and the hospital visits, he thought maybe they were doing IVF at the moment. It wasn't the sort of thing Donna would talk about, for fear of putting a jinx on it, but maybe that was the reason for her mood swings.

'It will happen, Mum.'

'You think?' she sniffed.

'Positive.'

Alf's confidence was totally meaningless because he really had no idea, but it seemed to give her comfort.

'Sorry, Alf,' she said again, wiping her eyes. 'I only want what's best for you.'

'No, I'm sorry. I should have discussed it with you.'

'It's your life.'

Didn't feel that way sometimes, but fair enough.

Mr Marriot decided that the final number, 'You're The One That I Want', was the most important to get right, so the first two rehearsals were all about that.

The new teacher, Miss Jones, rehearsed the girls in the sports hall and he rehearsed the boys on the stage.

When you'd trained since you were four years old you picked up choreography first time, so even though they had far more to do than the others, Alf and Sadie had their moves down immediately and even made up a few of their own. It meant spending more time alone with Sadie than Alf was comfortable with.

'So, are you seeing anyone?' Sadie wanted to know. She took a long pull on her cigarette.

They were standing in the courtyard where the teachers sometimes had a surreptitious ciggic.

'Why?' Alf asked.

'Just trying to make conversation,' she said.

Alf thought about Bryony. During the summer holidays he'd got a job renting out deckchairs on the beach, and she'd been serving ice creams at a nearby kiosk. It was when the conversation as they walked home was all about how many cartons of strawberry there were compared to vanilla, and the surprising popularity of mint choc chip, that he realized the relationship wasn't really going anywhere. Then Bryony and her family went to Majorca for a fortnight. While she was there, she posted a photo of her and a guy called Jorge, arm in arm with the hashtag #LoveIsland?

As break-ups went, theirs was about as good as it got. He was sure Sadie knew all this.

'Are you?' Alf asked her.

'Why?'

'Just making conversation.'

Normally, Alf found it easy talking to girls, but with Sadie it always felt like a competition.

'Thought I'd get it out of the way, because obviously we're going to have to kiss,' Sadie said, taking another drag and blowing the smoke at him. 'How do you feel about that?'

He wanted to say that he'd prefer it if she didn't smoke five minutes before, but he didn't think that would go down too well.

'I hadn't thought about it,' Alf said.

Cheap, but nevertheless a point to him.

When he was twelve, Sadie was the person he'd thought about kissing more than anyone in the world – after Flavia Cacace. But she'd been such a bitch in the intervening years; he thought maybe she was going to struggle more than he was with pretending to be hopelessly devoted.

20

November

LETTY

Fallen leaves crunched underfoot as Letty walked through the University Parks. A pale blanket of mist lay over the cricket pitch; the air, cold enough to chill her face, held a taint of rotting apples.

Letty was first in the reading room at the Bodleian. She had come to think of the desk – on the end of the first row in the second room – as hers, and didn't like the idea of one day finding someone else sitting there, so she always arrived at nine when the library opened. Gradually, the other regulars filtered in. The guy opposite always smelled slightly of malted breakfast cereal; the girl next to her of the first latte of the day. Letty wondered if they knew that she invariably ate a scrambled egg on a slice of buttered brown toast. Protein, fat and complex carbohydrate to fuel her for the day.

On weekdays, she worked until eleven precisely, then took a break for five minutes in the fresh air. There was never a day that Letty did not enjoy walking down the stone stairs worn shallow by hundreds of years of scholars' footsteps, and standing in the quad looking at the same sandstone carvings that students had gazed upon since medieval times. Each day at

Oxford felt like a privilege, yet she could not envisage herself spending her whole life in a book-lined study listening to students' essays, or eating her evening meals at high table with other dons, which it would be if she were to become an academic. And apart from her brief and totally unsuccessful flirtation with the idea of journalism, she hadn't had any other ideas for a career.

'Something will probably come up. A lot can change in two years,' the careers advisory service told her when she went along for the appointment they offered all students.

But nothing had changed much in the first year of being at Oxford. And in the Bodleian quad, nothing had changed for centuries.

Letty felt her phone vibrate in her jacket pocket.

As soon as she saw her mother's name on the screen, she knew something was wrong. Frances did not call during the day.

'Nothing to worry about,' said Frances, 'but Marina's in hospital.'

She could hardly have said anything to make Letty worry more.

'Just for observation,' Frances went on. 'The doctor said that he thought it might be a tiny stroke. Ivo's coming to take over. I've already missed a board meeting . . .'

'Shall I come down?'

'I honestly don't think that there's anything to panic about, and if there is, she's where she should be,' says Frances. 'But I'm sure she'd love to see you if you're not doing anything special this weekend.'

'I'll get a train after my lecture,' Letty told her, panicking anyway. Her grandmother was nearly ninety. If she was ill enough to be kept in hospital, there must be a risk of her dying.

Letty couldn't imagine a world without Marina. She was part of the fabric of the house in Belsize Park, as permanent as the stucco columns that held up the porch over the front door.

Letty couldn't even remember her being ill before. She was tall, opinionated, a force of nature. On her seventy-fifth birthday, when the family had gathered to celebrate, Marina had looked at the cake Frances had ordered with seventy-five candles and remarked, 'Well, Frances, you really know how to make me feel old.'

Letty, who was five at the time, had famously commented, 'But you're not *literally* old, are you?'

The station platform was crowded, and when her train finally arrived, Letty realized she was going to have to stand. It was a question of finding the best place. She ran down to the front where there were fewer people waiting, then saw that was because the carriage was first class. At least the corridor was less crushed. She managed to find enough room to sit on the floor, with her knees bent right up to her chest, and pulled out her tablet to review her lecture notes.

'Hello, down there!'

Letty didn't realize that the man was talking to her at first.

'It's Elle, isn't it?'

A pointed pair of tan brogues, red socks just showing beneath sharp blue trouser hems. She looked up. What was his name?

'There's a seat opposite me,' he told her, jerking his thumb in the direction of the first-class carriage.

'Actually, I'm fine,' said Letty.

'I have a table.'

'I haven't got a first-class ticket.'

'Can you see the guard bothering to push through this lot?' he said. 'And if he does, I'll stand you the fare.'

'That's really kind, but . . .' Letty couldn't actually think of a reason. 'Well, OK then. If you're sure?'

'Facing the direction of travel, or back to it?' he asked.

'You choose,' she said.

He opted for the former, and she wished she had chosen that, because now she would feel like she was backing away from him for the entire journey.

Very deliberately, Letty went back to the lecture notes.

'What's that then?' he said, peering at the words on her screen.

'Latin poetry,' she said.

'It's all Greek to me,' he said.

She smiled at the terrible joke and put her tablet down. Conversation was clearly going to be the price of her seat.

'So what are you up to in London?' he asked.

'My grandmother has had a stroke and I'm going to see her in hospital,' Letty told him.

'I'm sorry to hear that.'

'Thank you.'

'Are you close?'

'Extremely.'

'It's nice for grandparents, isn't it? They get all the affection, none of the worry, or the expense, for that matter. Apart from birthday presents, of course!'

'With us, it's a bit more than that,' Letty felt compelled to say. It seemed like almost a betrayal of Marina to let him assume that she was the same as anyone else's grandparent. 'She's the person I spent most of my childhood with. She introduced me to all the things I love . . .'

'Opera, culture,' he said.

It was a bit weird that he remembered, and she detected a sneer, as if he thought she was a terrible snob.

'She is Italian originally,' Letty said, as if to explain.

'I've never been to Italy,' he said.

'Really? You so should. It's beautiful.'

'Where would you recommend?'

'Depends if you like countryside or cities, I suppose. I mean, there's so much variety. Tuscany, Puglia, Rome . . .'

'I saw a programme about Rome. Looked like a building site. Have you been to Venice?'

'No. I long to, though.'

'I've been to the one in Las Vegas,' he said.

'That must be fun.'

'I've never been to an opera either,' he said.

'You really should. It's not as elitist as everyone thinks. I mean, in Mozart's day, operas were for everyone, more like musicals . . .' She hoped she didn't sound impossibly condescending.

'What's your favourite opera, then?' he asked.

'I suppose it would have to be *La Traviata*,' she said.

'What's that mean?'

'Literally, it means the woman led astray.'

'Tell me more . . .'

'It's about a courtesan who has to deny herself the man she loves because society doesn't approve.'

'Courtesan, eh?'

'Call girl . . . escort, if you like . . .'

Looking up at his sly smile, she saw that he knew exactly what courtesan meant – of course he did. She felt like a fool.

'Let me guess,' he said. 'He pursues her and they live happily ever after?'

'You really don't know much about opera, do you?'

'So what happens?'

'She dies. Most operas are about love and untimely death.'

'So why do you like it so much?'

Letty thought for a moment.

'Because the beauty of the singing allows you to experience such intense emotions, and . . .' She stopped mid-sentence when she saw he was grinning at her.

The train was slowing down on its approach to Paddington.

'OK, you've sold me,' he said. 'Let's go to the opera!' Had she inadvertently given the wrong impression in her enthusiasm?

'Umm. I'm pretty busy . . . I have exams next term . . .'

Why couldn't she just say no? He must know that she wasn't interested in that type of arrangement.

'I'd get so much more out of it if I went with you.'

Was he teasing her?

'I just don't know how things are going to be with my grandmother,' she said.

'Of course not. Sorry. Not the right time to ask.'

He held up his hands in apology.

'But it was a lovely idea,' Letty heard herself saying, since he'd been so decent about her refusal.

'Why don't you give me your number anyway?' he offered. 'I'll get tickets. You can say yes or no depending on how you're feeling?'

The train was pulling alongside the platform. Letty knew it would be easier to get rid of him if she just gave him what he wanted. If he called, she needn't answer, or she could block him.

She saw he had his contacts screen open and had already written 'Elle' in the name box.

She should have given him the wrong number, she thought, just after she'd told him the correct one.

When the nurse pointed to a bed with curtains drawn around it, Letty's heart stopped.

'Wait until they've finished doing her obs,' the nurse said.

When the curtain was swished back, Marina was sitting up in bed, looking rather cross. Seeing Letty, her face softened.

'*Tesoro!*' she said. 'What are you doing here?'

'I've come to see you.'

'But all this way!'

'It's only an hour. The train was packed but someone offered me a seat in first class.'

'A gentleman?'

Letty hesitated. Gentleman wasn't the word that came to

mind, but she supposed that was how he had acted in the circumstances.

A young doctor in a white coat was standing at the bedside.

'This is my granddaughter,' Marina told him. 'She's come all the way from Oxford.'

The doctor shook Letty's hand.

'We're fairly happy with you,' he told Marina. 'But we'd like to do a CT scan. We'll arrange that for tomorrow, and then we should be able to let you go.'

'I have to stay overnight?' Marina asked, aghast.

For the first time in her life, Letty saw fear fly across her grandmother's face, as if she'd had a sudden recognition of her mortality.

'I'll ask one of the nurses to get you a menu,' he added. 'It might be too late to order for tonight, but I'm sure we'll find you something to eat.'

'Don't worry, I'll go to the deli and get us something,' Letty intervened. The idea of staying in hospital was bad enough for Marina. Hospital food would be unthinkable.

'We'll have a lovely picnic!' she said, echoing the words Marina used to say to encourage her to eat. It was strange, feeling their roles reversed.

There was a part of Letty that wanted her grandmother to throw back the sheet, get out of bed and say, 'Don't be ridiculous! I'm going home.'

But Marina said nothing; the defeat on her face, the acceptance of powerlessness, the pale blue hospital nightie making her look suddenly old.

21

December

ALF

Apparently, Sadie was telling her friends that she had feelings for him, even though you wouldn't have known from her behaviour. They were great together performing, always had been, but when they kissed as Danny and Sandy, it wasn't proper kissing. For Alf, it was like another step in the choreography: put your mouth on hers, count four beats and break. He didn't lose himself in it.

'She does, mate,' Cal assured him. He was now going out with Kelly, Sadie's best friend, who was playing Frenchy.

How come everyone else knew and he didn't? Alf wondered. Even Miss Jones – Bridget, as everyone called her behind her back, because she was blonde, southern and a bit posh.

'You and Sadie were fantastic tonight,' she said in the car, after the final performance. 'And a little birdie tells me real-life romance is blossoming?'

'First I've heard of it,' Alf said.

'Sadie is very pretty . . .'

'You're not wrong.'

He decided he wouldn't give her anything more. He'd noticed Bridget and the girls all getting a bit giggly together. He thought maybe she was one of those teachers who wanted the students to like her too much. The way she drove her brand-new, bubblegum-pink Cinquecento, sitting forward very close to the steering wheel and stalling on the approach to round-abouts, was more like one of the girls in his year who'd just passed her test.

The rest of the cast had already gone to Mr Marriot's house where he was hosting the after-party, but, as usual, Alf and Miss Jones were the ones who had stayed behind to clear up and check all the lights were switched off.

'Used to doing it at my mum's,' Alf had told her, when she'd thanked him for helping.

'You've got a background in theatre, have you?'

'Ballroom dancing.'

Miss Jones wasn't from Blackpool, so didn't know things that everyone else knew.

'Oh, wow! I'm such a *Strictly* super fan!'

Since then, they'd had plenty to talk about: this season's celebs and new professionals, who their favourites were, who had been unfairly eliminated.

Cal handed Alf a bottle of San Miguel when they arrived at the party.

It was cool of Mr Marriot to allow them alcohol, and prob-ably quite risky for him as a teacher, but Alf didn't want to drink before the speeches. Sadie had organized presents. As the lead couple it was down to them to thank the staff on behalf of the students.

'You took your time,' she said, when Alf eventually found her and her mates in the conservatory at the back of the house, pouring tequila shots from a bottle they'd brought in them-selves. They were all still wearing their pink satin jackets with 'Pink Ladies' embroidered across the back, full stage make-up and their hair in fifties ponytails.

'I got a lift with Bridget,' he explained.

'Bridget thinks you're hot,' said Sadie.

'Let's just get the speeches done, eh?' he said.

There were bottles of wine in shiny gift bags for Mr Noakes and for the art teacher who'd painted the sets, and whisky for the caretaker who was going to have to dismantle them. There was a bottle of champagne in a box for Mr Marriot. Alf said a few words thanking each of them while Sadie handed out the gifts. Then they swapped roles, with Sadie saying the thank yous and Alf handing out bouquets of flowers, first to Mrs Marriot for hosting the after-party, and finally to Miss Jones for all her help with rehearsals. Alf kissed Mrs Marriot on the cheek, but when Bridget came up to accept her bouquet, he went for the left cheek, just as she was offering the right. There was a moment of hesitation; like people walking towards each other on the promenade who both sidestep the same way when they see they're about to collide, then sidestep the other, doing a little dance before one of them decides to stop and allow the other to pass. It was only a tiny moment, but Alf wasn't happy with himself for mucking it up.

Standing on a stepladder the following day, Alf wished he'd stuck to his original idea of not drinking at the party. Gary had woken him at seven, because the two of them were responsible for decorating the dance hall for the Christmas party that evening. Gary's Christmas jumper with reindeers on was too bright for that time in the morning.

His grandparents had put up the same decorations for as long as Alf could remember – hundreds of baubles dangling from a canopy of frosted white branches attached to the ceiling. When he was a kid, it had felt like walking into an enchanted forest that had appeared overnight. It was only in recent years, since he'd become the tallest in the family, that he'd realized how much work was involved in creating the magic.

Alf felt rough. Little snatches of the party kept coming back to him. He'd danced with Sadie, people clearing the floor for them to demonstrate their rumba, the muscle memory still there although they hadn't danced that routine together for more than five years. The last move was a slow drop to the floor, their faces close together. Somehow the floor came up quicker than he'd judged, and she'd hit the back of her head. Not badly. And at least there was carpet.

'You always were a fucking crap dancer,' she whispered into his ear before rolling him off her.

Had she bitten his ear? A little nip. Alf held his hand up to his left lobe, rocking the stepladder slightly. What was that all about?

He remembered being in the kitchen, hunting for more beer in the fridge, and Cal spotting the champagne they'd bought Mr Marriot and knowing they shouldn't . . .

Alf winced. As soon as the decorations were finished, he'd go and get Mr Marriot another bottle, which would mean another forty quid out of his savings, before he'd even started buying Christmas presents for his family.

'Coffee?' Gary suggested, when they'd done about half of the work.

'Thought you'd never ask,' Alf grinned. He stepped gingerly down from the ladder while Gary boiled a kettle in the tiny kitchen.

'Spare a thought for me this time next year,' Gary said. 'All tangled up in tinsel here, while you're sunning yourself on a beach.'

Alf and Cal had plans to travel round the world, spending winter in the southern hemisphere, but it seemed so far away, with A levels to get through, that it was no more real than a distant dream.

Was Gary looking forward to him leaving home? Couldn't

blame him if he was. They'd always got along pretty well, but he'd arrived too late to be a proper stepdad and a bit too early for them to be mates. Since Alf's growth spurt aged fourteen, he'd felt he was taking up too much room in Gary's two-up-two-down terraced house. His feet hung over the end of his single bed and if he forgot to duck, he hit his head on the kitchen doorframe. There wasn't the space on the glass shelf under the mirror in the bathroom for two razors, nor on the rack in the hall for his trainers. It was a house for a couple, maybe with a baby, but not for three adults.

When Sadie made her entrance, she looked at Alf as if he should be expecting her, and he wondered if he'd invited her the previous evening. Sadie's mum Leanne usually came along to the Christmas party because she was friends with Donna, but Sadie hadn't appeared in years.

She was wearing a backless fringed red dress, red satin high-heeled shoes and a Santa hat on her head. Sadie really was Blackpool's current queen of Latin, he thought, as he watched her doing a cha cha cha with his grandad to 'Rudolph The Red-Nosed Reindeer'.

When 'I Saw Mommy Kissing Santa Claus' came on, Alf led his mum onto the floor. They had danced to this one ever since he was a small boy and he'd had to go under her arm instead of her going under his. He didn't realize till the final twirl that Gary was filming them. Creating memories, as Donna would say, a phrase that irritated Alf, because it was like she was doing stuff in order to look back on it sometime in the future, rather than just experiencing it when it was happening. He didn't want to live his life with regrets, like she did.

He wondered what his mum would do the next year, with only the old men to dance with. They were great for a waltz or a slow foxtrot, but watching them jive, all pink and sweaty,

Alf sometimes thought they should keep a defibrillator on the wall by the fire extinguisher.

When 'Fairytale Of New York' began to play, it was his grandparents who took to the floor; the music starting slow, gradually increasing in speed until the chorus, which was perfect for a Viennese waltz where you needed breathers between all the twirling. From the back, with her slim body and good legs, Cheryl could have passed for a woman in her twenties. The song was long, but they kept going for the full five minutes. At the end, the whole room stood up and clapped as Cheryl pretended to collapse, but she'd hardly broken a sweat.

'Hope I'll look as good as that when I'm her age!' Sadie was standing next to him. 'Don't know what she's on, but they ought to bottle it.'

'Pilates,' Alf told her. 'She swears by it.'

Cheryl was also on HRT, but he wasn't supposed to know that.

'So, do I actually have to ask you to dance?' Sadie said.

'Didn't know if you wanted to,' he said.

'I'm the youngest, you're the second youngest, and after that your mum and Gary are the only ones here who aren't pensioners.'

Alf kind of wished that the song playing wasn't 'All I Want For Christmas Is You'. But it was good for jiving and jive was his best dance. He didn't want a repeat of the previous evening's rumba. When they finished, the applause was as loud as it had been for Cheryl and Chris.

'So what do you think?' Sadie asked, when they stepped outside to get some cold air.

'About what?' he asked.

'Show's over, you and Aimee are finished . . . we're "Two young stars we'll be seeing more of in the future".'

It was the caption under the photo that had appeared in that day's local paper. The reviewer had said *Grease* was the

196

best school production he'd ever seen. Donna had bought three copies: one for Cheryl and Chris, one for her to keep, and another to stick in a frame in the glass trophy cabinet.

'You want to partner up again?' Alf was surprised.

'Well, duh!' said Sadie.

He hadn't planned what he would do with all his weekends and evenings in the New Year. Last night's alcohol was still in his bloodstream, befuddling his thoughts.

'I'll think about it,' he said.

'Well, don't think too long,' Sadie said, clearly put out by his ambivalence. 'Offer ends on 31st December.'

She sounded like one of those competitions before the adverts on *X Factor*. Do you want a chance to win a cash prize and tickets for the tour? Do not call if you're watching this on catch-up.

Inside, he could hear Gary and the Stag Beetles starting their set with 'She Loves You'. They always played while people were getting their food from the buffet because it was surprisingly difficult to dance to Beatles songs – apart from 'Twist And Shout', and there were too many hip replacements in the room for that.

As they walked back into the hall, first Donna, then Leanne rushed up to hug them. Then Cheryl was there too.

'Lovely seeing you two together again,' his gran said. In her pink dress with huge net skirt, ash-blonde hair piled on her head, she looked a bit like the fairy godmother in a pantomime giving them her blessing.

Had a plan been drawn up that he wasn't party to? Alf wondered. Or had he missed something?

The New Year's Eve gala at the Tower Ballroom was as much a fixture of the family calendar as Christmas dinner with all the trimmings at Cheryl's. The tiered ballroom, with a big net of balloons suspended above the dance floor, never failed to impress. These days most of Blackpool's competitions took place in the Winter Gardens, but he didn't think there would be many people in the world's dancing community who would deny that the Tower Ballroom deserved the accolade of best ballroom in the world.

Everyone who went to the gala knew the popular sequence dances. There was nothing quite like the feeling of doing the Emmerdale waltz around the huge space with two hundred other couples all doing exactly the same steps.

The family always took two tables, and it was like being with Blackpool royalty as people came over to pay their respects to Cheryl and Chris. This year was the fiftieth anniversary of their first time dancing there. Donna had made Cheryl an ice-blue silk ballroom dress for the occasion, and she had a sparkling tiara in her hair.

For the past few years Aimee had come along, but now she had a boyfriend who didn't dance and she'd gone down to London to see the fireworks with him. Alf couldn't imagine how you'd get seriously involved with someone who couldn't dance at all. Dancing was so much a part of him; he didn't know what sex would be like if someone had no sense of rhythm or timing.

Gary couldn't dance when Donna had met him, but even he had mastered a passable waltz and had learned all the sequence dances. This year, he was having a go at the Tango Serida, which Alf, dancing with Cheryl, found it hard enough to remember the steps to – although Cheryl was pushing him through it, despite her mantra that the man should always lead. The third time through the sequence, he noticed Sadie dancing with her mum on the other side of the room. Sadie was in a short gold sequinned dress. She looked hot. And she was staring at him.

So that's what she'd meant by 31st December. Alf glanced at the clock. Two hours to midnight. What was he, Cinderella?

In his panic, he did a chassé instead of a rock step, felt Cheryl's disapproval stiffen through her hold.

He wanted to please his gran and his mum, and it was only for six months, so why not give them the pleasure of seeing him partner up with Sadie again, after all they'd done for him? And yet, and yet . . . if he had all those evenings and weekends free, he could earn enough money to see him through his year of travelling, and still maybe have some left over for London, if he got into the dance school he'd applied for.

After he'd taken Cheryl back to her seat, he went across to Sadie.

'So what's your New Year's resolution?' Sadie asked, clinking her glass of Prosecco against his orange juice.

Not to put things off in the hope that they'd go away, Alf thought.

'What's yours?' he asked. It wasn't midnight yet.

'Do what I've been wanting to do for a long time,' she said.

'What's that then?'

As soon as he said it, he suddenly knew what she was going to do, and he wished himself anywhere else because it just made everything more complicated.

Sadie put her glass down and kissed him full on the mouth.

Count to four, Alf thought, and break.

'Look, not sure how to say this . . .' Alf told her. 'But my answer's thanks, but no thanks.'

The way Sadie's face could change from light to dark was chilling, and for a moment he was fearful she'd want revenge. That meant he'd made the right decision, he reassured himself.

'I mean, I think you're great and everything . . . It's just, you know, I'm looking to the future now, not the past.'

22

January 2017

LETTY

It wasn't the prospect of studying in a room as cold as a fridge, nor even the upcoming exams, that made Letty reluctant to return to Oxford in January. It was more the feeling that her time with Marina was running out.

Marina had been diagnosed with atrial fibrillation which, when you googled it, was the medical term for heart failure. When Letty had returned home for the Christmas vacation, she'd found her grandmother slower and less commanding.

Frances and Ivo cooked the traditional family dinner on Christmas Eve, with Rollo supplying the special fennel sausages from Camisa on Old Compton Street, along with pretty tins of amaretti biscuits. Ivo got the *presepio* crib down from the loft, and at midnight, Marina herself placed the tiny baby Jesus in the manger. Everyone behaved so normally that Letty wondered if she was the only one thinking that maybe this would be the last Christmas they would all spend together. It made her all the more irritated that Frances couldn't just back down when, on Christmas Day, she and Marina had their traditional Christmas row – this time about the pudding – with Frances shouting, 'Trifle means jelly!'

'But it tastes so . . . synthetic.' Marina wrinkled her nose.

'By which you mean common,' Frances raged. 'Champagne bloody socialists!'

It was a variation on the usual theme. Frances, the child of an unemployed docker, had been dropped into bohemian North London society which, for all its liberal declarations, was as judgemental and difficult to penetrate as the milieu of the toffs they purported to despise.

Frances, of course, had a hand in shaping the narrative herself.

'Ask me anything about anything, as long as it begins with a letter from A to G!' was one of her favourite throwaway lines at dinner parties, because when she was growing up, the only books in her house comprised the first third of the *Encyclopedia Britannica*, which her dad had been persuaded to buy in weekly instalments by a salesman who came to the door, but had run out of money to complete when he was made redundant from the Ribble docks.

But Frances was an executive in an advertising firm, and that was surely about the most capitalist industry she could be in, Letty thought. She enjoyed going to the theatre and ballet, and eating out in fine restaurants. At some point, surely she had to acknowledge that she had become middle class herself. Anyway, how could anyone get so worked up about jelly?

The problem was – had always been – two matriarchs sharing one territory. Both clever, both strong, both extremely competitive. Ironically, it was Marina who had insisted that Frances and Ivo come and live there originally. For Ivo, the house in Belsize Park Gardens was home, but Frances had always felt like a guest that Marina tolerated, even though for many years now, it had been her income that had kept the household running.

What Letty had never really seen before Marina's stroke, was how much her father still behaved as his mother's child.

He rarely seemed to be at home these days, almost as if he was in denial.

'I think you worry too much,' he told Letty, when she raised her concerns. 'Marina will outlive us all!'

Letty developed a routine of revising during the mornings, then eating with Marina, as they had when Letty was doing her A levels. Now Letty was the one who brought lunch to Marina. Her grandmother did not go out much and had given up bridge, claiming that it gave her a headache, although Letty wondered if it was because she seemed to be losing her short-term memory.

Her memories from the past, however, were pin sharp, and she was still a brilliant raconteuse. Sometimes, as Letty listened to her anecdotes she wondered if she should record them for future generations. But she shied away from asking her, fearing that Marina might find it a mawkish suggestion.

When she met Letty's grandfather, Max, whom Letty remembered only as an old man arguing with other old men in a roomful of pipe smoke, Marina had been the hostess of a Soho restaurant which was frequented by artists, actors and intellectuals, the toast of 'le tout London'.

When Marina gave up her job to be a mother, the house in Belsize Park had become a social hub, where Marina held court with the same mastery as she had in the restaurant.

One lunchtime in the first week of January, Letty's phone buzzed with a number she did not recognize.

'Happy New Year!'

'Who is this?'

'It's Spencer. From the train,' he said.

'Oh! Hello!'

Letty stood up and walked across the room towards the window. Without Marina's care, the back garden was looking a mess.

'How's Gran?' Spencer asked.

Watching the sun going down behind the skeleton of the oak tree, it took a moment for Letty to realize what he was asking.

'She's OK, thank you.'

There was a pause.

'Look, I've done some research on *La Traviata*. Found a performance, but we'll need to discuss.'

Letty's immediate inclination was to say no. What could there be to discuss? she wondered.

'How about cocktails at the Sky Garden, tomorrow evening?' he was asking.

'The Sky Garden?' she repeated.

'Top of the Walkie Talkie. In the city. I'll see you there at seven, shall I?'

She had been out only once in her vacation, to Oscar and Raj's New Year's dinner, and it wasn't like Spencer was pestering her. It was six weeks since Marina had been taken into hospital, six weeks in which Letty had hardly given him a thought.

'OK then,' she heard herself saying.

'An admirer?' Marina asked brightly.

'Yes, I suppose so,' Letty replied, not quite sure how to describe Spencer. 'What does one wear for cocktails?'

Marina insisted that Letty try on some of her old dresses, which she kept in a shipping trunk at the foot of her bed. It was almost like being a little girl again, choosing costumes from the dressing-up box and parading in front of her grandmother. From the fifties, a deep green dress with a full skirt of watered silk, a tight lace bodice and three-quarter sleeves; from the sixties, a simple velvet little black dress with a boat neck; from the seventies, a lilac nylon number with long frilly sleeves. They all fitted perfectly, but they smelled of mothballs and they were far too fragile for a cold January evening.

Eventually Letty decided on her usual skinny black jeans and roll-neck sweater, worn under the black leather biker's jacket that had been Frances's Christmas gift. The shape of the jacket was traditional, with gold studs on the lapels, but the leather was as soft as butter and the designer label indicated that it had cost a fortune. Marina draped one of her old Hermès scarves in white, gold and green around her neck, and lent her a pair of long fake emerald earrings which, with Letty's hair scraped back into a chignon, dangled from ear lobe to shoulder.

'You look unreal!' Spencer said.

He was drinking a Mojito. He ordered one for her. It tasted summery in the vast greenhouse space. Looking at London spread out below was like being in a plane coming in to land, Letty thought.

The view gave them something to talk about as he pointed out various buildings, informing her how much the floor space cost per square foot in each postcode.

'Long story short,' he finally said. 'The opera you wanted to see is in New York. A place called the Met. It's sold out until the end of March, but I got two tickets for the first of April, which is a Saturday.'

This was too bizarre, Letty thought – to be sitting at the top of a skyscraper with a man she barely knew, who appeared to be asking her to go on a date to New York to see his first opera. Was the date significant? Was this some kind of early April Fool's prank? The answer should be a no-brainer.

'It's a big ask, I know,' Spencer was saying.

His disingenuousness was rather charming.

As he ordered another round, Letty tried to see him as someone else might. He was good-looking, well dressed and smelled of expensive cologne. He was the sort of man Frances might cast to advertise a brand of razor.

If she had met him at a party, Letty thought, she would have no reason to be suspicious of him. But she hadn't. She'd met him because he wanted to buy the services of a female student half his age, when he must have access to women he could date in the normal way.

Letty decided to confront the question. 'When we met in Oxford . . . I mean, why?'

He laughed.

'I could ask you the same.'

'But I asked you first,' Letty pointed out.

'Let's say I'm a bit like Rod Stewart,' he said. 'I've had two marriages. Ended up disliking them both and giving them each a house . . . you know that quote?'

Letty shook her head.

'You get the idea, though? I thought, if I'm going to be shelling out, I'll get what I want with no commitment.'

'And is that what you want from me? Because I was never going to become your sugar baby—'

'I knew that as soon as I saw you,' he interrupted.

'How?'

'No make-up, leggings – I'm sorry, but leggings? And then you couldn't get away quick enough . . .'

'How long did you wait?' Letty was curious.

'About ten minutes. I honestly knew I had more chance of scoring with the waitress than I did with you.'

Letty didn't know whether it was reassuring that he'd read her so accurately, or slightly unnerving.

'So, Elle.' He leaned towards her. 'I can't pretend I don't find you attractive, but I'm not expecting anything more than a broadening of my cultural horizons. You're the only person who's ever made me interested in seeing an opera. And it took some effort to get these tickets. In case you're wondering, I'll book us separate rooms in the hotel.'

She had been wondering. If he was that rich, he probably didn't even think about the expense.

It had always been her dream to go to the Met. She and Marina had seen most of the 'Live from the Met' transmissions at the Curzon cinema in Bloomsbury. The feeling of anticipation as the curtain went up, knowing that you were seeing a live performance beamed over by satellite, was thrilling, but the idea of being in the auditorium itself! Her exams would be over by then, she thought. Honour Moderations were said to be the longest exams in the world. If she survived those, surely she deserved a treat?

'So, you should know my name's not Elle,' she said.

'Just as well you told me before I booked the plane.'

'And I'll buy my own ticket,' she said, realizing that she had just agreed to go with him.

April was three months away, she thought on the Northern Line on the way home. She could always change her mind. He hadn't suggested meeting up in the meantime. She'd almost felt as if she was being dismissed when he'd looked at his watch, as if he had somewhere else to go on to.

Perhaps there was a whole string of other women who accepted his generosity?

'Did you enjoy your date?' Marina asked the following day.

She was sitting up in bed in her silk dressing gown, the four prints on the wall behind her. It was the same beautiful dark-haired Roman lady in each picture. When she was little Letty had thought it was Marina herself, but now she realized the slightly schmaltzy Pre-Raphaelite style was too old for that to be true. In each of the paintings the lady was wearing the same long dress, gathered at the waist, probably reimagined from the wall paintings of Pompeii, but the dress was a different colour. Tranquillity lolled in pink on a stone bench with a pink oleander beside her; Idleness was in yellow, twitching a long peacock feather for a ginger kitten to play with; Lesbia, Catullus's famous mistress, wore orange and held her pet sparrow aloft; and Violets, Sweet Violets, was in pale mauve, staring at a little posy of dark purple violets.

'It was interesting,' Letty replied, wandering over to the French doors that led out to wrought-iron steps down to the garden. It was raining. She stared at the globules of water running down the window, fascinated by how they stopped and started, ran into each other and made bigger drops, almost as if they were alive.

What would her grandmother make of Spencer? Letty half wished that she could bring him home for inspection.

'Would it be wrong . . .' She turned back to the bed. 'Would it be wrong to allow a man you hardly knew to take you to the opera?'

'You're asking whether he would expect payment of some kind?'

At ninety years old, Marina had pinpointed exactly what she was asking, but Letty hadn't expected quite such a direct response.

'I suppose so.'

'He will like being seen with you. That's all the payment he will expect, I think.'

'It's *La Traviata*!' she confided, expecting Marina to share her excitement, but her grandmother's expression did not change.

'What's that one about?' she asked.

'*La Traviata*,' Letty said louder. 'Verdi! We saw it together last spring!'

'Of course we did!' Marina said.

But Letty could tell that it was an artificial smile, and a shiver ran through her body.

23

February

ALF

The pizza restaurant where Alf worked had a Valentine's Day promotion lasting the whole month. Two heart-shaped pizzas for ten pounds. What they didn't tell you was that that was for the basic marinara. If you wanted additional toppings you had to pay extra. The chef wasn't happy. He prided himself on doing that thing of spinning the dough in the air. If you then tried to shape it, it came out looking more like a kidney than a heart.

It didn't really matter; walk-in business was slow. The rain had been sheeting down for weeks. The kids who delivered on mopeds were busier – nobody wanted to venture out. They sometimes got tips because people didn't generally open the pizza box until after they'd gone. Alf was the only one serving in the restaurant on weekday evenings, which meant a lot of listening to complaints and no tips at all when customers discovered the truth about the toppings.

Alf kept one pair of trousers and one black shirt just for work and he washed them every night when he got home, but he couldn't get rid of the smell of burnt cheese. His only perk above minimum wage was a free meal each evening, but he felt like he inhaled enough pizza to never want to eat it again.

There were two good things about working every night, though. One: you earned money. Two: you couldn't go out with your mates, so you never spent any of it. Which was just as well, because leaving home was going to cost a lot more than he'd estimated.

Alf had won a place at the dance school he wanted to go to, the only one where part of the degree course involved touring a show that the students created and performed. When he'd gone down for the audition, he'd been certain that London was where he wanted to be. Even in winter, the capital was buzzing. Walking down Shaftesbury Avenue on the evening he arrived, Alf couldn't believe how many theatres there were on just one street, and how many Chinese restaurants on the street parallel to it, and how many patisseries on the parallel street to the north side – one selling eclairs and nothing else, all decorated in pretty colours, more like a display of jewellery than cakes.

There was a drawback. London was unbelievably expensive. Being accepted onto the course – providing he passed at least two A levels – meant he could apply for student finance for the fees and also a maintenance loan, but he didn't like the idea of getting into a lot of debt and nor did his family. They couldn't see how you'd ever make enough as a dancer to have a hope of paying the money back. He didn't even tell them about rental prices in London. Alf knew that he was going to have to save to go there and get a part-time job while he was a student. He had decided to ditch his plans to travel with Cal, and Cal was getting in so deep with Kelly he didn't seem too bothered. The idea of lying on some paradise island in Thailand, or spending Christmas on the beach in Australia, no longer had the same pull. You didn't have to go that far to change your life, Alf thought. London was where he wanted to be.

It was the last Friday of the pizza promotion when Mr Noakes came into the restaurant with Miss Jones. Alf thought they were probably more embarrassed than he was, but by the time they'd spotted him they had already started taking off their coats.

'We can't go on meeting like this,' Miss Jones joked to Alf, as he pulled out a chair for her.

He hung back from the table while they were considering their order.

'Seems like a bargain,' said Mr Noakes.

'Not if you want extra toppings,' Miss Jones said, reading the small print.

'And I thought you taught English, not Maths!'

Alf cringed at the music teacher's attempt at flirtation.

'What are you having?' Miss Jones asked him.

'I think I'll have the spicy meat feast.'

'Oh, OK. I'll have the Four Seasons then.'

'Bit of everything,' said Mr Noakes.

Mr Noakes beckoned Alf over.

'A meat feast and a Four Seasons, please.'

'Wait a minute, what's the calzone like?' Miss Jones asked Alf.

'I think you'd do better with the Four Seasons.'

'OK then.'

'Thin base or Chicago style?'

'Oh, thin, I think,' said Mr Noakes.

'Good choice, sir. Plain crust or stuffed?'

The music teacher looked at him as if he was taking the piss.

'That's the final question, sir,' he said.

'Well, thank God for that. It's like being in a comedy sketch,' Mr Noakes said.

'Without the laughs,' Alf added.

Miss Jones giggled.

'Plain,' he said.

'And to drink?'

'How do you feel about a glass of vino?' Mr Noakes asked Miss Jones.

'Can't really, as I'm driving. You go ahead.'

'I might have a glass of your finest house red!' Mr Noakes told Alf.

Mr Noakes was clearly keener than Miss Jones was. It made sense because Miss Jones was in a different league. Attractive, good body, well able to look after herself. She'd been sent to cover Alf's English class for a lesson in the first week of January, and she'd surprised them all by striding into the class and announcing, 'I haven't taught you before, so there's three things you need to know. First up, I'm blonde but I'm not dumb. Second, I'm small, but anyone who messes with me goes straight to the Head. No three strikes and you're out with me, no yellow cards, no warnings. Three, and boys, this is for you' – she sniffed the air – 'these girls are all far too nice to tell you, but those adverts on television are lying. No woman ever fancied a guy because he wears Lynx.'

The girls had loved her after that and none of the lads had given her any trouble either, although Alf thought quite a few had gone down to Boots the following weekend to get themselves a different brand of body spray.

'Noakesy and Bridget?' said Cal, when Alf reported the sighting the following Monday.

'She's probably lonely,' Alf guessed. 'She came to my mum's classes at the beginning of the year.'

'Jesus, Alf!'

'What?'

'Not just the hottest girls but the hottest teacher too!'

'It wasn't like that . . .'

'You would, though?'

'I didn't even dance with her,' Alf said, wishing he hadn't mentioned it now.

211

'You would, though?' Cal repeated. He wasn't talking about dancing with her.

'Would you?' Alf asked.

'Are you kidding me? You know what they say about women in their prime? She's in her prime, mate, and you're in yours. It's eighteen for men. You might as well enjoy it, mate. It's all downhill from here.'

Donna always told her Ballroom Beginners, 'If you can walk, you can dance!'

It got them feeling confident at the start. Alf loved the way his mum was always so positive in her classes. He wished she could be more like that in the rest of her life. Donna was always careful with people's feelings, realizing how exposed they felt. It was the reason Donna was a better teacher for beginners than Cheryl. Most of them were varying degrees of hopeless, but they did improve if they kept coming. Miss Jones, not so much.

For a teacher, Miss Jones wasn't great at listening to instructions. The first time she'd appeared, at the beginning of January, Alf had deliberately not danced with her, thinking she'd be as embarrassed as he was. The following week, his mum asked him after class why he was avoiding the little blonde one.

'She's a teacher at my school,' Alf explained.

'Well, she's paying the same as everyone else. I need to share you around equally.'

There were always more women than men, so a lot of the lesson was spent with the women's arms stretched out in front pretending to be in hold. Alf would try to get around to everyone for at least a few bars of music, so they got an idea of what it felt like to dance with a partner.

Most of the younger women who'd seen *Strictly* and imagined the ballroom dancing world was full of fit guys dropped out pretty quickly. Alf assumed that Miss Jones was one of the

Lonely Hearts, as his mum called them, because she hadn't appeared since the third week of term. Now, the week after he'd seen her in the restaurant, she was back.

Alf was collecting the five-pound fees on the door.

'I've had a lot of preparation,' said Miss Jones, as if she needed to excuse her absence.

'Have you got a letter from your mum?' Alf asked.

She laughed.

'Take a step forward with your left foot, no, other left foot . . .' Donna started the class.

It was generally the women who had difficulty telling the difference between their left and right.

Alf thought it was probably worse for Miss Jones, with him standing there watching. He decided to get his obligation over and done with.

He guessed she wasn't used to struggling with things; she kept apologizing to him for getting it wrong as he walked her through the basic steps several times without music.

Donna went over to the sound deck. As soon as he heard the intro, Alf grinned.

'You should be fine with this one,' he said.

The track was 'Have You Met Miss Jones?'

It was that little bit of relaxation that seemed to untangle the knots she'd twisted herself into. For a few steps she managed to follow him, but it all went wrong as soon as he said, 'Look up, don't look at your feet!'

'Think of it like a spelling test,' he told her when the music stopped. 'You don't remember the words by staring at them – you remember them by not looking at them, don't you?'

'Thank you, teacher,' she said with a smile.

'OK,' Donna said. 'You all did well with that, so we'll have a go at the lock step. Alfie, can I have you back?'

He wished his mum wouldn't call him Alfie. Or that she'd at least save it for when they were in a family setting. It was his given name, but he'd always hated it, thinking it was more like the name you'd give a dog. When he was growing up, Cheryl's Westies were Albie and Bertie. At the age of five, he decided to insist on plain Alf because he thought it sounded more like a man's name. It was just before he went to primary school and, luckily, just before dancing competitively for the first time, otherwise he'd never have been free of it.

When he glanced inadvertently at Miss Jones, she gave him a conspiratorial wink, as if she'd noticed his discomfort and wasn't going to start calling him Alfie at school.

At the end of class, as he was helping everyone with their coats, she said, as if to emphasize their unspoken agreement, 'Thanks, Alf. I enjoyed this evening.'

'Glad to hear it, Miss Jones.'

'It's Gina,' she said. 'Outside school, obviously.'

24

March

LETTY

Spencer was standing at the check-in desk, just as they had arranged by text. He took Letty's ticket and upgraded it to business class.

'How did your exams go?' he asked, as they waited in the queue for security.

'Bit of an ordeal,' Letty said.

'But you survived!' Spencer said.

The subject was clearly over. It was refreshing to be with someone who had no idea about iambic pentameter or Homeric epithets and wouldn't have even understood what the examiners were asking, let alone how to answer.

'How's Gran?' Spencer asked.

'She's not too good at the moment.'

'Oh, I'm sorry.'

'She's old,' Letty said. Literally old now, she thought.

Marina had become an increasingly difficult and impatient old lady, with whom it was no longer a pleasant experience to spend an afternoon. The doctors were now describing her illness as vascular dementia, where a series of tiny strokes, or infarcts, knocked out bits of memory. Was it possible, Letty sometimes wondered, that there was an area in her brain labelled 'Love for Violetta', like a file in an old-fashioned cabinet, that would one day be randomly obliterated?

Part of Letty wanted to spend as much time with Marina as possible, knowing that their time was running out, but another side wanted to remember Marina as she had been.

As the plane took off, and there was no longer any chance of turning back, Letty felt a burst of relief. If her grandmother were in her right mind, she would approve, she told herself – hoping that was the truth, and not just a comforting platitude.

'Champagne?' asked Spencer.

It was two o'clock in the afternoon, but she was on a plane between two time zones with a man she hardly knew, on their way to a city she'd never visited, to see an opera she loved – so the normal rules, whatever they were, didn't apply.

'Let me pay for it?' she said.

She wanted to pay her share as much as possible. Upgrading to business class was totally beyond her means, so she'd let that go, but a glass of champagne was something she could afford and buying it would demonstrate a kind of symmetry, if not balance, in the situation.

Spencer laughed. 'It's free in business.'

At the luxury hotel there were, as agreed, two separate rooms, and they were the kind that had two double beds in each.

Letty had expected to feel tired from jet lag, but instead she was buzzing to get out and experience the city. She brushed her teeth and splashed cold water on her champagne-pink face before knocking on Spencer's door. Eventually he appeared in a towelling robe, his hair wet from showering, and when he saw that she was still wearing her leather jacket and jeans, a look crossed his face that made her feel as if she wasn't treating his generosity with quite the respect it demanded.

'Should I change?' she heard herself asking.

'People tend to dress up a bit more for dinner here,' he said.

'Of course,' she said, slightly flustered.

Letty had brought just the single carry-on bag allowed in economy. The silk blouse she'd borrowed from Frances to wear to the opera the following evening was the only item that would be acceptable for dinner, and he was hardly going to approve if she wore it twice.

Was there even a dress code at the Met? At the Royal Opera House in London, you could sit in the stalls in full evening dress or you could rock up in frayed jeans and a T-shirt and nobody would bat an eyelid, but maybe not here. Definitely not, as far as Spencer was concerned.

She remembered that he'd looked askance at her small suit-case at Heathrow.

'Is that it?' he'd asked. 'You're a lady who travels light!'

She'd thought his astonishment indicated approval, but perhaps she had got that wrong. Perhaps his suit bag contained a dinner jacket and formal black trousers with shiny black stripes down the side?

Now she was going to have to buy something the following day, which meant a further expense that she hadn't budgeted for. This evening, the blouse would have to do.

Letty hung it up, still in its plastic film from the dry cleaner's, feeling guilty for telling her mother that it was an American friend from her Greek sculpture course who had invited her to New York for the weekend, knowing exactly what Frances would say if Letty told her the truth.

Spencer had booked Robert, a restaurant at the top of the Museum of Arts and Design on Columbus Circle.

'You said you liked art,' he said.

Letty was touched at the care he had taken to try to please her. Was this what happened when you were with an older man? With Josh, the closest they had got to eating in the sky was candyfloss at the top of a fairground Ferris wheel, although at the time she had thought it the most romantic date in the world.

Glancing at the prices on the menu, Letty chose the least expensive item: a farmer's salad of fresh vegetables.

Spencer was good at making the kind of small talk she found almost impossible to initiate. Everything he said about New York seemed to relate to movie locations he assumed she would be familiar with. They should go to Little Italy, he said – did she remember that scene in *The Godfather: Part II*, because it hadn't changed a lot. Or Wall Street – didn't she agree that Leonardo DiCaprio had been robbed of the Oscar for *The Wolf*? Perhaps she was more interested in the romcoms? They could go for a walk in Central Park, like in *When Harry Met Sally*, or even have breakfast in that diner . . .

'Actually, I'm going to need to go shopping,' Letty told him.

'What a surprise!' he said.

What did it matter what he thought she was like, she asked herself, downing cold white wine like water to try to quell the strange buzz of bad and good nerves at the situation she found herself in? What was she like anyway? Sitting on the top of a glass tower in New York with a man she had met on a train, who had invited her to the opera, was like being in a high-concept romcom of her own. Why not be a different kind of person for a weekend?

Letty woke up fully clothed with a hangover. When she went to the bathroom and saw herself in the mirror, there was a discoloured patch on Frances's shirt just below the collar, where the shiny silk had gone matt with dark edges. She must have dribbled as she slept.

Bits and pieces of the night before flashed across her mind.

She thought she'd managed to bring it back whenever the conversation started feeling like flirting, but now she wasn't sure. She thought she remembered leaning across the table to taste a spoonful of his dessert, and the waiter arriving with another spoon for her.

She thought she remembered looking at his reflection in the mirrored lift back up to their floor, and him going to kiss her goodnight, and the kiss intended for her cheek landing half on her mouth.

Usually, Letty bought her clothes from Primark or H&M. Occasionally, Frances would buy her a designer coat, or shoes from Russell & Bromley, which made the cheaper clothes look more stylish. If they shopped in Selfridges together, it was always for Frances, and Letty never looked at the price labels, so she had no idea whether Saks Fifth Avenue was expensive in comparison; she only knew that it was totally beyond her reach.

When she asked one of the more approachable shop assistants if she knew of somewhere more affordable, the woman said she could try Century 21, but it was way downtown in the WTC district.

'Why don't I see you back at the hotel in a couple of hours?' Letty asked Spencer, forced to admit, when he asked what the problem was, that there was absolutely no way she could buy a dress here.

'But are there things you like?' he asked.

'I couldn't let you pay,' she said.

'Why?'

'Because I couldn't pay you back.'

'How's a dress different from an opera ticket?'

She was grateful he didn't add 'or a separate hotel room', 'or an upgrade to business', 'or dinner last night', but somehow all of those things were there in his question.

'It just is,' she said firmly.

'You know, you'd enjoy it far more if you just relaxed,' he said.

There was a slight edge in his voice now that made her suspect he was running out of patience with her random ethical qualms.

'Doesn't matter to me if you choose the lobster over the salad,' he told her, showing that he had observed her calculations the previous evening. 'What does matter is that you enjoy yourself. And I enjoy myself,' he added.

Was there an infinitesimal note of threat? Or was he saying that it would give him pleasure to buy her something, and who was she to deny him that? And then the decision was taken from her, as Spencer beckoned the shop assistant who was hovering, pretending not to listen.

'Could you help my friend find something suitable for the opera tonight?'

It was only when the lights went down and the orchestra started playing that Letty realized that there were, in fact, specific resonances with the romcom *Pretty Woman*.

Didn't Richard Gere take Julia Roberts to the opera in a long red dress that he'd bought her? Wasn't that opera in fact *La Traviata*?

Of course it was.

La Traviata, the story of a rich man who falls in love with a courtesan – or, in *Pretty Woman*, a street prostitute. In *La Traviata*, when love finally triumphs, it is too late because she is dying. Letty assumed that *Pretty Woman* had a happier ending, but she wasn't sure because it was always on telly so late she fell asleep halfway through, waking up with the jaunty music over the credits.

Spencer, she thought, with his extensive movie vocabulary, would be sure to recognize the theme. Perhaps he had devised this weekend as an homage? Perhaps he even assumed that she was consciously going along with it? He had preferred the red dress that the shop assistant suggested, although he had allowed Letty to opt for the black one.

Letty spent the first act of the opera arguing with herself. This situation was completely different because this rich man was not introducing the woman to high art. It was the other way round. More importantly, they had made no deal for her time. However, accompanying a man to the Met, wearing a thousand-dollar dress, felt far more compromising than any theoretical case she could argue.

The production had a stark modern set and made the chorus into a comic commentary on the central love story, rather like a Greek tragedy. Letty was slightly disappointed on Spencer's behalf that, for his first opera, he didn't get to see a more conventional staging.

At the interval, however, he was enthusiastic for exactly the opposite reason.

'I expected fat ladies screeching in flouncy dresses,' he said.

'Are you enjoying it?'

'It's something else,' he said.

It was strange, Letty thought, how she could spend an hour twisting herself in knots, only for them to unravel in a second. Spencer was not some scheming sophisticate but a straightforward guy who hadn't had the benefit of a middle-class North London upbringing.

Why did she always make things more complicated than they needed to be? Spencer wasn't the sort of person she was used to socializing with, but he was fun, and maybe that's what she needed in her life.

Afterwards, he let her buy them both hot chocolate in a cafe overlooking the park, and their goodnight kiss was perfectly sober and chaste.

Lying in a deep bath, Letty ran through the events of the day. They got on surprisingly well together, she thought, when she wasn't being neurotic. He was good at chatting about the things that were important to him, like watches. He appeared to own a fairly extensive collection, and stopped to look at the watch counter in each department store they had visited. He talked about them in the way that she might talk about art, knowing the makers, the designs and the prices. Even though she hadn't previously been the slightest bit interested, she'd found herself looking at men's wrists during the interval at the Met, trying to recognize a Rolex or a Patek Philippe. The eventual acquisition of a particular watch was for Spencer what getting a First would be to her. Not just a reward for hard work, but a fundamental indicator of status that he would have earned and that couldn't be taken away.

The sky was blue as they checked out of the hotel. They took the subway downtown – a dark, grimy, subterranean world just feet away from the glittering glamour of the city above. She was glad that he'd suggested the Staten Island Ferry as the final thing they should do, because it was so cheap that she could pay for it, and it was as unforgettable an experience to see Manhattan sparkling in the sunshine as it was to go to the Met.

In the car on the way to the airport, Letty craned her neck to see the iconic skyline fading into the distance, feeling almost tearful at leaving.

'Thank you *so* much,' she said to Spencer. 'I have had the best time.'

'Want to do it again?' he asked. 'I mean another city?'

Given what she'd just said, she could hardly say no, and yet she felt somehow that he was pressing home an advantage. Could she spend another weekend with him? When she thought about the shopping and the opera, she thought not; but when she thought about the Staten Island Ferry, how he'd stood behind her on the deck and taken a selfie of them both laughing with the wind blowing their hair back like in *Titanic*, she thought why on earth not?

25

April

ALF

The A level English syllabus was entitled 'Love Through the Ages'. Alf thought they'd probably chosen the theme because most of the students who did English were female. In their year, he was the only male candidate. In all the texts they were studying, the male characters were flawed bastards. Didn't matter whether it was a man or a woman who'd written it. Othello and Iago: both raving idiots; Heathcliff: a killer and a maniac. In *Tess of the d'Urbervilles*, Alec was a rapist and Angel Clare was a wuss. As far as Alf could see, Jay Gatsby was virtually a stalker.

The female characters weren't like that, though. Cathy in *Wuthering Heights* and Daisy Buchanan were both a bit high maintenance, but Desdemona was a loyal, understanding kind of woman and Tess was naive and innocent. The girls in the A level group could relate to the female characters, but he didn't recognize the male ones. True, most of the guys he knew didn't think in the complex way that girls did about relationships, so maybe you could say they were thoughtless, or even stupid, but not evil.

Alf had preferred the AS year, when they'd studied poetry.

He had never been a fast reader, so it was fewer words to deal with, and poetry was written about aspects of love that both sexes could relate to, like desire, longing, regret. They'd had some good discussions in the Lower Sixth. In Year 13, he felt like he was constantly under attack.

It was even worse when Miss Jones covered for the week Mr Marriot was at a conference.

Miss Jones wasn't used to teaching the A level syllabus, and she got flappy whenever anyone asked her questions. That made her vulnerable because the Pink Ladies could smell weakness a mile off.

'Got a question for you, Miss.'

'Go ahead, Sadie.'

'Are you dancing with Alf again tonight?'

It was a disadvantage for a teacher to be blonde, Alf thought, because pale complexions coloured and blue eyes were less opaque than brown.

Miss Jones was panicking.

'Yes, I'm going to my dance class,' she finally said. 'I'm not very good, but you get better if you work at things. That's a lesson you'd do well to learn, Sadie.'

Nice recovery, thought Alf. He'd come to quite admire the way she'd persevered with the dance classes. And it was true: she was getting better. A little bit better.

'Do you like being in Alf's arms, Miss?' Sadie asked.

Fortunately, the bell rang.

In the corridor, Alf caught Sadie up.

'Give it a rest,' he said.

'Oooh, sticking up for her now. Must be serious.'

'You're out of order.'

'I'm not the one who likes the teacher.'

'I don't like her, not like that!'

'What's that thing Shakespeare said about protesting too much?'

In the common room, Cal said, 'Just ignore it, mate. You'll never win with Sadie.'

'Yeah, and how did she find out about the dancing?' Alf was furious with him.

'I told Kelly not to tell.'

'Full marks, mate!' Alf walked off.

Miss Jones did not turn up at dance class that evening and, for the rest of the week, Alf skipped English, not wanting to embarrass her. When Mr Marriot returned, he gave him a ticking off. He understood that long bouts of concentrated reading weren't really Alf's thing, and even wondered if Alf had ever been tested for dyslexia, because he seemed to struggle more than he'd expect for someone of his intelligence. Alf told him that one of his primary school teachers had said the same thing, but he was always fairly near the top of the class, so his mum didn't think there was anything wrong with him.

He left Mr Marriot's office promising he'd make up the work, but feeling deflated. Was dyslexia just a way of saying he was thick? Mr Marriot was the teacher who'd always supported him. Was it unrealistic to think he was going to pass his English A level? And what would happen then? The dance school required him to pass both his A levels, Drama and English.

There was a cold wind blowing off the sea, and the air was heavy and wet, as if it was full of drizzle and salt spray but couldn't be bothered to rain properly. As he walked along the promenade, the rhythm of his footsteps helped to unravel tangled thoughts and work out what was important and what was not. He needed to spend more time studying. There was no point in earning the money for London if he failed to get there. He would cut down his nights at the pizzeria, and ask his mum if she could do without his help for the next couple of months.

When it finally started to rain, it was torrential and he had to make a run for it, with his backpack over his head.

The pink Cinquecento was parked about fifty yards down the street from the dance hall. Miss Jones was sitting in the driver's seat. She wound down the window and said, 'Can I have a word, Alf?'

She pointed to the passenger seat, leaned across and opened the door for him.

Inside the clean, dry interior of the small car, he felt very big and very wet.

'Alf, I'm sorry if I've caused you any embarrassment by coming to dance classes,' Miss Jones began.

The rain was coming down so fast now, it felt like being in a tiny glass room inside a waterfall.

'I'm the one who's sorry for telling Cal,' Alf said. 'I honestly wouldn't have done, but I thought you'd left.'

'I've decided not to come any more,' she said, staring through the windscreen.

'That's a shame,' he said automatically. And a bit of a relief.

'It's just, well, I've bought a flat on the other side of town, and it's keeping me busy.'

'People come and go all the time,' Alf assured her.

There was a long moment of silence. He looked across at her. She seemed vulnerable and a bit lost somehow.

'You don't want to take any notice of the bullies,' he found himself saying.

'Aren't I supposed to be the teacher here?' she said, sniffing.

He smiled at her, his fingers hovering above the door handle, wishing he knew what to say to finish up and get out.

'So, where's this flat you've bought?' he asked, trying to lighten up the mood.

'It's one of those new-builds on the South Promenade,' she said.

'Cool!'

'Want to see it?' She looked at him.

He wasn't sure how to say no without hurting her feelings.

'I'm working tonight,' he said.

'I didn't mean *now*!' She laughed, as if he was suggesting something improper. 'How about tomorrow? I could use someone tall to help me put up shelves and things.'

She was lonely and he'd made it impossible for her to come to dance classes. Wasn't it the least he could do?

'OK then,' Alf said.

He put the address into his phone and they arranged a time.

'See you at eleven, then,' he agreed, finally able to open the car door.

'Coffee,' she said. 'I may even be able to stretch to cake.'

It wasn't one of his mum's good days. The most promising Little Star had just announced she was quitting in favour of gymnastics.

'Dyslexia?' she said, when Alf told her what Mr Marriot had said. 'That's just a fancy word for laziness, isn't it? You've always been a hard worker. I don't know what's happened to you recently, Alfie.'

'Well, I'm spending a lot of time working at the restaurant, and helping out here . . .' he said.

'So it's my fault now, is it?'

'I'm not saying that.'

Sometimes he felt like he'd spent his life treading on eggshells round her, but when it came to giving him support, she wasn't there.

'What are you saying then?'

'Forget it,' he said.

'I don't need attitude from you, Alf, after the day I've had.'

'Yeah, well it's not been great for me either,' he said, unable to stop himself adding, 'Not that you'd care, because you never think about anyone else!'

227

His mum stared at him, then sank down onto a chair and started crying.

'I'm going to be late for work,' Alf said, and marched out.

It was the first time her tears hadn't worked on him, but he spent the evening feeling sore inside. By the time he returned home all the lights in the house were switched off, even the one over the front door you needed to see your key into the lock. Donna and Gary had gone to bed. Cheryl always said you shouldn't let the sun go down on a row.

When he got up, his mum had already left for the private classes she took on Saturday mornings.

Gary was in the kitchen, hunched over his cornflakes.

'I didn't mean to upset her.' Alf was the first to speak.

'It's been a tough few days,' Gary said. 'She lost another pregnancy.'

How was he supposed to know if nobody told him? Alf felt terrible for what he'd said.

The florist was selling red and yellow tulips, two bunches for five pounds. He asked if they could put a bit of tissue and ribbon around. But the studio was already locked up when Alf got there. He looked at his watch. It was gone eleven and suddenly, he remembered that he was supposed to be on the other side of town, at Miss Jones's flat.

'That's so sweet! You really shouldn't have!' Miss Jones said when she saw the flowers. Barefoot, and wearing a short dress, she looked much younger and prettier than she did at school.

He didn't want to mention the stuff with his mum, so he just handed the flowers over.

Miss Jones indicated that he should take his trainers off. He hoped his feet didn't smell.

The flat was so new it looked more like a computer-generated image than a place where someone was living. The main room had French doors leading out onto a balcony over-looking the sea. There was a sofa on the wooden floor still in its plastic packing. The master bedroom had a cream carpet and a big window with another sea view. The double bed was covered with a white cotton duvet cover. It was like something you'd see in a posh hotel, except for the blue kitten, white rabbit and soft furry hedgehog propped up on the pillows. Miss Jones showed him a remote control that made a television screen rise out of the tailboard. He'd only ever seen that in adverts.

Alf knew you'd have to have a lot more than a teacher's salary to afford a place like this.

'Coffee?'

Miss Jones had one of those machines that George Clooney advertised, where you put capsules in.

She took three mugs from a cupboard and arranged the tulips in one of them.

'Hadn't even thought about vases,' she said. 'Who knew how much work it is making a home!'

She'd bought him a Victoria sponge in a box. He wondered if she'd stopped to get it on her way home yesterday after-noon, after inviting him over. There didn't seem to be anything else in the fridge apart from a two-pint bottle of semi-skimmed milk. She cut him a big slice, then didn't have a plate to put it on.

The way she fussed about the kitchen, opening the empty cupboards as if crockery would somehow miraculously appear, reminded him a bit of nursery school, where the girls always spent their golden time in the Wendy house playing at being mummies, offering invisible meals on doll-size plastic plates and pretend cups of tea.

There was nowhere to sit down, so he stood leaning over the sink, trying not to drop crumbs.

'So what do you want a hand with?' he asked.

'That lot,' she said, pointing to a pile of boxes containing flat-pack furniture.

'You're very good at this,' she said, as he screwed the legs into one of the dining chairs. 'I wouldn't have a clue!'

'Wait till you've tried it,' he said. 'It might collapse!'

It didn't. She sat down, kicking her legs straight out in front of her.

'Next?' he asked.

'How much time do you have?' she asked him.

'I'm not working till this evening,' he said, then wondered if he'd just committed himself to staying all day.

'You really don't mind?' she asked.

'Pleasure,' he said.

The polite response was automatic, but he was happy enough. The bare room with its view of the sea felt calm after the trouble at home; he was too pissed off with Cal to want to spend Saturday afternoon watching the football in a pub with him. He quite liked the slight feeling that he shouldn't be there, although he couldn't say why not. He was eighteen. It was his free time.

Removing the packing, Alf lined the pieces up on the floor with the correct Allen keys. He'd done quite a lot of stuff like this with Gary.

'Bloody hell, Alf,' said Miss Jones. 'Is there any way you're not perfect? A man who can dance and put up shelves!'

'Not that good at English,' he said.

'If you want, I'll give you extra lessons,' Miss Jones said.

She held his gaze and he couldn't tell whether the offer was for real, or whether she was teasing him.

At first, he was hesitant about asking her to hold stuff steady, or hand him the correct fixtures, but she was easy to chat to, not sarcastic like some of the older teachers. When he asked why she'd chosen teaching, she admitted that she'd wanted to be an actress, but after spending two years as a waitress and never getting any of the roles she went for, she decided there were better ways to earn a living. Then, as if remembering that he wanted a career in theatre himself, she added, 'It's a precarious existence, Alf, but you're so talented, you'll be fine. And to be honest, you're a much better waiter than I ever was too!'

With the shelves and coffee table assembled, the living room looked less like a show flat.

'Do you mind if I watch *Final Score*?' he asked.

'Be my guest.' She waved towards the bedroom.

'I just want to see how Blackpool did.'

He switched on the television, and sat on the very edge of the bed with his feet on the floor.

After a few minutes, Miss Jones walked in, went around the other side and lay on top of the duvet, propping herself up on the pillows. She patted the bed.

'Make yourself comfortable,' she said.

Alf lay there feeling anything but, with only the three cuddly toys separating them.

Was she coming on to him? She was nice and pretty and fun, and if it had been anyone else he knew behaving like this, he would have known. But she was a teacher. The rules were different.

Alf tried to think down the erection he was getting. All the league teams beginning with A. Aston Villa, Arsenal, Accrington Stanley. There were guys at school who'd pay money to be where he was now. Blackpool, Birmingham, Brentford, Bury, Bolton Wanderers, Burnley. It had been a while since he'd had sex. Chelsea, Coventry, Chester, Charlton Athletic. Eight months. Derby. Surely there must be more Ds than Derby? Everton. He couldn't think of any more Es.

'You know what Sadie said?' Miss Jones asked.

Was that what this was all about?

'You don't want to take any notice of Sadie, Miss Jones!' he said. Then, glancing across the pillows, he saw the dismay on her face.

'I mean, most of the guys think you're really fit,' he told her.

'But you don't . . . ?'

'It's not that I don't. But . . .'

But what? he thought. But I'm a good boy? But you're a teacher? She was fit. She knew what she was doing. He was eighteen. An adult. He hadn't had sex for months.

'I think about you all the time, Alf,' she said, looking at him with her big blue eyes.

'Miss Jones?'

'Gina,' she said.

Then the cuddly toys were on the floor and her face was so close to his he could smell that she'd just brushed her teeth. The only thing she was wearing under her dress was a black lace thong.

26

May

LETTY

It was almost as if by imagining a friendship with the American woman at the sculpture lectures, Letty caused it to happen. The day after she returned from New York, she ran into Molly browsing the new fiction table in Blackwell's. They struck up a conversation. Molly was taking a Liberal Arts Masters. They talked about the production of *La Traviata* at the Met, which she had also seen. She confessed that the abstract modern design had not quite worked for her either. Molly provided tips for if Letty ever visited the Big Apple again, and Letty advised Molly about the lesser-known art galleries and theatres of London she should check out during her year in the UK.

When they'd parted outside the King's Arms, Letty felt she'd found someone who genuinely shared her interests.

The majority of Letty's fellow Classics students were public schoolboys who saw Oxford as a rite of passage before becoming lawyers in Bloomsbury. No one admitted to a passion for their subject. In fact, when Letty had used the word at their first seminar, the students around her had wrinkled their noses with distaste. During her first year in college, meals in hall, where most people made and developed friendships, had been torture for Letty. Letty had always been first in, first to sit down, first to finish and escape. One or two boys had been confident enough to try to chat her up, but Letty's serious demeanour was a barrier that nobody was patient enough to penetrate.

After becoming friends with Molly, Letty finally began to enjoy the social life that most students had taken for granted from day one. She thought perhaps it was because Molly's crowd were all American, so they didn't consider her any more peculiar than other English people. They were mostly Rhodes Scholars who'd got fraternities and sororities out of their system in the States, and valued the old-fashioned traditions of Oxford, such as visiting each other for tea, or punting on the river.

If you weren't doing exams during the summer term, the pace of university life slowed down. Students who were involved in drama spent their days rehearsing for garden productions and evenings performing; others simply revelled in the beauty of the college gardens, doing archery or playing croquet on the lawns.

One Thursday afternoon, at the end of the fifth week of term, a group of them were in a punt hired from the Cherwell Boathouse. The air was filled with birdsong and when Letty's phone rang, she found herself apologizing to five frowning faces as she fumbled in her bag to answer it. Her nerves were jangling. The ringing of her phone indicated urgency. She was always half expecting a call telling her that Marina had taken a turn for the worse, so when the name that appeared on the screen was not Frances, she answered with relief.

Apart from an acknowledgement of the text she had sent to thank him, Spencer had not been in touch since they parted at the airport. She had slightly mixed feelings about it – on the one hand, hoping that she hadn't said or done anything to offend him; on the other, relieved not to have to make more decisions about their association.

'Cut to the chase,' he said after their initial greetings. 'Are you doing anything this weekend?'

She couldn't even claim that there was an essay to write.

'I'm thinking Venice,' Spencer said.

Less than an hour before, it had crossed Letty's mind that sitting in a punt with a brawny man in a striped T-shirt at the helm must be rather like being in a gondola. The coincidence made the phone call seem almost predetermined.

'Venice?' she repeated.

Opposite her, Molly raised an eyebrow. She was the only person Letty had told about Spencer, and she thought her friend disapproved but was also a tiny bit envious.

'Know it's short notice,' Spencer was saying.

It made Letty feel less obliged to him. Presumably he had been stood up by some other woman and was looking for a replacement. She wondered how many phone calls he had made before getting to her.

'When?' she heard herself saying.

'First flight out London City airport tomorrow. I can't promise separate rooms – it is the Danieli. But I'm sure there'll be a sofa. Bring a dress this time.'

There was something about his tone that made Letty immediately wish she'd declined, but when she analysed it she couldn't think of a logical reason why. It was her own fault that she hadn't packed carefully for the New York trip. It had cost him a lot of money. Surely he had a right to remind her?

Marina was propped up against a bank of pillows. Her nightie had a tea stain down the front, but her face lit up when Letty entered the room.

'To what do we owe this pleasure?' she asked.

Her language appeared to have reverted to the more elaborate courtesy of a bygone era where most of her clear memories now resided.

'I'm on my way to Venice for the weekend,' Letty told her.

'La Serenissima!' Marina smiled.

It was always a nice feeling when she connected with something in a positive way.

'He bought me lace in Burano,' Marina suddenly declared. 'And we danced in the piazza.'

Her watery eyes sparkled.

'How romantic!' Letty said, trying to picture her grandparents dancing. Her grandfather was considerably shorter than Marina. 'Was that the lace for your wedding dress?' she asked.

'We could not marry!' Marina said crossly. 'He was from a very old Venetian family. A *conte*!'

Now Letty regretted asking; Marina was agitated.

'I was wondering if I could borrow a dress?' She attempted to calm her grandmother with talk of clothes.

Opening the trunk at the foot of the bed, she held up dress after dress, bringing the ones that Marina nodded at over for closer inspection.

'This is the one!' her grandmother finally said.

It was made of glazed cotton with horizontal blue stripes dotted with pink roses, waisted, with a small white collar and buttons down the front, and a skirt so full it stuck out as if there were a crinoline underneath. It fitted Letty perfectly.

In the cupboard that contained racks and racks of shoes in a rainbow of colours, Marina gestured at a pair of pointed white slingbacks that suited the dress. How was it possible, Letty wondered, that the fashion part of Marina's brain remained perfectly intact?

'Yes,' she said, gazing at Letty. 'The colours match Burano. You must wear it there.'

'Burano?'

'Of course!' Marina seemed very certain.

The dress was so different from any of Letty's monochrome clothes, yet she loved the swishy feeling that it gave her as she twirled like a ballerina on a musical box so that Marina could inspect every angle. Had her grandmother really worn the dress in Venice? She liked the idea of returning Marina's style back to her home country.

Bring a dress, she thought, wondering whether she would dare to wear it, and what Spencer would say if she did, but packing the black georgette cocktail dress he had bought her just in case she lost her nerve.

Motoring across the lagoon in the launch from the airport, Letty felt the kind of wonder she had experienced seeing the skyline of Manhattan; it was so like it was supposed to be that it almost felt unreal. The hotel Danieli, Spencer informed her, was where Daniel Craig had stayed in *Casino Royale*, and Johnny Depp in *The Tourist*. Housed in a large Venetian palace a stone's throw from St Mark's Square, it was as opulent inside as out. Their room looked over the lagoon towards the Palladian basilica of San Giorgio. On the water outside, a mismatched assortment of gondolas, water taxis and *vaporetti* continuously dropped and picked up myriad tourists. Letty thought that if she stood at the window for long enough she would see every person she had known, or would ever know.

'What do you want to do?' Spencer asked.

'I could stay here forever and watch this view.'

'Shall we get them to send up some lunch?' he asked.

'Why don't we just wander?' she suggested. 'See what we find?'

The guidebook that she had bought at City airport said that the best thing to do in Venice was get lost, and it was remarkably easy in the maze of canals and passageways and bridges which, to a newcomer's eye, all looked very similar in their decadent beauty. Within fifty metres of St Mark's Square the density of the crowds thinned out, and there were canals where the only sign of human life was washing strung on lines, the smell of frying onions, the sound of mothers summoning their children to eat, and the clatter of eager footsteps in hidden kitchens nearby.

They found a bar selling tapas-like portions called *cicchetti* and bought several small plates, most of which Spencer consumed, along with glasses of white wine.

'Eat up!' Spencer urged her. 'We won't have time for dinner.'

'Why's that?' Letty asked.

'I've only got us tickets for La Fenice.'

He pronounced it La Fenniss.

'La Fen-ee-chay,' Letty said automatically, realizing too late that she'd both offended him and ruined his announcement.

'How come it isn't Ven-ee-chay, then?' he asked defensively.

'Because Venice in Italian isn't Venice at all, it's Venezia,' she said.

'What does La Fen-ee-chay mean when it's at home?' he asked.

She was quite pleased that she didn't know the answer to that, because it went some way to restoring his dignity.

They looked it up on Google. It meant the phoenix, a mythical bird that rises from the ashes. Which, she thought, was quite appropriate, because she knew the theatre had burned down several times in its history. Or perhaps that was why it was called that? Maybe it was just a nickname given to it by the people of Venice.

'Wasn't it incredibly difficult to get tickets?' she asked.

Now he looked pleased.

'Yes, it was. We're seeing *La Traviata*, by the way. La Fenice is the first place it was ever shown,' said Spencer.

'You have done your research!'

'Happy?'

'Very happy,' she said.

'Then it was worth it,' he said, reaching across the table and taking her hand.

Letty's smile froze, her hand captive under his.

He'd bought tickets for *La Traviata* at La Fenice, for good-ness' sake. It seemed ungenerous not to let him hold her hand, and yet, and yet . . . It was their first physical contact, apart from a peck on the cheek, and it felt so much more intimate, especially here, in this intensely romantic setting.

This was the city of masked balls and Casanova, Letty thought as they walked into the pink marble foyer with its huge chan-delier. It was a place where the serene beauty of the exterior concealed undercurrents of duplicity and base desire. Aside from trappings of contemporary consumption – tiny quilted Chanel handbags on chains, jewels from Bulgari, and all the luxury watches that Spencer could ever aspire to – these people could be back in the eighteenth century, glancing at each other over their programmes, checking out the other boxes through their opera glasses.

What assumptions did they make about her and Spencer? she wondered. What was actually going on here? Spencer was the sort of person who had a business plan, an endgame. At some point the question of sex was going to arise, and she couldn't bear the idea of it getting to the point where it was requested as an explicit part of the deal. This had to stop, and yet sitting in a gilded box surrounded by golden cherubim, looking up at a sky-blue ceiling with the Graces floating above, felt like being in heaven.

'It's funny how times change, isn't it?' Spencer said as they wandered back to the hotel. 'I mean, in those days, the guy's reputation was going to be ruined by him shacking up with a prostitute. Now, it's no big deal. So the story doesn't really make sense any more.'

Letty felt slightly alarmed by this analysis.

'My main problem is nobody would sing like that if they

were about to die, would they?' Spencer said. 'Maybe next time we can do something I like and you know nothing about.'

'Maybe . . .'

'I could take you to a football match.'

'What makes you think I don't know about football?' she asked.

He stopped in the middle of a bridge.

'Who did Dennis Bergkamp play for?'

'Arsenal and the Netherlands,' she said.

'Bloody hell! He was my childhood hero! Have you ever been to a football match?'

'Just one, at White Hart Lane,' she told him.

'You're a Spurs supporter?'

'No. A friend of mine was.'

'Because that could be a problem . . .'

'In what sense?' she asked.

He laughed. 'Well, I couldn't introduce you to any of my mates, could I? Then again, maybe I want to keep you all for myself.'

Tell him now, Letty thought, as they walked past a shop window full of Carnevale masks, some elegant, some grotesque. With their bare black eyes staring at her, she couldn't seem to find the words.

In the room, Letty made straight for the bathroom, showering, brushing her teeth and changing into the long white T-shirt she wore to sleep in, grateful to find luxurious fluffy white robes hanging from the door. When she came back into the room, she was relieved to see that Spencer had transferred a pillow to the sofa.

She sat on the edge of the bed, conscious of his gaze on her back, then slipped the robe off and herself under the sheet in as quick a movement as possible.

She heard him stand up and go into the bathroom, and

when he came out, he switched off the lights and lay down on the sofa.

'Goodnight!' she said.

The dark silence felt loud with the injustice of the situation, Letty knew she would never sleep.

After a few minutes she sat up.

'Look, I'd much rather sleep on the sofa myself.'

'I'm fine.'

'I want to make it clear that I don't want to have sex . . .'

'I'd gathered that.'

'But, it's a huge bed . . .'

Unable to say anything more, she lay down again, turning to rest on her side right at the edge of the bed, leaving at least five feet of space for him.

For a while he did nothing, but then she heard him get up and climb into the other side of the bed, making no attempt to kiss or touch her. She lay listening to the rhythm of his breathing change and snatches of conversation from the street below becoming less and less frequent, until the only sound was the shift and creak of boats against their moorings. She had never actually fallen asleep in bed with a man before. With Josh it was always in the afternoons, after school. They'd had to keep as quiet as possible, stifling giggles with pillows so that Marina would not suspect. The only time they'd gone to his place – the final time – they'd used his mother's bed. Probably because he didn't want the world to see his single bed with its Spider-Man duvet. The frilly pinkness of Josh's mother's taste, the mock rococo white and gold headboard to which he'd tied her willing wrists with chiffon scarves they'd bought in Poundland together, hardly able to keep their hands off each other in the shopping aisle at the thought of what they were about to do, the incredible turn-on of trusting someone so much . . .

Letty squeezed her eyes shut, trying to stop the images racing through her brain and the sound of her pleading with him, 'Yes, yes, do anything you want, give it to me, more, more, more . . .'

It had followed her down every corridor and into every classroom.

When she woke in the morning, she was surprised to see Spencer already up and dressed.

'I'll see you downstairs,' he said.

A gentleman, Letty thought, thinking of Marina.

He did a double-take when she appeared at breakfast wearing the fifties dress and the white slingbacks, her hair scraped up into a high ponytail.

'You look unreal,' he said.

She'd realized in New York that this was his phrase for paying a big compliment, rather than a comment about her being weird.

'Can we go to Burano?'

'Is that the island where they make glass?' he asked.

'That's Murano, I think. This one is further away.'

'Any particular reason?'

'My grandmother recommended it.'

'Good enough for me,' he said. 'Let's get a gondola.'

'Oh, I think it's miles too far for a gondola,' Letty told him. 'We have to go there by *vaporetto*.'

'Vrrooom,' Spencer said, making a speedboat kind of gesture with his hand.

The journey took almost an hour, and when they arrived Burano was not at all as she had expected. It no longer felt like Venice; more like a humble coastal village, a community for artisans and workers out of sight of their wealthy aristocratic employers. The main streets were canals, but they were only large enough for little boats. What was beautiful about the island was that all the houses were painted in bright paintbox colours – blue, pink, yellow, green – making it feel almost like a child's drawing of a place.

'You match the houses,' said Spencer, stopping to take a selfie of the two of them against adjacent pink and blue dwellings.

Marina's exact words. Letty had the almost eerie feeling that she was walking in her grandmother's footsteps. She was aware that she looked so unusual in her grandmother's dress that people were stopping to take pictures of her, but with her eyes behind dark glasses, it was almost as if it wasn't really her, just a role she was playing.

On the main street, there were tiny shops selling table linen made of Burano lace.

Letty bought a single round doily for Marina's bedside table. Spencer pondered over a tablecloth and napkins, finally deciding against.

'People don't use tablecloths any more, do they?' he asked, making Letty wonder who he'd had in mind for the gift.

In the square, where they sat at a pavement table drinking glasses of light white wine, an old man was playing the accordion, a couple of little girls dancing round and round in a circle.

Letty didn't know if it was the heat, the dress that smelled faintly of age, or the alcohol so early in the day, but she had the strangest feeling that her life was swirling around her, as if somehow she was supposed to be in this place, that it held a profound significance for her, but she couldn't quite grasp what it was. Had the old man with the accordion always played here? she wondered. Had he been a young man when Marina had danced here? She was certain that she had been here in this spot. She could feel it so strongly.

When they started walking back to the *vaporetto* station, Letty realized that wearing a pair of pointed shoes with slingbacks and no tights on a hot day had been a silly idea. Puffy blisters were turning to sore wet patches on her heels and toes, making walking in the shoes impossible. The boat was about to leave and *vaporetti* to the island were infrequent.

'Do you want a piggyback?' Spencer asked.

He carried her to the quayside, earning a round of applause from the delighted Italians already on board.

Back at the hotel, she went to the bathroom to wash and tend to her feet. When she came out, he was standing at the window. When he turned, he looked disappointed.

'What?' she said, looking down at the shorts and T-shirt she'd changed into. Surely there wasn't a dress code for the gondola ride he'd booked.

'You looked so sexy in that dress,' he said. 'It was all I could do not to fuck you all the way back across the lagoon.'

It was a curious relief to hear the words finally spoken.

He was a good-looking man who was incredibly generous to her, she thought, and now the cards were on the table and she had to make a decision. It wasn't that he was unattractive, more that she saw him with the same detachment she might look at a film star who was inarguably handsome but not her type.

It couldn't be worse than what had happened with Josh, could it? Perhaps it might even be preferable to have sex without love. Perhaps her mistake had been to think that one was inseparable from the other.

They were in the Danieli with the Venetian lagoon lapping outside, in the city of Casanova and James Bond. It was almost weirder not to have sex, wasn't it? They were grown-ups. What had she got to lose?

She looked straight at him, then suddenly he was pushing her back onto the bed, pinning her arms behind her head, and when she tried to say, 'No! Not like this,' pulling her shorts down over her narrow hips, tearing her panties aside and entering her, panting on top of her for what was probably only thirty seconds, but felt like a lifetime of powerlessness.

*

The following morning, Letty returned to the house in Belsize Park, limping because of the blisters on her feet and the rawness inside that went all the way from her groin to her belly button. She was about to put her key in the door when it opened.

Her father's face was streaked with tears.

'I'm so sorry, Letty,' he said.

27

June

ALF

Gina had been dropping hints about her birthday. She was going to be twenty-five, but she kept calling it 'a big birthday'. In some ways, she seemed younger; in others, older and more sophisticated. It was grown up for a twenty-five-year-old to own a flat and a brand-new car, to order things like Chanel soap on the internet because they didn't sell it in Boots, or buy him Ted Baker shirts that he couldn't wear except at her flat, because people would assume that he'd shoplifted them. But she was also really easy to please, and Alf loved seeing her face light up when he bought her a gift, even something as cheap as a white chocolate Magnum from the garage. He planned to do something special for her birthday, not just to even things up a bit, but because he enjoyed the buzz he got from surprising her.

He had organized the weekend off work weeks before, wanting to be fresh for his A level English exam on the Monday. He was spending so much time out of the house his mum wouldn't even realize he was away. She assumed he had a girlfriend. She'd always been cool about him sleeping over, after giving him a strict talking to about contraception when he was fifteen. Donna was maddening in some ways, but she wasn't a hypocrite.

Relations at home had stabilized, maybe because he wasn't around much. Occasionally, his mum muttered about making sure he was doing enough schoolwork, but he always turned up on time to help her with her classes, so she couldn't push it. The hostile words they had spoken to each other still seemed to hang in the air, like a slight smell of drains – always there, not quite bad enough to call the council – but since Alf had secretly been seeing Gina, he felt so much more relaxed about life, it was just easier to pretend there wasn't a problem.

When you hadn't had sex for a while, you could forget how much difference it made. Since the first time, he and Gina never stopped. The more they did it, the more they wanted it.

Gina was good at sex. She knew a lot of tricks and she was up for anything. There was an urgency to her enjoyment, as if she wanted to get as much of him as she could and then some. Alf often found himself remembering what Cal had said about her right at the start.

'She's in her prime, mate, and you're in yours. They say it's all downhill from here.'

At school, Alf was good at covering his tracks. He'd had a lot of practice during boyhood. By the time people had discovered he was a dancer, Alf was such a well-established footballer the other lads were more curious than critical, occasionally trying to do pirouettes themselves and realizing how much skill was involved. And if any of the rugby players ever accused him of being gay, he was old enough by then to say, 'So how come I've got my hands on a good-looking girl every night, while you've got your head stuck up another boy's arse?' Which was a line he'd got from Sadie.

It was ironic that, in a way, Sadie had made it happen with Gina. Gina said it would have happened anyway. She said she knew from the first time she saw him at the audition. Alf had slightly altered his own chronology to make out he'd always fancied her too. Fact was, he had never given it serious thought until the black lace thong, but since then he'd thought about little else.

Secrecy gave the relationship an added buzz of excitement. It turned him on when he and Miss Jones walked straight past each other in a school corridor, and he caught a waft of the perfume he'd watched her spraying around her shoulders that morning, as she stared at him in the mirror when he was getting out of the shower.

Sometimes it felt a bit surreal, just the two of them in a glass box overlooking the sea, like he was fucking a fantasy woman. But afterwards, Gina would snuggle up next to him in the white cotton sheets that she got laundered each week and delivered back all fresh and smelling of ironing, and chatter away about the holidays they'd go on when he finished school. A friend of hers had been to the Maldives and said it was incredibly romantic; Gina had always wanted to see the Galapagos Islands where the turtles were. He'd lie there thinking that they were big plans given that they'd never even caught a tram up to Fleetwood, but not wanting to spoil the make-believe.

It was her longing to go away somewhere together that gave him the idea for her birthday present. His first thought was a show in London, but Gina's dad lived in London and he was minted. A hotel at the very top of Alf's budget would still fall short of what Gina was used to. And going down to London would involve catching the train, where there was always a risk they'd be spotted. If he couldn't give her luxury, Alf decided he'd give her beauty. The Lake District was drivable. During term time, it was unlikely anyone from school would pitch up in the same place on the same weekend as they were there, especially not if he booked a cottage, not a hotel. He got it all planned without her knowing.

On the Friday, the biggest bouquet anyone had ever seen was delivered to the school for Gina, causing all sorts of speculation about who had sent it.

'Dad always used to send me birthday flowers at school,' Gina told him. 'If people know it's your birthday, they're nice to you all day.'

There must have been two hundred quids' worth of flowers, Alf estimated, and when he woke her up in the morning and told her what they were doing, Gina insisted on taking the flowers with them. So it was the bouquet in the front and Alf lying along the back seat of the pink Cinquecento until they got out of Blackpool, as if he was in a getaway car.

The cottage near Buttermere looked picturesque on the photos. What he hadn't paid enough attention to was the main road it was on, which was why it was so affordable. But there were roses round the door and a bunch of wildflowers in a vase on the table. The OTT bouquet from Gina's father looked completely out of place.

The woman who met them with the keys pointed out the pint of milk in the fridge and, in the cupboard, some teabags, coffee sachets and sugar.

'You've thought of everything,' Gina said.

She wasn't even exaggerating. Gina was the least practical woman Alf had ever known. Her idea of cooking was stabbing a few holes in the film of a ready meal before putting it in the microwave, or ordering in a pizza. She had never bothered to replenish the coffee capsules after the complimentary box you got when you bought the machine ran out.

'Checkout time is noon,' the host said, handing Alf the keys, leaving him and Gina alone.

'Which bed shall we sleep in?' Gina asked, bouncing on each of the three beds upstairs, like Goldilocks.

'We could try them all?' Alf suggested.

'Oh God, Alf,' she said, wrapping herself round his body. 'I love being with you.'

There was a whole world of difference between 'I love being with you' and 'I love you', and they were both careful to stick to the first, although when she looked at him with those liquid blue eyes, he sometimes thought she wanted to say it. He didn't know how he'd reply if she did, but he thought he'd probably go with 'I love you too', because he felt great with her, and he wanted to protect her, not upset her. And that's what love was, wasn't it?

They locked the door carefully, making sure that Alf had the keys, and went for a walk. It felt weird being out in the open, and he wasn't sure if he should maybe put his arm around her. They knew each other's naked bodies inside and out, but the simple act of holding hands, fully clothed, felt charged with a risky kind of intimacy. Each time a car drove past, it was like both of them held their breath, fearing they were going to be seen together.

When the path divided, they automatically veered off along the fork that took them by the lake, and the nerve-wracking noise of approaching cars was replaced by birdsong and the lapping of small waves as the wind blew across the water. It felt nice, wandering along, occasionally stopping to say how lovely the view was, then dropping a kiss on her lips, before walking on again. It helped calm him about his upcoming exam. Gina had now read the books on the syllabus so that she could help him, and they ran through the key points he needed to remember. A few hikers passed them going in the opposite direction, giving them odd looks which Alf assumed was because neither of them were wearing suitable clothes. Gina was in white jeans and silver ballerina-type flats that were her only concession to practicality, since she usually wore heels. He was in jeans and trainers. Neither of them had bothered with jackets because the sun was shining when they left the cottage.

He estimated that they were about two thirds of the way round the lake when the sun suddenly disappeared, leaving only bright curls of light around the edges of dark thunderclouds. Then the skies opened. They stood in the scant shelter of a tree, trying to decide whether it would be quicker to go back the way they'd come, or continue the last bit of the circuit. Then Gina remembered you weren't supposed to stand under trees in a storm, so he thought they'd be better off choosing the shorter route. It was low-lying and boggy. Gina's jeans were spattered, and the squelching mud kept grabbing her pumps from her feet. He could feel the wetness seeping into his trainers and creeping up the legs of his jeans. He hadn't brought another pair. He was cross with himself and a bit irritated with Gina screaming every time there was a clap of thunder that they should have gone the way they knew.

When they eventually got back to the cottage, he let Gina have the first shower, and by the time it was his turn the hot water had run out. He had to put his wet jeans back on. The cottage felt cold and damp as a continual stream of traffic sloshed along the road outside.

'We could light a fire,' Gina said, looking at the logs in the fireplace.

'I think they're ornamental,' Alf said. He'd never lit a real fire and was quite sure Gina hadn't either. He didn't want to take the risk of trying in case the chimney hadn't been swept, and setting the whole place ablaze.

'Shall we order in a Chinese?' Gina asked.

'I'm not sure they do delivery in the Lake District,' he said.

'So I'm going to have to drive us, am I?' she said.

'Looks that way,' he said.

All the preparation and he'd still managed to muck it up.

*

The sky was clear again on the Sunday morning, the sun coming round the edge of the floral curtains. Alf tiptoed downstairs to make a cup of coffee.

He'd wanted it to be perfect for her and it hadn't been, but, as she'd said, this way it was like being in a romcom where everything goes wrong. It hadn't gone *that* wrong, but he knew what she was getting at.

Gina stretched and yawned when he put the coffee down beside her.

'Today is my treat,' she said. 'Girl can't have too many treats on her birthday, can she, and Dad sent some money for us to have a good time.'

'Did you tell your dad about us?' Alf asked, shocked.

'He suspected something was going on. He's cool about it.'

While he was downstairs in the kitchen, Gina had been looking up spa hotels. The place she drove them to was so swanky Alf felt embarrassed about walking into reception given the state his trainers were in, but they were immediately issued with robes and slippers wrapped in plastic. Gina had booked side-by-side massages at two. Alf had never had a massage in his life, but after the initial fear of getting a hard-on, he thought it was something he could get used to. Gina, who'd started out chatting to the masseuse, gradually stopped talking, and the room was incredibly peaceful as they lay face down in a haze of essential oils, surrounded by gentle music that sounded like the sea.

Afterwards, they had tea in a conservatory with palm trees – three tiers of plates with finger sandwiches, scones and cream, and tiny cakes that tasted intensely of chocolate and passionfruit and a pink flavour he couldn't work out, until Gina told him it was rose.

'Guess what?' She leaned across the table. 'I've booked to stay the night.'

'But my exam is tomorrow afternoon!' he said.

'And I have to be at work in the morning. So we can chill, get an early night. We can even do some revision if you want. We'll leave early tomorrow morning. Traffic will be better when we're not stuck with everyone who's returning from their weekend in the Lakes. You'll have plenty of time to go home and freshen up before the exam.'

'But . . .' Alf was sure there was a logical objection flitting around at the back of his brain, but he couldn't seem to pin it down.

'Come and see the room at least,' Gina said.

The bed was enormous, the pillows as soft as a cloud.

'I'll make sure you get a good night's sleep,' Gina said, loosening the belt of his towelling robe.

28

July

LETTY

One of Frances's colleagues had given her a piece of paper with a pie chart called the Grief Wheel, which showed the progression of bereavement. It was clearly a comfort to Frances to have a written document demonstrating that Letty's reactions were not abnormally extreme and that shock, protest and guilt would one day give way to acceptance. For Letty, unable to tell her mother that her feelings of loss and hopelessness were not just because of Marina's death, the regular appearance of the Grief Wheel was an additional irritant, which she wanted to grab from Frances's hand and tear into tiny pieces.

Frances advised Letty not to get rid of the dress she had been wearing when Marina died. She was angry now, and that was natural, she said, but she had nothing to be angry about and in time she would see that.

'I'm not angry,' Letty shouted, driving Frances from her room, because Letty never usually raised her voice.

She was not angry with the dress, nor with Marina, but she was angry with Ivo, and with Oscar and Raj, who were planning to go ahead with their wedding in Greece. How could they even think of celebrating? But mainly she was angry with

Frances, because it was always Frances who made the decisions in the family. And they had decided not to tell her until she got home. They didn't want to spoil her lovely weekend, they said. But if they had, she would have received the message on the boat on the way back from Burano, and everything would have been different.

'Were you trying to warn me?' Letty sometimes asked the empty bed, where she would often kneel and talk to her grandmother as if she was still there.

Then the logical bit of her brain would prevail. There was absolutely no way Marina could have willed the massive stroke that killed her, in order to get Frances to ring Letty in Venice to summon her home, thereby avoiding the horror of that night.

After the first rushed time, she'd locked herself in the bathroom at the Danieli trying to decide what to do for the best, certain that Spencer would want to do it again, if only to prove that he wasn't the sort of guy who prematurely ejaculated, like a frustrated teenager. After the way he'd pinned her down, she didn't think he was going to take no for an answer. She didn't have her phone in the bathroom to see if there were any flights that evening, and if there were, she probably couldn't afford them. She certainly didn't have the money for a water taxi to take her back to the airport, and by the time she'd worked out the public transport options she was pretty sure the last flight would have left. If getting out of Venice wasn't an option, maybe leaving the hotel was, but again, it would involve getting her stuff together. Would he allow that? When she thought she heard the door to the bedroom close, she wondered if he had gone out, and decided to make a dash for it. But when she opened the bathroom door, he was standing with a champagne flute in his hand and another beside an ice bucket on the table, trails of tiny bubbles rising through pale gold.

'To us!' he said, raising the glass.

'I've got a headache,' Letty said.

'Champagne's the best cure I know.'

He didn't believe her, and why should he? The headache was invented and she wasn't good at pretending.

'I'm really sorry, but I think this was a mistake . . .' she started.

Spencer put his glass down on the table, his expression darker than she had seen it before.

'You really are the worst kind of cock-tease,' he said.

'I'm sorry,' she said, willing herself to cry – surely he'd take pity on her if she cried? – but fear had somehow switched off her emotions.

He picked up the second glass of champagne and brought it over to her. Taking her right hand from her side, he put the glass into it.

'Have a drink,' he ordered.

When room service arrived with a whole dressed lobster and another bottle of champagne, he was on top of her. The fact that he got up, pulled on his robe, and let the waiter into the room, tipping him generously, while she lay right there in the bed, made her feel more degraded than the way he turned her unresponsive body whichever way he wanted it. When she tried to fight him off he held his hand over her neck, thumb and forefinger splayed, not hard enough to bruise, but with just enough pressure to show that he could if he wanted.

'You know, you'd enjoy it far more if you just relaxed,' he said.

Letty counted three times, but maybe it was more than that. The champagne dulled the pain, so she drank more, drifting towards oblivion only to wake up with the feeling that she was suffocating because he was inside her again.

In the morning, he stood at the window drinking cappuccino, as a cruise liner as big as a block of flats glided surreally past behind him and the room vibrated.

'They'll kill the golden goose with those things, if they're not careful,' he said.

There was another cappuccino on the table, which he brought over to the bed, presenting it to her, then reaching over to stroke a strand of hair back from her face.

'You're beautiful,' he said, smiling as she instinctively flinched away from him, then leapt out of the way as she suddenly put her hand over her mouth and ran to the bathroom to throw up.

When she finally emerged he said, with a worried look, 'You are on the pill?'

Surely he didn't think you got morning sickness just hours after? It was a bit late for him to be concerned now.

She nodded, even though she wasn't, unable to bear the idea of him thinking for a second that he might have got her pregnant.

Letty's periods had been erratic since her eating disorder. She bought a pregnancy test, not trusting the result until several more tests had proved negative. She also knew she ought to be checked at the STD clinic. Even though she was symptomless, she must be at risk from a man who didn't even consider using protection when sleeping with a virtual stranger.

The clinic was in the same hospital that Marina had been admitted to. When Letty was looking for directions, she saw the young doctor who had diagnosed her grandmother's first stroke approaching with a smile on his face, which faded as she walked straight past him, heading into orthopaedic outpatients, where she waited for several minutes before venturing back into the corridor.

The nurse's expression did not change when Letty admitted to unprotected sex with someone she didn't know very well, but looked concerned when she said, 'I didn't want it.'

She left the hospital with a leaflet for the rape crisis line.

Had she been raped? Letty asked herself. Could consent be given and withdrawn within ten seconds? The answer was technically yes, of course, but it wasn't relevant as nobody would believe her.

The leaflet said that it helped to talk to someone. She couldn't risk telling Frances. She would probably think she should press charges, and then she'd have to tell her that she'd accepted not just one but two lavish weekends abroad from a man she'd met through a website designed to put young women in touch with sugar daddies. What was she thinking? How could she have been so stupid? And wasn't it the case that the woman's background was always held against them? Josh's film was probably still somewhere on the internet. She was stuck in a never-ending loop of shame.

It was a mistake to take the dress to the charity shop, but not for the reasons Frances said. It was so beautiful that they put it on a mannequin in the window. Driving to the funeral parlour to help choose the coffin, or the florist's to decide on the flowers, or to Rollo's to discuss the order of service, her father always seemed to select a route that took them past the shop, so it was a more constant reminder than it would have been if Letty had put the dress back in the trunk at the bottom of Marina's bed.

The third time she passed it, Letty felt a new rush of panic as it occurred to her that there was a risk Spencer might also drive past. It could be on his way to work for all she knew, and he would see it, and then he would know the area where she lived, which she had never told him. Since Venice she had switched off her phone, not daring to look and see if he had tried to contact her. After a sleepless night, she decided to go back to the shop and buy the dress back herself. But when she got there, it was no longer in the window. Letty asked the shop assistant where it was and was told it had just been sold.

'To a woman?'

The shop assistant gave her a funny look.

'Someone famous, actually. I can't tell you who, obviously. Let's just say model, lives in Primrose Hill.' She winked as if Letty would know who she was talking about.

Apparently whoever it was had paid a hundred and fifty pounds for it.

Letty found herself staring at the chart on the wall behind the till, trying to work out what proportion of a goat or a bee-hive or a school in Africa that would purchase. Then she walked out in a kind of daze.

Marina's death split the family, even before her failure to leave a new will was discovered. Rollo wanted Marina to be buried with their father. Frances insisted that Marina had told her that she wanted to be cremated, and her ashes scattered in Italy. Letty supported her, but Ivo said he couldn't remember his mother expressing any strong views to him.

'I don't like taking sides,' he said.

'But you are taking bloody sides, don't you see?' Frances screamed at him. 'Because unless you agree with me, then your brother will have it his way! What you don't like taking is responsibility,' she told him. 'But for God's sake, your own mother . . . !'

'I had no idea you two were so close,' her father said sarcastically.

'Well, fuck you!' Frances shouted. 'Just trying to do what she wanted, but after all I am only a woman, and so was she, so our views – even on this! – don't really count . . .'

'Only you could turn this into an issue of sexual politics!'

'Please, let's just make a decision,' Rollo had said.

Marina was buried, after a Catholic mass – with Frances, ironically, the only one who knew when to kneel and when to stand up, because her upbringing had been Catholic whereas

Ivo and Rollo's father Max had insisted on raising them as atheists.

It was a dismal ceremony, followed by a dismal wake in an Italian restaurant that Marina had never even been to.

For several weeks, Letty couldn't get out of bed, even though she found it hard to sleep. She couldn't eat. The thought of food made her sick. Her tears were so near the surface that totally inconsequential things could trigger a convulsion of sobbing. Her books remained untouched on her desk, as she no longer found any consolation in literature.

One night, she dreamed that she was standing at the window in Marina's bedroom, and her grandmother, lying on the bed behind her, said, 'Beautiful women are always cast as madonnas or whores. It is the way men try to control them.'

Letty woke up absolutely convinced that she had heard her grandmother speaking to her, and for a blissful moment she wanted to rush into Marina's room and tell her everything. Then she remembered she wasn't there.

Perhaps Marina had actually said this, Letty thought, closing her eyes, trying to remember. Perhaps one Sunday lunch during some discussion with Frances? Perhaps explaining the plot of *La Traviata*, which Marina had taken Letty to see when she was an inquisitive nine-year-old who wanted to know why her namesake Violetta could not be with Alfredo, the man who loved her.

Marina was still with her, she thought. Not as a ghostly presence in the house, but because they had spent so much time together. Letty knew what Marina would say, even if she was no longer there to say it. People lived on – not just through their genes, but in their stories. And that was such a comfort.

29

August

ALF

When Alf went to school to get his A level results, his nerves were worse than they'd ever been before a performance, even though he knew what was going to happen. His fingers shook as he opened the envelope. There was one surprise. He'd got an A for Drama and he hadn't expected that. There was a different examining board for the English A level. His grade was on the second piece of paper, beneath the Drama result. He knew what it was going to say, but until he looked he could still hang on to the hope that there would be a way out.

Around him, girls were screeching and hugging each other. Nobody approached to ask how he'd done, maybe because of the look on his face, maybe because he'd kept his distance since they formally left school for the revision period. Alf hadn't gone to the prom. He didn't want to be in a position where he had to dance with Sadie, or talk to her. If anyone could guess what was going on, it would be her.

Alf left the building envelope in hand, but stopped himself looking until he was outside the grounds.

Unclassified.

Which meant he had failed.

It felt like he'd been winded.

Now he had to face telling his mum, and her crying and her anger. She'd say the exam result didn't matter, but lying to her face did.

But if he hadn't lied, Gina would have lost her job. And losing her job would always be on her record, whereas Alf failing his exam didn't have to be permanent. Mr Marriot could appeal to the examining board; Mr Marriot adored him. Or he could retake. Or the dance school would make an exception . . .

All the reasons Gina had come up with, standing knee-deep in stinging nettles on the hard shoulder of the M6, had seemed plausible enough at the time.

Now, staring at the stark reality of his result on paper, Alf knew none of that was going to happen. After all the thinking he'd done, he still hadn't a clue how to justify it without dumping it on Gina, and the whole point was to avoid that, so all he'd done was put off the moment.

They'd had a blow-out on the journey back from the Lakes. They were in the middle lane and Gina had done well not to panic. She'd kept the steering wheel steady and turned on her hazard lights, remembering to look in the mirror to check the traffic behind her before bringing the car safely across to the hard shoulder. It was only once they'd come to a halt that the danger they'd just escaped had hit her. It had taken a while to calm her down enough to call the RAC. The telephone operator had instructed them to get out of the car, climb over the barrier and wait. But it was Monday morning rush hour, and by the time the breakdown service had turned up, there was no way of getting back to Blackpool in time for the exam.

At eight o'clock in the morning, Gina had called the school to let them know she would be late.

If Alf had been thinking straight, he probably should have called Gary to come and give him a lift. But with Gina screaming at him that they couldn't be seen together, he'd decided to wait and hope that the rescue service would turn up in time. When they still weren't there by noon, he phoned the school to say that he had a stomach bug and he didn't think he was going to be well enough to sit the exam.

What he hadn't reckoned on was Mr Marriot dialling his home number to ask how bad Alf really was, because the exam was so important, and Donna ringing Alf to ask what the fuck was going on. Then he'd made it worse by telling her he'd been in an accident, so she was panicking, even though he said he was fine.

The trouble with lies was that a little one could so easily become an intricate web of deceit. When he finally showed up at home, Donna was so happy to see him back in one piece he didn't have to go into too much detail. When she asked what would happen about the exam, he told her it would be fine. He could retake it if necessary.

Mr Marriot wasn't as easy to fool. Perhaps he'd heard rumours. Perhaps it was too much of a coincidence that Miss Jones hadn't come into work on the very day that Alf had missed his exam with a clearly fictitious excuse.

'I can't make a case for you if I know you're lying to me, Alf,' he explained patiently, maintaining eye contact, even though Alf was doing everything he could to avoid looking at him. 'So I'll ask you again. What's going on here? You're a decent chap, Alf, but please don't sacrifice your future on behalf of someone else.'

Alf reckoned that they couldn't do anything to Gina if it was just speculation. If he admitted nothing, she'd be fine.

Mr Marriot said he was very disappointed in him, which felt worse than if he'd been angry.

Gina was convinced Mr Marriot was just saying that, and would relent.

Now, as Alf stood outside the school gate with his results in his hand, he saw the Head of English get into his car and his hopes lifted for a few seconds, but Mr Marriot drove straight past him, without even winding down the window to see how he'd done. He already knew, Alf thought. Teachers got the results the day before the students did, so they could ring up and advocate for the ones who'd missed their grades. Mr Marriot was cutting him adrift.

In a way it was a relief, Alf thought, because now he could think properly about what he was going to do. He started walking towards Gina's flat, then turned back towards home, realizing that Gina wasn't the person he wanted to be with – she would be all sex and cuddles and reassurance that everything was going to be all right. He knew it was about not wanting to see him unhappy, but it was also about not wanting to feel guilty herself, which was why she always had to make it seem like it wasn't such a big deal.

What he needed to do was to tell his mum. Lying to her all this time had eaten into him. Now at least it would be out there. I'm sorry I've disappointed you. I'm sorry I've thrown away an opportunity. But I will make you proud of me, Mum. Promise.

He wanted to feel her hug, and to hear her say, 'I'm always proud of you.'

Even if she didn't quite mean it right now, but she was his mum, and that's what family was for, wasn't it? To be there for you, whatever happened.

Donna was sitting at the kitchen table where he'd left her that morning before going up to school. She was pretending to act normal, except that it wasn't normal for her to be doing nothing. With the breakfast things put away, the washing-up done, the table wiped clean, she'd usually have the sewing machine out, or be struggling with her invoices on the software Gary had downloaded for her that was meant to make things easier but was twice the work, as far as she could see. As Alf walked in, she was trying hard to keep her facial expression neutral, but her eyes were darting between happy expectation and fearing the worst. At that moment he loved her so much, and felt so bad at letting her down he couldn't look at her.

'Failed English.'

'You're joking? You *are* joking, Alf?'

'Not joking. Got an A in Drama though!'

He was trying so hard not to cry it came out sounding flippant.

'You failed?!'

'It was the exam I missed.'

'But you can retake . . .'

'Can't. Not going to.'

'So which is it? Can't, or not going to?'

'Decided not to go to dance school.' Alf still couldn't answer the question directly. 'Don't want to have all those debts.'

'But Gary and I have been saving for you, and Mum and Dad have got a bit put aside too. We're all going to help you—'

'Can't see the point.'

'Can't see the point? The point is, you've got a gift! Point is, we all believe in you . . . Alfie . . . what's happened to you?'

He'd thought his mother didn't want him to go down to dance school in London. Nobody had told him that they were planning to support him. But how could they have done? For the past few months, he'd rarely been at home long enough to have a proper chat.

Alf couldn't hold the tears back any more. They came out in great coughs, as if he was choking out all the lies that had stuck like phlegm in his lungs. He could feel his mum hovering beside him, not knowing whether to touch him or not. And that was his fault too, because whenever she asked him something he didn't want to answer, he'd accused her of nagging him. So she no longer knew how to comfort him. He'd spent his life walking on eggshells round her, and now he'd made her do the same round him. He hated himself for that.

'Alfie,' she said softly. 'I need to know. And I promise I won't tell anyone. Are you on drugs?'

How out of touch they'd become that she could even think that.

'No,' he said, sniffing back tears.

'Is it a woman?'

He said nothing.

'Is she married, Alf?'

He felt ashamed that he'd allowed his mum to develop fears that were much worse than they needed to be.

'No. She's not married.'

'Is she in trouble? I mean . . .'

She meant pregnant.

'No! Course not!'

'Who is it, then?'

He owed it to his mum to tell her. He wanted to tell her. He wanted to say that it wasn't what it looked like. But he'd promised Gina.

'I'm the one who fucked up the exams,' he said. 'It's on me.'

The silence in the kitchen felt deep and sticky, like it was clutching at him, trying to pull him in, like he couldn't free himself from it without telling the truth.

He went to the fridge for a drink. In the door, next to the four pints of semi-skimmed, stood a bottle of proper champagne.

He turned round and saw that there was an envelope with his name written on in his mum's lap.

They had believed in him; they had bought champagne and a congratulations card. For all he knew, they'd organized a surprise party at the dance hall in his honour. Alf had never felt so rotten in his life.

He closed the fridge and backed out into the hall.

'We don't deserve this, Alf,' his mum said, her voice rising as she realized he was going out again. 'If you leave now without giving me an explanation, then don't bother coming back!'

She was bluffing, he thought, as the front door closed behind him.

'So, I know it hurts now, but really, it'll be easier with you living here, won't it?' said Gina.

She came across from the kitchen area and sat next to him on the sofa, taking his hand. It was generous of her to offer instantly to share her home, but he was expecting a bit of a discussion, a bit of sympathy maybe. Living with someone was a step you made together out of choice, not necessity. He didn't like the idea of swapping the feeling that he was taking up too much room in one place with feeling indebted in another, and not really having a home that felt like his.

'I can't be in hiding all my life,' Alf said.

Gina smiled, smoothed his hair back from his face.

'So, you've finished with school now. You're almost nineteen. I mean, I'm not saying we put an announcement in the paper, but we don't always have to be looking over our shoulder any more!'

It took a moment for the meaning of the words to sink in.

'You could have said that before!'

It came out sounding angrier than he meant. Gina shifted away from him on the sofa.

'You didn't ask,' she said. 'You never even bothered to text me about the A in Drama, which you seem to be forgetting in all this, Alf. I mean, an A in Drama is really good. It's not like you've got nothing.'

She made it sound as if he was being ungrateful.

'You knew?'

Of course she did. She'd been in school the previous day,

preparing her classroom for the new term. Had she actually asked Mr Marriot? Alf wondered.

'Why don't we go away for this last week of my holiday?' Gina suggested. 'When we get back, if anyone asks, we've just hooked up.'

He wasn't going to London now, so he could. The idea of getting away appealed. But then he'd have to come back, and nothing would have changed.

'I can't just go away and leave my mum,' he said.

'I thought she'd kicked you out.'

'She hasn't really, not if I explain . . .'

'You mean tell her I'm the reason you failed your exam?' Now Gina was the one who was on the verge of tears.

'I wouldn't say that!'

'That's what she'll think, though,' said Gina.

It *was* what Donna would think. Because in a way it was true, wasn't it? If Gina hadn't decided to book them into the luxury hotel, the situation wouldn't have happened. But you couldn't turn history back. If the tyre was always going to blow out on the motorway, who knew how things would have been different in busy traffic on the Sunday evening? They might really have been in an accident. Things might have been worse. You couldn't live your life thinking 'if only . . .'

No one died, as Gina often said.

'Let her cool down a bit . . . tell her when we get back.' She shifted her bottom back along the sofa. 'Everything will be all right, I promise, Alf,' she said, taking his hand and guiding it under her summer dress. She wasn't wearing anything underneath.

All his peers would be going out clubbing tonight, or celebrating with their families. Alf would probably serve some of them later in the pizzeria. Their lives were changing, but it felt like his had just stopped. And yet he knew that if he asked any of his mates if they'd rather be out getting rat-arsed at 'Spoons right now, or shagging Miss Jones, most of them would say he was the lucky bastard.

When he returned to Gina's after work, she'd already booked tickets for a week in Lanzarote, leaving him just a day's notice for his boss at the restaurant, who wasn't best pleased.

Another bridge burned, or another fresh start. It depended on your perspective.

There was nobody at home when Alf went back to get his passport. He'd flown without his mum a few times when he and Aimee competed in the Baltic countries. Donna always texted him – *Safe journey. Love you always* – before the flight, as if in case anything went wrong, it would be the last message that he'd see. And he always texted her – *Landed* – as soon as they touched down. He couldn't get on a plane without telling her.

He sat down at the kitchen table, trying to compose a note, but nothing seemed to begin to cover what he needed to say. Eventually, he wrote:

Dear Mum and Gary,
Need a break. Going to the Canary Islands. I'll text when I
get there.
I'm sorry.
Love, Alf

Turned out they would have known anyway, because the taxi driver who picked them up at five in the morning from Gina's for the airport was Terry, the drummer in the Stag Beetles, who didn't seem to get that Alf didn't want to chat. But when he finally stopped firing questions at him about what he was up to these days, Alf wished he'd kept him talking because he could see Terry checking Gina out in the rear-view mirror. It was early in the morning, so she wasn't wearing make-up and she looked young, but the matching suitcases weren't what you'd expect someone of Alf's age to own. Alf knew that a report would go back, and he wondered if 'petite, pretty, blonde, nice luggage' would be enough to give the game away.

There was no text message on his phone before he switched it off for the flight. He still texted *Landed* when they touched down, but didn't receive a reply.

30

October

LETTY

A new academic year, a new beginning, Letty thought, as she walked through the Parks towards the Bodleian on the first Saturday of her third year at the university.

The sky above the honey-coloured colleges of Oxford was almost as blue as it had been in Greece, where Oscar and Raj got married.

'Very *Mamma Mia!*' was the way Oscar had wanted it, which had turned out to be a literal description; one of Oscar's first jobs in theatre had been assisting the producer on the first run of the ABBA musical, and many of the guests had, at one time or another, starred in productions all over the world.

The wedding was perfect. The sun shone, the wine flowed, and several of the actors sang songs, giving it the vibe of a fantasy karaoke party where the singers sounded exactly like the original artists. Everyone was beautiful and happy. Real life felt a very long way away.

Frances had rented a villa with a pool at the top of a hill, which had an uninterrupted view of the sea. There were fig trees in the garden laden with green fruit that split to reveal luscious pink flesh inside, or fell to the ground and lay drying to a sticky toffeeness in the sun. With yoghurt and honey from the adjoining farm and lamb chops grilled on the barbecue, Letty's appetite began to return.

Swimming hundreds of lengths in the pool, she gradually began to re-engage with her body. In the afternoons, Frances donned a big straw hat and sat in the shade reading the Booker longlist on her Kindle. Letty lay feeling the sun on her skin, and started on the reading list for her third year, choosing to concentrate on Ancient Greek texts in the place where they had been written. The alphabet and a lot of the vocabulary of Modern Greek was the same, so when she went down to the village she could read the street signs and the local newspaper. But the pronunciation was so different that even when she practised sentences in advance, she still had to make do with pointing in the village shop.

It was as if the family had come to an unspoken agreement not to mention Marina or the fate of the house in Belsize Park, but to enjoy a two-week holiday away from everything, including mobile phones. Frances, who always rose to a challenge, declared after just two days' abstinence that it was the best thing she'd ever done. Letty hadn't even bothered to bring her phone with her. So she was a little surprised to see Ivo, who generally used his as little as she did, standing in the square near the water trough in the village early one morning with his handset pressed to his ear, speaking in an agitated way.

'OK then, Rollo,' he said, quickly switching it off when he saw Letty approaching.

'Dad!' she scolded.

'I know,' he said, smiling at her. 'Me of all people! Promise you won't tell your mother?'

It was like the pacts they'd made on childhood holidays. Can I have another gelato? Only if you promise not to tell your mother. Letty readily agreed, and they walked back up to the villa arm in arm.

*

On the evening they returned to London, Frances could wait no longer to reveal a plan that she'd obviously been devising all the time they'd been away. She had decided to propose to Rollo that they convert the house into three flats. One could be sold and the money split between both parties; another could be Rollo's to do what he liked with. She, Ivo and Letty would downsize, converting the basement and raised ground floor into a duplex, which would give them ample space. If there was enough money, they might even be able to go into the roof, converting the property into four flats instead of three, one of which could be for Letty after university.

It sounded like a huge amount of work to Letty. She was surprised Frances was so keen to hang on to the house. Letty had lived there all her life, but it didn't feel like the same place without Marina. Maybe they should all move on?

What surprised Letty was Ivo's decisiveness.

'Actually, I don't think it would work,' he declared. 'Surely it would be better for everyone to have a fresh start.'

It was uncharacteristic of him to express such a definite opinion.

'What about what I think?' Frances demanded.

'You can't always get what you want . . .'

'But you're getting what you want.'

It was the same old argument, but Letty wasn't as certain that on this occasion Frances would win. Ultimately, it was her father's family house. This was the one instance when his view would trump hers, especially since his agreement was needed in order to have any hope of bringing Rollo round to her plan.

Letty was quite relieved to escape back to the attic room in North Oxford, with its sunny view of treetops turning from gold to terracotta.

Having enjoyed swimming in Greece so much, Letty found a pool in Summertown and bought a second-hand bike to ride there. Physical exercise gave her an appetite for food. It was a way of ensuring she ate without having to think about it too much, and became as much a part of her routine as being first into the lower reading room of the Bodleian each morning.

On Saturdays, the library opened at ten instead of nine, so Letty took her break at midday instead of eleven. She caught sight of him just before he spotted her, but it was only a second or two, not enough time for her to do an about turn and find safety behind the security gate that barred access to non-students. She could feel her heart beating against her ribs.

'Long time, no see,' said Spencer.

She'd dreaded a moment like this, but when weeks had turned to months without him appearing, she'd grown complacent, persuading herself that he had got what he wanted and forgotten all about her. A man like him wouldn't have any problem finding a willing partner for lavish mini-breaks. Problem was, she realized now, she'd never really known what sort of a man he actually was.

'Coffee?' he said.

'No thanks.'

Why hadn't she rehearsed a plan of action? Something to say to him, at least?

'Lunch, then?'

She could turn round and go back up to the reading room, she thought. But he might wait, and by the time the library closed it would be getting dark and there would be fewer people around.

Better to get it over with.

'I'm not hungry,' Letty told him. 'But a quick coffee . . .'

'How about the King's Arms? I could murder a pie.'

It was early enough for them to find a table, although the only one left was very near the fruit machine, which kept playing short bursts of electronic tunes, its icons randomly flashing potential money prizes.

While he was at the food counter, she found herself thinking it was odd that he knew the name of the pub, the type of food it served and where you ordered it. Had he been there before? Had he come up to look for her before the beginning of term? It was a pub, she told herself. Pubs usually served pies. Perhaps he'd noticed the name on his way to the library. Had she ever told him she worked in the Bodleian? It would be easy enough to find out the principal Classics library, but the idea that he might have done research troubled her.

They would have a conversation, she tried to reassure herself, then it would be over. She stared at the clock. Ten past twelve. By one o'clock she would be free. She took a sip of her coffee, glad that he wasn't there to see her hand shaking so much she had to put the cup back in a puddle of liquid.

'How's Gran?' he said, returning to the table.

She'd always hated it when he referred to Marina like that.

'She's dead,' she said.

'Oh. Sorry to hear that.'

She said nothing.

'Had a good summer? No, obviously. Sorry,' he said. 'Anyway . . .' He raised the pint of beer he'd brought back from the bar. 'Here's to happier times.'

Letty stared towards the door, not wanting to make eye contact with him.

'So, any other places you'd like to visit?' he asked.

Was he actually thinking she would say yes, or was it a wind-up?

'I think we want different things.' She finally found some inadequate words.

'Really? What sort of things do you want?' he asked.

She had to be brave enough, Letty told herself. Be like Frances, not like Ivo. Sometimes confrontation was necessary.

'I don't want to see you any more,' she said, feeling a moment of triumph that she'd finally got it out.

'God, you're such a cock-tease,' he said, putting his hand on her knee under the table where no one else could see.

She shifted her chair sharply backwards, almost knocking over a man carrying three pints.

'I'm not. I really don't want to see you again. I don't even like you.'

Too far.

'You don't have to like me,' he said. 'I pay for your services, remember?'

'I didn't ask you to.' Letty could hear how weak those words sounded, how his response was there, unspoken but understood. *But you accepted it.*

She tried another tactic. 'You could have any woman you wanted.'

'But sometimes I only want you. It's like I can go for months without a curry, and then I just fancy one and nothing else will satisfy.'

'Surely not if I don't want you?'

He answered her question with a horrible smile.

It suddenly occurred to her that she didn't have to sit there with him if she didn't want to. She stood up. 'Goodbye.'

She stopped outside the pub, trying to decide whether to go back to the library or head to her room, or perhaps seek sanctuary in one of the colleges, where he wouldn't be allowed. In the second of deliberation, he had come out after her.

'We have fun,' he said, trying to catch her hand. 'So what's the problem?'

'The problem is that I don't like you,' she said, stepping away, wondering why the cruel words seemed to bounce right off him.

'You think you're better than me,' he said. 'But you're just a slut.'

That word, Josh's word, the cool girls' word, as degrading as a slap across her cheek, the word that had pursued her relentlessly until she found herself behind the locked doors of a psychiatric hospital.

How could she still be a slut, Letty wondered, when she was saying she didn't want sex?

'Please leave me alone,' she said, her voice rising to indicate that she was prepared to shout it if necessary. Surely somebody would help her if she screamed?

'I'm not going anywhere,' he said.

'I'll call the police!'

He laughed.

'I don't think the police would be interested if they knew about our arrangement, do you?'

'We don't have an arrangement.'

'So you say . . .'

He took out his phone, scrolling through his photos and stopping on the one of them he had taken on the Staten Island Ferry, then the one of them in Burano with the pink and blue houses behind them.

And then, suddenly, like an alarm going off, his phone rang as Letty was staring at the screen, and there was a green band displaying the name of the caller. Gina.

Spencer snatched the phone back and swiped the screen, turning away from Letty.

'They didn't?' he said.

Letty could hear a woman crying at the other end.

'Don't worry, I'll sort it out. Hey, calm down, princess. I'm on my way . . .'

When he turned back to Letty, she could see he was rattled.

'Got to run,' he said.

Was Gina his wife? Another girlfriend? Someone at work? It didn't sound like someone at work.

'I'll be back,' he said, before turning and walking away.

I'll be back. It was a line from a movie. *Terminator*. He was always referencing movies.

Letty returned to the library, but couldn't concentrate for the rest of the afternoon.

She took a different route back to North Oxford, looking over her shoulder every couple of seconds. Approaching the junction with her street, she walked straight past, doubling back further up the road when there were no other pedestrians in sight.

Upstairs in her room, as the light faded, leaving her in total darkness, she struggled to think of a plan. Then, after preparing a script in her head, she called her uncle Rollo. She was phoning on behalf of a friend, she would say, to ask his advice.

'It's very honourable of you to ring, Letty,' Rollo began. 'But I've come to a settled view, I'm afraid. And I don't think your pleading, understandable though it is, will change the verdict.'

'I'm really not calling about the house,' Letty tried to interrupt. But Rollo was used to arguing his case.

'I'm well aware that *prima facie*, it seems unfair. But I don't really see why I should simply agree to Frances's demands . . .'

Letty almost felt like shouting 'Objection!' as they did in American crime series, to shut him up.

'I have made my best efforts to be reasonable,' Rollo continued. 'Believe me, I am sympathetic to the situation Frances finds herself in. Especially now she's been made redundant.'

'Redundant?' Letty repeated.

Why hadn't Frances told her? Why did everyone in her family always think that she needed to be protected from bad news? Why didn't anyone treat her as a grown-up? What was she supposed to do now? Ring home innocently and try to get Frances to tell her? Pretend that they'd never had this conversation? But what if it then emerged that Rollo had told her and Letty had just carried on regardless?

Why didn't families ever just tell each other the truth, instead of creating whole ecosystems of deception from the tiniest seed of a secret?

'Was there something else?' Rollo asked.

'It's not really that important,' Letty said, ringing off quickly.

Rollo would probably think that she – or the 'friend' she was intending to ask on behalf of – was overreacting. Spencer had said, 'I'll be back!' but he'd made no physical threat. He'd been distracted by a phone call and he'd left. Of course the police wouldn't be interested.

But as she lay in bed that night, Letty didn't feel safe.

31

November

ALF

The worst time was when the school was deciding what would happen. Alf got a job labouring on a building site because he couldn't face serving people he knew in a restaurant. It was cold brutal work, starting and finishing in the dark as the nights drew in. It exhausted him physically, but he welcomed the exercise because he didn't even get two hours' dancing a week now that he and his mum weren't speaking. He developed muscles he'd never had before, which impressed Gina, who spent her mornings at the gym. In the afternoons all she seemed to do was internet shopping, and he didn't feel he could criticize, because it was her money and she didn't have a lot else to do.

Donna had gone up to the school to see Mr Marriot as soon as Terry reported seeing Alf and his new girlfriend. Ironically, it was the pink Cinquecento parked outside the flat rather than Terry's description that had given her away. When they returned from Lanzarote, the Head had ordered Gina not to come to work until a review had been carried out. With Alf now living with her, it was pretty clear what had been going on, but the mitigating factors were that, apart from a couple of cover lessons, Gina hadn't actually taught him; and Alf had been eighteen, and not an immature or inexperienced eighteen-year-old either. In the absence of any evidence or a formal complaint, nobody wanted to bring the police in. Not even Donna, who was furious but not vindictive.

'Just stick to denying that anything of a sexual nature happened until you'd finished school and you should be fine,' was the advice Gina's father obtained from a lawyer in London.

As it was, nobody asked him, so Alf didn't have to lie.

The week before half term, it was mutually agreed that Gina would leave the school voluntarily. The Head suggested that a different career might suit her better. Gina railed at the injustice of his decision, almost as if she'd come to believe that because no evidence had been produced, she'd done nothing wrong. But Alf thought she'd probably been lucky. And Stuart clearly felt the same.

'It's all about moving on now, princess. Chalk it up to experience.'

Stuart was amazing. He negotiated a deal with a local estate agent to let the flat out. It wasn't a good time to sell, but the rent would give Gina a bit of an income cushion until she got herself sorted out. He said they could stay as long as they liked with him in London.

Gina decided that she didn't want to rush into a new job. It had all been so stressful, she thought they deserved a break. Her best friend Sally had been in touch and suggested visiting her and her boyfriend in Rome. Alf had always wanted to travel, so why not start there?

Alf didn't have any better suggestions. He had a couple of thousand pounds saved from working. Lots of people his age took time off. So why not? He couldn't see a future for himself in Blackpool either.

Gina had so much stuff to drive down to London that there wasn't room in the car for him and his backpack, so he offered to get the train. It suited him to spend a few hours on his own.

There were goodbyes he wanted to say, although he didn't tell Gina that.

His mum wasn't at the dance hall, and she wasn't at home either. His bedroom hadn't been touched since he left it, although the bed had been made up with clean sheets. His schoolwork folders were stacked as he'd left them on the desk. In the cupboard, his dance clothes were still hanging in their plastic coverings. On the windowsill, his football trophies had gathered a layer of dust. With its single bed, football wallpaper and team photo of the Tangerines during their brief time in the Premiership, it was like looking at a snapshot of his childhood with nostalgia for something that was lost. But the child's bedroom didn't quite tell the whole truth about his life, he thought; a bit like the photo in the dance hall cabinet of him when he was a little boy and his mum dancing ring o'roses on the beach, laughing into each other's faces like they hadn't a care in the world.

'She's changed you,' his mum had said the last time he saw her, when he'd gone around to plead with her not to make a formal complaint against Gina.

Was that it? Or was the truth that he'd grown up, and neither of them had handled it that well? All squashed together in Gary's house, little issues became a big deal. They should probably have sat down and talked it all through, but they didn't know how to do that, so they both pushed each other away instead. He closed his bedroom door. Too late now.

Sometimes he wondered whether if he'd passed his English A level, he and Gina would even have continued, with him down in London and her up here working. Now that it wasn't secret, the sex didn't have the same incredible sinful urgency. But it was still great. And the controversy had forged a kind of bond between them, like it was them against the world. They'd both given up so much they had to stick together now, otherwise it would have been a waste.

*

Cheryl's dogs were pleased to see him, at least. They jumped up and down around his legs, and his gran's face lit up when she saw him standing alone in the porch. But her face set back into a pursed grimace as soon as he told her he'd come to say goodbye.

'You'd better come in,' she said, but she didn't show him into the living room, or offer him tea in the kitchen as she always used to.

'Do you know where Mum is?'

'I do, but I won't tell you if she hasn't,' Cheryl said cryptically.

'There's nothing wrong, is there?'

'There's nothing wrong.'

The words 'apart from you' seemed to hang in the cold hallway air.

'I didn't want to leave without saying goodbye,' he said.

'For whose benefit?'

'Does it matter? Mine, probably. You're the one who says not to let the sun go down on a row.'

'It wasn't a row, Alf. We all believed in you, supported you, trusted you. We never thought you'd lie to us.'

'I know,' he began. 'And I am truly sorry. I mucked up.'

'But you're still going with that woman who's ruined your chances.'

He'd come in peace. He didn't want to go through it all again.

'It's my life,' he said quietly.

'And we have our lives too, don't we?'

'Fair enough,' he said.

If Gina were there, she'd say that it proved her point about the women in his family bearing grudges. He didn't accept that from her, but he couldn't accept what they said about Gina either, when they didn't even know her.

'Can you tell Mum that I came?' he said, seeing as they weren't getting anywhere.

'I'll tell her that.'

He wanted to say, 'And tell her that I love her too. And I love you.' But he knew he wouldn't be able to say it without crying, and he wasn't going to cry. Everyone left home, didn't they? It wasn't such a big deal.

His gran kept a perfectly straight back as he hugged her.

'All the best,' she said.

He could hear the dogs still barking as he walked down the street and Cheryl ordering, 'Back to your basket!'

There was a bitterly cold wind blowing in off the Irish Sea as Alf wandered one last time along the promenade. The illuminations went up every year in a brave attempt to extend the summer season till November, but once they'd gone dark, it always felt to him like the town had admitted defeat to the elements for another year.

Cal had got himself an apprenticeship as a trainee manager in a hotel on the front. When Alf walked into the lobby, he was planning the entertainment schedule for their 'Tinsel and Turkey' weekends in the run-up to Christmas.

'I can only give you five minutes,' he said, self-important in his three-piece suit and hotel-branded tie.

'Only came to say goodbye,' Alf told him.

'Where are you off to, then?' Cal asked.

'London first, then Italy – Rome.'

'Jammy bastard,' said Cal, dropping the hotel-manager language.

Their friendship had taken a knock, but it had only needed a gesture for it to be back on track again. Why couldn't families be this uncomplicated? Alf wondered.

'You and Kelly?'

'Engaged, mate.'

'Bloody hell!'

'Stop her going on about it – for a while, anyway. I reckon

I've got at least four years before we can afford the sort of do she's after.'

Alf laughed.

'What about you and Miss . . . Gina?'

'Miss Gina's all right!'

They both laughed.

'Jammy bastard!' Cal muttered again.

'Maybe you'll come visit?'

'Maybe,' said Cal.

Both of them knew that was never going to happen.

They shook hands, and Cal helped him lift his backpack.

'Bloody hell, you've got your whole life in there!' he said. Then, as Alf was going out through the revolving door, he heard Cal calling, 'Great news about your mum, mate!'

The last person Alf would have chosen to run into at the station was Sadie. To his relief, she was on her way down to Liverpool, where she was doing a degree in Musical Theatre at LMA, so they were getting different trains.

'London, is it?' she said.

'En route to Rome,' he said.

'En route?' she mocked.

He waited for the inevitable banter about learning new words from teacher or something like that. He knew she was thinking about it, deciding she was too sophisticated to stoop to that now.

'So, how did your mum get on today?' she said, as her train was announced over the speaker.

'Fine,' Alf said automatically, not having a clue what she was talking about.

'Did she get a photo? One of my mates Instagrammed hers. Not sure about that, are you?'

'Not really,' said Alf.

'Oh my God, you don't actually know, do you?' said Sadie, reading the expression on his face.

'Know what?'

'It probably shouldn't be me telling you . . .'

Why was it that everyone seemed to know something about his mum that he didn't?

'. . . it's her first scan today,' Sadie informed him.

'Scan?' he repeated.

'Donna and Gary have only gone and got themselves pregnant!'

The doors to her train opened.

'So it's just as well you're off really, isn't it?' Sadie said. 'They'll need the room.'

Gina's dad was well into his forties, but he was like a kid with a PlayStation showing Alf how to operate all the gadgets in his house. If he was out, he could do it all from his mobile phone – switching on the heating, raising the blinds, telling the toilet to clean itself.

'I'm kidding about the toilet,' said Stuart. 'My cleaner does that.'

When he saw the adverts on telly, Alf had never been able to picture who would seriously ask Alexa to order tissues, or play a track. Stuart was that person. Alf could see the point when the whole house was designed with smart technology in mind. When you lived in a two-up-two-down with draughty windows and a ten-year-old fridge, it looked like something in a future you couldn't yet imagine. In Stuart's house, it was the present.

Stuart's garage led straight from the kitchen. You could see his lime-green Porsche sitting there, almost like it was another guest. There was space for another two cars; Gina's pink Cinquecento was parked up beside the Porsche, the colours bright, like toy cars in a Barbie house.

On their first evening, Stuart ordered in pizzas. With thin, charred crusts, spread with tomato sauce that tasted like tomatoes, and loaded with white cheese that tasted like cream, they weren't recognizable as the same category of food that Alf had served. Stuart opened a bottle of Barolo and then another, and afterwards he poured shots of Limoncello and proposed a toast.

'To your new life in Italy!'

Alf had never had good red wine before. It made him feel warm and sleepy.

Gina's bedroom had mirrored wardrobes, a remote control for the blinds, and underfloor heating. Rabbit, Kitten and Hedgehog lay in their usual places on the bed. There was always a moment of anguish on Gina's face when Alf swept them onto the floor, as if he should treat them with more tenderness, which was quickly replaced by gleeful anticipation.

Alf was first down the following morning.

'Latte? Cappuccino? Americano?' Stuart asked.

'Couldn't have a cup of tea, could I?'

'You can take a bloke out of the North, but you can't take the North out of a bloke.'

Alf wasn't sure if it was a criticism or a compliment. Stuart was from the North himself, wasn't he?

Stuart boiled the kettle, put a tea bag into a big mug, and handed it over. Alf went to the fridge to get some milk. In the swish fitted kitchen, with its granite surfaces and drawers that closed when you gave them the slightest hint of a push, he couldn't see a bin.

'Alexa, what do I do with my tea bag?' Alf asked.

'Re-ordering tea bags,' came the reply.

There was a moment when Alf feared he'd pushed his luck. Then Stuart's expression relaxed.

'Bin's under the sink,' he said.

Stuart drank his espresso in one gulp.

'Don't suppose you get hangovers at your age,' he said. 'Nothing a mega fry-up won't fix. Get your jacket.'

'Gina's still asleep.'

'If we waited for Gina, mate, we'd miss the match.'

It was an early kick-off for the Arsenal match. Alf wondered why, if you'd got plasma screens as huge as Stuart's, you would go out to watch the match in a pub.

Turned out they weren't going to a pub. They were going to the Emirates Stadium itself.

They sped along the North Circular in the Porsche. The car was so in-your-face and the volume of the Foo Fighters so loud Alf thought that all the people in the ordinary cars they passed were probably wondering whether it was someone famous behind the tinted windows, perhaps even a Premiership footballer.

'Saw them at Glasto,' Stuart said.

'Cool,' said Alf. 'Did you camp?' he asked.

'Glamping,' said Stuart. 'Need a bed at my age!'

He was a cool guy, Alf thought, wondering if he had a girlfriend, maybe more than one. They weren't close enough mates yet to ask.

Stuart rented a garage in Highbury just so he could put his car there on match days. It cost him two hundred pounds a week. When Alf couldn't hide his astonishment, Stuart said, 'Have you any idea what the insurance excess is on this?'

The cafe they went to for breakfast was at the other end of the scale: a greasy spoon with Gunners flags on the walls and everything in red and white, from the mugs and plates to the Formica tables and chequered tiles on the floor. Stuart introduced him to his four mates. There was another estate agent, a City trader and a car salesman. They were minted and much older than Alf, but it didn't matter because they were all lads talking about football. They sympathized with him supporting Blackpool, but respected it when he declined the loan of an Arsenal shirt. Alf wanted to fit in, but he wasn't going to wear another team's strip.

It was the North London derby, Arsenal versus Tottenham, so the atmosphere in the stadium was electric. When the first goal went in, the cheers were huge, but a one-goal lead wasn't enough to calm the nerves. When the second goal went in, everyone was on their feet,.and Alf could see they were proper fans even though he'd always thought of them as a bit soft and southern before.

'You can come again,' one of Stuart's mates told him as they all shook hands at the end, as if his presence had brought the team luck.

Driving back round the North Circular with Radiohead at top volume, Alf glanced across at Stuart. He was a cool dad. For the first time ever, Alf found himself wondering if his own dad would have been cool too. He'd always assumed that his dad would be solid and reliable, like Gary was, but Kieran had ridden a big motorbike and in the only picture Donna had of him, he was wearing a biker's leather jacket, looking mean.

It occurred to Alf suddenly, just as they were going past IKEA, that he was now older than his dad had been when he died, so nobody could have had any idea what sort of father he would have become.

Maybe Alf's life would have been completely different, because his mum always said Kieran didn't like dancing. He probably wouldn't have appreciated the thought of his son in Lycra. He was an apprentice plumber. Maybe he would have gone on to have his own business, or come down to London where the money was, and ended up with a Porsche himself? Or maybe he would have lived his whole life fitting bathrooms. When he set off that night on his motorbike to see Donna, it probably seemed like the world was opening up for him.

'You OK, mate?' Stuart smiled across the dashboard at him.

'Yeah, good, thanks,' Alf replied, his eyes fixed on the road ahead.

32

March 2018

LETTY

In the months following Marina's death, Frances had gone through her own periods of anger, blame and exhaustion, but now she seemed to have accepted the loss and was making plans for the future. The process was very like the Grief Wheel, Letty thought, except that for Frances, it was the loss of the house rather than the loss of Marina that she was adjusting to. In a way, the two were inseparable.

Relations in the family had normalized to the extent that they spent Christmas together. It was one of the most harmonious Christmases Letty could remember. Gone were the superficial arguments in the kitchen about olive oil or goose fat for the roast potatoes, or jelly for the trifle.

It was decided – by Frances – that everyone was too old for presents, and guests were forbidden to bring any more stuff into the house. *Stuff* was Frances's latest adversary. As she was no longer working, clearing up had become her principal day-time occupation. The house was so big the family had never had reason to throw anything away, so the task had a Herculean quality, the wardrobes Narnia-like, with boxes behind the rails stuffed with clothes, and the enormous loft looming overhead, still to be investigated.

If Ivo lent a hand at weekends, he seemed to create more problems than he solved by picking through the boxes packed up in the hall ready to take to the charity shop, pulling out items that held specific memories for him, brandishing battered old Dinky Toys, saying, 'Aren't these worth money these days?' as if Frances were, in her drive for clearance, devaluing his legacy.

'Not if they're in such poor condition without their original box,' Frances would protest. 'We did actually watch *Antiques Roadshow* together.'

By the time Letty returned to London for the Easter break, the house was clear enough to invite estate agents around to value the property, although they had yet to make a start on Marina's rooms.

'Ivo's still in denial,' Frances told her, 'and Rollo says to just bin the lot, but it's difficult being ruthless on someone else's behalf.'

Frances was still wary, Letty thought, of trespassing on her mother-in-law's territory.

'Shall we tackle it together?' she volunteered, and was surprised to see gratitude spreading across Frances's face.

They were making a start on the trunk at the foot of the bed when the doorbell rang.

'That'll be the final agent,' Frances said, glancing at herself in Marina's mahogany cheval mirror and trying to smooth her hair down. 'God help us!' she said, clearly disappointed with what she saw.

The doorbell rang again.

Frances set off down the hall to open it.

Letty heard her mother's voice becoming a touch posher and more confident, as it always did with visitors.

'You'll have to excuse my appearance,' she said. 'Endless clearing . . .'

'It's a pleasure to meet you.' The man's voice was uncannily familiar.

'Shall we start here?' Frances said, showing him into the main reception room.

Marina had occupied the two back rooms of the raised ground floor of the house. The large room with a bay at the front had been used by the whole family. Their voices were more muffled in there. Letty stood behind the door to Marina's bedroom, trying to hear what was being said.

The estate agent was making the right noises, but his voice was all wrong. Northern vowels overlaid with a twang of Essex.

'Lovely space! There can't be many of these houses that are still a single dwelling. High ceilings! Must be thirteen feet? Fifteen, is it?'

Letty hadn't heard the voice for six months. Six months of bracing herself in the Bodleian when she went for a break. Six months of walking out of the back exit and down the alleyway between Brasenose and Exeter colleges, then turning right onto Turl Street instead of walking straight out onto the Broad, for the simple illogical reason that it was a different way from the route they had walked together. Six months of getting the coach instead of the train when she came home for weekends. The fear was not as acute as it had been, but the avoidance strategies had become habits that, because they'd proved successful, she hadn't been able to drop.

'Period features! Original fireplace, cornicing . . . You pay a lot for the square footage, but there's no substitute for quality . . .'

Letty realized she was trapped. If she closed Marina's door and locked it, her mother would call out, 'Letty?' Escaping upstairs would mean running the risk of bumping into them as they came out into the hall. There was no room under

Marina's bed. The cupboards were still full. There wasn't time. The French doors! Letty ran across the room, trying to turn a key that was stiff with disuse. Frances and Spencer were now in the hallway; she could hear the changed timbre of their voices in the echoey space. Please turn, please turn, she pleaded with the lock. Finally it clicked. She pushed the door open and ran down the corkscrew steps, knowing there were only moments before they looked out of the window at the garden.

Only partially hidden under the wrought-iron lattice, her back pressed against the wall of the basement, she could hear Frances saying in the room above, 'Garden's a mess. I'll get someone to clear it before the photos.'

'It's a good size, though,' he said.

And then the voices drifted away and Letty could breathe again. It was beginning to drizzle and it was unlikely that he'd now want to inspect the garden, she thought, unless they came out onto the patio outside the basement dining room. Letty inched her way round the corner to the side of the building, flattening herself against the wall, praying that the narrow corridor of garden at the side of the house was too overgrown for him to want to explore. The guttering above her head was leaking. As drizzle turned to rain, sporadic drips onto her head became a constant stream of water. Finally, after minutes standing under a freezing waterfall, she heard the front door opening.

'We'll be in touch,' said Frances.

'I look forward to it,' he replied.

'Do you want to borrow an umbrella?' Frances asked. 'Actually, I've got about a hundred – I could even give you one.'

'Thanks. I'll be fine,' he said.

The front door closing. Splashing footsteps on the black-and-white tiles of the stoop. A glimpse of pointed tan brogues, red socks, the hem of a sharp blue trouser leg. Footsteps echoing down the street, getting more distant until she wasn't sure whether she was just imagining them.

Letty went back round the building and ran up the wrought-iron staircase, banging on the glass door, which Frances must have closed.

'What on earth?' Frances asked, returning to Marina's bedroom.

'I'm locked out.'

'What are you doing out there?'

'Needed some air.'

Frances sniffed.

'It does have a bit of an old-lady pong,' she said. 'I wonder if he noticed?'

'You're not going to go with him, are you?'

'Stuart?' said Frances.

'Stuart?' Letty repeated.

'He's offering by far the best deal. I think things must be worse than they're saying in the housing market . . .'

'He sounded so sleazy.'

'He's an estate agent, darling.'

'But . . . I had a bad feeling about him.'

'You didn't meet him!'

'I didn't want to meet him . . . I could just tell . . .'

'You think he might put buyers off? I know what you mean. He's just the wrong side of the line between charming and creepy . . .'

How could Frances have seen in ten minutes what she hadn't?

'Please don't,' she urged.

Frances gave her an exasperated look.

'All right,' she sighed. 'The one on England's Lane is nearer, and slightly more civilized, I suppose . . . and Stuart's given me the ammunition to negotiate the commission down, hasn't he?' She suddenly brightened at the prospect of doing a deal.

*

It started with not being able to sleep and Letty trying to re-member mindfulness exercises to slow her breathing, calm the agitation, make her focus on the present. But the anxiety wouldn't go away. Every night she lay awake, turning the de-tails over in her mind. Had something she said led him to their house? *Slut*. Had she told him they were selling it? Again, she didn't think so, but he knew that she lived with her grand-mother who had died. Perhaps he had made the connection? And yet, if he'd really wanted to stalk her, he surely could have found her in Oxford? *Slut*. Was she just letting her imagination run away with her? This man was Stuart, but she knew him as Spencer. She was sure it was him. Perhaps it was a name he'd made up for the role, like she had made up Elle? Spencer had said he was a property developer, not an estate agent. Per-haps he did both? Or perhaps all estate agents had aspirations to be property developers. Perhaps it was like altering your name, just slightly, to pretend you were the version of yourself you'd like to be.

Letty tried to concentrate on clearing Marina's rooms, but every book, every ornament, every item of clothing seemed to hold a memory that she wasn't yet willing to discard. Some-times, when Frances put her head round the door to check how it was going, Letty would realize that she had just been sitting, staring. When Frances suggested going for a walk, get-ting some air, she found some excuse, not wanting to go out and run the risk of bumping into him. If he operated in their area, he was bound to visit other properties, making valu-ations, conducting viewings with clients. Perhaps he had spotted her in the street and followed her home?

Her appetite disappeared. At mealtimes, she could feel Frances watching her push food around her plate.

One evening, as she was sitting at Marina's desk, staring at her own reflection in the dark window, she overheard her mother's agitated voice in the kitchen downstairs telling Ivo,

'You talk to her! She listens to you! Suggest she goes back to the therapist.'

A few minutes later, her father popped his head around the door.

'Everything OK, Letty?'

'Fine.'

Then her mother's hiss of sarcasm, so loud it was clear she had tiptoed upstairs and was standing right behind him: 'Oh, well done! That's so very reassuring!'

Letty stared at the pictures above Marina's bed. Tranquillity, Idleness, Lesbia and Violets, Sweet Violets, all lolling prettily among Roman ruins.

Why not escape? There was still a month before Trinity term began. It had been invigorating reading Greek in Greece. Why not Latin in Italy? She didn't want to ask her parents for money with all their financial worries, but there was the legacy that Marina had left each grandchild: five thousand pounds to be used for travel. She was sure her grandmother would approve. Maybe she could even take a class in Italian? Learn the language that Marina had spoken as a little girl but had to erase from her identity. Within seconds, the fleeting thought had become a plan, almost as if Marina was showing her the way.

Running downstairs, she found her parents in the kitchen. They had both clearly heard her footsteps because they were smiling artificially at her as she came through the door, the words of some interrupted argument hanging in the air, as obvious as if someone were trying secretly to fry bacon.

'Would you mind if I went away for a while?' Letty asked.

'Away?' said Frances.

'I feel I need some space, a break from everything . . .'

'Sounds like a very sensible idea!' said Ivo immediately.

Frances shot him an exasperated glance.

'Where?' she asked.

'I was thinking Rome.'

PART THREE

May 2018

33

First week

ALF

Afterwards Alf will wonder why he didn't just drop his back-pack and run down the street with Letty, instead of staying to face the confrontation he had been dreading. In that moment of indecision, he lost her.

'Someone's in a hurry,' says Stuart.

'Gina, can we talk?' Alf says.

'About what?'

All his instincts are to keep this conversation until they are somewhere private, but in Italy, people are always having arguments in the street. Nobody's looking, nobody's bothered. They might as well do it here.

'I'm sorry, Gina, I'm leaving . . .'

He prepared his speech as he sat on their bed waiting for her. Quick and clean. Don't get into a fight.

'For her?' she asks, pointing down the street.

Did she see him kissing Letty? Is that why she kissed him so ostentatiously? Staking her claim?

'I didn't mean it to happen like this. Wanted to explain to you properly.'

Gina looks pointedly at his backpack.

'I left you a note . . .'

It sounds so weak.

Unable to look at Gina, Alf glances at Stuart, but cannot quite read his expression. He looks almost as if he's enjoying this. Alf wonders if he knew, or at least suspected. Has Stuart been following him?

'You can't leave me,' Gina says. 'Not after all I've given up for you.' Her voice is quiet, like she's trying to piece it all together.

'I didn't mean you to give anything up,' Alf says.

'So now you're saying you didn't ever want to be with me?'

'Of course I wanted it,' he says. 'I just didn't think it would be for . . .'

He doesn't want to say the word. He feels like he's going back on a promise, even though he never made a promise.

'I just didn't think it would be forever!'

'But I lost everything because of you!' Gina's voice rises.

Suck it up, Alf thinks. She's got every right to be angry.

'I've lost stuff too,' he says quietly.

'Like what?'

'My family . . .'

'Your bitch of a mother!' She's suddenly on the attack.

Now Alf's angry too. He should never have had to choose.

'She was only trying to look out for me!'

'She was trying to destroy me!' Gina shouts.

'Oh, get over yourself!' he says. 'You're not the victim in this!'

That sounds like he thinks he was the victim, and he doesn't mean that. But Gina can't just rewrite history.

'You . . . you . . . bloody bastard!' Gina flails at him. 'Well, go on, Mummy's boy. Go back to your mummy. See if she still thinks the sun shines out of your arse!'

'Gina . . .'

'Go!' She's shouting now. 'Just go!'

300

He doesn't want to leave her hysterical.

'I think you'd better go, Alf,' Stuart says firmly, standing between them.

'I'll get you my share of the rent,' Alf tells Gina.

'It's not about the bloody rent! The rent doesn't matter!' she screams at him.

'It does to me.'

And then she's sobbing and he hates it when she cries. But he forces himself to pick up his backpack and walk away.

He hears footsteps chasing him. Stuart grabs his arm, spins him round, then lets him go, laughing as he sees Alf automatically duck from his reach.

'You're not worth it, mate,' Stuart says. 'You struck gold with Gina and you threw it all away on that little tart.'

'Don't you dare call her that!' Alf shouts.

There's a leering smile on Stuart's face that he's never seen before. He can't figure out what he ever liked about him.

'Slut, cock-tease!' Stuart goads him. 'You'll find out soon enough. Looks like an angel, behaves like a whore . . .'

The force of the blow sends Stuart reeling, clutching at his face.

'Jesus!' he says, sitting on the pavement, fear in his eyes.

Alf stares at his own fist in shock. He hasn't hit another bloke since he was at primary school, doesn't know where it came from.

'Sorry,' he says.

Stuart gets to his feet, brushes himself down.

As Alf turns, he shouts after him, 'Don't even think about coming back when she's bored of you, you bastard!'

They were about to get the one o'clock train, so it has been less than an hour. Alf stands outside her building, pressing the number for her apartment. When she doesn't answer, he waits, hoping to be able to slip into the building behind one of the other residents, convinced that if he can talk to her, he will make her understand. Eventually, the old man with the stick who they'd shared the lift with returns, smelling of a boozy lunch.

On the tenth floor, Alf gets out, knocks on the door of Letty's loft.

'Please talk to me, Lets. Please allow me to explain . . .'

He waits there, knocking again and again, until the next-door neighbour comes home from work, catching him with his ear pressed against the door. In two hours, the toilet has not flushed, the blinds have not been raised or lowered, and Alf has heard no footsteps. The ceiling fan is not on and it is a hot afternoon. He cannot sense her presence just a few feet away from him. Perhaps she did not come back here because she knew that this was the first place he would try to find her?

But where has she gone?

By the time he gets back to the school, it is closed for the weekend.

Alf gets the cash he needs from a Bancomat and takes the Metro to Piramide, walking the last few hundred metres to the apartment.

He takes a deep breath before climbing the four flights of stairs for the last time. Five minutes, he thinks, and then it will be over. He remembers thinking the same thing early this morning. Was it only this morning? It seems like much longer.

Gina isn't there. The bed is still unmade. Perhaps she went straight to work from Stuart's? Perhaps she called in sick, or handed in her notice? Alf sees the letter he wrote earlier, seemingly untouched. He screws it up, pockets it: no point leaving it now when they've already said all there is to be said. Stuart will take her back to London. He'll look after her, Alf thinks, as he leaves the cash and his keys on the kitchen table.

*

As he walks to the tram stop, he realizes he's now homeless in Rome. He still has enough money for a couple of weeks, more if he works. He takes the number three tram to Porta Maggiore, goes back to Letty's apartment building again, then, when there is no reply to the entryphone, he tries the Sardinian restaurant. The proprietor has not seen her.

When it gets dark, the lights do not come on in Letty's tenth-floor loft.

Alf hauls his backpack to the tram and travels all the way around Rome to the other terminus at the Villa Giulia, staring out of the window in case he spots her. He sits on a park bench on the steps that lead up to the Villa Borghese in a kind of dazed limbo, then gets the last tram to Porta Maggiore. Her windows are still dark.

The one thing everyone always warns you about Rome is not to stay near Termini station, but it's cheap and he needs somewhere to leave his stuff. It's near the school. If he hasn't found her by Monday, he wants to be there in the morning when she arrives.

There's no air conditioning and each new hour he hears the desperate panting of a different man with the prostitute in the next-door room.

In the morning, he's back at the apartment building. One or two of the residents are beginning to eye him warily.

Alf wanders round Rome, revisiting the places they went to as if searching for clues in a crazy treasure hunt, convincing himself each time that this will be the place she will be waiting for him.

He walks through the Villa Borghese, remembering her overtaking him recklessly on the Segway, her hair flying behind her. Yuri greets him enthusiastically and asks after *la bella signorina*. She has not been there.

He takes the bus to Tivoli, where he first put his hand on

her waist and taught her salsa, and she trusted him when he said that people had probably been dancing here for centuries, even though he'd just made it up because he was so desperate to find a way of touching her. He stands in the caves at the top of the fountain, listening to the rushing water, where he first felt overwhelmed by his attraction to her, then ruined it by speaking clumsily.

In the dingy bus trundling back to Rome, he recalls the exact sensation when she said she'd felt something too, like he was levitating.

In the Piazza Navona, the accordionist is playing the same tune they waltzed to, when she followed his steps as if they had been dancing together for years, and a crowd gathered around them and clapped, and it had felt good that they were beautiful together in other people's eyes.

Alf stares at the lines of tourists queuing for the Bocca della Verità, remembering how cold and dank the air felt when he put his hand in and asked it silently, 'Is this for real? Is it even possible that she could love me back?' and how stupidly happy he had been when his hand wasn't bitten off.

Was it there that desire became inevitability? Or was it earlier than that? Was it sitting on the number three tram, or before, on the street outside the school, watching her ballerina walk, or even the first moment he brushed past her outside the director's office – *colpo di fulmine* – that he felt the axis of his life shift?

Alf's last hope is the Forum, the place where they first had a proper conversation. If she wants to see him, that is where she will have gone.

He sits on the steps near the triumphal arch of Septimius Severus, listening to a tour guide explain about the *damnatio memoriae* of Geta by his brother Caracalla.

The obliteration of memory. The destruction of all traces of a person, as if they never existed.

In the House of the Vestal Virgins, Alf takes a photograph of the empty pedestal.

On Monday morning, when she does not appear at the school, he is certain she has left Rome and he has wasted precious time with his searching, kidding himself that if he thought about her enough, she would somehow materialize in front of him.

Unfortunately, it's the strict receptionist, Olivia, who looks up and says, '*Prego?*'

'*Sai dov'è Violetta?*'

As far as he can understand from her rapid explanation, Violetta left a message on the answerphone. She's not coming back. It's strange because she's paid for a month. Perhaps there has been a family emergency? They are writing to tell her that they will suspend the week she has already paid for.

Alf asks for a contact number.

They only have an email address.

Her email, then?

They're not allowed to give out personal details.

Even though he produces his most winning smile, which would probably work on the giggly receptionist, Olivia is unmoved.

Alf returns to her apartment building one more time, remembering the bear of a caretaker, who is back at work after the weekend.

'The English girl? Gone away! Friday afternoon!'

She asked him to call a taxi. To the station, he thinks. Or it could have been the airport. She had luggage with her.

Which? Alf demands. '*È molto importante!*'

The caretaker thinks it was the station.

At Termini, Alf looks up at the departure board, trying to decide. There is a train leaving for Florence in five minutes. He remembers Heidi was in Florence for the weekend, and she and Letty were friends. But the weekend is over now.

There is a train to Naples in one hour. They were going to go to Ischia, he thinks. Perhaps that is where she has gone? Perhaps she will be there waiting for him? Of course! It is so obvious to him now he doesn't know why he didn't think of it before.

With time to spare before the train leaves, Alf walks across the square to Feltrinelli, the international bookshop. The book he wants is there, in a long black line of Penguin Classics.

34

Second Week

LETTY

Milan has a different vibe from Rome. The roads are wider, the buildings more modern, the people generally taller, fairer. Someone of Alf's height and colouring wouldn't stand out here. A couple of times, Letty spots a man with blondish hair on a passing tram, or walking a few yards in front of her on a crowded street, and her heart races, and she's not sure whether to hang back or confront him until the moment he turns, and she sees that it is someone else, not Alf at all, and there's a torque in her chest, relief twisting against disappointment, that makes it difficult to breathe.

There's absolutely no way he can be here, she tells herself, unless the attraction between them is so strong it is somehow telepathic and has drawn him to her. But that would be like believing in fairy tales.

Letty has chosen an anodyne chain hotel. Her room has the decor of countless other rooms all over Europe; the buffet breakfast she makes herself eat is the same as it would be in Berlin or Madrid. It's not the sort of place that anyone stays for more than a night, but she has been here for three. Suspended in time. During the day, she goes to see places mentioned in her guidebook, checking behind her every few yards that she isn't being followed, taking the backstreets, making it more difficult if anyone is looking for her. She walks for miles, deliberately exhausting herself because the only comfort she can find is in the oblivion of sleep. Each morning, she keeps her eyes closed as she wakes, trying to hold Alf's presence with her, putting off the moment when she has to face the reality that he has not miraculously materialized through wanting him so much. And when she eventually opens her eyes, grief balloons in her chest, bringing convulsions of tears and snot and uncontrollable sobbing.

This morning she will visit the cathedral. She has been saving this most iconic landmark, seeing all the other sights first, because after the Duomo there will no longer be a valid reason to stay in Milan. She does not know where she will go next.

Her route takes her past the opera house, La Scala, where *La Traviata* is playing. She cannot decide whether it would comfort her or make her sad to buy a ticket for the evening's performance. In her head, she can hear the duet '*Un dì, felice, eterea*'.

One day, happy and ethereal, you appeared in front of me and ever since, trembling, I have lived from love. Love that's the mysterious heartbeat of the universe.

Croce e delizia.

Torture and delight.

I hate and I love, Letty thinks. All bound up in one.

For a moment, she allows herself to imagine seeing the opera one day with Alf, certain that he would think it as beautiful and passionate as *Manon*. And afterwards, making love, their bodies would move, flesh to flesh, soul to soul, in harmony, becoming something more beautiful than their individual selves, like two voices in a duet, transcendent, ethereal.

'*Prego?*' The box office attendant interrupts her daydream.

Watching the opera alone, she knows she would be transported to the last time she saw it – sitting next to Spencer, smelling his aftershave, keeping her muscles taut so that their thighs would not accidentally touch.

'*Mi dispiace. Niente.*'

She hurries away across the piazza.

How did Spencer find her? However hard she tries to concentrate on the guidebook, or the paintings in the Pinacoteca, or the stories of the contestants on television gameshows she watches in her hotel room, it always comes back to that. She had just about persuaded herself that it was possible he had appeared at her home in Belsize Park because he is an estate agent who covers their area. Coincidence, bad luck, something like that. But his presence in Rome could not have been chance. To turn up unexpectedly in one place could be regarded as misfortune; to turn up in two looks suspicious, to misquote Oscar Wilde.

She thought she had escaped. But she had not.

And he knows Alf.

This is as inexplicable as it is terrifying.

Letty looks at her map and sees she needs to walk through an arcade to get to the Duomo. It's a beautiful space, as ornate as a cathedral itself with marble mosaic floors and painted vaulted ceilings, but she does not stop to admire the architecture, because high-end shops selling sharp suits and expensive watches is Spencer's territory. She hastens, not quite running because that would draw attention, and when she reaches the exit she feels as relieved as if she was trapped in a dangerous cave but found a way out into the air.

The piazza dazzles in the sunlight; little children are running around; there is a vendor with a huge bunch of helium balloons – pink, green, gold, silver circles – floating like an art installation against the intricate Gothic filigree of the Duomo facade. Above, the bluest of Italian blue skies makes her feel that nothing bad could happen to her here. Yet still she hurries towards the huge doors of the cathedral, as if to seek sanctuary there.

Inside it is much darker than she anticipated, a vast greeny-grey Gothic vault. Her eyes take a moment to adjust. The only natural light filters through stained-glass windows projecting their brightly coloured images onto the gloomy columns. Letty gazes up, thinking about how miraculous it must have been to see the sun shining through the stained glass for the first time, how it would make you believe that God was anointing the building with his blessing.

Sometimes she wonders whether if she had faith, her life would be simpler. Her grandmother went to mass every Sunday and she always feels closest when Letty is in a church. Did Marina really believe, she wonders, or did she simply find it comforting, as she does, to reflect quietly in a peaceful space filled with centuries of reverence? It's strange how when someone dies, there are all sorts of questions that you never thought of asking.

Letty remembers sitting in Santa Croce in Gerusalemme on her first day in Rome, not even a month ago. She is a different person now.

It is as if part of her has been freed by love and yet part of her is still paralysed by fear, and she cannot find a balance, constantly trying to stop herself tipping between delusional joy and hopeless despair.

Sometimes, in her anonymous hotel room, she wonders whether she has dreamed it all.

These facts are certain.

She went to Rome. She fell in love with Alf. And she was sure that he loved her back.

Then Spencer appeared.

It was definitely Spencer, or Stuart, or whatever his name

really is. He was staring straight at her as he approached with a horrible smile on his face, relishing her fear.

And Alf knew him.

Her only choice was to run away.

Why Spencer was there, how he knew she was there, is a mystery. Alf told her he had things to sort. She presumed a girlfriend. Was that the blonde woman who was holding Spencer's arm, but kissed Alf as if she owned him?

Whatever narrative she invents to explain the collision of the four of them there in that sunny Roman street, changing it, in a second, from Paradise to Hell, all lead to the same conclusion: her relationship with Alf is over. Alf knows Spencer and, whether he was part of a plan to lure her, or whether he was an innocent pawn in whatever game Spencer is playing, he will discover what sort of woman she really is, and he will not want her after that.

The last thing left to do in Milan is go up on the roof terraces of the cathedral.

There's airport-style security at the entrance, a queue for the lift, a walk along the gulley beside grey Gothic buttresses, then a narrow staircase up to the highest terrace, where Letty steps out into a place of such light and serenity she feels almost airborne. Stretching before her is an avenue of delicate spires, dozens of them, all pointing towards Heaven, each impossibly narrow spindle of stone topped with the statue of a saint, ornamented and delicate, like white lace against the sky.

She notices that visitors fall silent as they arrive, the beauty literally breathtaking as they struggle to comprehend the skill and devotion of craftsmen centuries before. She sits on a stone ledge feeling totally safe in this celestial place, never wanting to leave.

Far below, the tiny figures of pedestrians traverse the geometric patterns of the square, going about their daily lives.

Down there in the human realm, life weighs heavily, whereas here among the saints she feels light and insubstantial, as if the burdens have been lifted.

Letty wonders if everyone who looks down thinks about jumping. It would be so easy to end all the pain. Just one step, one leap, to disappear forever.

35

FRANCES

The view from the warehouse apartment is breathtaking: the City skyline directly opposite; below the balcony, the Thames. It's high tide. A tourist boat passes by, snatches of the commentary blowing in on the breeze.

Living here would be energizing, Frances thinks. There's a kind of rhythm to the river flowing past. With boats going back and forth all day, it would be like living on the heartbeat of London.

Each flat she has seen offers her a different future. There's a part of her that would like to spend the rest of her life viewing properties, imagining how she would look in them. Like trying on clothes.

'Great for summer parties,' says the estate agent, who's called Ben. He's in his early thirties. She's cheered by the fact that he thinks she's the sort of person who has parties – which, after all, she is, or was, or will be, anyway.

Ben's been showing her flats for the past couple of days. They've developed a bit of a flirtatious relationship.

'One very spacious bedroom,' he says, throwing open the door to a room with a huge double bed and a wall of mirror behind.

'Yes,' says Frances.

She sees her reflection next to Ben's. She's wearing a navy blue sleeveless shift dress. Classically smart. She's never quite sure that her arms are still good enough, but from this distance they look fine. Her hairdresser says the fringe takes years off her. How many years she didn't specify.

'Your problem,' says Ben, looking directly into Frances's eyes in the mirror, 'is you don't really know what you want, do you?'

Frances wonders if she correctly detects a slight frisson of invitation. How far would he be prepared to go to make a sale?

'So true,' she says, returning his gaze.

It's been quite a shock realizing how little she can get for her budget in any of the central areas. The only thing she knows for sure is that she wants to be able to walk to the theatre; that's what she likes doing, so why shouldn't she? But that means sacrificing a bedroom for a view. She thinks she'll be happier with a view, although she was tempted by a little Georgian attic duplex in Lamb's Conduit Street, where the neighbourhood is more bookish and Bloomsbury.

'Thoughts?' Ben says into the mirror.

'What do *you* think?' Frances says, attempting a coquettish smile.

'Well, if you were *my* mother,' he says, 'I'd probably say go for the duplex, although with that, there are the stairs.'

In the mirror, Frances sees the smile drain from her face.

She's almost tempted to put in an immediate offer for the hipper apartment they're standing in, just to show him how fucking youthful and cool she is.

Instead, she says tightly, 'I'm going to have to do some thinking. Cast my net a little wider, possibly.'

By which she means to imply leaving him for another estate agent, but she sees that the old-fashioned expression has simply confirmed his view of her. She probably should have said 'reset her filters' or something.

'Not a problem,' he says.

It's an expression that makes her furious, with its implication that she has troubled him but that he's prepared to let it go. It's his bloody job to show her properties, she wants to scream. And as a matter of fact, it *is* a problem for him, because she probably won't be buying through his company now, and the market's dropping with all the uncertainty and more to come.

'Can you bloody believe it?' Frances says to Oscar at lunch.

She's glad they've come to the Delaunay, where the atmosphere is civilized, the waiters professional, the decor reassuringly timeless. It's balm for her frazzled nerves. The thought crosses her mind that if she bought an apartment in Covent Garden she could come here for breakfast, lunch and dinner if she so pleased. She quite likes the idea of having a table where she always sits.

However, her budget wouldn't buy her much square footage in this area.

'To be fair,' says Oscar, 'you are old enough to be his mother, darling, even though you're looking fabulous!'

Frances gives her son's hand a squeeze across the table.

'I think it was the mention of the stairs that finished me off,' she tells him. 'It was like he was saying, next stop retirement home, you know?'

'Frances, he's an estate agent whose ambition is probably to be a contestant on *The Apprentice*.'

'He wears loafers with no socks.'

'What more do you need to know?'

'What is that all about anyway?' Frances asks. 'How bad do those shoes smell at the end of the day?'

'An estate agent with stinking feet! Frances, you can do better than that.'

'It's not that I wanted to,' she says. 'It would just be nice to feel that someone finds me attractive, you know?'

She knows she shouldn't be asking her son for reassurance, even if he is gay and nearly forty.

'Frances, you are gorgeous and Ivo is a sad bastard,' says Oscar. 'If you want to find someone, it won't be a problem. Now, I hardly dare tell you my news . . .'

Frances is grateful for him taking charge. She despises neediness.

'What news? Tell me something to cheer me up.'

'We're having a baby!'

It's almost exactly the same feeling she had when Oscar brought his first boyfriend home. The moment that the two boys came in and stood together in the kitchen, all she could think about was that she absolutely must have the right reaction. Then she ended up being so over-the-top enthusiastic it looked as if she were overcompensating, as if she didn't approve, when in fact she was delighted it was all out in the open.

'Oh, darling!' she says now, her eyes welling.

'Sorry, I should have left it for another day.'

'No, of course not,' says Frances, sniffing. 'It's nothing to do with me being a grandmother.'

Although of course it is.

'Are you adopting or getting a surrogate, or what?' She struggles to find normal questions to ask.

'Turkey baster with a lesbian couple we know. We're going to share the parenting.'

'Are you sure?'

'About what?'

'The turkey baster.'

'Why?'

'Oh, I don't know, I just have this theory that happy children come from great sex.'

'Well, that's a bit weird, really, and kind of impossible in this case.'

'You're completely right,' Frances says. 'And I am delighted. I really am. Do tell Raj I am, won't you?'

'I will. It may not happen for years, though.'

'I won't start knitting just yet, then.'

For a moment Oscar looks worried, and then they're both laughing at the joke. Good God, thinks Frances. I really am getting old if he thinks for one millisecond I'm taking up knitting.

'How's Letty?' Oscar asks.

'Letty seems to be having an absolute ball. She sends me photos, which seems like a good sign, don't you think?'

'Great stuff!' says Oscar, as the waiter arrives to take their order.

'I'm going to have the chicken salad,' says Frances. 'I never usually eat salad out because it's such a bore dealing with lettuce and talking at the same time. Here they chop everything up into little pieces.'

'Next stop retirement home?' says Oscar.

She laughs. Oscar always makes her feel better about herself, somehow. They bounce off one another. He doesn't tolerate her self-doubt.

'Letty and I did such a fun thing the other evening,' Frances tells him, once the waiter has gone. 'There was a live relay from Covent Garden. I was at the Opera House. Letty was watching in a cinema in Rome. In the interval, she WhatsApped to say that the camera was on the stalls, and where was I sitting? So I went down to the front by the orchestra pit and waved at the camera, and she saw me and WhatsApped that she was waving too! It's funny – hundreds of miles away from each other, but standing there on my own at the front of the Opera House waving like a mad thing, I felt closer to her than I have in years.'

'Which opera was it?' Oscar asks.

'It was a ballet, actually. *Manon.*'

'Letty went to the ballet?'

'Yes, that's what I mean. She texted and said, guess what, I'm seeing *Manon* in Rome. Just wondered if you were there. It's a good sign, don't you think?'

Both of them are always cautious about being too optimistic about Letty, because in the past, whenever they've thought a problem was over, something worse seems to have happened.

The waiter brings their food, tops up their glasses, then disappears without disturbing them.

Oscar squeezes lemon over his schnitzel.

'Does she know?' he asks, allowing the elephant that has been stalking the sides of the room to come charging to their table.

Three and a half weeks ago, the evening after Letty left, Ivo said he wanted to talk to Frances about their future. He made a nice dinner, opened a bottle of wine, then told her that he had been having an affair for the past seven years and would be leaving her once the house was sold.

Seven fucking years. It was the length of the deception that had killed Frances, rather than the deception itself. Ivo's a good-looking man. Good for his age too. She wasn't dumb enough to think that he wouldn't have had temptations, especially since the menopause had put her off sex. But that had only been for the past two years, and she never thought that he'd leave her because of it. Maybe find some other woman for sex – sometimes she'd even felt it would be a relief if he did, so she wouldn't feel so guilty for always being tired – but not a relationship. Seven years! She's tortured herself by replaying every single moment that they've spent together during that time, in the context of his duplicity and her stupidity.

'I haven't told Letty yet,' Frances informs him. 'I can't bear to spoil it when she sounds so happy for once.'

'Do you think that's wise?' Oscar looks concerned.

'Why should it be me that tells her?' Frances takes another tack. 'He deliberately left it until after she'd gone.'

'True,' says Oscar doubtfully.

'He's moved in with her, you know.'

'Yes. He told me.'

'Are you in contact with him much?' Frances tries to make the question casual, although inside she's burning with indignation.

'I've spoken to him a couple of times. He asked me if Letty knew,' says Oscar.

And what else did they say to each other? Did Oscar give his father hell? Or were they perfectly civilized? Man to man. You know how it is. These things happen. A knife of jealousy slices through Frances. What she hates most about the whole thing is how she now feels in competition with Ivo for their children's love.

'You do know,' she says, hot with anger, 'that what he really wants is for *me* to tell Letty. Because even he can't think of a way of spinning that he's been having an affair for the last seven years – even when Letty was ill, even when she was in hospital – with a woman who's closer to her age than his. But I'm not going to.'

The tears that are always there these days, particularly, she's noticed, when she's decided on a firm, considered position, start to fall, and she's trying to keep them back with the fingers of one hand to stop her mascara running, like one of those soppy contestants on reality television, while the other hand searches for a tissue in her bag. Not in the Delaunay, for God's sake!

'Frances . . .'

'No, it's fine,' she says, finally locating a tissue. 'It's just . . . it's just . . .'

She knows she shouldn't say what she wants to because it will sound like it's all about her, not about Letty, but she can't stop herself.

'It's just . . . I'm terrified that Letty will take his side.'

'Of course she won't!' says Oscar, so emphatically that a piece of the schnitzel he's slicing flies across the table. 'Anyway, there really aren't sides, are there? You're our mother and we're here to support you. He's a lying bastard, but he's still our father – we'll just see you separately from now. We're not children.'

'She'll think I deserve it for being such a shrew . . .' Now the tears are unstoppable. 'She always thinks I'm the unreasonable one.'

'Frances, you're not unreasonable, you're strong. You've had to be. God knows, you had to hold your own with Marina.'

'Sometimes I wonder if it would have been better to act like a docile little Catholic wife,' Frances sniffs. 'Not that Marina was ever that herself.'

'Frances, you're brilliant in all sorts of ways, but docile wife is not something you'd be capable of for more than a minute. And Ivo wouldn't have wanted that either. He loved that you were a proper feminist. He was proud of you.'

'Only because it meant he didn't have to face any confrontation, or pay the bills. He sub-licensed that to me, while all the time looking like a right-on man. It suited his self-image. He's always been so vain. And now he's looking like a man who's attractive to women half his age. God, it's such a mid-life fucking cliché!'

'You were happy too, though. Weren't you?'

The thing Frances most hates is people trying to make you see the positives when something really awful has happened. She doesn't want mediation, she wants endless undiluted sympathy and loyal ganging-up. She supposes it's a natural human instinct to try to heal someone who is in pain. But it seems to have the opposite effect on her.

'I thought I was happy,' she concedes. 'But he's destroyed that, and I don't feel like being reasonable and grown up about

320

it. And actually, I would like you to take sides!' Frances tries to make a joke out of it, while at the same time meaning every word.

'I'm always on your side, whatever. You know that,' says Oscar calmly. 'And Letty will be too. I'm just not sure it's fair to keep her in the dark, especially when we're always telling her to be open with us.'

'But I'm only doing it so she can have a nice time without worrying.'

'But isn't that why we all hide things from our family?' Oscar says. 'Thinking you know better is where it all starts to go wrong.'

How lucky she is to have Oscar, Frances thinks, as she watches him walking away down Aldwych towards the Strand. She's thought it since the moment he was born, but at the same time been surprised at thinking it. Growing up she'd never had any strong maternal instincts, but that feeling of being fortunate, blessed even, to have somehow produced such a special being, is as powerful now as it was when she first held Oscar in her arms in the delivery room. He was a tiny infant and she didn't know what sort of mother she would be, but she always somehow knew that they would get each other through the experience. And that is how it has been.

As if he knows she is still there watching, Oscar raises his arm high in the air and waves backwards at her as he walks past the Waldorf hotel, then disappears beyond the crowd of people waiting at the bus stop.

Was she actually happy with Ivo all those years? She didn't really stop to think about it. She was too busy. Now, Frances wonders if she derived her validation as a person from work rather than from her family.

Being made redundant in a marriage is very different from being made redundant from work, which wasn't great, but at least she saw that coming. Revenues were down; the whole industry was changing. Advertising simply couldn't be delivered in the same way any more. Though she had tried to keep up with digital this and social-media-platform that, if you were someone who'd grown up with books not screens, you never really got it. The young people who did were valuable and deserved big salaries which, frankly, in the new world, she didn't any more. If it hadn't been financially advantageous for her to stay there until the CEO finally called her in to talk about 'restructuring', she would have resigned long before. And perhaps that would have been better for her self-esteem. She'd seen what was going on at work, but she hadn't had a clue what was going on at home.

Walking past the Royal Opera House box office, Frances decides to see if there are any returns for this evening, knowing that ballet will distract her for a few hours. There is a single seat available, close to the stage. Frances always feels slightly guilty about going to the ballet because of Letty, but she has never lost the tingle of excitement as the lights go down and the curtain swishes up. The programme is a triple bill. The first ballet is contemporary and plotless. Frances is impressed by the technique but unmoved. Occasionally, though, it's nice to see something that she's not blown away by. It allows her to think that the life of a ballet dancer might actually be quite boring at times.

The second ballet is a revival of Ashton's *Marguerite and Armand*, and Frances is thrilled to see from the cast list that prima ballerina Marianela Nuñez is dancing the role of Marguerite, and the brilliant young Russian principal, Vadim Muntagirov, is Armand.

The story is based on Dumas's *La Dame aux Camélias*, a kind of mini version of *La Traviata*. A young man and a courtesan fall passionately in love, but his father insists he leave her. When the young man hears she is dying, it is too late for their love to triumph.

322

It's strange, Frances thinks, reading the plot summary, how most ballets are concerned with young men falling for women who are either innocent victims, like Giselle or Odette, or tragic whores, like Marguerite or Manon. Women in ballets are stereotypes and they almost always die. It's unbelievably sexist and yet she still adores it.

Why? Frances tries to rationalize. Perhaps art transcends political correctness? Maybe it's because those are the tropes of fairy tales that are embedded in girls' psyches as soon as they are born? Or is it because she's a secret romantic hiding in a cynic's body?

The dancers light up the stage. The Russian's musicality and phrasing is so natural that he metamorphoses into something that's more air and artistry than human being, his body becoming a kinetic expression of passion.

For the second time in a day, Frances finds herself grappling with her bag for a tissue as her eyes fill with tears. The performance feels so intensely redemptive she decides not to stay for the final ballet, but leave with the music and emotion still playing in her mind.

Wandering along Floral Street towards the tube, she sees Muntagirov leaving from the stage door. Dressed in jeans and a hoody, his hair wet from a shower, he's now recognizable as the boy she saw at Letty's first end-of-year performance. Part of her feels she should congratulate him, as if she somehow knows him because she has seen him grow up. You have become a fine young man! I always knew you would be a sensational dancer!

It would be ridiculous.

But she did see something special in him then, something almost miraculous: a shy teenager who turned into pure grace and elegance when he danced. He stood out from all the others.

There was usually only one brilliant male ballet dancer per generation – Rudolf Nureyev, Mikhail Baryshnikov, Carlos

Acosta. She remembers wondering whether this boy was going to be the next, and then having the treacherous thought that Letty would never be good enough to dance with him. Letty was a little taller than the rest of her year, but she just didn't stand out. She was beautiful to look at, and yet you lost her on stage.

Frances remembers sitting in the audience of proud parents suffering a terrible dawning of reality and guilt. Why had she ever encouraged her daughter to do this thing that she was not going to succeed at? Who was it for? Was it really for Letty? Or was it for herself, because she loved the idea of having a daughter on the stage, because it's what she had wanted to do?

She'd taken Letty to *The Nutcracker* when she was only three years old, not knowing that you weren't supposed to bring children under five. But Letty was so disciplined and contained even then, she could sit still for hours concentrating. She remembers the look of wonder on Letty's face as she saw the Christmas tree growing out of the stage at the children's party.

At the interval, Letty had asked, 'Can I be one of those children?'

And Frances had said, yes, of course she could, if she worked hard enough.

Frances sits on the Northern Line as it trundles from the West End to North London. It wasn't just her; they'd all encouraged Letty to pursue her ballet dream, she tells herself. Marina, and Ivo too. As a matter of fact, Frances was the only one who'd voiced concerns about the inevitable loss of a proper academic education. Letty was a clever girl. What would happen if she had an accident or something?

Afterwards she had wondered if it was the very act of articulating that thought that had somehow brought about Letty's injury and deselection, which was when things started to go downhill for her.

Never mind 'you're only as happy as your unhappiest child', Frances thinks. That's a convenient phrase that fathers use to show that they care. It is the fate of mothers to feel responsible for their children's unhappiness, as if it is all their fault.

But now Letty is happy in Italy, Frances reminds herself. She doesn't need to worry so much about her.

The light is on in the basement. She probably left it on this morning. But as Frances opens the door, she senses that someone is downstairs. She's felt every emotion in this house, but never fear, and for a moment she's furious with Ivo for leaving her like this, for putting her in danger as well as humiliating her.

There must be a protocol for what you should do if you surprise an intruder, but she can't think what it is. Should she shut the door and ring the police? Or would that be overreacting? It's possible it's just Ivo, who's come back to get something. He still has keys. Or even Rollo. The place is half his, after all, although she doesn't think he'd come over without asking her.

Frances puts her keys in her bag and slings it over her shoulder so that she can run if necessary. Then, still standing on the threshold but holding the front door open, she calls out, in as loud and aggressive a tone as she can muster, 'Who's there?'

'Hello!'

It is Letty's voice that floats up from the kitchen.

36

Third week

LETTY

Letty wishes she had never gone away. At least her mother wouldn't have had to suffer alone. Not that she's much help. They've never had the sort of mother–daughter relationship that could be described as a friendship. Letty has always felt as if Frances regards her as a curious and slightly tiresome creature. But in the past week, Letty has witnessed her mother's grief as well as her resilience, and she is beginning to think it is she who has judged unfairly.

Communicating with Frances was a challenge she'd generally tried to avoid. It was always easier to bask in Marina's unquestioning love or Ivo's uncomplicated affection. Letty had never observed her mother vulnerability before returning from Rome. Now, seeing her mother in an old tracksuit with no foundation to mask the wrinkles, and a narrow stripe of grey roots at the parting of her curly red hair, Letty wonders if this exhausted, fragile-looking person has always existed beneath the professional gloss.

It's strange to be home. She still feels in transit somehow, with no idea of a destination. She still feels afraid to go out by herself. She doesn't know how that's ever going to stop. She wonders if she should tell someone about Spencer following her to Rome. But who?

Frances would only overreact, and she has enough stress to cope with. For all that it wasn't perfect, Frances and Ivo's marriage lasted almost forty years, and Letty knows that whatever Frances used to say about him being weak or not taking responsibility, she loved him, supported him, allowed him to lead the life that he seemed to want. Letty used to wince at the criticisms Frances would level at Ivo, but now they seem insightful rather than harsh.

Seven years! It was seven years ago that she sustained her injury. There's a tiny part of her that wants to know whether her father had already started his affair when they went skating together. Or whether her accident somehow provided the excuse, the catalyst for him to betray them. She cannot ask him because she doesn't want to see him. Since he has been lying to them all for seven years, she's not sure whether she would believe his answer anyway.

Letty sits at Marina's old pedestal desk, wishing her grandmother were still here. Everything seems to have fallen apart without her. The house, the family. Did Ivo only stay because he feared his mother's disapproval?

Wearily, she opens the first drawer of the desk, half tempted to empty its contents straight into a black bin liner as Frances would. Her mother has become ruthless to the point of abandon, but for Letty it is more than just stuff; it is the catalogue of a life, a life she only glimpsed, she realizes when she unearths the photograph.

It's in a manila envelope with no writing on it, under a pile of similar unused envelopes in one of the bottom drawers.

As she pulls the photograph out, she feels as if Marina is standing behind her.

The photograph is in black and white. In the foreground a couple are dancing around a modest piazza of rectangular

327

houses. The woman's long dark hair is flowing behind her. She is wearing a waisted dress with a small white collar, buttons down the front and a full gathered skirt made of striped fabric with roses. The tall, handsome man, in high-waisted, wide-legged trousers and a short-sleeved shirt, is smiling into her face. Their bodies make a perfect V shape from the waist. In the background, old men sitting around a cafe table smile with pleasure; a few women with shopping bags have stopped to watch. One of them, with a pram, has her hands clasped excitedly together over her chest, as if she is clapping. The photograph has the slightly blurred quality of the famous Doisneau shot of two lovers kissing on a Paris street, captured in their own spontaneous rush of perfect romance, unaware of the day-to-day world going on around them.

It is a beautiful evocation of a time, a place, a love affair.

The longer Letty stares at it, the more she feels torn by conflicting loyalties. She has discovered something she is sure Marina never meant anyone else to see, and she is the only person who could have found it. Anyone else would have chucked it away, along with all the other brown envelopes that smell of age and whose glue has dried to uselessness.

Did Marina mean for her to see it? Or had her grandmother forgotten the photo was there? Or did she sometimes lock her door, take it out of the envelope and sit thinking about her long-lost lover?

Letty feels as if her identity is suddenly fluid, mercurial, slipping from her grasp.

'Come and have a look at this!' she calls to Frances, but her mother is talking on the phone.

Letty stares at the photo lying on the leather-topped desk. Is this delay a sign that she should not tell? But it is not her secret. It belongs to the family. Marina cannot simply hand the responsibility to her.

I'm sorry, she tells her grandmother silently.

'That was the estate agent,' Frances says as she comes into the room.

Letty feels her heartbeat accelerating in her chest, her neck, her head.

'We have an offer for the house. Short of the asking price, so I've told him to up it,' her mother continues.

Letty grips the edge of the desk.

'Which estate agent?' she whispers.

'The one on England's Lane.'

Relief whooshes through Letty's body, but she's still shaking. Is this another trick?

'You didn't tell the other one I'd gone to Rome?'

Frances frowns, bewildered by her peculiar reaction.

'Of course I didn't!'

The phone rings again, saving Letty from her mother's inevitable questions. She can hear her mother talking, but cannot seem to process the information. Whenever she thinks she is free of Spencer, he somehow insinuates himself back into her life. How is she ever going to be rid of him?

When Frances presses the off button, her face lifts with a smile. 'I only got us the asking price!'

Letty waits. She keeps thinking there is going to be a 'but' . . .

Frances's face falls.

'You hate the idea of moving, don't you, darling? I'm so sorry . . .'

'No, no, it's not that,' Letty tries to reassure her. 'You are an amazing negotiator!' She gets up from the desk, arms tentatively outstretched, offering her mother a hug.

Since she grew, hugs always felt awkward, with her being taller than Frances. But they've hugged quite a lot in the last week, and now Letty's not sure which one of them likes the feeling more.

Frances pulls away suddenly.

'I am too bloody impatient,' she says. 'What I should have done is rung Ivo, and when he said, "Accept!" I should have asked for anything I managed to get on top. Why didn't I think of that?'

'You could always do it now,' Letty suggests. 'He doesn't even know they've called.'

'Letty!' says Frances, surprised. 'How incredibly devious of you!'

Letty feels a little lift of pride at confounding the version of herself as a goody two shoes who never does anything wrong, except through weirdness or naiveté.

'I don't think I could do that,' Frances decides. 'I'm not going to be the liar in this relationship. I think I'll just take the gratitude and be satisfied with that. What's this?' she asks, peering at the photo on the desk.

'I found it,' Letty says.

'Mother and beloved son dancing,' says Frances bitterly. 'I wonder where that was taken . . .'

'It's not Ivo, though,' says Letty. 'It can't be. Look at what they're wearing. Look how young Marina is.'

Frances snatches the photo back.

'Oh my God!' she says, reeling as the implications occur to her, just as they did to Letty. 'Did you know?'

'Of course not!' Letty protests.

'I just thought, you know, the dress . . . isn't that the same one you were so keen to get rid of?'

'Yes. Because I was wearing it when Marina died. In Venice. In the very place this photo was taken!'

'It doesn't look like Venice.' Frances looks more closely at the photograph.

'It's Burano. Marina told me to go there. It's as if she knew . . .'

A shiver runs down her spine.

'You were always very close,' Frances says, putting her hand over Letty's, sensing she's disturbed without knowing why. 'Weird things happen like this sometimes, darling. Some people call it fate; I prefer the notion of serendipity, don't you? It sounds so much less portentous, and it's such a lovely word. I once tried to create a campaign around it.'

'A campaign for what?' Letty asks.

'Hummus and taramasalata, initially,' says Frances. 'Seren-DIPity, you see. There were plans to roll it out to guacamole . . .'

It's so very Frances to go from presentiments of death to party food in a sentence.

'Would have been a horrible waste of the word, really. And of course the world would never have been blessed with Dip a dee doodah, Dip a dee day . . .' Frances sings the jingle from a Christmas campaign Letty remembers but never realized was her mother's creation.

'Sorry, darling.' Frances realizes she's become sidetracked. 'So, let's work this out,' she says, holding the photo up so they can both look at it. 'Here we have Marina, in, what, the fifties? Must be. Clearly in love with a man who looks exactly like Ivo, who was born in 1958. Marina and Max were married in 1952. Poor Rollo looks so much like Max did – he must be his son. But Ivo, well, I never could fathom it. Marina must have met this man at the restaurant . . .'

'When I told her I was going to Venice, Marina said something about an Italian count,' Letty remembers. 'He bought her lace in Burano. And they danced in the piazza. She said she couldn't marry him because he was from a very old family . . . I thought she was confused.'

'He couldn't marry her because she was already bloody married,' says Frances. 'God, what a hypocrite in her bloody mantilla on a Sunday, and all her advice about how to be a good wife . . .'

'What advice?'

'Men's egos are fragile, Frances. You must not tread so heavily, Frances . . .'

331

Frances's imitation of her mother-in-law's voice is so spot on it feels almost sacrilegious in Marina's room.

'I was supposed to pretend that I wasn't the one supporting the family or making the big calls, in case poor Ivo felt emasculated. Although, in hindsight maybe she had a point. Maybe it's my fault he's fucked off with totty half his age! You won that one, Marina,' Frances calls out, looking up at the ceiling.

'Do you think Ivo knows?' Letty asked.

'God, there's a thought!' says Frances. 'I'm sure he doesn't. But then,' she adds wistfully, 'I was sure he and I would grow old together. Should we tell him?'

Letty thinks it's the first time she and Frances have been the 'we' in the relationship between the three of them. It feels odd, but also nice.

'Why don't we put it on the pile of things he has to deal with?' Letty suggests.

'Good idea. Of course, knowing Ivo, he'll probably just deny it looks like him and do nothing,' Frances says.

'But we're pretty sure, right?' says Letty. 'Because if we are, it means I'm more Italian than I thought.'

'Goodness, yes!'

Frances looks again.

'Oh! I've just had a wonderful thought! That dreadful old bore Max was always implying that you children got your intelligence genes from him. Well, it seems rather unlikely he had anything to do with it now!'

'Isn't intelligence supposed to come from the mother's side, anyway?' Letty says.

'Quite!' says Frances, beaming at her.

It's almost as if the photo has released her mother from a lifetime of being made to feel inadequate by Ivo's family.

'Come on,' she says. 'Let's go and find ourselves somewhere to live.'

*

Frances has decided that, rather than a flat on the river or a tiny rooftop garret in Covent Garden, they will look for a small house. She has settled on Stoke Newington, which is near enough to civilization – by which she means less than thirty pounds for a taxi home after the theatre – and also has decent restaurants and parks.

They're viewing a terraced house on a street called Palatine Road.

'What?' asks Frances, when she sees Letty's face.

'Palatine . . . I was there, just the other day . . .'

'And that's a good sign, or a bad one?'

Frances is so sharp. But she hasn't asked why Letty returned ahead of time, even though Letty knows that she is itching to. And Letty has not volunteered anything.

'A good one, I think,' Letty replies, knowing that if she says a bad one, she will have to explain.

On their return to Belsize Park, Frances makes an offer that is way under the asking price, and settles for a midpoint between.

'Now we can move on!' She hugs Letty, then calls Oscar to tell him the news.

Letty goes back to Marina's bedroom. There's a new urgency now to packing up. She can hear her mother talking excitedly.

'Oh . . . and you'll never guess what, darling. The strangest thing . . . Letty, can you send it to Oscar?'

Letty takes a picture of the photograph and WhatsApps it to her brother, feeling treacherous as she sends Marina's private moment of joy out into the digital cloud, allowing the potential for it to be accessed by millions of strangers, when it has lain hidden for so many years.

'Exactly!' she hears Frances saying. 'Do all families exist in a permanent cycle of secrets? Do you think that's what Tolstoy meant when he said that happy families are all alike, but every unhappy family is unhappy in its own way? Is there even such a thing as a happy family, darling?'

Letty envies the easy way her mother and brother talk to each other. She wonders if Frances will ever feel comfortable enough to talk to her like that.

'Oscar and I have decided no more secrets,' Frances calls out. 'What do you think, Letty? Can at least the three of us try to be honest with each other from now on?'

Letty stares into the garden. She has come to think of secrets like irises, Marina's favourite flowers, that wither after blooming but stay underground, sprouting tubers that may push up in unexpected locations when the time is right. Except that secrets, unlike irises, are almost always ugly and destructive when they come to light.

'Does that mean all secrets from this moment, or do we have to tell the ones up until now?' she asks for clarification.

Frances relays what she's just said to Oscar. They both obviously find it very funny.

'God, Letty, sometimes we have no idea what goes on in that clever brain of yours! How about this? Oscar suggests we declare an amnesty on all secrets until today, but a ban on future ones?'

'Agreed,' Letty calls back.

She stares at the photo, focusing on the V shape formed by Marina and her lover. They are waltzing, Letty thinks. Flowers in a vase. She remembers vividly the wonderful sensation of twirling, being literally swept off her feet, Alf's beautiful face smiling into hers, the current of electricity that arced between them from that moment on.

She recalls the crowd that gathered around them as they danced in Piazza Navona with eyes full of love, just like Marina and her Italian count. And she suddenly thinks: did someone in the crowd capture them on camera? Did a picture of her and Alf dancing fly around the world on Instagram? #dancingcouple

#Rome #love. And did Spencer see it, and remember Letty's love of Ancient Rome? Unlikely.

But Spencer knows Alf. And Alf is on Instagram. It's a logical link.

Since Josh, Letty has stayed away from social media, but now she finds herself trying to envisage the Instagram handle printed on his T-shirt. @rometourguidealf. It doesn't take long to find him.

She scrolls quickly back through the photos on his grid. Tivoli – no sign of her there; Bocca della Verità, the Trevi Fountain. Scrolling through the images is like reliving their love affair; the snack van in the Villa Borghese, the rose-pink city at sunset. But there are no photos of her. She asked him not to. He respected her wishes. She goes right back to the date they met, the postcard view from the window of the classroom. The following day, he posted a video. The frame on the grid is paused on Masakasu's face, contorted with the effort of singing. Letty clicks to open it. The Japanese boy is straining to hit the high notes of 'Nessun Dorma' and, in the background, she sees herself watching this most unexpected performance in amazement.

The caption reads: *Cool guy in my Italian class #opera #Rome #Roma #singer #BGT #Italy'sGotTalent?*

It has by far the most likes.

Among Alf's followers, Letty finds someone called Stuart who describes himself as 'Fan of Arsenal, Porsche, Property'.

He has put up posts from New York, and Venice, including the colourful houses of Burano. But, she is relieved to see, none with her. There are many with the blonde woman he was with, the woman who kissed Alf so proprietorially, who Stuart describes as 'My beautiful Gina'.

Nervously, Letty clicks on her handle. But the account is private.

Enough, Letty thinks. And yet she cannot resist going back

to Alf's feed, gazing again at the photos that tell the story of their Roman romance.

And now, looking more closely at the dates, she sees that the most recent photos were posted after she left. They have captions, but no hashtags.

Beneath the photo of Tivoli, he has written: *Dancing fountains*.

Beneath the photo of Piazza Navona: *Like a magical ballroom.*

Beneath the Bocca della Verità: *I didn't tell the whole truth, but I didn't lie.*

Beneath the empty pedestal in the Forum, the caption reads: *Where have you gone?*

Beneath the photo of the Trevi Fountain: *Come back!*

The most recent photograph, posted just yesterday, is not a view she recognizes. It's an empty beach beside a very blue sea. Above the photo, it says *Ischia*, and underneath he has written: *How many kisses will satisfy my love for you? As many as the grains of sand . . .*

It is a quotation from one of Catullus's most famous poems, a message only she will understand.

37

Fourth week

ALF

Alf has never seen a beach that sparkles in the way the Maronti does, the sand reflecting the sunlight like a million tiny mirrors. He thinks it must be something to do with the long-dormant volcano that looms over Ischia – it appears benign, with its slopes clad in forests, but constantly issues little reminders of its red-hot core through warm springs in the island's spas and the fumaroles that puff out smoke near Sant'Angelo, the picturesque village on the headland, where he has rented a room.

Alf takes a water taxi to work each morning, a little wooden boat with an outboard motor and Tino at the helm, who speaks to him in such a strong dialect that Alf can only understand one in a dozen words. Alf stays on the Maronti all day, lying in the sun from dawn till dusk, only stirring when somebody asks for a lounger, which he takes the money for and sets up with an *ombrellone*. But there are very few tourists around. The season doesn't really kick off until June, according to his boss Mario. Initially, he only offered Alf work in the afternoons, when he takes a siesta. Alf thinks there is a lover involved, because he always returns with a big smile on his face and a slightly animal smell wafting around him. After a week, he asked him to come along in the mornings too. Alf's presence allows Mario to chat and smoke with his friends in the restaurant, without losing customers to the rival *ombrelloni* outfit along the beach. In turn, Alf is granted breaks to go for a swim, although Mario thinks he's mad because in his opinion the sea's nowhere near warm enough.

There's a gentle current running along the shallows, and if Alf walks about a kilometre to the headland and gets in the water there, he can be back by the stack of orange loungers in about ten minutes without swimming at all. Alf loves the sensation of drifting on the water, his arms and legs spread, his eyes closed against the glare of the sun. He feels happy in this place on the edge of sand and sea, this liminal place – he remembers Letty's word – or as happy as it is possible to be without her. But he still sits up sharply whenever he hears the diesel engine of the island bus as it drops people off at the top of the small cliff above the restaurant, and the sound of English voices coming down the steps to the beach. If someone is visiting the island, they are bound to come here. The problem with moving around was that he could never be certain Letty had not just left the place he was arriving at. The rational side of him now thinks that if she ever came to Ischia, she was gone before he got here. But he still lives in the hope that she will return.

And he has nothing better to do. Alf had only got as far as deciding that what he wanted in life was to be with Letty. He hadn't thought about after that. There is nothing for him at home. It occurs to him that he is doing exactly the same job as the one he had in Blackpool the summer he was seeing Bryony. The two places couldn't be more different. The money Mario gives him, and the tips, pay for his room. For lunch, Alf eats whichever dish the restaurant wants finished, usually pasta with a seafood sauce. They wave away his attempts to pay. Whether there is a formal link between the restaurant and the sun loungers he doesn't know. It could just be that they are kind. After his siesta, Mario always returns with an ice-cold bottle of Nastro Azzurro for him. It's a pretty easy existence. As the sun goes down and Tino announces his final ride, Alf wades out again to the water taxi, and together they chug towards the setting sun, until it disappears below the horizon and the little harbour of Sant'Angelo is suddenly lit with a string of golden lights against the deep blue of the night sky, a colour that Alf has never seen in any place outside Italy.

If Letty were here, it would be perfect.

Each time he posts a photo on Instagram he feels he is sending it to her, in case one day she may happen upon it, like a message in a bottle, and read his captions and realize how much he loves her, and how sorry he is that he mucked up. But Letty does not do social media. She does not like photographs. She is as likely to receive his Instagram posts as she is to pick up a discarded vessel on some desert island beach.

The twins have arrived. Two identical little girls. Cheryl sent him the photos as email attachments; apparently Donna and Gary have decided they don't want the babies up on Instagram, which Alf is pleased about. He feels eternally grateful that his childhood happened just before 'sharenting' – he would have hated to have an online record of himself as a boy in a tail suit, or a samba shirt with frilly sleeves. The glass cabinet in the dance hall is embarrassing enough with its pictures of him holding silver cups half his size, grinning with no front teeth, his hair slicked back like some miniature matinee idol from the 1930s.

Their names are Isabella Cheryl and Dorabella Christina, his gran told him.

Alf wrote his mum and Gary a postcard instead of emailing to say congratulations, choosing a view of Sant'Angelo with a pink oleander in the foreground.

So happy to hear about the arrival of two beautiful little sisters!

Then he tore that one up, not quite knowing whether he was allowed to claim them as sisters, and thinking it would look a bit odd to put an omission mark and insert the word 'half' before 'sisters'. He bought another identical one and sent it with the message: *Happy to hear about the arrival of two beautiful little girls! Sure you've got your hands full! I'm in Ischia, near Naples. Have split with Gina. Hope you are all well. Love, Alf.*

After he'd sent it, he thought he should probably have said more about the babies and not mentioned him and Gina, but he didn't want them to look at the beautiful beach and imagine her sunning herself there. And then he wondered if it seemed as if he was asking for sympathy, or forgiveness. But he consoled himself with the thought that people never really read the words on postcards anyway, and it probably wouldn't arrive for weeks, if it arrived at all.

Then he decided to send a text as well: *Congratulations on birth of twins! They are beautiful! Hope all good with all of you! Love Alf xxx*

Alf lies in the shade of an orange *ombrellone* with his book. The Penguin edition of the poems of Catullus has a Roman mosaic on the front cover, an image of two lovers kissing, the woman's dress falling off, exposing her bottom.

When Mario sees it, he raises an eyebrow and asks what the book is about.

'*L'amore*,' Alf tells him.

Mario gives him a knowing nod, more *Playboy* than poetry, but he's got a point because some of the work is quite graphic in describing sex.

It has been hard work trying to understand the poems, even translated into English, but Alf has found a few really good ones he can relate to. If you get past the bits that refer to people in Ancient Rome, and the allusions to mythology and stuff, Catullus could be a modern poet. The emotions are the

same. Alf particularly likes one of the early poems, when Catullus and his lover, who he calls Lesbia – although, according
to the introduction, she was a married woman called Clodia –
are in the first throes of passion. He thinks the very short
poem Letty said she liked so much, that afternoon they spent
together on the Palatine Hill, must have been near the end of
the relationship, or even after the love affair was over.

I hate and I love.

He remembers Letty saying that it summed up everything
she felt about love.

Alf wonders if she first read it after the dickhead boyfriend
put up the video.

For Alf, the words speak of his love for Letty and his hatred
of himself, two simultaneous emotions contained in his body,
equally acute and equally painful, and he cannot seem to feel
one without the other.

I hate and I love.

It's tearing me in two.

Just sometimes the balance tips towards love, flooding his
body with a glorious smiling sensation of happiness, but for the
most part the heaviness of self-hatred feels as if it's drowning
him in his own stupidity and guilt.

He promised to be kind. He lied. Instead of explaining the
situation to her, his cowardice allowed Letty to see Gina kissing
him and jump to the wrong conclusion.

Who could blame her for running away?

Another thing Alf has noticed is that Catullus is preoccupied
with older men trying to spy on his relationship with Lesbia.
There is a poem about curious eyes or evil tongues bewitching
their love.

For some reason, every time he reads it, Alf thinks of Stuart
chasing him down the street. He's Gina's dad, so he was
angry – Alf gets that – but the words he spat at him were ugly,
almost like a curse.

'You struck gold with Gina and you threw it all away on that little tart.'

Alf's mind keeps revisiting the image of Stuart with Gina, strutting towards them. It didn't seem as if they were looking for where the school was; it looked like they knew. Or one of them did. Is it possible Stuart had been checking up on him? Did Stuart even go to the school and find out that Alf wasn't attending? What was Stuart up to when he was meant to be driving racing cars? On the very same day, Alf remembers, that he met Letty out of school and they went back to her place and made love in the sky. Was there any way Stuart could have known that?

No. He's overthinking. Stuart's the kind of bloke who makes sexist remarks without a second thought, and the school is scrupulous about not giving out contact data.

Every day Alf calls, hoping that Chiara the receptionist will pick up the phone, but so far it has always been Olivia who answers. Alf has given up pleading with her, and now simply disconnects. Today, when he rings, slightly later than usual, it is finally Chiara who answers.

'I'm sorry, it's not possible,' she says.

'*Ma dai, Chiara, cara,*' Alf pleads. 'It's me, Alf. You know me. I'm not a bad person. I'm in love!'

He senses the slightest hesitation.

'I beg you, please just give me the email address . . .'

Whether she takes pity, or she can't bear listening to his poor Italian any longer, Chiara finally relents. He hasn't heard it from her, she whispers. Does he understand?

'Heard what?' says Alf, his heart somersaulting with joy.

After his boat ride home from work, Alf sits outside a bar in Sant'Angelo with a beer, listening to the gentle lapping of the sea against the harbour walls and the *chink chink chink* from the rigging of the small yachts that are moored there. He had thought that having a way of contacting Letty would solve all his problems, and yet with her address typed in, Alf cannot think of a title for his email, never mind the words.

Should he put 'Sorry' or 'I'm so sorry' or 'Forgive me' or 'I know what you must have thought, but . . .' or even 'I love you' or, better still, 'Please believe that I love you and I never meant for this to happen'.

He tries to imagine her sitting opposite him and pictures her face, frowning as she thinks seriously about the answer to a question, searching for a logical explanation. He cannot write anything flowery, because that will annoy her. It has to be something that will stop her from simply deleting it.

He eventually decides on 'Please read this!'

And then there is the remainder of the blank screen to fill.

Alf's as nervous as he used to be when confronted with the title of an English essay at school, having done all the reading and worked out what he thought, yet still frozen, not knowing where to begin, not trusting himself to be able to convey what he wanted to say to the reader. Mr Marriot used to tell him, 'Just start, Alf. Don't think about creating the perfect first sentence, just get something down and you can always make it better later. To write, you have to start writing.'

It's good advice. Alf decides he'll get everything that he wants to say written down, then come back to it. It has been weeks now since he saw Letty. He's impatient to contact her, but it can wait another day. It's probably the most important letter he'll ever write in his life. He has to get it right.

Dear Letty. No, too formal. *Hi there!* Too glib. Maybe start with nothing. Just go straight in.

I'm sitting on the waterfront in a place called Sant'Angelo. It's on the west side of Ischia, where we were going when I last saw you. It's lovely here. Perhaps the most beautiful place

I have ever been to, but, without you here, Letty, it feels like looking at a postcard of a view instead of really experiencing it.

Before I met you, I didn't even know, but now it feels like I was just riding along on the surface of life. When I started getting to know you, it was like everything suddenly got meaning. In the mornings, I didn't wake up thinking 'another day', I woke up excited about what I was going to learn that day, and excited about seeing you, and even more excited about dancing with you, and . . . well, making love with you, that was like being taken to another dimension . . . I've fallen for you, Letty. Never knew why it was the word 'fallen' before, but now I do, because it's like there's an inevitability about it and I don't have control of what I feel, it's just happening to me. I've never been in love before. I didn't know it was possible to admire and desire someone so much that they occupy all your thoughts and emotions . . .

Trouble was – and here's the stupid bit that I'm still putting off saying, even though what I should do, should have done, is come right out with it – I was already in a relationship. I should have told you right from the start. I don't know now why I didn't. I knew almost immediately that I wanted to split with Gina, but it wasn't really because of anything she had done, it was because I had met you, and it just didn't seem fair to let her down . . . So, as it's turned out, I've made everyone unhappy, and I lost you . . . I hate making people unhappy, but losing you feels like losing the life I'd only just realized was possible . . .

Alf writes until the bar closes, pouring all his emotions onto the screen, and for a moment he is tempted to just click send. But he stops himself. He thinks of Mr Marriot again.

'What's your aim, Alf? Where are you going with this? What do you want your reader to think at the end?'

It's not an exercise in explaining his feelings to himself; it's his only hope of getting Letty back.

'Let it rest. Come back to it later. You'll be surprised how much better you can make it.'

Just after he closes the email app, a notification appears on the icon. He has received an email. For an excited moment, he allows himself to believe that it is from Letty, that the two of them have been thinking the same things at the same time and miraculously connected in cyberspace.

Then he taps the icon and sees that the message is from his grandmother.

Dear Alf,

We all thank you for the postcard, which was kind of you. It looks very nice where you are. I'm sorry to hear about you and Gina. I don't know if it was her decision or yours, but I do know it's always difficult when you break up with someone. And even though you know my thoughts about her, I believe you felt strongly about her, so that can't have been easy either way.

I'm sorry it all got out of hand, Alf. I know that your mother is sorry too. Sometimes these things happen in families and it all blows up, and once terrible things have been said, it's hard to go back. Whatever anyone tells you about the university of life, nobody gives you lessons and there aren't exams you have to take, so we all muddle through as best we can.

I'm going to be honest now, Alf, and say I don't know if I'd of been in the mood to apologize yet if we didn't need you so much here. Donna has been diagnosed with post-natal depression. I think she must have had it with you, Alf, which was why she was always crying. You were such a patient little boy with your mum. We thought it was Kieran's passing that was making her upset, not a medical thing, but now I'm not so sure. It was bad then, but it's much worse now. You think of depression as when someone's really, really sad, but apparently

345

it can come with other things like psychosis, and that's what Donna's got now. So, she keeps thinking she's a bad mother and she's going to harm the little ones, and she's terrified. At first we thought that she was just tired from the birth, and trying to feed two babies is no joke. We thought if she got some rest she'd calm down. But it's more than that, Alf. It's a mental illness. She's getting treatment now and she's had to go into hospital. Gary's doing his best, but he's self-employed so he doesn't get paternity leave like the government's always going on about, but they don't think about men like him who can't just take weeks off. Grandad isn't a teacher, as you know, and the worry about Donna seems to have made his arthritis worse, so he's really only good for doing the admin and keeping the books. I'm helping Donna full time, but I can't teach as well, and if it goes on like this, we're going to have to close the dance hall.

So, Alf. Could you come home and help us? I know it's a big ask. But I know you're a good boy. Always have been. I think because you were so much the centre of all our lives, Alf, we couldn't believe it when you lied to us, but all teenagers lie. Donna did. She knew I wouldn't approve of her going out with a biker, so she didn't tell me, so that was a lot to find out all at once, I can tell you, and relations weren't the greatest then either.

I'm sorry about being so hard, Alf. And I know in her heart of hearts Donna is too. Grandad and Gary always thought we went well over the top anyway. We'd all be so grateful if you could help us.

Love from your gran, Cheryl.

Alf wipes away the tears that have been running down his face.

It's nearly midnight, but that's only eleven in the UK. Cheryl has just sent the email to him so she must be up. He taps her mobile number, but it rings unanswered. Perhaps she's with Mum at the hospital?

Alf looks up flights out of Naples.

Then he clicks reply:

Dear Gran,
I can get a flight the day after tomorrow. Please send my love to Mum and tell her I'll be there as soon as I can. I'm looking forward to meeting my little sisters. I will do my best to help you.
  Love, Alf.

38

Seventh week

LETTY

They are saying on the news that it is the hottest prolonged spell of weather since the summer of 1976, which her parents' generation always remember with nostalgia. It has been hard work trying to get the last bits of stuff cleared, which Frances refers to as 'pockets of resistance', as if she is engaged in a war of attrition with the family's possessions. Each day, Letty wakes up to another piercingly blue sky, sunshine beating against the now curtain-less windows. The unrelenting heat is making her feel constantly exhausted and a little queasy. She hangs out of her bedroom window in a vain attempt to breathe fresher air, but it is already thirty degrees.

Letty picks up her phone, a small part of her hoping that the email she received late last night was in fact a dream, so she won't have to do anything about it.

And yet, it was wonderful to hear from him again, after weeks of trying to forget.

Please read this!
I'm sorry it has taken me so long to write. It took weeks of
persistence to get the school to give me your email address. And then

I found out that my mum was ill. So I'm back in Blackpool now, trying to help out here, and Italy feels like a million miles away.

There's so many things I want to tell you, Letty, but the main one is sorry. Everything I said to you was true. I love you. I've never felt this way about anyone before. I want to be with you more than I've ever wanted anything.

But there was stuff I left out as well. And that was stupid of me.

I was already in a relationship with Gina when I met you. Please believe that I tried to finish it that morning we were going to Ischia, but Gina wasn't home when I got back. I know it's no excuse because I should have told her before, but it was bad timing because her father was visiting Rome, and that made it more difficult because she was out with him, or he was there too, and it was never the right time. I never expected Gina and Stuart to come looking for me. That was too weird, seeing them and you, and then you running off. I panicked. I thought I'd better tell Gina then and there and get it done with. But I should have run after you and explained. By the time I did, you'd disappeared . . .

The email goes on about his longing for her, how she changed his life, how he wishes they could be together, but realizes that they probably can't because she will not be able to forgive him. He says that he respects that, but all he wants is for her to give him the chance to prove himself.

At the end he writes: *I am reading Catullus in translation, like you recommended. I hate myself and I love you, Letty. And I am torn in two.*

Tears roll down Letty's face.

Please don't hate yourself, she wants to tell him. What I love about you is that you're happy with who you are.

She reads the email again, searching for hidden clues. Un-less it is the most Machiavellian wind-up – and she doesn't believe Alf is capable of that – it is clear that he doesn't know about her relationship with Stuart. Stuart is Gina's father. It's as simple as that. And yet, she knows it's not. Stuart had come to Rome to find her, she's sure of it.

And there is Alf assuming that the reason Letty ran away was because she saw him with his girlfriend. She wants to write immediately and tell him it wasn't that. She wants to say that she always suspected he had a girlfriend, and she believes that he was going to finish it. But she knows that if she gets in touch with him again, she will also have to tell him about her relationship with Spencer, who is Stuart, because she wouldn't want to have secrets from Alf, and it wouldn't be fair for him to think that he is the guilty one.

If she contacts Alf, she will have to tell him. And he will not love her then.

Letty hears her mother calling up the stairs.

'Come and have some breakfast!'

FRANCES

Letty's obviously been crying, and she is doing that thing of looking away whenever Frances tries to make eye contact. She is eating a plain yoghurt. It takes all the energy Frances can muster to pretend not to count the spoonfuls, fussing around, running the tap, boiling the water, making tea, opening the fridge, staring at its virtually empty shelves, enjoying the coolness, sitting down at the table, pretending to read the paper.

It's not in Frances's nature to say nothing, and yet she knows that saying something might make things worse.

Since Letty's been home, she's hardly left the house. She hasn't even mentioned going back up to Oxford and Trinity term must be in full swing by now. She's not eating properly. Whenever Frances suggests she go for a walk or a swim, Letty makes some excuse and returns to her room, where she seems to do nothing but lie on the bed staring at the ceiling.

The medical term is 'ruminating', she remembers. And it is not healthy.

Is it still the aftershock of Marina's death that has Letty in its grip? Or the idea that Marina wasn't quite who she thought she was? Or is it the trauma of her parents' marriage failing? Or the reality of leaving the house she has lived in all her life? Aren't death, divorce and moving supposed to be the most stressful things?

Or is it whatever happened in Rome? She seemed so happy there when they spoke on the phone and Frances had dared to breathe a sigh of relief, allowing herself to believe that maybe Letty had finally become an independent person that nobody had to worry about any more.

Why did she allow herself to feel relieved? Surely that can't have caused this, Frances thinks, wondering how a perfectly rational grown-up can, even for a second, believe in jinxes. Is there a small, irrational part of the human brain, she wonders, that magnifies when stressed, making a person think that bad things are their fault? Or is it just her? Is it her own massive inadequacy, because she's always been the one who fixed things? Her job, their house, Ivo. What a joke! Now everything's gone wrong, and her daughter is sinking, and she's never been any good at fixing Letty.

This bloody heat doesn't help. Nor does the fact that she and Letty are living in a limbo-like space where they've not quite left one house and are not quite certain of the other. There are stacks of boxes in every room. Most of them are going into storage along with all the furniture, because, typically, Ivo and Rollo cannot decide what to do with the stuff their family has accumulated over the past seventy years. Rollo's wife doesn't want their house turning into a museum; Ivo and his mistress have not decided where to buy a place, or whether to buy at all.

'I'm really much happier in a one-bedroom flat with nothing,' he told Frances proudly the last time he showed his face, as if she should award him a Scout badge for slumming it or something. 'Perhaps we should put everything into an auction?'

'Nothing to do with me,' Frances said. Because even though she hates the indecision, the disorder and the delay, she is not about to start ringing up Sotheby's on his behalf, which is what she would have done in the past and what he hopes she'll do, although of course he'd deny it.

Frances is taking nothing with her except her clothes, shoes and books, along with a single box of treasured mementos of the children's lives. The first programme Oscar's name appeared in; the tiny violet tutu Letty wore for the Flower Fairies ballet at her pre-elementary class.

It will be exciting to start again from scratch, she tells herself, and yet she dare not look forward to it too much in case it doesn't happen; any number of things can go wrong with buying and selling property.

Pretending to be absorbed in the newspaper, Frances turns to the Arts pages.

'There's a live relay of the new *Swan Lake* this evening,' she announces. 'It's supposed to be wonderful. Would you like to go?'

'With you?' Letty asks.

'Well, I'd like to see it . . . We can go separately if you wish.' Frances does her best not to sound hurt.

'No, no! That's not at all what I meant!' says Letty. 'I'd love to go if you're going?'

LETTY

Trafalgar Square has turned into an open-air auditorium with a giant screen in front of Nelson's Column.

Letty cannot believe the thousands of people here.

Up on the screen, she sees that it is Vadim Muntagirov who will be dancing the role of Prince Siegfried.

'Lucky us,' says Frances, as they find a spot on the steps down to the square, which make a natural amphitheatre for the show. 'He got the most amazing reviews everywhere.'

'He was so wonderful in *Manon*,' Letty says.

She remembers watching the final act – the soaring music, the heartbreaking emotion that the dancers expressed through their bodies.

'It was the most beautiful and passionate thing I have ever seen,' Alf said.

She aches with longing for him.

He is back in the UK. Perhaps he is even watching the live relay in some cinema in Blackpool?

'I adore him.' Frances is still talking about Vadim. 'His dancing is just so free and lyrical and beautiful. It's like getting a shot of pure joy. Apparently the company nickname for him is Vadream!'

When she was a teenager, Letty used to think her mother chattered away incessantly simply to annoy her, but she has realized recently that it's because Letty's silences make her nervous. She doesn't know what Letty is thinking, and Frances likes to be in control. The more Letty tries to avoid conversation, the more Frances has to fill the empty space. It's irritating, but Frances is trying so hard to be friends Letty forces herself to try harder too.

'I had a crush on him at school,' she admits. 'I had this fantasy of dancing a pas de deux with him. Not that I even met him or anything, because he was years above. Except on the last day – I just had to rush up tell him he was amazing!'

Frances is staring at her.

'What?' Letty asks.

'That just sounds so unlike you! Weirdly, I almost did the same thing the other day. I saw him coming out of the stage door and only just managed to stop myself fangirling madly.'

The lights in the auditorium on the screen go down. There is a brief round of applause for the conductor, and then the haunting music begins, and the curtain sweeps up to reveal a wicked sorcerer turning a princess into a helpless swan.

FRANCES

All the good press Frances has read about the new production of *Swan Lake* is spot on. The sets are stunning, the costumes lavish, and the entire Royal Ballet is on terrific form. It's a pity, she thinks, that the music is so familiar from the thousands of adverts it's been used in. How amazing it must have been to hear it for the first time.

'What do you think?' she asks Letty in the interval.

'Loving it!' says Letty. 'I don't envy the swans though. It's not just the dancing, it's the standing in rows, not moving a feather between steps. Must be sheer agony on the legs.'

'Do you ever imagine yourself up there?' Frances asks, then winces inwardly at the tactlessness of her question.

Letty thinks before answering in her own considered way.

'When I was thirteen, the only thing I wanted in life was to be one of them. But I never would have been good enough.'

'Don't you think?' Frances says vaguely, unwilling to agree or disagree.

'I didn't have it,' Letty said. 'You can practise as much as you want, but you have to sparkle on stage. And I didn't, did I? Honestly? So, in a way, now it's more relief than regret.'

She says this as if she has just thought of it, but Frances wonders whether she always knew she wouldn't make the grade. Frances says nothing. She's not going to protest falsely.

Letty's dancing was lovely, precise like everything she does, but too careful, always somehow contained in her body. She never took flight.

'I'm sorry I stopped dancing though,' Letty goes on. 'Because dancing was good for me. I was never going to be a prima ballerina, but dancing was part of me, and I denied it. I think I should find a class again.'

There are so many things she doesn't know about Letty, things that she never dared to raise with her because she was frightened of making things worse. She always thought Letty's problems stemmed from having to give up ballet. It was why they avoided the subject, as if ballet had become an unmentionable secret, whereas they probably should have talked much more about it.

'I danced with someone in Rome,' Letty suddenly says. 'Not ballet. Waltz. We waltzed round Piazza Navona . . .'

Her daughter gives her a shy little sideways smile, but her eyes are sparkling.

For God's sake, Frances tells herself, do not say the wrong thing. And yet say something! Keep this unusual sharing of information going. Do not balls it up!

'What a lovely image!' she manages.

Letty blushes.

'Yes, I was literally swept off my feet,' she says.

'Can I ask who by?' Frances ventures.

Wrong. Too soon. The sparkle switches off and Letty refuses eye contact.

'Just someone I met at the school,' she says. 'He's a ballroom dancer. His mother has a school in Blackpool so he grew up dancing.'

Frances longs for more. Age? Looks? Gay? Straight? What were the exact steps leading up to this unusual event?

But Letty is now staring up at the screen where the third

act is about to begin, and Frances knows if she asks any more now, she will be shushed.

The set is so opulent that the crowd break into a spontaneous round of applause as the curtain rises. The dancing is dynamic, scintillating, and yet, whilst Frances smiles and admires, she is not transported to a state of forgetting where or who she is, as sometimes happens to her when she is watching ballet, because part of her brain is fixated on getting more out of Letty about what happened in Rome. Who is this dancer? Is he the reason for her abrupt return?

LETTY

Letty watches as the prince is duped into swearing love for the sorcerer's daughter Odile, whom he believes to be the swan princess Odette.

It's getting dark now, and the temperature has dropped a little, but the square is buzzing with the kind of energy you get in an Italian piazza, where it's a way of life for people to spend evenings outdoors. It only takes a few days of good weather for London to feel like a Mediterranean city too.

'Do you want a sad ending or a happy one?' Frances whispers, as the curtain comes up on the bleak lakeside scene of the final act.

It's not as ridiculous a question as it sounds, because *Swan Lake* can either have a happy ending where true love triumphs and the sorcerer dies, or a sad one, as in most English versions, where the lovers sacrifice their lives for their love, but the final bars of music hint at reunion in the afterlife. In this new production, the ending is unremittingly tragic, with Odette throwing herself to her death, and the prince surviving to live in guilt at his betrayal.

Letty was hoping for a happy ending, because the performances were so believable; she was totally invested in the story and longed for their love to survive.

'The final pas de deux was wonderful, but the ending was a bit of a let-down,' Frances pronounces, standing up and stretching after being seated on stone for such a long time. 'I like my fairy tales to have happy endings. Honestly, Letty, I'm beginning to think I'm a terrible old romantic under my cynic's clothing.'

'I suppose the producer was trying to make it as realistic as possible.' Letty tries to work out the reasoning behind it. 'In real life, it wouldn't have a happy ending, would it?'

'In real life, a princess wouldn't be turned into a bloody swan, would she?' Frances points out.

Letty laughs.

'Shall we walk along the river?' she suggests, as the crowd head towards the tube. She doesn't feel like getting into a packed train when it's still such a lovely evening.

The balmy temperature of the air makes strangers smile at each other in the street, as if acknowledging their mutual good fortune at being out in this wonderful city at this time of night with no need for a jacket or umbrella. It's as if the personality of London has opened up.

'It was a summer just like this when I met your father,' Frances muses, as they wander across Charing Cross footbridge towards the South Bank, the river slopping along beneath them.

Frances used to present herself to the world with such attitude that, even though she was physically small, nobody would have dreamt of messing with her, Letty thinks. Now, it's as if she's allowing her vulnerability to show, even in the way she walks.

'It was so hot nobody could sleep, so we'd just wander round Oxford after the show, talking and talking. We seemed to have so much to say in those days, so much we wanted to do . . .' Frances sighs.

'Did you fall in love with him straight away?' Letty asks.

Frances thinks about it.

'I fancied him rotten,' she says. 'He was *so* good-looking, and of course he was charming and radical, although I sometimes wonder whether his politics really went much further than wearing a Che Guevara T-shirt. But I don't know if I really fell in love with him until we danced . . .'

'Danced?'

'I don't mean like you. Not properly dance, but Ivo could do LeRoc and he was the best slow dancer ever.

Letty's not sure she wants to hear any more details, but perhaps it will be good for Frances to talk.

'Our last summer at Oxford,' Frances continues, 'there was a May Ball in his college. Tickets cost a fortune, but I'd been waitressing Saturday nights, so we thought, why not? We'll never be students at Oxford again, will we?'

Letty has never heard this before.

'It probably wouldn't seem like much to the festival generation today,' Frances recalls, 'but for me then, a working-class lass from Preston, it was like stepping into *The Great Gatsby*. There was an actual fairground with dodgems, a carousel, the lot, and a live band, but we weren't that interested in jumping up and down in a marquee, so we walked round the college walls, me in a hired ballgown, an apple-green chiffon number, I seem to remember, Ivo in a white tuxedo, planning our future. What we would do . . . how many kids we would have . . .'

'You planned children?' Letty asks. She's always assumed that Oscar was an accident.

'We already knew I was pregnant. We hadn't planned that, obviously, but isn't that the difference when you're in love? I mean, it's not just having sex, is it? It's that you want to have his children.'

Letty says nothing.

'Two kids, a boy and a girl. So we got that right in the end, didn't we?' Frances gives Letty's arm a little squeeze.

'Afterwards, there was a disco in the cloisters. Most people had crashed out by then. We were the only couple left in the quad, and I remember so clearly it was "Dance Away", and it felt like Bryan Ferry was actually in the cloister singing it just for us,' Frances says. 'God! That's a song I'd take to a desert island . . .'

Letty suddenly realizes where this is heading. Frances is so clever. She knows that waltzing round the Piazza Navona isn't something that just happens. She has offered her own intimate story of dancing because she wants Letty's in return.

Why not tell her? Letty thinks. What's the point of keeping it to herself? Didn't she promise no more secrets from now on? She stops walking and says quietly, 'I fell in love in Rome.'

As the words escape, her chest seems to inflate with a rush of excitement at allowing herself to speak about Alf.

'With the dancer?' Frances asks.

Letty smiles.

'Yes, of course with the dancer! His name is Alf.'

'Alf,' Frances repeats. 'I like that.'

'He's really a wonderful person, and when I'm with him I feel amazing, somehow. Like normally, I'm trying to hide or disappear, but with him it's like I'm present, engaging with the world . . . if that makes any sense?'

Frances nods enthusiastically.

'When I was waltzing with him, it was so brilliant I was actually telling myself to remember exactly how it felt, because I knew it was the best moment of my life!'

Glancing sideways at Frances's face, she sees her mother look so pleased Letty can hardly bear to let her down with the real-life ending to her fairy tale.

'Thing is. It was never meant to be,' she says, choking on

the words, as if saying them out loud has made the ending of their story inevitable.

'Isn't that a touch melodramatic?' Frances asks.

'It's over. I ran away.'

'Wait a minute – did he hurt you?'

'No! Why do you always think it's the man's fault? It's my fault. You have no idea what I'm like or how stupid I've been!'

'I know you have a tendency to think things are your fault when they're absolutely not,' says Frances. Her hand stretches towards Letty, but Letty rejects it, turning sharply away.

'It was nothing like that,' she says.

Frances sighs.

'So, what does Alf do in Rome?'

'He went home too,' Letty says.

'And you don't have any plans to see him?'

'No! I've told you!'

'Are you sure, darling?'

'Of course I'm sure!'

Why did she ever get manipulated into mentioning Alf? Now Frances is never going to let it go.

'You see, I had this . . .' Letty searches for a way of closing the conversation down. 'This thing with another man . . .'

'You were only there three weeks!' says Frances.

'Not in Rome!' Letty tries to clarify. 'It's complicated! Please don't ask for details. I'm ashamed enough.'

'Jesus, Letty, why can't you just have a normal relationship for once?' Frances blurts.

Letty feels her lower lip quivering. She stands holding the railing, her eyes blurring with tears as she stares at the lights of the London Eye twinkling in the inky water below.

She can sense her mother's hand hovering a few inches from her back, but she shrinks away, as if one comforting touch would shatter her into a thousand pieces.

FRANCES

It's so hot Frances cannot sleep. The window is open, but there seems to be no difference between the temperature inside and out. She switches on the fan, and then off again as the whirr annoys her.

The air is sticky as treacle, her thoughts held in its viscous grip. She cannot let go the image of Letty staring down into the river.

The swan princess throws herself in the lake because she cannot be rescued by the prince's love.

Is that what was going through Letty's mind?

Is that why she suggested going down to the river? Was it some kind of a cry for help that once again Frances failed to hear, as she rattled on about the summer of '76, when she should have been thinking about the more recent hot summer of 2013.

She remembers sitting beside the hospital bed the night Letty was taken in. The drip in Letty's arm. Letty's foot poking out from under the sheet, the heart with a knife through it, so at odds with the Winnie-the-Pooh mural on the wall behind. Still young enough to be in the children's ward, but with a bloody tattoo.

Frances remembers the looks the nurses gave her. What sort of mother was she? Her daughter was dangerously dehydrated and underweight. She had been talked out of jumping into the river by a passer-by.

How could she not have noticed? How could a stranger who had never seen Letty in her life have known she was in danger when Frances had not?

Frances tried so hard to be a good mother, but she never got it right with Letty. She read all the books about difficult teenagers, knew it was important to let them make their own mistakes. She tried to give her independence. Perhaps too much. Perhaps that was the problem? But whenever she tried to get more involved, ask about her life, she could feel Letty's irritation, her posture stiffening as the defences went up.

Nothing has changed. In the cab home last night, Letty shifted as far away as it was possible to be without hanging out of the window. The driver was banging on about the weather. It took all Frances's strength to stop herself telling him to shut the fuck up, even though silence would have been worse.

It's light when Frances finally falls asleep. She wakes up with a start, knowing what she has to do. Then sinks back into the pillow, trying to figure out if it's a crazy idea.

Everything seems to be exaggerated in this heat, as if they're living in the pages of *A Passage to India*, where events can be magnified and made into something they might not be.

She needs space to think rationally, away from the empty house and its silent dramas. But she can't risk leaving Letty alone.

Maybe it's about time Ivo took some responsibility.

Without allowing herself a chance to change her mind, Frances picks up her phone.

'For God's sake! It's five o'clock in the morning!' Ivo mutters.

There's a petty part of Frances that's pleased she's woken him up and hopes she's woken his mistress too.

'I'm going away for a few days and I need you to come and stay with Letty because I'm worried about her. She's not eating. She cries often. She seems . . . somewhere else, somehow . . .'

'Somewhere else? For God's sake, Frances, don't you think you worry too much?'

Frances feels as if her blood has gone from hot to boiling point.

'What is the point of saying that?' she shouts into the phone. 'What does it even mean? I'm telling you Letty's in distress. She needs help. I don't know how to help her. What's not to worry about?'

'She's twenty-one!'

'God, you are so gutless.' Frances spits the words down the phone. 'The fact that Letty disapproves of your behaviour doesn't absolve you of responsibility towards her! And don't tell yourself that really it's me that's the problem, so it's OK to do nothing. This isn't about me.'

'For once,' Ivo says.

Frances wants to tell him to fuck off. But she knows that is exactly what he is trying to get her to do, so that he feels justified in putting down the phone.

'Listen, Ivo,' she says, trying to sound icily calm. 'You have a daughter with a history of eating disorder and depressive illness – which isn't your fault, I'm not saying that. But what you do have to do is acknowledge it. It's all very well going on a march to protest NHS cuts, but you need to share the burden of care . . .'

'That's not fair! I used to do everything with her!' Ivo protests. 'It's Letty who doesn't want to see me.'

'You used to do the nice things, like brunch in Hampstead and matinees at the Everyman. And skating, of course . . .'

'That's below the belt, even for you, Frances!'

'Below the belt? I haven't even started!'

'Don't shout!'

It's what he says when cornered, and it's so middle class, as if somehow it's more important to appear polite than to address the issue.

'I'll ask Oscar then.' Frances puts down the phone.

After a couple of minutes Ivo calls back.

'OK. I'll come over. Where are you going anyway?'

'None of your fucking business.'

For a moment, she feels better for swearing at him, but the sense of release is fleeting, as her mind returns to the memory of Letty staring down into the river.

39

ALF

'There's nowhere better than Blackpool on a day like this,' says Cal, as he and Alf walk along the promenade.

Alf thinks of the little boat chugging across the beautiful blue water of the Bay of Naples towards the sparkling Maronti beach. But he knows what Cal means. During these days of constant sunshine, Blackpool beach looks golden and the sea is almost as blue as the Mediterranean, even if it will take a while for it to warm up to a temperature that Alf can tolerate for anything more than a quick dip. The weather is so unusually hot that visitors walk around with permanent smiles on their faces. Children play happily, shrieking with the joy of making sandcastles and eating ice cream, rather than whining that they are freezing as they shelter from the rain in the amusement arcades. The evenings are light and warm enough for people to walk about in shirtsleeves. The pizzeria where he used to work has put tables on the pavement outside, and the pubs are serving pitchers of summer cocktails with strawberries floating on top. If Alf had a pound for the number of times he's heard the words 'nowhere better' he'd be a rich man. There's a pride in the way it's said, as if people always believed that

Blackpool had this potential, and finally, after enduring many chilly, drizzly summers, their faith has been rewarded. In the evenings, the sun setting over the sea, tinting the water myriad shades of pink and blue, is as breathtaking and unique as any sunset anywhere.

It isn't exactly good to be home, but it isn't bad either.

At first, he and Cal don't quite know how to be with each other. His old friend is a little defensive, as if he expects Alf, having lived abroad, to think himself a cut above the rest of them. When he hears the reason Alf has come home, though, he's quick to offer sympathy.

Donna's admission to a psychiatric ward has not become gossip. Alf's beginning to realize that all the stuff about mental illness not being treated the same as physical illness is true. It's not just that it's under-resourced by the government; it's that people try to avoid talking about it. Yet when you do open up, almost everyone has a story of someone they know who has suffered. Apparently Cal has a cousin who got depressed and he's on medication. It took a while, but now he's fine. It's the same thing the doctors are saying about Donna. She will get better. It just takes a while to find the right meds.

The weird thing is that some of the time, Donna seems just like herself, like when Alf walked into the ward, and her face lit up and she said, 'What brings you home?'

But when she starts worrying about things, there's no reasoning with her. Even though Cheryl had warned him that nothing he said would make any difference, Alf still did what they all apparently did at first, which was try to reassure her, and prove that she was wrong. And it was as if his mum was just refusing to listen, which was frustrating, and he had to force himself to think how frightening it must be, to stop himself being annoyed with her.

Cal listens, which is all a mate can do really.

'Do you miss Italy?' Cal asks.

'A bit,' Alf says.

'So, you and Miss Jones . . . ?' Cal finally asks.

'Over.'

'Sorry, mate.'

'My decision,' says Alf. 'I met someone else.'

'You jammy bastard!' says Cal.

'She left me.'

'Oh. Sorry to hear that.'

'Yeah.'

'Still, plenty more fish.' Cal gestures at the sea.

'Yeah!' Alf tries to give the laddish smile Cal is looking for that will mean they won't have to discuss relationships any more.

It's over. Letty hasn't replied to his email. He can make up excuses – Chiara got the address wrong, or he wrote it down wrong, or Letty hasn't looked at her phone or her computer – but he knows that the most likely explanation is that she doesn't want to see him any more. And he doesn't want to become a pathetic, pining pain. So that's that. The best thing to do is keep occupied so that there are other things in his brain to fill the void of her absence.

The twins are staying with Donna in hospital, because it's important for them to bond with their mother and also important not to reinforce Donna's belief that she'll harm them. Cheryl is on hand almost constantly during the day.

Gary is working again, and visiting in the evenings. Alf is running the dance school almost single-handedly. In the mornings, he goes to the hospital and takes the twins out for a walk in the double pram. He felt a bit self-conscious about it at first because it's very pink, but he's found the best way of dealing with that is concentrating on his half-sisters, not on what people might be thinking of him. He explains the stuff that they're looking up at, like the leaves on the trees, the blue sky, streetlamps, seagulls flying over, so they'll get used to his voice, even though they can't understand, obviously. A couple of days ago, he received his first smile from Dorabella, who's usually the most alert one at that time of day, and he never knew how brilliant a baby smiling at you could feel.

In the afternoons, he usually takes a couple of Donna's private lessons, then, after the end of the school day, it's the kids. The big classes have dwindled because of the weather. No child who isn't dedicated wants to be sweating in a dance hall when they could be on the beach, but there are a couple of juniors, Mia and Toby, that Donna has high hopes for, and he can see why.

He's become much stricter than he ever thought he could be, barking out corrections in a stern voice as Donna always used to do with him and Sadie. He understands now that it's only when kids have got that special something that you really want to push them to make sure they achieve their potential.

In the evenings, it's the adult classes. Since the weather's tropical, Alf has decided to go with a Caribbean vibe, buying a couple of fake palm tree decorations from the party shop, and offering tall glasses of non-alcoholic fruit punch during the breaks. He's concentrating on teaching the rumba because it's slower than the other Latin dances, and it's the one that most women prefer. In the weeks since he's been home, the numbers have increased.

'You're a natural, Alf,' Cheryl tells him happily, when she pops in to check on how it's going.

He was shocked to see how much his gran had aged when she first picked him up from the station, but some of her frown lines have smoothed out since his return, and she's wearing make-up again, which shows she must be feeling more like herself.

On the plane home, he'd wondered whether there were going to be recriminations or some kind of drama, but everyone's too anxious and busy for that. It's like, you're home, you're family, get on with it – and he's glad it's that simple.

Alf's out with the twins on Saturday morning when he spots someone vaguely familiar jogging towards him, but it's only when he's a few yards away that he recognizes Mr Marriot, who he's used to seeing in a suit, not a vest and shorts. Alf swerves the pram to one side to allow him to pass, but when Mr Marriot sees that it's him, he stops running but stays jogging on the spot, breathing heavily, looking from the babies to Alf.

'My sisters,' Alf says quickly, as he sees his teacher's thought process.

'Ahh!' says Mr Marriot. 'So you're back?'

'I'm back.'

'And Gina?'

It's the first time anyone in Blackpool has referred to her by her first name since he returned. To Cal and Donna and Cheryl, she will always be Miss Jones. It's odd that his teacher's the only one to call her by her first name.

'I don't know,' Alf says.

'Oh . . .' Now, Mr Marriot's the one who's looking awkward.

'We went to Rome,' Alf tells him. 'Didn't work out.'

'I'm sorry to hear that.'

'No, you're not,' Alf says, but nicely, smiling.

'You're right, I'm not.' Mr Marriot smiles back.

It's all they need to say, and it feels good to re-establish respect without having to explain.

'So what are you up to?' Mr Marriot finally stands still.

'Don't let me stop you, sir . . .'

'You're not. Too hot.' Mr Marriot wipes his brow with his forearm.

'Helping out at home. My mum's in hospital.'

'Oh, now I *am* sorry to hear that, Alf.'

Alf can hear the genuine concern in his voice.

'If there's anything I can do, really anything, please let me know,' his teacher goes on.

'Thank you. I don't think there is.'

'Well, the offer stands. Even if it's just to talk. If you were thinking of having another go at your A level English, I'd be only too willing to help.'

'That's very kind, sir. I'm not – not right now, anyway. Got a lot on.'

'Yes, I expect you have.'

There's a moment of hesitation, where it's time for them to move on but neither of them quite knows how to. Then Alf holds out his hand and Mr Marriot shakes it, smiling as if he's the one who's grateful they've made up. And then he's off again, and Alf listens to his footsteps echoing all the way down the street.

'Teacher,' Alf says to Isabella and Dorabella. 'Good bloke.'

The woman calls late on Thursday afternoon while Alf is coaching Mia and Toby through their ballroom tango. He recognizes the routine Donna has choreographed for them; it's exactly the same as the one he used to do with Sadie at their age. But he's looked up the rules and seen that they could add a chase, which is one of his favourite moves, and always impresses the judges, so they're trying to incorporate that.

'Hello, Donna's Dance Hall, Alf speaking,' he says, picking up the landline receiver, reminding himself that he ought to put his mobile number on the website.

'So, here's the thing,' says the woman at the other end of the line. 'There's this cruise I'm going on next week, and I've left it rather late, and I need to learn to dance, at least the basics, pronto, by which I mean this week. Do you have any lessons available?'

'We're pretty short staffed right now,' Alf tells her. 'But if you don't mind me, I have a few slots available.'

'Why should I mind you?' she asks.

'Well, I'm not a qualified teacher, but I was Junior Ballroom and Latin champion, so I know what I'm doing.'

'Perfect!' she says.

They arrange an hour the following afternoon.

'Do you live in Blackpool?' Alf enquires.

'Why do you ask?'

'I'm wondering if you know where we are?'

'I have the postcode from the website, so I expect I'll manage to find you,' she says, and rings off, leaving Alf staring at the receiver, wondering why he feels like she's the one doing him a favour.

He realizes that he didn't say how much a private lesson with him will cost. Should he charge Donna's rate, as he does with the clients who already know him? Or even more, since she's desperate? He's going to have to negotiate when she arrives, which isn't ideal.

'What are you two doing?' he shouts at Mia and Toby, who have stopped mid-tango at the other end of the dance hall.

'You were on the phone . . .' Toby falters.

Did they hear him explaining that he wasn't a qualified teacher?

'And that's a reason for you to take a rest because . . . ?'

'Sorry!'

'Thank you,' says Alf, trying to sound as stern as Cheryl. 'Now, bent knees! Come on, you can do better than that!'

Alf would put his new student in her late fifties. She's small and slim and carries herself well. On the fourth finger of her left hand, there's a pale ridge where a wedding band has been worn. He wonders if she's recently widowed, or divorced, which is often why women of her age choose to go on dance cruises. There are usually a few male dancers employed to take them round the floor and make them feel better about themselves. It's a job he has considered for himself once things are sorted out, because you get to travel while you work.

'Before we start,' he says, 'it's thirty pounds an hour.'

'Any reduction if I buy in bulk?' she says.

'I'm not Costco,' he says, without thinking. She is his first-ever independent adult student, but he's not going to be a pushover.

She gives him a cute little smile, as if she secretly admires his stance.

'OK then,' she says, handing over three ten-pound notes. 'Let's see if you're worth it.'

'So which dances do you want to learn?' Alf asks.

'What do people normally start with?'

'How about a waltz? You'll need a waltz. Then for Latin, we normally teach cha cha cha—'

'Oh no, I'm far too old for Latin!' she interrupts.

'Let's concentrate on the waltz then,' he says. 'I'm Alf, by the way.'

'Yes, I know that!'

'And you're . . . ?'

She hesitates for just a second. Perhaps she's one of those women who wants to be called Mrs – by a younger man. But he doesn't think so. Her personality seems younger, not older, than the age she looks.

'I'm Fran,' she says.

'OK then, Fran,' he says. 'What I need you to do is stand behind me and follow exactly what I do. This is your basic waltz step.'

'Isn't it different for a woman?'

'Yes, and that's why I'm teaching you the woman's step. I know the man's steps. I don't need to learn, do I?'

That silences her.

He watches her in the mirrored wall. Her feet are pretty good, her face frowning with concentration.

'Look up!' he says, then raises his hand for her to stop. 'Watch me, and really concentrate on sliding that foot past your ankle. You can plonk it down like you're doing and get round the floor, or you can place it beautifully from the start.'

'Plonk' was probably going too far, Alf thinks, but he's keen to establish who's boss on the dance floor.

'So,' he says, standing in front of her with his arms outstretched, 'You know what the most important thing is in ballroom dancing?'

'The hold,' says Fran.

'Right,' says Alf. 'So put your left hand here . . . it's not on the man's shoulder, it's at the top of his bicep muscle.'

She moves her hand to the right place. Getting into hold can be a nervous moment. He always likes to get the woman to touch him before he touches her. A lot of women are very tentative, but Fran seems confident enough.

'OK, now give me your right hand.' He grasps it firmly and swings his right arm into position in the middle of her back.

'Ta daa!' she says.

'Comfortable?'

'Yes,' she says.

'Well, you shouldn't be,' Alf tells her. 'It requires a lot of strength from the woman as well as the man to keep in a good ballroom hold, and by the end of the lesson your muscles should be aching.'

'You're really selling this,' she says sarcastically, but he likes that she's serious about learning properly.

When she's mastered a natural and reverse turn and a change step, he goes to the music desk and puts on the waltz track that begins with 'Moon River'. Then he comes back and takes her in hold again. She manages to get all the way down the hall without making a mistake, but when he says, 'Great!', smiling down at her, she loses concentration for a second and stops.

'OK,' he says. 'We're going to try that again. Don't look down – your feet won't tell you where to go, you have to tell your feet. It's all here.' He points to her head.

He glances at the clock. Probably just enough time to teach a chassé and then lead her into a spin turn.

The chassé is straightforward, and she has good timing. The woman's steps for the spin turn are difficult unless you know what it's supposed to feel like.

He takes her into hold, but she resists going with the spin, trying to turn him instead.

'Listen,' says Alf, dropping his arms, 'I'm sure you're much better than me at most things, but I am better than you at dancing, so believe me, the only way we're going to get around this floor is if you follow me.'

Her face has this way of going from cross to mischievous in a second. It's quite attractive.

'Blimey,' she says. 'You're masterful!'

And then they're both laughing and, grabbing the opportunity while she is relaxed, he takes her in hold and spins her, then continues, calling out the moves, 'Natural, reverse, change, and natural and chassé and into spin turn.'

The music has now segued into the 'Tennessee Waltz'.

They manage a complete circuit of the floor and, finishing on the final notes of the tune, Alf bows to her and she bobs a slightly mocking curtsy at him.

'How was that?' Alf asks.

'Bloody amazing!' she says. 'Can we do it again?'

Her glee is childlike.

'Best to leave on a high,' he says.

The children's class are beginning to filter into the room, all the girls in pink leotards and net skirts, and one reluctant little boy in a Manchester United strip who comes along with his sister. Alf thinks he has the potential, but not the confidence, to stick at it and suffer all the taunting.

'Are you free tomorrow morning?' Fran wants to know. 'Maybe two hours?'

Alf thinks about it. 'I don't normally teach in the mornings . . .'

'But you'll make an exception for me?' She's used to getting her own way. 'It's just I don't have much time . . .'

'All right then,' he concedes. 'One hour. And you're going to need some ballroom shoes,' he tells her. 'We don't mind trainers here, as long as they're non-marking. But on a cruise . . .'

'Oh. Well, if you say so,' she says.

He writes down the name of the shop and tells her that she'll get a 10 per cent discount if she mentions Donna, Cheryl or Alf.

'Cheryl?' she says.

'My gran,' he says.

'We're doing this a bit different today,' Alf tells the twins the following morning. 'We've got a lady coming to learn the quickstep, so you're going to be good while I teach. We'll have some nice music on. I think you're going to enjoy it.'

Today, Isabella is the more alert one.

'Might as well get used to it, girls,' he says, lifting the pram up the steps, putting his key in the lock, and pushing the door open to inhale the familiar combination of floor polish, hairspray and a slight hint of sweat, all overlaid with rose potpourri, that always smells like coming home.

Alf gets the music lined up before the lesson this time.

When Fran arrives, she gives the pink pram a pointed look and demands, 'So what's the story here?'

'They're my half-sisters. I look after them in the mornings. That's why I don't normally teach. We'll give it a go, but if they

375

don't take to it, then I'll teach you this afternoon instead. Deal?'

'Deal.'

'I'm hoping they'll be used to the music because they heard it for nine months,' Alf says. 'So, the quickstep. Important you learn this one because at any social dance, the host or hostess will put on a bus-stop quickstep. So this is what happens: all the women wait at the "bus stop", which is just the corner of the room, for a man to come along and take them round the floor, then he drops them back again at the end of the queue for another bus.'

'How incredibly sexist!' says Fran.

'That's one way of looking at it,' Alf says. 'Another is that if there are more women than men in the room, which there invariably are, you get to dance with all the men instead of being stuck with some old geezer with bad breath who thinks he's better than he is and massacres your toes.'

'Jesus! When you put it like that . . .' she says. 'Anyway, I suppose ballroom dancing's not exactly noted for its political correctness, is it?'

'Not really,' Alf agrees. 'Doesn't mean it isn't dominated by some very strong women, though. If you think I'm tough, you should meet Cheryl.'

'Your gran.'

They're probably not that much different in age, Alf thinks. He wonders whether they'd get on, or whether Cheryl wouldn't take to another alpha female on her territory.

Once Alf has taught Fran the basic step, he puts on the music, but almost immediately Dorabella starts crying.

'Sorry,' he says, dropping his hold and going to the pram to pick her up. As soon as he does, Isabella starts crying too.

To his surprise, Fran comes across and picks Isabella up.

'There, there,' she says. 'Did that loud music surprise you? It's fine. Alf's going to make it much quieter now.'

Miraculously, Isabella stops crying, and looks at this new face curiously.

'Magic touch,' Alf says.

'It's called being a mother,' says Fran.

He didn't have her down as maternal, but he's not sure why now; she looks very comfortable with a baby in her arms, and softer, somehow. Not as fearsome.

'How many kids do you have?'

'Boy and a girl,' she says. 'Big gap between, though.'

Fran gently lowers Isabella, then she takes Dorabella from him and puts her back too.

'Is there any way of sitting them up a bit so they can watch? They'd like to see the glitter ball and their big brother dancing, wouldn't you, little ones?'

So Alf raises the back of the pram a little and puts the music back on, and at first the twins appear to be watching them, and then they fall asleep again.

'I always think half the reason babies cry is nothing to do with being hungry or having a nappy full of crap – they're just bored,' Fran says. 'Give them a distraction, and just like the rest of us they're happy.'

Alf can't work out where Fran comes from. There is definitely some northern in her accent, but she's got a kind of caustic confidence that seems more southern to him. No woman of her age round here would say 'crap' to a virtual stranger.

He adds ten minutes to the lesson for the interruption, and then says it's time for him to be getting the babies back to their mother.

'Does she work in the mornings?' Frances asks.

'Er, no. Actually she's in hospital,' Alf tells her.

'Oh. I'm sorry to hear that.'

There's a slightly awkward pause. He thinks she's probably thinking it's cancer.

'Post-natal depression,' he says.

'Oh dear,' Fran says.

'How about another lesson this afternoon?' he asks.

'Are you sure?'

'Yes. There's one condition, though.'

'Which is?'

'You'll try a jive. Honestly, you're going to need one Latin dance and you'd love the jive.'

He thinks it would suit her go-for-it personality.

'I used to do a dance called LeRoc at university,' she admits. 'All the cool guys who'd done a year abroad and snogged a French girl fancied themselves at it.'

'It's probably very similar,' Alf says. 'Where were you at uni?'

'Oxford,' she says. 'Not bad for a girl from Preston, eh?'

As she reaches the dance hall door, she turns and waves at him, and he gets a moment of powerful déjà vu, as if he's seen her waving before.

When she returns in the afternoon, they practise the quickstep, and he's impressed.

'You're a natural dancer,' he tells her.

'Oh, behave!' she says, but he can see she's pleased.

When she's relaxed, her face lights up and she looks much younger. He thinks that she was probably very attractive in her youth. She's not exactly pretty, and red hair isn't generally his thing, but she's quick and a little outrageous, what Cheryl would call a real live wire.

As he predicted, she gets the jive straight away, and he's able to teach her some quite complicated moves because she's now got the hang of following him.

'Actually,' she says breathlessly, when he congratulates her, 'it's far easier when you put yourself totally in the man's hands. Maybe this is where I've being going wrong all my life.'

Their hour is almost up.

'Do you have plans for the rest of the evening?' she asks.

'Er . . .'

His expression must have given away his slight alarm, because Fran says, 'Oh, please! I only meant could you give me another hour? I'm leaving tonight.'

'Your cruise starts Monday?'

'Exactly,' she says.

'Well, if you're sure you're not too tired.'

'I'm not that old!'

'That's not what I mean. Three hours is a lot for anyone.'

'Are you saying you're too tired?' she demands.

Alf *is* quite tired, as a matter of fact. It's more dancing than he's done in a while, but he's not about to admit that to her.

'So what did you have in mind?' he asks.

'The dance I've always wanted to do is the Viennese waltz,' she says. 'I know they say it's the most difficult, but do you think I could try it?'

'The steps are quite simple, in fact,' he tells her. 'But I don't think it's something they'll generally do on a cruise, because not many people can do it well. It takes a lot of energy.'

'Oh, bugger the cruise!' she says. 'I mean, I'm never going to get another opportunity, am I?'

The last time he did a Viennese waltz, Alf remembers, was in Piazza Navona, and as they'd twirled faster and faster, it felt like everything he ever wanted was there in that moment. He's reluctant to spoil that perfect memory.

But he's got Fran here now, who couldn't be more different from Letty, in age and looks and everything, and he likes her, and he knows that she'll be able to do it, and it will make her so happy, and, for some reason, behind the bluff exterior, he thinks there's a lot of sadness in her life.

When he's taught her the steps and they've practised, he puts on Cheryl's Viennese waltz selection, which begins with 'Where Do You Go To My Lovely?'

'Oh my God!' Fran cries, as the first few bars of Parisian-like accordion music tinkle through the speakers. 'I remember this so well. The guy who sang it on *Top of the Pops* was all moustache, but it stayed at number one for an age.'

'Ready?' says Alf, taking her in a firm hold.

She nods, endearingly nervous.

'And, off . . . we . . . go!'

He can't close his eyes and pretend he is with Letty: you can never close your eyes ballroom dancing, and it would be a disaster with the Viennese because you need to keep spotting so as not to fall over. Fran is much shorter and less natural, so the experience is totally different, but holding her determined little frame in his arms, hearing her shrieking half with joy, half with fear, as if they're on a waltzer at a fair, is a lot of fun. He doesn't think it's possible to feel unhappy when you're doing a Viennese. Maybe that's what Donna has been missing, with the pregnancy and then trying to feed two babies. Dancing was his mum's life. Alf decides that as soon as she's able, he'll take her for a spin round the dance floor, or even the courtyard at the hospital, and see if that doesn't help take her mind off all her worries.

As the music trails off into dee da das, Fran practically collapses against his chest.

'That . . . was . . . absolutely . . . brilliant!' she says, completely out of breath. Her face is pink, tendrils of her curly red hair stuck to the sweat on her forehead.

He smiles down at her.

'Not many people can get right to the end of that track,' Alf tells her, which is true. With Fran, he thinks, it's a little about ability, but mostly about determination. It's like, give her a challenge and she'll rise to it, because she won't be beaten.

'You could be a good dancer, if you wanted,' he tells her. 'You could do your medals.'

'I'm too old for medals, darling.'

'Well, you'll enjoy your social dancing anyway,' he says.

'If I can get past the halitosis and the stamping feet?'

Alf laughs.

'So, here is your money.' Fran hands him three twenty-pound notes.

'Let's say fifty for the two hours, shall we?' he offers.

'Sweet of you, but I only have twenties.'

Alf looks in his wallet but he doesn't have any smaller notes.

He shrugs.

Fran holds out her hand. He shakes it. And suddenly, he feels a little sad that she's going.

'It's been real,' she says.

And then she walks across the floor, and when she gets to the door, she turns and waves with both hands in the air.

And suddenly Alf remembers where he's seen her waving before.

'That's her!' Letty had pointed at the cinema screen where a small figure was standing in front of the orchestra pit, waving not just one hand, but both.

Instinctively, he'd waved back, then stopped as Letty shook her head at him.

'That is *so* cool. Your mother is one cool lady,' he'd said.

'Wait!' he calls out now.

Fran stops.

Letty called her mother by her first name, but what was it? Thoughts are racing through his mind.

Not Fran. He's sure it wasn't Fran.

She's looking at him, expecting an explanation for why he's called out.

'Buy you a drink? I mean, with the extra ten quid?'

'So, really I'd be buying you one,' she says.

He grins at her.

'OK, why not?' she says.

'I'll just switch everything off here,' he says.

She sits down on one of the chairs near the door.

Preston, Alf thinks, as he makes sure the taps are not dripping and the kettle is unplugged in the kitchen. He's sure Letty said her mother came from Preston. He can't have made that up, can he? Is the heat doing funny things to his mind?

And she went to Oxford, he remembers.

They were walking up the Via Veneto. Their first walk together. When Letty mentioned Preston, he'd thought he was in with a chance. When she said Oxford, not so much.

Frances! It was Frances!

Alf switches off the music desk.

So, the real question is, what is she doing here?

The sunshine is still bright as they stroll along the promenade. The beach is packed. He can see a lot of bright pink flesh that's going to hurt later on. All the deckchairs are out. It's going to be a lot of work getting them all back in and stacking them. He doesn't envy the kid who's got his old summer job.

Alf can't think of where to take Fran. She's too posh for a pub. He doesn't want to go to Cal's hotel bar.

'Blackpool Tower!' she says, as they approach it. 'The home of ballroom!'

'Have you ever been?' he asks.

'Not inside.'

Alf looks at his watch.

'This, you have to experience,' he says, taking her hand to run across the seafront road. He pays for two tickets, and they run up the stairs.

'Oh my God!' says Frances as they step into the ballroom. She gazes up at the ornate tiers, the huge stage where the Mighty Wurlitzer is up and the organist is playing 'Isle Of Capri'.

'It's bigger and better than I ever imagined,' she says. 'It's like a fairy-tale palace!'

'Wait till you try the floor. It's very springy.'

'We're going to dance? Here?' Her excitement is almost like a little girl's.

'Not this one – it's a tango – but there's bound to be a waltz up soon.'

'How do you know?' she asks.

'Tea dance always finishes with a waltz, so we'll get at least one in.'

He leads her over to an empty table near the dance floor, pulls out a chair, bows as she sits down.

'I love it!' she says.

'Tea?'

'I'll just have some water.'

He goes to the bar and brings back two glasses with ice and a jug of water.

'Do you come here often?' she says.

'Every New Year,' he says. 'There's a gala.'

'I think I'd come here every day if I lived in Blackpool.'

The next tune is a slow foxtrot. Another one that's impossible unless you know it. They both sit watching the couples dance. They're mostly old ladies dancing together, but they clearly know what they're doing. On the other side of the room, one of his mum's regulars waves at him. He hopes she's not going to come across and ask him to dance. Fran sees and instinctively turns to talk to him, as if to take possession.

'So, a good-looking boy like you,' she says. 'Are you going to be a dance teacher in Blackpool all your life?'

Is this the reason she is here? Alf wonders. To check him out?

'I don't think so,' he says carefully. 'I'm just helping out while my mum's in hospital . . . after that, I'm not sure. I'm thinking of maybe going to dance school myself. I'd like to be in musicals.'

'My son produces musicals,' she tells him.

He remembers Letty has a brother, a much older brother. What did she say? He was the reckless-passion baby; she was the biological-clock baby. And he thought at the time, what kind of a mother would say that to her child? But now he's met Fran, it doesn't seem quite so mean. It's just the kind of thing she would say.

'In Preston?' he says, deciding he'll play her along for a while.

'Preston? Good God, no! The West End. You should meet him . . .'

Her voice trails off, as if she's giving away too much.

'So, what about you?' Alf asks. 'What do you do?'

Frances sighs.

'At the moment, all I seem to do is move house,' she says.

'Hence the cruise . . . ?' He's teasing her now.

'Obviously,' she says, remembering her story.

'The fact is, my husband and I have just split up,' she tells him.

Letty's parents have split up? Could this be why she hasn't replied to his email? Here he is thinking that all she's got to worry about is him and Gina, when . . .

'So we're downsizing,' Frances says.

'We?'

'Myself and my daughter, actually.'

He can't do this any more.

'How is Letty?' Alf asks.

He thinks it's probably rare for Fran to be lost for words.

'Now this,' Alf says, as the organist on the Mighty Wurlitzer segues into 'Can't Help Falling In Love', 'is a waltz.'

He stands up, offers his hand, takes her into hold.

'You're not supposed to look at me,' he reminds her, pushing her head to the left. 'Lean back! Flower in a vase!'

She's so flummoxed that her legs have turned to jelly, and he's practically dragging her round the floor like a mop. But gradually her posture returns as she concentrates on following him. He admires her grit.

At the end, he bows, and shows her back to the table as a cha cha cha comes on.

'How long have you known?' is her first question.

'Just now,' he says. 'In the dance hall, when you waved goodbye. I saw you do the same wave from the Royal Opera House, when I was watching *Manon* with Letty. But even before that, nothing about you added up . . .'

'What do you mean?'

'You're just not the sort of person who goes on cruises.'

'Lucky I didn't pursue a career in acting,' she says.

'And you say things like that,' he says. 'So the question is, why? And how did you find me? I'm thinking of all the dance halls in all the world, you didn't just walk into mine.'

'I figured there can't be that many Alfs who were brought up dancing, so I started ringing all the dance schools in Blackpool. You were the third. The woman at the second one suggested it. You're obviously famous here.'

'Small world, ballroom dancing,' Alf says.

'I suppose I wanted to see what all the fuss was about,' Frances says.

Fuss? Is fuss good or bad? His heart is racing and there's a question he wants to ask so much, but he's afraid of the answer.

'Does Letty know you're here?' he finally dares.

'God, no! She'd murder me.'

'But she has mentioned me?' He feels pathetically needy saying it.

'She mentioned dancing in the Piazza Navona . . . I suppose I wanted to see if you were genuine . . .' She looks at him and smiles. 'Tick!' she says.

He can hardly dare speak – it sounds like there's hope.

'How is Letty?' he asks again.

Frances sighs and she looks different, fearful, and he's suddenly frightened of what she is about to tell him.

'When I heard about your mother, I decided not to tell you. I think you've got enough on your plate . . .'

'Tell me,' he says.

'I think Letty is ill. She's been ill before, you see. Seriously ill, in hospital. I don't know if she told you?'

He nods.

'God, I'm the last person to think that a man can be the solution to her problems!' Frances says, pushing her hair back from her face. 'And I don't know what went on between you, but I think you were important to her and if there's any way you could bring yourself to see her, I think it might make a difference . . .'

For a second, Alf feels like he's jumped in the air and taken flight.

'But of course, knowing Letty, there's always the chance that it's the last thing she wants,' Frances says. 'And I don't know if it was right to come here.'

Now she's looking up at the high ceiling, the ornate chandelier, as if she's trying to keep the tears that are shining in her eyes from falling.

'But I had to do something, I couldn't just watch it all happen again and not even try to save her.'

40

Sunday

8 a.m.

Letty is sitting on the toilet, staring at the awards for campaigns that Frances won during her years in advertising, and wondering why her mother allowed her achievements to be consigned to the walls of the loo. She feels partly to blame herself, because she never challenged the narrative that her father's family created to explain Frances's abrasive presence in their midst: she was a brash, difficult woman who'd come from nowhere because she was clever, but used her intelligence to make money rather than doing anything truly creative or worthy.

It was so unfair. Frances wasn't privileged like her father's family. She'd never been to concerts or opera or ballet when she was growing up. Everything she knew when she arrived at Oxford was self-taught. She had no idea which cutlery to use at formal dinners, nor what sort of conversation was acceptable at sherry parties and what was not. She thought students at Oxford were supposed to have opinions and air them, but she didn't realize that was only in certain social contexts.

'It was as if everyone else had a rule book left in their room, like a Gideon Bible, but they'd run out of copies when they got to me,' she remembers her mother telling her when Letty first went up. And Letty had wondered why she was making such a fuss about it, and what on earth did cutlery matter anyway? What she'd never done was put herself in her mother's shoes, a diminutive female redhead arriving in a city she'd been to only once for interview, ill equipped to deal with rich, entitled posh boys. In that position, you'd consciously have to create a brave identity in order to survive.

Letty thinks of what her mother said about dancing with Ivo after the May Ball, with Bryan Ferry crooning just for them as the sun rose over the ancient cloisters. She imagines their bodies moving together to the sensual serenade, both of them young, optimistic, idealistic, and still protected from the realities of life outside by those medieval walls of privilege.

They already knew Frances was pregnant. They had clearly decided to keep the baby.

The way the story was always told, or not exactly told, she thinks, but hinted at, by Marina, was that Frances got herself pregnant to ensnare Ivo. But this was the end of the seventies. Nobody had to keep a baby then.

'Isn't that the difference when you're in love?' Frances had said the other evening. 'I mean, it's not just having sex, is it? It's that you want to have his children.'

Letty recalls the feeling of Alf deep inside her, and her craving for him to go even deeper, so far that he would become part not just of her body but of her soul, and atoms of Alf would become all mixed up with atoms of Letty, their bodies entwined, their souls indivisible. Then she looks at the wand in her hand. Was that why this happened? Or was it just chance, serendipity, the expired use-by date of the last cherry-flavoured condom, which they'd only read afterwards?

'I don't think I'm very fertile,' she'd told him.

388

And he'd smiled at her and said, 'Let's not worry, then.'

But she's pretty sure he wouldn't feel the same way about a positive pregnancy test.

9 a.m.

Frances lies in bed, wondering why Letty is spending so long in the bathroom.

What can she be doing in there all this time?

When Frances arrived home the previous evening, Letty was asleep. Frances crept into her room, staying for a moment to make sure she was breathing, then remaining a little longer, liking the feeling that nothing bad could happen while she was watching over her.

Ivo wasn't there, of course, although in a way that was a relief, because Frances was too exhausted to parry questions or dissemble, too tired even to decide if dissembling was what she was going to do.

She'd taken the last train out of Blackpool with a connection to London, changing at Preston. Alf insisted on accompanying her to the hotel to pick up her small suitcase, and then he carried it to the station for her.

There's something rather old-fashioned and chivalrous about him, which Frances thinks must be the dancing. She's always loved the *révérence* at the end of a ballet class, and with ballroom, it's similar. As the dance finishes, he bows to her. It feels rather nice. And God, he's so handsome it's almost impossible not to get girlishly giggly when he smiles at you. What's lovely about Alf is that he's obviously aware that he's good-looking, but there's nothing calculated about his smile. He's not flirting, he's not patronizing and he's not arrogant either. It's not that he's guileless, exactly, but there's an openness about him that's very attractive.

Perhaps he's so at ease with himself because he's grown up

with two strong women as the main influences in his life? A single mother is obviously going to have a close relationship with her son, especially as she was so young when she had him. But there's also the grandmother Cheryl, whom he obviously respects and who's clearly a piece of work.

When Alf told her why his mum was in hospital, Frances instantly abandoned the idea of revealing who she was or why she was there. She's still concerned that it's not fair on him.

But it was Alf who said, when they talked about Letty's condition in the Tower Ballroom, 'I understand what you're going through, Fran. I mean, I know it's worse for the person who's ill, but it's difficult being the one who loves them, isn't it?'

'That doesn't put you off? Letty, I mean?' Frances heard herself asking.

'It's part of who she is, isn't it?' Alf said. 'I mean, I don't want her to be ill, but you can't pick and choose bits of someone, can you?'

A couple of tears had filled her eyes when he said that, and spilled down her cheeks.

'Come on.' Alf had stood up and offered his hand. 'This is a Viennese. It's the one Debbie and Giovanni did for their American Smooth in the last series of *Strictly* . . .'

And so they'd danced to 'Memory', which Frances had always considered a terrible schlocky old Andrew Lloyd Webber crowd-pleaser; before she was swept around and around Blackpool's Tower Ballroom, when it became one of the tracks she'd put on the fantasy playlist she is always updating, to take to a desert island.

10 a.m.

Alf is standing on the platform at Blackpool station.

Now that his old room at home has become the twins' nursery, he's staying at Cheryl's, so they usually have breakfast together. His gran was happy to hear he was going down to meet up with some friends in London. They decided not to bother worrying Donna with it. Gary's there to take the girls out for a walk. Maybe even take Donna out too. It will be good for them to do something as a normal family. Apparently, his mum had held both of the babies in her arms the previous evening. And she'd managed to feed them and burp them, and first Dorabella, then Isabella, had smiled at her as she changed their nappies, and she'd said, 'Did you see that, Mum? I'm so lucky, aren't I?'

So, as Cheryl says, baby steps, but it looks like they're on the right road.

Alf remembers the last time he took the train down to London, when he didn't even know about his mum being pregnant until Sadie told him. That seems like a lifetime ago now. He felt nervous then too; not like this, but because he knew he wasn't doing the right thing leaving without saying a proper goodbye. He thinks they've got over that now. It was always going to be difficult making the break between childhood and being a man, and he made mistakes. As Cheryl says, maybe they could all have handled it better. But that's behind them. It feels like they're onto a different stage of their lives now.

This time, he knows he'll come back, and he'll stay until he's no longer needed, and then . . . he doesn't know what. That's the future.

Now he's in the present. He looks at his watch. The train journey takes three hours to Euston. Then he has to get the tube, then walk the short distance from the station to the house. He can't believe that in less than four hours' time he will see Letty.

11 a.m.

Letty finds Frances standing in the kitchen, halfway through a slice of toast, making a pot of tea.

'You look refreshed. Much better!' says Letty.

'Thank you! And what about you?'

'I'm well, thanks.'

'Did Ivo come over?'

'For about an hour. He said you were worried about the illness coming back.'

'Bloody hell!' says Frances.

'It's not that,' Letty tells her.

'Letty, please don't exist in a state of denial. You're not eating properly. You're depressed. Don't tell me I'm imagining it.'

'You're right, I haven't been eating and I am preoccupied. But that's because I've been feeling nauseous. Especially, if you must know, in the mornings . . .'

Frances is about to speak, but then the words sink in and she drops the remainder of the piece of toast on the floor.

'Fuck!' she says, stooping to pick it up. 'Why does it always fall marmalade side down?'

For a moment, Letty wonders if Frances did actually hear what she said, and then her mother asks, 'Have you done a test?'

'Yes. This morning. I've done two, in fact. Both positive.'

'Is it Alf's?'

'Who else's would it be?'

'The other guy . . .'

'That was over a year ago!'

'Then why . . . ?' Frances asks, bewildered.

'Please don't ask,' Letty says. 'My problem now is, should I tell him?'

'Alf?'

'Obviously, Alf.'

'Well, it may be obvious to you, Letty . . .' Her mother's face has gone all lined and frowny again as she tries to compute the information and the available options.

Eventually she says, 'I suppose it really depends, doesn't it?'

'On what?'

'On what you want to do.'

'You mean, on whether I want to keep the baby?'

'Yes!'

'It's only a few weeks. I may lose it. Or it may be a false positive.'

'I don't think you get false positives, Letty. False negatives, maybe, if it's early . . .'

'So, I have thought about it.' Letty resists another wave of nausea. 'I don't think I could go through with an abortion.'

'Why not?' Frances demands.

'*You* didn't!'

'I could have done, though.'

'And what made you not?'

'Ivo and I loved each other. If we were going to have babies, it seemed mad to get rid of one just because the timing could have been better . . . and residual Catholic guilt, I suppose.'

'The last thing I wanted to do was get pregnant. It never even crossed my mind,' Letty tells her. 'I am not ready to have a baby, and yet . . . I don't feel I'm ready for anything. I don't know what being ready even feels like . . . I'll need support, of course.'

'Was it great sex?' Frances asks.

'What?'

She's used to her mother saying inappropriate things, but this is too much. She's perfectly entitled not to support Letty, of course, but . . .

'The thing is, I have this theory that happy babies are made by great sex,' Frances explains. 'Oscar's always been so equable and . . .'

Her mother stops mid-sentence, as if she realizes the inevitable implication of what she's just admitted.

'And it wasn't so good when I was conceived.' Letty finishes the thought for her. 'That really is too much information!'

'The trouble is,' Frances tries to backtrack, 'once we'd decided that we'd like another one – and we really, really wanted you, darling – time was running out and it didn't happen straight away. And frankly, there's nothing that kills your sex life more than plotting your ovulation cycle. It's like, we have to do it tonight or else, and—'

'Stop!' cries Letty. 'I get the idea . . . And if you must know,' she admits, after a long pause. 'It was unbelievable sex!'

12 p.m.

Well, this is awkward, Frances thinks, looking at her watch. Alf said he'd try to get a train at around ten, and the journey takes three hours, three and a half if you include the tube. That means he's probably going to arrive in two hours' time, and now she's even less sure that she's done the right thing. In fact, she is quite certain that it was wrong of her to interfere, and she only hopes that she hasn't put a jinx on the whole relationship.

Alf will probably think she knew about the pregnancy!

Never mind that. It's Letty she's concerned about. It obviously took a lot of courage for her to talk to her about it, especially at such an early stage. And when she actually asked her for support, all Frances could give her was her totally illogical pet theory about happy babies!

She's always longed for her daughter to trust and confide in her, and she just did, and Frances blew it.

'I really think you should tell Alf,' she says.

'Surely it's my choice what I decide to do?' Letty says.

'Of course it is!' Frances says.

'Because I'm a hundred per cent sure that Alf won't want to be with me,' says Letty.

'Of *course* he'll want to be with you!' says Frances.

She really is going to have to tell Letty what she's done,

Frances thinks, and she's got less than two hours to do so. 'You mustn't be so hard on yourself, Letty . . .'

'That's such a stupid thing to say! You don't know anything!' Letty suddenly shouts, and runs upstairs.

1 p.m.

Frances is knocking on Letty's door.

'Letty, darling,' she says. 'There's something I have to tell you. I've done a really bad thing.'

'I just need some time, Frances . . .'

If she just had enough time and peace of mind, Letty thinks, she would see her way through this. It's so hot and oppressive in the house, and yet she doesn't want to go out for a walk on her own that might clear her head.

'Just let me tell you this one thing, and I'll give you all the time in the world,' Frances is saying.

Her mother sounds so miserable, on the point of tears almost, that Letty gets up off her bed and opens the door.

Frances comes in and sits down on her bed.

'So, I've done a mad thing. I think it must be the heat,' she says. 'I didn't mean to . . . well, initially, anyway. I needed a couple of days away to cool off, so I checked into the Renaissance . . .'

'You were in a hotel just down the road?' she says.

'To begin with, yes,' Frances says. 'But I had this thought that wouldn't go away.'

'Thought?'

'That I might be able to find Alf, check him out, persuade him to come and see you.'

'What? Why?'

'He sounded good for you . . .' Frances falters.

'But how?' Letty asks, still dumbfounded.

'You said he was in Blackpool. I thought, how many dance

395

schools can there be? Quite a few, as it happens . . . and I've always secretly wanted to learn ballroom, as you know . . .'

As she tells her, Letty can't help admiring her mother's tenacity. Who on earth, apart from Frances, would ever think she could fix this?

'Are you serious?' she asks, when Frances tells her about ringing the dance schools in alphabetical order.

'So, third time lucky. He answers the phone . . .'

2 p.m.

Alf takes the Northern Line to Belsize Park.

The exit from the tube is on a hill. It looks pretty much like any number of suburban streets, if it weren't for the fact that there are no empty storefronts, and only one charity shop. The rest are all estate agents, coffee shops, florists, restaurants; it's obviously a prosperous area.

Letty's street is a tree-lined avenue of white stucco houses, a bit like where the children live in *Mary Poppins*. Each is five storeys high, if you count the basement and the windows in the roof. Each has tiled steps up to a large porch that's supported by columns. They're the sort of properties that Stuart sells to oligarchs and rock stars for millions and millions of pounds.

He always knew Letty was out of his league, he thinks. But not this far. It's never going to work between them. The gap's too big. She never even replied to his email, so why on earth did he ever think this was a good idea?

It all seemed so straightforward when he was talking to Frances. He likes Frances. And she was a girl from Preston, wasn't she? And she managed to fit in here, didn't she? He tries to breathe through the nerves, before climbing the steps to the shiny black front door with its brass lion knocker. His hand hovers over it.

Still time to change my mind, he thinks. Then a movement at the curtain-less bay window makes him glance to the side.

Letty smiles at him from the empty room. Dimples. He has thought only of the horror on her face as she turned and ran away from him. He had forgotten the dimples. But then the smile fades and she disappears. The front door opens and she's standing just a couple of feet in front of him, and yet she seems as unreachable as when he first saw her.

'I believe you already know my mother,' Letty says, as she shows him downstairs to the kitchen where Frances is sitting at a big table. She looks as if she's been crying, Alf thinks. They both do.

'This house!' Alf says.

'You're not seeing it at its best,' says Frances.

'No, I mean, it's huge!'

'Oh, don't worry, we only own about a tenth of it.'

'We're moving to Stoke Newington,' Letty informs him.

'To Palatine Road,' Frances adds.

He doesn't know what he's supposed to say.

There's a silence, then Frances says, 'Tea? Or something stronger? Or' – she pushes back her chair – 'why don't I just leave you two to it?'

'Would you like tea?' Letty asks, once they've heard Frances going upstairs.

'The British answer to all awkwardness,' he says.

She looks taken aback.

'I didn't mean . . .' he says.

'No. You've every right,' she says, looking at the floor. 'Shall we go for a walk?'

3 p.m.

'Which way?' Letty asks him as the front door closes behind them. 'That way' – she gestures with her left hand – 'is Hampstead Heath. The other way is Primrose Hill.'

'Where you went sledging?' he says.

'Yes!' She's forgotten telling him about that.

'Has to be Primrose Hill, doesn't it?' he says.

It's a relief, but it's also a stay of execution, Letty thinks.

The advantage of Hampstead would be that it's where Stuart's estate agency is. So the subject would arise naturally, and it's better to get it over and done with, surely? But the thought is even more terrifying now that Alf is here, in the flesh, even more gorgeous than she remembered him, with his tan and his hair all blond from the sun.

'So you went to Ischia?' she says, as they walk along the road.

'Yes.'

'What's it like?'

'Stunning,' he says. 'I thought you might have gone, you know, after—'

'No,' she says quickly. 'I took the first train out of Rome to Milan. Stayed there a few days, wondering what to do.'

'No wonder I couldn't find you,' he says.

Their footsteps echo on the pavement, silent thoughts reverberating in the air.

'What's Milan like?' he asks.

They've gone back to comparing notes on places they've been, she thinks.

'I liked it,' Letty says. 'The cathedral is amazing. It's very dark inside, but when the sunlight comes through the stained glass it makes these incredible coloured projections on the stone. You can go up on the roof, amongst all these unbelievably delicate spires and statues of saints. It's like being in Heaven . . .'

She doesn't tell him that when she was up there, she imagined how easy it would be to throw herself to the ground and make all her problems and mistakes go away.

But how she dismissed the thought, picturing how upset her family would be, and Alf, if he ever found out, and how it would ruin all their lives and make a horrible mess on the beautiful piazza, which would be incredibly selfish of her. And how that moment had felt like an epiphany up in the sky, surrounded by saints, because that's when she realized that she wasn't ill, just sad. Because when she was ill, she'd thought that her dying would make it easier for everyone.

4 p.m.

They are standing at the top of Primrose Hill, with London spread out below them. The grass is dry and brown after the unusually long spell of constant sunshine, and the hill is almost like a beach, with people on towels sunbathing, and groups of mothers with small children sleeping in pushchairs in the shade of sun umbrellas.

Below them is the zoo and then Regent's Park, says Letty, pointing to the near and middle distance.

'And what's beyond?' he asks.

'Well, central London,' she says. 'The river Thames. Look, there's the London Eye ... and Big Ben, behind that scaffolding.'

She indicates familiar shapes that seem very small on the horizon.

He remembers looking out of the window of her amazing loft in Rome, and finding the Vittorio Emanuele monument in the far distance. And he remembers what they did straight after that. And he so wants to touch her now, kiss her. But when he shifts slightly closer to her, she moves away.

Suddenly she's running down the hill, with her arms

stretched out like a child being an airplane, her long hair flowing behind her. He launches after her, swerving and leaping and stumbling over uneven hillocks, until finally falling and rolling over and over until they are lying side by side on the parched earth, gazing up at the blue sky, laughing.

He props himself up on his elbow beside her, looking down at her beautiful serious face. She stretches out one hand to run her fingers through his hair and pulls him down, hugging him so tightly he can feel her heart beating against his chest. And it feels so right. As if all his life was leading to this moment, the past gone, the future opening up. When they break apart, he touches her face, gently tracing the outline of her cheek that is wet with tears.

'What?' he asks.

'I just want a little bit more time with you!' she says.

'You've got it!'

'No . . .'

She pushes him off, sits up abruptly. Looks the other way.

'Too much has happened that can't be changed.'

'I'm so sorry about Gina,' he says.

'I thought all along there was someone . . .' she says.

'I'm so sorry.'

She takes a very deep breath, like a backwards sigh.

'Alf, it's not Gina, it's Spencer.'

'Spencer?'

'Stuart. I know him as Spencer . . .'

He doesn't understand what she is saying.

'You know Stuart, how?' he finally asks.

'It's a long story and at the end of it, you won't like me any more and—'

He puts his finger lightly on her lips.

'Don't say that.'

She takes his hand from her face and turns away from him again, not able to look at him as she begins to tell him about her first meeting with Stuart at the Randolph hotel and how she walked out and left him. And then, their subsequent chance meeting on the train.

'I was compromised as soon as I sat with him in first class,' she says.

Alf wonders if it was chance at all.

And then she tells him about all their meetings after that. The Sky Garden, New York, the opera, Venice, the opera, their boat trip to Burano, and what happened in the hotel room that was so close to the lagoon she could hear the water lapping and the gondolas clunking against their moorings.

Her weeping is all mixed up with blaming and berating herself, and when he tries to comfort her she pushes him away crossly, so he sits and listens, until gradually her sobs subside with one big breath and there is silence between them.

He knows it is crucially important to say something. The longer he doesn't, the less she will believe him, but he can't find anything that doesn't sound like a trite cliché.

'Letty . . .'

He dares to touch her hand, and when she allows that he draws her to him, and her tears soak through the shirt he is wearing, right to his skin, as he holds her against his chest, never wanting to let her go again.

5 p.m.

For the longest time Alf says nothing, and Letty doesn't want to move because she loves feeling his hand holding her head against his chest, and the wonderful smell of him. Then finally, he speaks. 'In a way we were both seduced.'

'Both?'

He stands up, pulling Letty to her feet, and says, 'Let's walk down to the river and I'll tell you about how I met Gina.'

He tells her about the audition for *Grease*, and driving to the after-party in her brand-new pink Cinquecento, and how by chance she turned up at his mum's dance school – but Letty wonders if it was chance at all – and how he helped her make up flat-pack furniture in her brand-new apartment on the seafront, and how it was thrilling to keep their secret affair from his mates at school, and how, when it all blew up with his family, it was Alf who felt guilty for getting Gina into trouble, but how it was too late, then, to turn back the clock.

In the Italian Gardens, they stop to sit for a while in the shade. Someone must be watering the plants, Letty thinks, because there are bright cascades of petunias spilling from stone urns.

There's a long silence in which Alf seems to be figuring it all out.

'I think we should be grateful to them,' he finally says.

'How do you work that out?' Letty asks.

'Neither of us would have been in Rome without them, would we?' he says. 'We never would have met . . .'

Is this what love feels like? Is she understanding him correctly? She's been wrong before. Didn't she think that Josh loved her? But that was different, because with Josh she was always trying to be someone different, the sort of girl she thought he would like.

With Alf she has always been herself, in all her neurotic loneliness. And he still seems to like her.

Holding hands, they walk through the elegant Georgian terraces of Fitzrovia, then the narrow streets of Soho, which was once the red-light area of London but is now full of clubs and cafes.

Letty stops walking suddenly, forcing herself to ask the direct question she needs him to answer.

'Doesn't it bother you that I slept with Stuart?'

'Of course it does,' Alf says.

Her chest sinks. She knew it was too good to last.

'Because I hate the idea of you ever being with anyone else,' he says. 'Doesn't it bother you that I slept with Gina?'

'He paid me,' she says, 'I was his sugar baby.'

'He thought that. You didn't. You thought he was taking you to the opera. Gina paid for a spa day in a hotel. Does that make me her gigolo?'

'Why is gigolo a much nicer word than whore?' Letty wonders.

'We're not in the eighteenth century any more,' Alf says. 'Nobody's going to send us to a penal colony . . .'

It's a reference to *Manon*, she realizes, and for a moment she thinks of Des Grieux, Manon's devoted lover, dancing with desperate, mournful passion.

'I'm not saying you're like Manon,' Alf says. 'And I'm no romantic poet either. So here's the thing: we can live our lives regretting what we've done or we can move on. It's like hearing a song, trying to decide whether you'll dance or not. If you wait too long, the music's over, you've missed your chance, and you'll never get that moment back.'

6 p.m.

He can see her thinking about what was just a throwaway line, examining its logic.

'But what about . . . Stuart?' she says. 'It feels like he's stalking me . . .'

Alf thinks of what Stuart said about Letty, and the expression on his face when Alf hit him. How Alf suddenly recognized him for what he was. A cowering, spiteful misogynist. He wonders now why it took him so long to see it. He was so bowled over by the success Stuart had made of his life and the wealth he had accumulated, when all he was was a pathetic middle-aged bloke with a James Bond fantasy.

'Stuart's a bully,' he says. 'Bullies are usually cowards. I

403

don't think he'd dare do anything. It's the chase he obviously enjoys. Probably not capable of any kind of relationship, not even as a stalker . . .'

He hopes that's true. He's not going to live his life intimidated by the thought of an Arsenal supporter with a lime-green Porsche.

They cross Trafalgar Square and take a route through Charing Cross station that looks dark and unpromising, but suddenly becomes a footbridge across the river Thames.

The tide is high and the water churns beneath them. In the distance, he can see the dome of St Paul's Cathedral surrounded by the glass towers of the City, their windows glinting in the evening sunlight.

There's been something that he's been practising saying, in case he ever saw her again, and if there's ever going to be a moment, this is it. And it's easier walking, somehow, when she won't be staring straight at him and wincing when he gets the pronunciation wrong.

'There's something I want to say to you,' he says. 'Please bear with me.'

There's a small enquiring frown on Letty's face. She's still nervous, expecting the worst. He hopes that in time, she will relax with him again, like she did in Rome. He clears his throat, suddenly very nervous himself, and takes her hand.

'*Vivamus, mea Letty, atque amemus, rumoresque senum severiorum omnes unius aestimemus assis.*'

Now she is smiling at him. Dimples.

'Let us live, my Letty,' she laughs, 'and let us love, and put no value on the gossip of horrid old men.'

It's weird, Alf thinks, how the words seem even more appropriate now than before he knew about Stuart.

'*Soles occidere et redire possunt; nobis, cum semel occidit brevis lux, nox est perpetua una dormienda.*'

'Suns may set and rise. For us, once the brief light has gone, we will sleep forever.'

404

'Da mi basia mille, deinde centum, dein mille altera, dein secunda centum, deinde usque altera mille, deinde centum. Dein, cum milia multa fecerimus . . .'

'Give me a thousand kisses, then a hundred, then another thousand and a second hundred, then yct another thousand, then a hundred, then when we have kissed so many times . . .'

Her violet eyes are shining in amazement that he has remembered all the words and she looks so happy, he wants to stop walking and kiss her, but he has practised the poem so many times, he is determined to get to the end.

'Conturbabimus illa, ne sciamus, aut ne quis malus invidere possit, cum tantum sciat esse basiorum.'

'So that we confuse the total and not know it, and no bad person can envy us, when he realizes our kisses are so many.'

They stop in the middle of the bridge. He looks at her. She takes a step towards him, and he lifts her off the ground so that their faces are level and they kiss for a long time.

Dozens, hundreds, thousands of kisses.

'How did you find Catullus in Latin?' she asks eventually.

'The internet can be very useful,' he tells her.

'That is the loveliest thing that anyone has ever done for me!' she says, beaming at him.

And then she draws away, her face suddenly anxious again.

7 p.m.

It's just twelve hours, Letty thinks, since she discovered she was pregnant, and realized that her life had changed completely and she was going to have to change herself. She was going to have to be strong now, because it was no longer acceptable for her to muck up. It wasn't just about her any more.

But there is a part of her that longs to wallow in the unbelievable happiness of the past few minutes for just a little longer. Just this evening, maybe, just tonight. Or maybe even for another month, until it's more certain. Because she knows that what she is about to say will change everything again, risk everything.

But Frances knows.

So Alf has to know. No more secrets.

She listens to the water lapping below and the hum of the city. Alf's arm is around her shoulder, his forefinger gently stroking her skin under the sleeve of her T-shirt. She wishes it were possible for them to stay in this perfect moment, in this liminal place, forever.

'I'm pregnant, Alf,' she says.

She feels the slight pressure of his hand as he turns her to face him. And then he looks into her eyes for a long time, before dipping his face and kissing her so softly, his eyes closed, as if he is concentrating on pouring his love into her. For a moment, she feels nostalgic for the time, just a minute ago, when they were carelessly in love, and it was just the two of them and there was no need to be sensible at all.

Then he says, 'The weekend after we spent that Friday afternoon on the Palatine together, I was walking by the Tiber and there was this graffiti, *Non cercavo niente, ma con te ho trovato tutto! Sei il mio tutto. Ti amo!* When I read it, it was only you I thought of. And I thought, how can I love her, how can she be my everything when I've just met her? But you are my everything. I love you.'

They amble hand in hand along the riverbank and watch the sunset from Waterloo Bridge, then wander into Covent Garden piazza, where there are tables on the pavements, and people are smiling and toasting each other with Prosecco. The air is so warm and balmy they could be in Italy.

They both hear the music at the same moment.

It is the Ed Sheeran song, 'Perfect', sung by a busker who's standing in the colonnaded portico of a church that looks a bit like a Roman temple.

'Viennese waltz,' says Alf, suddenly stepping in front of Letty, taking her into hold, pushing off with his right thigh against hers, so that she has no choice but to follow him as they waltz around and around the cobblestones.

They are dancing in the dark, with her feet somehow following his, her hair flying out behind her, the honey gold of the market and the floodlit white of the Opera House racing around like images in a magic lantern against the indigo blue of the sky. She can feel the ground beneath her feet, Alf's arms strong enough to support her if she stumbles, and, as they twirl and twirl, fear turns to courage, and surprise becomes a giddy sensation of such elation that when the song finally ends, she collapses against his chest, breathless and laughing. And it is perfect.

EPILOGUE

Thank goodness for that! Frances thinks as she hears them come in. She can tell by all the whispering and laughing and shushing that they have had a lovely time.

She remembers when she came to this house for the first time, how exciting it was to be at the start of a great adventure with Ivo. They couldn't make each other happy forever, but that didn't make the beginning and the middle any less wonderful.

Alf will be a good father. He was perfectly sweet with the twins.

It won't be easy, but they will manage.

Perhaps they'll all live in Palatine Road, and who knows, maybe she'll be able to help look after the baby, so that Letty can finish her degree, and he can go to dance school?

And maybe Oscar will give Alf a job. He's certainly got the looks for a West End leading man. Oscar will absolutely adore him! She wonders if Alf can sing, but she knows that now is not the time to barge in and demand to hear him.

Maybe Oscar and Raj will bring their baby round too? She'll operate a family crèche! She will buy a twin pram and push the babies round the little park at the end of the street, and get to do the bit of mothering she missed out on.

Grandmothering, she reminds herself.

But she must only be involved if they want her to be, Frances promises herself. She will try to be a good grand-mother, not one who watches every move and offers her unsolicited opinions.

Alf lies awake, listening to the unfamiliar creaks and echoes of this huge house.

He will get a job. It will be easy enough to find work as a waiter in London. If he's working in the evenings, he'll be able to look after the baby during the day, and Letty will be able to finish her studies. Maybe they'll swap around when the baby is a little older, and he will study, or teach, or both. There must be plenty of dance schools in London.

Donna will be a gran and Cheryl will be a great gran! He's not sure whether she'll like that. But they've got enough on their plate at the moment, so he will wait a while to tell them. Those two tiny girls will be aunts!

And he will be a parent and so will Letty. And they will both rise to the challenge because he will give her the confidence she needs, and she will have high expectations of him and each day will always be interesting.

And they will make love, and they will dance.

Letty lies staring through the bare window at the night sky, thinking how strange it is that they are the same countless stars that twinkled over them in Rome.

In a year's time, there will be a baby; in two years, a toddler; in three, maybe they will return there with a little girl or boy, and take a picture of him or her on the empty pedestal.

Or none of that may happen.

That is the future.

Letty closes her eyes and snuggles into the warmth of Alf's body.

This is the present, and it is lovely, and she is the happiest she has ever been, living in the moment.

ACKNOWLEDGEMENTS

I am lucky to have the best professional team supporting my writing. Thank you to my clever, intuitive agent and friend Mark Lucas, and to Niamh O'Grady, Araminta Whitley, Alice Saunders, Annette Murphy and everyone at The Soho Agency; to Nicki Kennedy, Sam Edenborough, Jenny Robson, Katherine West, Alice Natali and May Wall at ILA; to Stephanie Cabot at the Gernert Company in New York.

It's a joy to be published by Mantle and Pan Macmillan and I am fortunate to have Sam Humphreys as my editor. Thank you, Sam, for being so thoughtful, intelligent and kind. Thanks also to the whole dynamic team especially Rosie Wilson, Sarah Arratoon, Josie Humber, Maria Rejt, Alice Gray, Natalie Young and to Claire Gatzen for her sharp-eyed copy-editing.

I am grateful to Iris Tupholme at HarperCollins Canada for her incisive thinking and care, and to every one of the international editors who have loved my work and published it all over the world.

Thank you, Carol Dunbar, for teaching me to waltz and thank you, Nick, for the lovely times we shared at Blackpool Tower Ballroom and elsewhere.

I have been going to see the Royal Ballet for many years. Usually, I have watched from slips seats in the amphitheatre which cost less than a cinema ticket. We are so lucky to have this wonderful company as part of our cultural life in the UK, and now their performances are regularly screened live around the world. Do go see them. Thanks to the entire company for your beautiful dancing and commitment to perfection. Thank you, Sarah Lamb, for the moving performance of *Manon* that I describe in this book. I am indebted to Carlos Acosta, the greatest dancer of his generation and a brilliant man. My heartfelt thanks to Marianela Nuñez, not only for her virtuoso dancing, but also for her sparkling and generous personality on and off stage. I am especially grateful to Vadim Muntagirov for his extraordinary grace, soaring leaps, dazzling artistry and beautiful character.

Thank you to Connor's friends, for giving me feedback and helping me with my research. I'm talking about you Dr Michael Bussell, Liam Donachy, Simon Card, Jacob Webster, Jamie Knowles, Sam Drew and Beth Nicholas.

To my lifelong friends Martha Kearney, Lucy Tuck, Isabel O'Keeffe, Debra Isaac, Charles Elton, Nick Marston, Rod McNeil, Dee Slade, Molly Friedrich, Anne McDermid and Felicity Bryan, thanks for all the good times.

Finally, I could not have written *Only You* without the support and love of my amazing, loyal, wonderful sister Becky and my gifted, charming, altogether marvellous son Connor, who is my favourite dancer of all! You know how much I love you – the entire universe and beyond – and this book is for you.